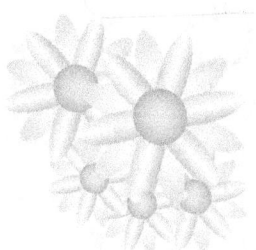

eloves me, eloves me not

A novel by L. A. Johannesson

First Printing, 2012

ISBN 978-0-9874365-0-4

Published by: Linda Johannesson, Sydney, Australia

www.lajohannesson.com

DEDICATION

I dedicate this book to the man I love. We met when this story was only an idea. Thank you for being at my side as both it and our own love story evolved. Chris, your support and encouragement have been instrumental in helping me to keep moving the cursor to the right. You have also shown me that almost anyone can be your 'once upon a time', but it takes someone incredibly special to be your 'happily ever after'.

This story is also dedicated to everyone who has searched for love. The journey can be incredible and exhilarating, discouraging and challenging. The search for love comes complete with its highs and lows, its ebbs and flows. When you find it, I hope you will see that it was all worth it – every step, every tear, every effort, every disappointment and every hope, dream and prayer it took to get you there.

A wise friend once offered these words of hope; "If I had to go through all the heartache, all the disappointment, all the dating false starts to become the person I was when I found myself in the situation where I met the love of my life, and he fell in love with exactly who I was at that moment, then it was all worth it. And it was all necessary."

eloves me, eloves me not

ACKNOWLEDGEMENTS

So many people have provided inspiration, encouragement, ideas, editing and moral support throughout the development of this novel. The idea for this book had been ruminating for a while but it was in taking a creative writing class that it came to life.

I'll start there and share my gratitude to fellow author and inspirational instructor, Lynda Simmons, who has taught and inspired me.

Chris, you have provided encouragement since Chapter One. Thank you.

Jasmina and Carol-Anne, I am grateful for your feedback in the early chapters as I struggled to find my voice.

A huge thank you goes out across the globe to my international review team for your feedback on the first draft. In Canada, thanks to Marina, Donna, Kelly, Linda and Judy for your ideas, suggestions and reader reviews. I'm also grateful to Emma in New Zealand and Brenda, Kim, Amy, Sarah, Amanda, Beryl and Chris in Australia and to Wanda from Russia.

My sincerest appreciation goes out to all the designers who participated in the book cover design competition for their incredible creativity, especially Milan Djakovic for your winning design. I am so grateful that you were able to bring my vision to life. And Chris your technical support is appreciated more than you know.

Thanks also to A.T.H. Webber, author, for his guidance in manoeuvring the self-publishing space and to Jennifer for making this introduction.

Finally, my gratitude goes out to every person along the way who asked, "How's the book coming along?" Your interest and support helped get me here.

I am happy to say that this novel is now finished and ready for you to read.

eloves me, eloves me not

CHAPTER 1

Any bets on whether he'll show?

I thumbed this text message to my best friend Chloe partly to distract myself as I waited and partly to give voice to my mounting scepticism. Maybe he wasn't coming. Maybe this was a waste of time. The message-sent indicator read 7:22pm. Even if his arrival was imminent, he was already over 20 minutes late, so we wouldn't be off to the best start.

Why had I agreed to this?

Why did I continue putting myself in this position?

I knew why.

The answer was simple.

I wanted the end result. I had always wanted it. I deserved it.

I wanted to find love – crazy, overwhelming, 'permanent grin on your face', 'can't wait another second to see each other', 'wonder how I ever lived without you' kind of love.

I wanted to be in love, to give love, to feel love.

I just couldn't understand why it had been so elusive.

It wasn't that I hadn't tried. In fact, I had become intimately familiar with the process of looking. But now, at 39, I found that my otherwise optimistic, happy and naturally romantic self was growing weary and disillusioned with the quest.

This is what I had learned about the journey. I knew that before you can marry the love of your life, you must first have a relationship. To have that relationship, you need to meet the right man. To meet the right man, you have to date a lot of men and in dating a lot of men, you meet far too many of the wrong ones. In meeting too many Mr. Wrongs, your romantic notions begin to fade and your patience wanes, feeding the fear that you'll never actually meet Mr. Right.

Was I just too being too picky?

I didn't think so. I preferred to think of it as being selective. I had a lot going for me. Shouldn't the man I choose to share my life with be all of those things too? The truth was that while I wanted a man in my life, I was pretty sure that I didn't need one.

Perhaps this was the real reason I was still single.

There had been many times when I was ready to abandon my search but then some well-intentioned friend or co-worker would introduce me to someone new. Or I'd meet a new guy at volley-ball, or catch a smile from a handsome man in a bookstore or the gym, and the sparks of my optimism were rekindled once more.

It's amazing what one can do with 20 minutes, standing in a restaurant foyer. I had busied myself powdering my nose, re-applying a thick coat of frosted cocoa gloss, straightening my brown billowy blouse, adjusting my necklace and removing stray fluffs from my newest butt-hugging jeans. I practised my 'hello, it's wonderful to meet you' smile until it was the perfect blend of sincerity and mischievous flirtation. I sifted through dozens of old text messages, rereading them, deleting the work ones, saving the personal ones. I sorted out my wallet only to be left with a fistful of garbage and no garbage can to deposit it in. I scanned the restaurant menu for new recipe ideas, making mental notes for the next romantic dinner I would prepare. I eavesdropped on the conversations of other patrons as they strode by. Based on the quick glimpses of their faces, a brief clothing assessment and the snippets of dialogue my ears plucked from the air, I constructed individual scenarios for each group. I guessed at how they were related, who had made the plans, why they chose this venue and what they might be celebrating.

My imagination ran free to fantasise about my own situation. It conjured up hopeful romantic notions of coming back here on this same day the following year to mark the anniversary of our very first date. It had been a long time since I celebrated an anniversary.

I peeked out the open door again and wondered if the man I saw approaching was Roger.

He was about the right height. His hair was 'dirty blond', as Marnie had described. I disliked that term, because the 'blond' always seemed to get lost in the 'dirty'. It led me to wondering why there were no 'clean' blonds walking among us.

He made his way from his sensible navy four-door sedan that was parked in the very far corner of the lot, a safely buffered distance from any other vehicle. As he moved closer I observed that he was handsome enough, tall, well built, with a sandy complexion and strong, squarish features in keeping with his German heritage. Physically, I thought Roger, if this was him, was reasonably attractive. I could feel a small glimmer of possibility flicker inside.

Last week I had reluctantly agreed to yet another blind date.

Marnie and I both knew the loneliness that came with 'single-dom', especially when you longed for a relationship. Together we had formed a pact last November just after learning that partners were welcomed at the office Christmas party for the first time ever. We both felt the humiliation that came with having no 'significant other'. We bonded over discussions about how out of place singles felt at these formal functions. Sometimes it felt as if single people had no place in a life that was neatly arranged in tables of twos and fours.

So there at the office coffee machine over a chai tea and a café Columbian, we committed to helping each other find love. Whether we accompanied one another to singles events, cheered each other on after bad dates, went on shopping expeditions in search of the ultimate rendezvous outfit, or arranged introductions and blind dates, we were there for each other from that point forward.

She was the first of us to find it just two weeks into the new year.

Marnie was even more motivated to help me find love as a result. She had just learned that her brother's friend Roger was available. He was a family friend from way back but she didn't know him all that well now. What she did know was that he was tall, looking for a relationship and she thought that we might have some common interests. Roger was somewhat outdoorsy. He worked out at the gym, hiked, skied and took the occasional camping trip. He was an architect that she described as leaning more toward the creative than the engineering side of his profession. I was reluctant when she told me he was a little bit shy, yet relieved when I learned that he liked women who were not. I was definitely not. She went on to add that he was naturally handsome but lacked a certain contemporary metrosexual polish that she preferred in her ideal man.

The combination of his shyness and his lack of polish set off some sparks of reluctance. But the burning flame of my perpetual optimism overpowered them and won out.

On some level I knew my Mr. Right did exist. He was still out there somewhere. I held dearly to the possibility that the next man I met might just be 'the one', my forever guy, my lifelong lover and the man I had been waiting for since my first real kiss in Mitchell Morgan's basement, 28 years ago.

I wondered if Roger could be him. If he was, I would have to draw the line at taking his last name. There were many surnames I would gladly assume. Clooney had a nice ring to it. But I could not go through life, blissfully married or otherwise, being 'Kathleen Overmeyer.'

He took a long time to get to the door. Obviously he was not a fast walker like me. He had much more of a slow and deliberate swagger than a purposeful stroll. I watched him intently as he entered my life holding his mobile phone to his right ear, chatting, chewing gum and scanning the parking lot from left to right and back again.

As he entered through the doors of the restaurant, I could see that his shoulders were broad and his arms were noticeably muscular as they sprouted from beneath the constricting confines of his moss-green short-sleeved, body-hugging soccer jersey.

At first glance, I liked what I saw.

Or did I?

It was then I noticed it. A black and yellow beer crest dotted the right lapel and a greasy stain almost the same size marred the left one. His baggy brown thick corduroy pants just met the tops of his scuffed black leather loafers. He stood a slightly slouched 6' or thereabouts.

Marnie's phrase, *'lacked a certain contemporary metrosexual polish,'* echoed through my brain.

Eeewww! Did he just pick his teeth? Yes he did AND he was going in again!

His cavernous mouth opened wide to allow for the entry of his rather large left fist, baby finger outstretched on a quest to hunt down and eradicate some offensive piece of leftover sustenance that was most likely lodged between his two rearmost molars.

Nice first impression.

He caught my glimpse and nodded. I hoped that my expression had not revealed my repulsion but feared it had. I tried quickly to replace it with my signature warm and welcoming smile that had been perfected over way too many first dates so very similar to this.

Why did I do this? Was it really worth it? Really? I could do without this, couldn't I? I have so far. Isn't it just time to pack it all in and just stop trying?

The scent of the air changed from the enticing allure of a flame-grilled burger that had passed by atop a server's platter just moments before. Still talking on his mobile phone, Roger now stood beside me, and so did the heavy aroma of onion. Or was it garlic? Yes, it was definitely garlic. He glanced from my calves slowly up to my eyes and mouthed a questioning "Kayte?"

I nodded silently, fighting my inner urge to answer "Kayte? No, never heard of Kayte. I'm Tania. And there's my ride. Gotta go. See ya. Bye!"

But I refrained.

"Yep… uh huh… yeah… right, right." He was obviously in agreement with whoever was still on the other end of the phone. He was not making a good first impression. Not in the least. I got the feeling that one might have to pry the mobile phone from his face to get a proper hello.

The hostess came over and asked if we were ready to be seated. This was my chance to turn tail and run, but instead, I responded with, "Uh… um… yes… please". He nodded and then gestured with his free hand a rather quick and dismissive 'off with you' gesture and then fell in behind me.

I vacillated between being impetuously judgmental by leaving immediately and staying, holding dearly to the teeniest shred of possibility and giving this guy a fair chance. I was not impressed so far.

As his hand gestured past my eye, I noticed that there, wedged under his baby fingernail, hung this huge green leaf-like object.

Ewwwwwww. What was that?

My guess was that it was the offensive remnant he freed from its hiding place between his back teeth just moments before. Judging by the garlic smell, my speculation was that it was a stray piece of lettuce from a recently enjoyed Caesar salad.

I decided to refrain from eating anything on this date. That made the Merlot mandatory.

We arrived at the table, he gestured for me to sit first, which was a polite and welcome reprieve. *Okay, maybe he wasn't so bad.* I was just about to place my butt cheeks into the contours of the formed wooden chair when I was interrupted by a thunderous guffaw erupting from his garlicky mouth. I flinched, jolting the table and knocking over the menu, salt and pepper shakers and the promotional signage.

I straightened the table, regained my composure and when the laughter subsided, he ended the call with a perfunctory, "Roger that!" He hit the end button and then placed the phone into its home dangling from the right side of his belt.

Did he just say "Roger that"? And was he seriously wearing his phone? 'Lacking a certain metrosexual polish...'

Yep, he was lacking all right!

"So, you're Kayte?"

"Yes, that's me." The words squeaked out of my tight lips that were feigning an interested smile.

"And you know Marnie?"

I know her all right and I hate her right now. I'm fantasising about how I will make her pay for this!

"Yes, we used to work together." My smile continued. "And

you're a friend of the family's, I understand?"

"Yep, they pretty much adopted me when I was young."

We sat across from each other giving us both the opportunity to conduct the dating 'size up'. Roger was handsome enough with a long rectangular face, angular jaw, thin, slightly pursed lips, olive-toned skin and huge green eyes. His hair was unkempt and a little greasy but luckily for him the tousled look suited him. The light above our table shone directly on him, emphasizing the sprinkling of dandruff flakes across his shoulders. It was obvious that he was not a meticulous type. I got the feeling that the dishevelled look was the rule not the exception. It certainly suited his rather coarse personality.

He had long, shapely eyebrows that framed the large sockets which showcased his amazing emerald eyes, by far his most attractive feature. I was looking deeply into them when I noticed that there was a small wad of sleep at the edge of his left eye.

Eeeewww. Didn't this guy ever look in a mirror?

Look at his forehead, Kayte. Look at his forehead.

"So, you're still single huh?"

Like it was a curse. "Yes, I am. Single, but hopeful!" I added.

"You must be too picky."

Oh there's something I've never heard before. Thank you, Roger. You have solved 'The Mystery of No-Date Kayte – The Single Saga'. The reason she's not paired off is that she has standards. What an astute observation and arrived at within only minutes of meeting me. He was good. That settled it. I was too picky.

If I settled for anyone I could be doing the matrimonial march tomorrow. If let's say I were to marry Roger, perhaps there would be a smattering of green freshly picked tooth refuse lining the aisle rather than a stream of lovingly tossed red and pink rose petals.

The truth was this: I was ready to settle down, but I was

definitely not ready to settle.

"Define what you mean by 'too'..."

"Hello there. How are you doing today? I'm Brittany. I'll be your server. Can I take your beverage order to start?"

Our perky little 20-something waitress had hopped over to our table and was looking down at us. She was wearing tight black pants and an equally tight bosom-hugging red pullover that was the standard restaurant uniform.

"Give me a vodka and diet coke." Roger then motioned with an upward palm to me and raised his eyebrows as if to ask, "And you?"

"A glass of Merlot, please."

It might be the only way I'll make it through this date.

Brittany hopped away.

"So, Marnie tells me you're an architect. That must be fascinating. What do you like most about it?"

"It's interesting. I like the idea that I design functional art. I see the world as my gallery and I'm the artist designing distinctive masterpieces for the average person to interpret, admire, appreciate, use, live in, work in, play in. It's the ultimate interactive art form. It gives me a real sense of power. Plus the pay's not too shabby either."

Hmm... an interesting and thoughtful response, albeit a little artsy. An intelligent vocabulary and did I detect a hint of sense of humour? I'll try to keep an open mind.

With that his phone rang to the tune of "I'm too sexy".

"Tell me..." was how he greeted his caller.

Open mind, now closed.

Thankfully, Brittany reappeared with our drinks. Mine barely had time to touch the table before I lifted it to my lips. I was looking for a reason to stay seated rather than bolt for the door, head home and rearrange my cutlery drawer.

My own phone subtly vibrated against my leg through my bag. I peeked in to find that Chloe had responded with a text of her own.

I'll put $20 on him to show and another $20 that says you'll fall madly in love.

Roger was nodding and exclaiming "no way" repeatedly to the person on the other end of the call while he looked over and winked at me. In my head, I also chanted, those two little words. As in there would be 'no way' this date would last much longer and 'no way' would there be a second one and 'no way' was I about to fall madly in love. It had taken me all of 18 minutes to come to those conclusions. At least I had become very efficient!

"Roger that!" He took the phone away from his ear and placed it on the table.

He stared down at his glass and almost shouted, "Man, I forgot to ask for the most important part". With that he looked around for our waitress and, to my shock, lifted his right hand, dandruff flakes falling to the table as he snapped his fingers three times to get her attention.

I was mortified.

"So are you looking to get married?"

I choked on my wine. "Wow. No verbal foreplay with you huh?" I was proud of my witty retort.

From him there was no response, no smile, not even a tiny chuckle. He just sat there and stared like a detective using his best 'just answer the question' gaze.

When he realised I wasn't responding any further he added, "I am. I'm not like most guys. I actually want to get married. I want to settle down, have a house – that I've designed, of course – have some kids, do family stuff."

"That's refreshing to hear. I really think I want that too."

But not with you – that's for sure!

"Would you still want to work?"

What kind of question was that?

"Yes, of course, my career is very important to me, it's a huge part of who I am."

"Well, I'd let my wife work, as long as she could do that and have a clean house and dinner on the table when I got home."

I played his words over in my head.

What century did this guy think he was living in?

He was smiling. I had hoped he was even half joking, but my single-gal-great-catch sense had not even registered, so it suggested he wasn't.

An obviously perturbed Brittany made her way back to our table. "Yes?"

"Can you grab me five olives for this, doll? I forgot to tell you that when I ordered."

Her mouth said, "Sure, coming right up." But her face said what my mind was thinking. She turned on her heel and padded across the polished oak flooring toward the bar, as Roger stared after her, following her butt with each step.

Moments later, she returned with five olives skewered on a saucer and dropped it on the table. "Here you go."

I wondered if she had licked them, rubbed them under her armpit or dropped a splash or two of Tabasco on them.

"Roger that!" he inserted where a 'Thank you' ought to have been.

He removed a green speckled wad of gum from his mouth and placed it in the dish. Roger began picking olives one by one off the skewer and tossing them up in the air, catching them, chewing them with an open mouth, then washing them down with a noisy slurp of his drink, all followed up with a proud "ahh".

eloves me, eloves me not

Charming. Was he for real? Or was Marnie hiding somewhere, filming this, laughing her ass off, and pulling some big practical blind date joke on me?

His attention was back on me and mine was waning – no, wandering, or was that wondering what the heck I was still doing there?

I wanted out.

Roger was obviously another 'Mr. Couldn't Be More Wrong'!

He did not appear shy at all. However I was uncharacteristically quiet, not asking him many questions because I didn't care to know the answers.

"So you haven't said yet. What do you think?"

I think you could use a shower, some fashion advice, some lessons in manners and a toothbrush!

"What do I think? About what?"

"Me. Am I what you expected?"

No, if I expected this, I definitely would not have come.

"I'm not sure what I expected."

How else could I get out of answering this question without being rude and appearing ungrateful to Marnie?

"Am I what you like? You're pretty cute Kaytie – bet you're a good kisser."

Yep, but you'll never have the pleasure. I can assure you of that. And just who do you think you are calling me 'Kaytie'?

"Thanks. What makes you say that?"

"You have great lips, very full, very soft I'll bet. Yep, you're a good kisser. Plus, being single at, what did Marnie say you were, 39? You've probably had tons of practice. So how many guys have you dated anyway?"

That was it. I had had enough.

I wanted to toss my wine and add a fresh contribution to his shirt stain collection but I took a huge gulp instead. I leaned in nice and close to Roger, stared him straight in the eyes and then whispered in my most seductive voice, "Hmm... how many guys have I dated? Should I consider this a date?"

The garlic stench was choking me.

"Roger that. I'm paying. And I might want to try out those great lips. So yes, it's definitely a date."

I took the final sip of my Merlot. I locked my gaze and stared deeper into his eyes, trying to ignore the sleep goop that had now become crusty. "Then, let's see, that would make for a grand total of..." The pause was long and purposely theatrical. "...one too many."

I grabbed my bag, stood up and said, "Goodbye Roger".

"You're leaving?"

With a sarcastic closed-mouth smile and a deep stare I put it in simple words he'd understand. "Roger that".

I turned and was gone.

I caught a glimpse from Brittany on my way out. She had obviously been eyeing our exchange. She gave me a knowing 'you go girl' sisterhood smile and an encouraging thumbs up.

That was it. I was done with blind dates. Finished. Over them. I was never going on one again. Never. Ever.

Maybe I was even done with dating.

CHAPTER 2

"Do I seriously have to give you the twenty bucks?"

"Well, he did show." Chloe responded.

"But you also said another twenty that we'd fall madly in love. And that just ain't gonna happen!"

"Honey, from the sounds of that little escapade you earned it. Keep your money. We'll call it even."

As I recounted the details of the Roger meeting to Chloe, I almost couldn't believe it myself. But it was true. I was there. I had lived through it exactly how I had described it.

"I don't think I'd have the stomach for dating these days. But I have my man, so I don't have to." She made a good point.

"Okay chickee, as your best friend and biggest cheerleader, I proclaim that it's high time we change your dating luck. Now powder that nose of yours, get up off that couch and prepare to meet the man of your dreams. I am about to introduce you to scads of single men who, just like you, are searching for l-o-o-o-o-o-v-e!" In true Chloe style, her emphasis was on the drawn-out, sing-song way she said "love!" Her words almost sang in tune with the smooth Spanish jazz sounds drifting from the speaker in the background.

This was why I loved her. Chloe was quite a character. She had more energy than a three-year-old hopped up on Easter morning chocolate. It was little wonder she and I were such great friends. Personality-wise we were cut from the same vibrant cloth. More than that, though, we were proud of the permanent places we had earned in each other's hearts and lives.

Despite our steadfast friendship, our lifestyles could not have been more different – where Chloe lived in the city, I lived in suburbia. You'd think it would have been the other way around; the single girl would live in the city and the family in the suburbs. I lived where I did mainly because affording a decent house with a yard in the city you needed two incomes. While Chloe had two wonderful kids that kept her busy each day, most of my affection was spent doting on my golden retriever, Dylan, the reason I needed the yard.

While Chloe worked from home offering a before and after school program for a dozen or so children whose two parents were out making enough money to pay for their city home, I spent my days interacting with demanding clients and time-starved, over-stressed executives who often acted like kids. Perhaps the biggest difference of all was that I slept alone while Chloe cuddled up each night with Bruce, her loving husband of 18 years. His friends often referred to him as "Boomer" because of his deep hearty booming voice.

"Scads of men huh?" I replied. "Well you could have given me a little more warning. Had I known, I would have had my legs waxed! So, my happily hitched hydrangea, just how are you planning to introduce me to all these eligible men? Where are you taking me? And, more importantly, whatever will I wear?" I joked in my best southern belle drawl as I raised my well manicured eyebrows, tilted my chin downward, pursed my lips and batted my lashes in Chloe's direction.

"Aha, my single little sunflower, therein lies the beauty of my plan." Chloe smiled. "We don't even have to leave your lovely little home!"

I glanced around the comfortably furnished living room where we sat enjoying our monthly girlfriend's day. Even in the soft, dim, evening light I saw that it was a lovely little house and I was proud of how the décor had come together. The soft scents of vanilla and cranberry candles wafted through the air, crossing sensory boundaries and blending perfectly with the colour scheme. On the main floor, the butter yellow walls provided a cheery canvas that was punctuated with the warm dark woods. An eclectic mix of artwork adorned the walls – from photographs I had taken to impressionist garden scenes that invited you in for a stroll – all expertly framed. The curtains and upholstery were a calming neutral taupe that anchored the room. There were a dozen or so healthy plants breathing their life into my surroundings. The recently installed beech wood flooring had been carefully chosen to both mask and match Dylan's abundant stray fur.

Although I loved my little house, it was clear that something was missing. It was obvious to me every time I left it and again when I returned. It was missing another.

At first, it had been liberating and fun to be in my own home, living the single life, just me all by myself. I made all the decisions, chose all my colours, stocked the fridge with all my favourites, decorated how I saw fit, watched what I wanted on TV and filled every single closet with my stuff. Now it cried out for a man to infuse some balance. Living alone had lasted about ten years longer than I'd ever imagined it would and had become terribly lonely and taxing.

I didn't know why I was still single. I was taught that love comes along precisely when you're ready for it to find you. Frankly, I felt I had been ready for years now.

Who was I kidding? It was way overdue.

My thoughts returned to the impending man invasion. "Well if scads of men are coming here, I'd better chill more beer and hide the remote."

"Enough chitchat, let's get to it. Grab your wine and follow me." Chloe reached down and gave Dylan a pat on the head.

"What's this black thing lying beside Dylan that looks like a butt plug?"

"Butt plug?" I glanced to see what she was referring to. "Oh, that's his Kong. It's a toy made of super strong rubber that even he can't chew through. And you can wedge cookies into it or fill it with peanut butter. It keeps him busy licking for hours trying to get whatever is in there out. Butt plug? Does it really? And how do you even know what a butt plug looks like?"

"Wouldn't you like to know," Chloe taunted as she stepped over all 30+ blond hairy kilos of Dylan and his butt plug and proceeded upstairs to the room I had dedicated as my office. My curiosity demanded I follow.

There in waiting, on the large oak desk, laid my computer. I was unaware that it would be the vehicle that would launch us off on an exciting cyber journey.

I gave Chloe the look – the glance that said 'I know you so well. I can usually read your mind but now, here on this rare occasion, you have me stumped. Just what the heck are you up to?'

"My friend Michael told me about this great dating site that he's been using," Chloe said. "Since he broke up with Melanie, he's been looking for ways to meet new women and he swears by this one. So I thought we'd have a peek given you're going through a bit of a – how shall I say it – dry spell. Oh, and this way the old married lady gets to have some fun and live vicariously through her best friend. You know how I love that!"

"A dry spell? Yes, Chloe, I would wholeheartedly agree that four long months without sex, without a single date – well except for the Roger incident – without so much as a peck on the cheek definitely constitutes a dry spell. It's so bad that I even broke Phil last week!" I sadly admitted, shaking my head.

"So much for relying on your vibrator to 'Phil the void!'" Chloe laughed. She revelled in this kind of repartee, the kind that could only be created between the best of friends.

As I passed the mirror in the hall, I stopped to defend myself and uttered aloud, "It's not like I'm some homely or worse, ugly, woman with a great personality or anything. I'm not unattractive. I'm tall and relatively fit, and yes, I have some womanly curves. I've got nice breasts and long and muscular legs that men seem to be drawn to. I'll admit to having a little too much around the middle." My defence had risen to more of a rant. "With my looks, personality, and lovely chocolate locks, I shouldn't have dating troubles."

Getting even closer to the mirror, I examined my reflection more critically and mused, "I have beautiful azure blue eyes, smooth even skin and full lips. I dress well. I'm smart, sociable, funny, and I'd say darn right sexy. There is no reason that a woman of my calibre should continue to live in chastity-ville! None whatsoever. Well, no reason other than that whole lack of humility thing!" I laughed at myself, or was that with myself? Chloe happily joined in.

"Here's to ending KitKat's dry spell," Chloe toasted as she raised her glass and clinked mine which was now only half full of this tasty, newly discovered Australian Chardonnay.

I raised my glass. "Here's to getting wet!" This nearly caused Chloe to shoot wine through her nose!

We clinked again before Chloe sat herself down at the keyboard and we both took our spots behind the computer and settled in, set to begin what we hoped would be an exciting adventure.

"I'm driving," Chloe said as she placed herself in the power position with hands on the keyboard. She double-clicked on the web browser icon, knowingly typed in **www.wheresinglesfindlove. com** and hit return.

In a matter of seconds, the internet worked its magic and the site appeared on the screen. Although I knew many people who had experienced some success with online dating, I had only pondered the idea once and never followed through on it. Chloe started browsing through the photos on the homepage and I dared to wonder if this might finally be my gateway to meeting the one, the man for me, the one who would love me like no other. Would this be the road to finding that one man who was everything I hoped and dreamed my perfect mate would be?

I couldn't stop my optimism from rising to the surface, just as it had so many times before even after so many ultimately unfruitful attempts. Let's see – what else had I tried? Hmmm, there were personal ads, telephone date lines, singles dances, speed dating, singles adventures, blind dates, suppers for singles, hiking with singles and even date night at the grocery store! I had tried virtually every avenue I could think of to meet the right man, but never the online dating thing. Maybe Chloe was onto something. Maybe this could finally be it. Please finally be it. Please, I pleaded silently.

The words **Meet sexy singles now – sign up for FREE!** appeared on screen, calling out and grabbing my attention. Chloe's hand was on the mouse, the cursor placed over the 'click' button, her forefinger poised; ready, set, left-click. The journey had begun!

The screen redrew quickly and responded. **Before you can connect with singles, please take a moment to fill in the form below.**

"Okay, your turn to take the wheel," Chloe said as she surrendered the power position and then moved to the chair on my right and began rolling around the office.

"Great," I growled. "Even this comes with its own version of requisite paperwork!"

Create a Member ID to login: Your Member ID must be at least 4 characters.

"And rules to boot," I added. "Hmmm what will my member ID be? I assume that's what others will see listed as my name on here, right? Chloe, what do you think about 'katontheprowl'?"

"M-E-E-O-O-O-W-W-W – very slinky, indeed. I like it! Okay, what's next?"

Create a password. Your password must be at least 6 characters.

"Chloe – turn your head please, for not even you will know my password to love," I taunted, borrowing Chloe's singsong tone as I uttered the word love. I typed 'readyforlove'. **Re-enter password** came the next command.

"What? You didn't get it the first time?" My impatience had begun to surface but I complied and typed again, acknowledging my overdue readiness.

"Just get to the good part. I'm almost out of wine and we haven't even seen any hot men yet!" Chloe was now flipping through the pages of one of my self-help books she had just retrieved from the shelf.

Country, City, Postal Code, email address, date of birth.

"Should I tell the truth or do you think I could pull off 35?" I asked as I populated the blank fields on the screen with my personal information.

"Oh, Kayte, just be honest – geesh, I'm aging just watching you type."

The final line asked, **Are you over 18?**

"DUH, ya – see above! And yes, I have read and agreed to the Terms of Use and the Privacy Policy."

"Okay, Chloe, drum roll please!"

Fingers tapping the desk, Chloe gladly obliged.

I clicked the submit button. **CONGRATULATIONS you are now a member of Where Singles Find Love! But we still need a few more details before you meet sexy singles in your area.**

The online message window broke in. And the vivid orange bar called out for attention as it flashed at the bottom of the screen.

Bigbadwolf says:
Hey girl 'sup?

Bigbadwolf says:
Feel like a visit from the Big Bad Wolf tonight?

K8 says:
Sorry hon, no can do, I'm just on my way to Grandma's house!

K8 says:
Seriously, Chloe is here & she's holding my hand as I finally listen to all you guys & take the plunge into the online dating waters. So, I'm a little busy.

"Who's that?" Chloe asked as she put down the photo of my nephews and slid back over toward the desk to get a better view of the screen.

"It's Roman."

"Kayte, you know so many people. I get confused. Is he the guy from volleyball, or from somewhere else all together?"

"Good memory girl! I met him at volleyball last season. He's the guy who works for Luxor Automotive, the mechanical engineer, lives in The Village. He's a good guy, a little rough around the edges, but a good heart. He's single too and if I remember correctly, I think he's used online dating too."

Bigbadwolf says:
Chloe's there? Even better – a 3some! I'll B right over – LOL!

Roman finished with a wink.

K8 says:
Can I take a rain check?

K8 says:
Just 2 clarify, that would be on the visit, NOT the 3some.

Bigbadwolf says:
Of course! But you gotta tell me how your virgin voyage into the online dating waters goes

Bigbadwolf says:
& if U R lucky my little Leibchen I'll share rule #1 from the
coveted book of Roman's Rules of Online Dating.

K8 says:
From the WHAT?

Bigbadwolf says:
The Book of RROOD (pronounced RUDE) – Roman's Rules of
Online Dating, my personal compendium of not yet published
protocols I plan on sharing with online neophytes just like you.
Surfing these online dating waters for 3 years, I've learned a
thing or two. And you know me. I must share, especially with the
ladies! Hey, maybe I'll even teach a class.

The nerd smiley appeared on the screen.

K8 says:
I'll gladly B your protégé oh wise master. But gotta go. We have
to finish my profile. More importantly, we need more wine! Later
Gater!

Bigbadwolf says:
TTFN

K8 says:
Kayte-OUT!

"Okay, now where were we?" I asked.

"Maybe it's time to get some more vino and have that sushi we
picked up for dinner. I'm thinking that if we don't eat now, the
wine will go to our heads and we'll be writing you a profile you
might regret. One that I'm sure will get some attention but maybe
not the kind of attention you want."

Dinner over, wine glasses topped up, Dylan guarding the front
door, we returned to the computer, as full of optimism as we were
of sushi.

"Okay, let's enter the basics. Height, 5'10".

Body type? Given there was no 'big boobs and some jiggly bits' section I ticked 'average'. Smoking habits? N-E-V-E-R! Religion? Where was the 'born Catholic, but don't get to church much anymore, usually only at Christmas and Easter' button? Ethnic background? Caucasian. It only took seconds to click all the appropriate boxes.

"Finally the good part, writing my profile. They suggest you start with a powerful opening line if you want to maximise the number of responses. Chloe, we better make this one a crowd stopper."

"How about 'Tall lady well worth the climb'?" Chloe offered. "Or perhaps something more romantic; 'let's watch the sun come up'? Or better yet, 'I like my men like I like my coffee – hot and sweet!' – that's nice and sassy!"

"For a happily married woman, Chloe, you are spouting these off way too easily. I'm going to write the profile and you keep thinking about opening lines. Remember it has to be smart and grab their attention. Personally, I'd like to make them laugh. Just like marketing, you need to evoke an emotion right from the start."

"How 'bout 'Tall drink of water, looking for her glass'?"

"How 'bout you just keep thinking," I replied as I poked around my computer for my personal files and dug out two that I hoped should really help in the profile writing process.

The first file was my ideal mate list. I had read scads of books on finding a mate, finding love, achieving romantic bliss. One in particular that I had read a couple of years back professed that you must create, in vivid detail, a clear vision of who it is you're looking for before you can find him. It suggested you visualise him in as much detail as possible, physically, spiritually, emotionally, intellectually and think about the kind of life you'd like to have together. Did you want an active sort, a sports enthusiast or more of an intellectual who challenged your mind or touched your soul? It suggested defining what physical characteristics you find yourself most drawn to. What economic, social characteristics were your biggest priorities? Were there demographic, racial or religious factors that had to be considered? It suggested including those too. Being a big believer in visualisation, I figured the exercise couldn't hurt so I obliged. I thought about what would be the best personality type and physical match for me and wrote a detailed list of what my ideal mate would be like. Although it had been several years since I'd written this list and hadn't looked at it in a while, I was reassured to find that it had remained pretty consistent over the years. It was a rather lengthy collection of random, but meaningful, adjectives that read:

Kayte's Dream Guy!

Male, tall (over 5'11"), strong build, broad shoulders, sexy arms, hairy chest, full lips, laugh lines, sexy eyes, easygoing, outgoing, sociable, positive/optimistic, enthusiastic, great sense of humour, intelligent, communicative, balanced, loving, strong yet gentle, honest, loyal, affectionate, demonstrative, an awesome kisser, romantic, adventurous, lots of interests, confident but not arrogant, down-to-earth, spiritual, community minded, high energy level, within 6 years of my age, non-smoker, social drinker, strong family values, outdoorsy, athletic, sexy, passionate, energetic, sexy voice, caring/respectful, somewhat domesticated, health conscious, committed to personal growth, an accomplished lover, local, fun, patient, honours commitments, trustworthy, monogamous, truly appreciates me, animal lover, law abiding and drug free.

The second file I found was the profile I had drafted the last time I had considered trying online dating. I had spent two weeks labouring over what to say – I grappled with whether it should it be serious, funny, short, detailed, flirty, down-to-earth? I pondered what I would have to say to catch the attention of the right guy.

I remembered thinking back when I wrote that first draft that there were so many ways to position yourself. Back then I'd had a really tough time deciding. The profile I came up with was hardly the work of a consummate marketing maven like myself. It should have been a cinch to put together. It should have been easy for me to craft the copy that had been swirling around in my head for years. But when it was personal it was a very, very different challenge. I remember editing it and editing it again. I just couldn't create something I was happy with.

It was a few years ago but it must have taken a dozen edits before it was finally ready. I felt so strongly that I had finally crafted the online profile that would end my single days and find me my dream guy. Five years ago, I was ready to post my first-ever online ad. It sat proudly at the top of my 'to do' list for the following Sunday morning. But we all know what happens when you make plans!

That Friday after work, a number of us went out to say goodbye to a co-worker, Derek, who was leaving for an international post with the global alliance division, based in Australia. I was tired and really didn't feel much like going out, and would have preferred to have gone straight home, put on my jammies, curled up with Dylan, made a big bowl of popcorn, watched a sappy chick flick and gone to bed early. But I fought the urge to hibernate and I joined in dutifully, albeit reluctantly, and trotted off to the Urban Fountain for finger food and cocktails with a half dozen of the gang from the office. Derek's friends were meeting us there. There were five of them – two women, one being his heartbroken girlfriend who wasn't making the trip with him, his cousin and two quite handsome guys from back in his university days.

The one who captured my attention most was definitely Simon. My heart actually leapt when I first saw him. Then he smiled at me with his sensual glistening eyes and gleaming white teeth and as he introduced himself he warmly took my hand in his for a little longer than others might have deemed socially appropriate, but I enjoyed it. My visceral reaction to him moved to my stomach where I could feel the butterflies flitting about. I think it was about two hours later, after an incredibly entertaining yet eerily familiar-feeling conversation with Simon, when my physical reaction to him moved lower still.

I knew that night that I'd be removing at least one item on Sunday's to-do list. I fantasised that I'd never have to join that online dating community because I truly thought that I had finally met my Mr. Right, in the flesh, in the club on that Friday night and his name was Simon.

Wasn't that always the way? When you didn't want to do something, but you pushed yourself and went along begrudgingly, it seemed to switch on some communication channel with the universe to deliver some sort of karmic payoff for your extra effort. It had happened too many times in my past to be merely coincidence.

There was no room for entertaining thoughts of Simon now. This was about the future, not the heartbreak of the past, the broken trust, or the shattered dreams that became drenched in disillusion. Those had vanished. The future held fresh promise for me and for love. I'd learned from my dating past, some painful lessons, some not so painful but equally enlightening. I now knew what I wanted, what I wouldn't tolerate, and what could make me happy. All that was left was to find it.

With tools in hand, I constructed my online dating profile.

Hi there – thanks for stopping in! If you look a little closer you'll find a fun, energetic, optimistic, sexy, outgoing, sociable and big-hearted lady who is looking to connect with her male counterpart, especially of you're not afraid of adjectives.

Like me, you are tall, attractive and in decent shape. You'd be open and communicative, have strong values, a rapier wit, and still have a need to enrich your life through interesting adventures and experiences.

You believe in balance and you hold strong to your convictions. Yet you'd never be described as 'narrow minded' or 'set in your ways' – you're not your father... YET!!!

If sports like volleyball, rollerblading, running, cycling,

hiking, and snorkelling are your cup of tea, then great, we can drink from the same pot. If travel, culture, dining out and experimenting at home with new recipes/wines/music... are on your favourites list, then all the better.

If home improvement is more than a concept to you and it actually might be somewhat of a hobby, then you get BIG bonus points – especially if you have tools and aren't afraid to use them!

If you prefer sand to snow, dogs to cats, friends to acquaintances, houses to condos, brunettes over blondes, making love over having sex, and actually meeting someone face-to-face over drawn-out 'e-lationships', then maybe we should connect.

But know this, I'm looking for a relationship. I may be ready to settle down, but I'll never settle. If this scares you then I'm probably not the woman for you. However, if you too are seeking an amazing and passionate relationship, then introduce yourself.

Either way, good luck with your quest!

"DONE! And the only editing I had to do this time was for grammar and typos."

"Yay." Chloe literally applauded. "For your opening line, how about 'If at first you don't succeed, sky diving is NOT for you!' Or 'My glass is always half full, want to take a sip'?"

"Here, have a read." I turned the screen in her direction.

She read my profile, nodding all the way through. At the end, she proclaimed, "Now that's a *tall* order!" and right then, right there, my opening line was born. "I think it should be called 'Tall lady - Tall order. Looking to take love to new heights.'"

"Love it." I nodded, winked and gave her two thumbs up. "Now we need to choose the picture."

In my head, the advertiser and amateur photographer in me had narrowed it down to three shots I had been using as my display pictures for my instant-message chats. I had sorted and sifted through the mass of online photos I had collected over the years. I must have looked at over 100 of them to find three I liked.

The first was very sultry with make-up perfect, the hair just gently tousled with an emphasis on my shining full lips. Very nice except there was a bit of the flash showing in the top corner and I thought it looked a little too much like I might have taken it myself, which, of course, I had.

The second was pretty natural. I was tanned, it was just a head-and-shoulders shot but you could see the mischievous look in my eyes and my lips were pouting a little. My hair was unusually curly; it must have been a humid day.

Our third choice was me with the dog. This one showed an awesome smile. I was in jeans and a casual black top and you saw both my love of animals and more of my body, but not my belly. Yay!

"Chloe, you choose. I do this for work all the time but when it's personal it's so much harder. I think it's between two and three."

"Hmm – I like them all. They all look like you, just different sides of you. I can't choose. I like both the ones you do, but I'm not a guy. What one do you think men would prefer?"

"C'mon Chloe, really, think about it, if I knew what men preferred, would I still be single?"

"Hey, I have an idea. Is Roman still online? Let's see what he thinks."

"Let's see." I opened up the instant message contact list and saw that thebigbadwolf@socialarity.com was signed in as 'Online but Away'. I tried him anyway, because even when he showed as 'Away', half the time he was still home. Living in a small apartment, Roman could still usually hear his computer and he'd answer the instant message call anyway and within seconds he responded.

Bigbadwolf says:
U reconsider that 3-some thing? LOL

K8 says:
"Ah, let me see. That would be a big... NO, but thanks for asking!

K8 says:
But would like to ask a favour of you – we need the male point of view.

Bigbadwolf says:
Happy to give it.

K8 says:
We can't decide which photo of me to use for my profile. We've got the opening line, the profile itself, just need to decide on the right picture.

K8 says:
I'm sending two files to you right now – let me know what you think.

Technology performed its magic and forwarded through two images of me to Roman's computer in seconds. It astounded me what we could now do from our home computers.

Bigbadwolf says:
Definitely #2. That look is so HOT. (The word HOT displayed on screen in a different font, complete with flames, and it flashed for added effect.) While U look kind of innocent and natural, U can tell there's a she-devil inside. Guys like that look."

Bigbadwolf says:
And your hair is curly – mmmmmm – noice – makes me want 2 grab a handful of it and give it a tug while I'm...

K8 says:
Okay too much info Roman

K8 says:
But thx

Bigbadwolf says:
You are welcome Liebchen, and there U have learned Rule #1 of my online dating rulebook. There is nothing more important in your profile than the photo. It is the ultimate power to attract or repel.

Bigbadwolf says:
Agonise over your profile name and opening line, pick your categories, choose every word with great care, but men will be men. We are visual creatures. Give good photo and you'll get our attention.

K8 says:
Thanks Wolf. I appreciate the advice oh wise one!

Bigbadwolf says:
Anytime babe. Perhaps we could arrange some small recompense - a 3some on another day perhaps?

K8 says:
NO, NO, NO

Bigbadwolf says:
Can't blame a guy 4 tryin'

K8 says:
No... but you knew that would be my answer... Kayte-out!

"What's with the Wolf references?" Chloe asked as she raised her head and gave her best howl to the moon.

"It's short for Wolfsky, his last name. A good Ukrainian boy."

"Gotcha!"

"Well, girl, there we have it straight from the horse's mouth."

"Really? I was thinking it sounded like it was coming from the other end!"

"Let's find you a man before mine gets here to pick me up, shall we."

"Okay, I think we go here to enter our search criteria. Wow, this is really customisable. It's almost like ordering from a menu! Let's see, I think I'll place my order for men within a 40 kilometre radius who are non-smokers, stand over 5'11", looking for a relationship, and are between the ages of 30 – no, 32 and 42. That should give us a few to choose from."

I hit enter and it was then that I received the biggest shock of my dating life (and, believe me, there had been quite a few before that). The unexpected happened. My very own computer, in my very own office, in the comfort of my very own home presented me with a list of men, single men. These guys were online, on this site, looking, like I was, to connect with someone. They were looking for dating, relationships, and possibly even marriage. This list contained not just 10 men, not 20, not even 30. It was bursting with a grand total of 337 men who were on this site, who met my criteria and who might be looking for someone just like me. Jackpot! Man, was I going to be busy.

"Holy guacamole. Does that say 337 matches?" Chloe blurted.

"Uh-huh. It most certainly does. I was a little sceptical but I want to thank you darling. For in one night you have introduced me to more men than all of my other friends combined have managed to do over my entire lifetime."

"You are welcome. But before you gush all grateful, are there any hotties on that list?"

Sitting side by side, we began the sorting, sifting and selecting process. Some guys were attractive and got my immediate attention so I clicked through their photo to read their profile. Guess guys weren't the only visual creatures.

Some were just not my physical match and I knew at a glance. I had always preferred attractive, tall, dark haired, casually dressed, well-built men who were on the muscular side. And if they had blue eyes, full lips and a hairy chest, then all the better.

We were greeted by 'Imyourcowboy'. His photo popped up to say 'howdy'. Was that a blue and black checkered lumber jacket he was wearing underneath a long denim outback coat? And did those sideburns extend down his face as far as his mouth? Nope, definitely not my cowboy.

And then there was 'mulletman' – my profile name for him, not his.

Some of guys were handsome but their profiles were lacking,

and there were those few who just didn't 'speak' my love language.

There was one who was, as his handle suggested, handsome. But were those Star Trek posters all over the wall behind him? Yep. Okay, perhaps we'll meet in the next galaxy 'captainhandsome'.

What was it with these downtown dudes who didn't have a car or didn't even drive? I didn't think 'Cuddlecat' was a match either. Apparently this little kitty was unlicensed. I was not prepared to be 'Driver Dog' on all our dates.

Then there was the guy who had his girlfriend in the photo. I thought he was just too lazy to edit the woman out of the photo but no, she was part of the deal. The profile read:

We are an attractive professional married couple who are looking for a sexy, open-minded woman to join us for some erotic times in our home. Candles, a lovely dinner, wine and jazz will set the mood for our encounters. Other fun times for the three of us would include trips to the cottage and sailing. Sporting, rock and live theatre also await us.

He might have been perfect if he wasn't a he-plus-a-she! I wanted to *be* a couple not *be with* a couple.

Some guys openly admitted to fetishes and sexual practices that I couldn't ever see myself involved in, let alone advertising to the world that I sought others to join me in. I didn't care what anyone said – potatoes just were not THAT versatile a food.

As I travelled from screen to screen, looking at profile after profile, I realised that this was a visual medium and the photo was the key. Roman was bang on. The right photo made all the difference, especially when there was so much competition. Some guys had very compelling photos, but others were using really bad ones where you couldn't even see their faces. Some were using pictures that were of celebrities and not of themselves at all, others were showing lovely travel shots and landscapes and some chose to not even post one. Some had presumably their old girlfriends beside them. But others were thoughtful enough to go that extra step and black out the girl's face. Some men had their photos with their children, some with their pets or parents. Some were half naked sprawled across a bed or standing in the shower, some were dressed to the nines. Others added unique photo-edited elements to theirs, and others even added headings, titles and call-outs. Then there were the men who had photos but they had to grant you access before you could actually view them.

Yep, this was certainly an interesting insight into contemporary dating life and endlessly entertaining to boot. I almost didn't care if I actually met a man from here or not because the simple act of browsing through the list was proving to be even more amusing than anything they called reality TV. Okay, so I said 'almost'! Yes, yes, yes, I desperately wanted to meet a man from here, or from anywhere, for that matter. It was time. It really was.

As I scanned from photo to photo, I repeated, as much as I hated to admit it, that Roman was right. The picture really was the first sort. I, like others on here, decided if I wanted to know more solely based on my reaction to a tiny thumbnail photo. I wondered if this made me shallow or if it was just a necessary reaction to being presented with so many options?

I drew great pleasure from reading their profile names and opening lines too. They combined to give me another sense of who these guys were. The opening lines were definitely phase two of the selection process. I found myself thinking that if the photo got my attention, did the opening line keep it? I couldn't help seeing things this way. I had spent the last 15 years working in marketing and I needed the visuals to match the words and vice versa.

I groaned when I read 'R U the cure for bacheloritis?' posed by one man's opening line. I chuckled as another joked, 'Bad spellers of the world – UNTIE!' Then there were the more romantic breed who promised hope by asking things like, 'Are you ready for your last first date?' and yes, I drifted into that romantic notion for just a moment. *Ah. The last first date. Now that would be heaven.*

Blink. Blink. Blink. The 'new message' button at the top of the screen called out to me. I had my first message. I could feel the anticipation rise in my chest. My eyes got a little wider and a smile crept across my face as I saw the flash of opportunity blink before me.

"I think I've just got my first message. Let's read it together," I called out over the thwang, thwang, thwang of Chloe who was relieving her restlessness by bouncing on my stability ball out in the hall.

Sending the silver orb flying into a not-too-amused Dylan, she leapt off it and rejoined me as she squealed, "Let's see. Let's see."

The hopeful romantic in me opened the message half expecting it to be from the hottest guy on the system proposing we jet off to Bali the following weekend to a tranquil setting where we could focus solely on getting to know each other. Click. The message window opened. **Welcome to wheresinglesfindlove.com. We are so happy that you chose us to accompany you on your journey into finding lasting romance… to view our members' success stories, click on the link called Our Happiest Hearts.**

"I don't think so. They can't be serious. Who writes this drivel? It's a good thing we're drinking wine, because this kind of cheese needs a little something to wash it down." I closed the window and hit delete. It was then that I noticed the sender's address was 'admin'. *Note to self; admin is not your dream guy.*

"Mr. Right, oh Mr. Right, where are you?" I borrowed Chloe's sing-song style and went back to whittling down my list of 337 Mr. Maybes.

"Well hello 'Shaunisdabomb'!" Chloe chimed in blowing 'Shaunisthebomb' air kisses.

"He's very handsome. Look at that strong jawline and nice dark full head of hair. Rugged yet polished, good teeth, 6'2". Hey it seems like we even have a few of the same interests – volleyball, hiking and photography. Okay, I'll put him on my favourites list."

I continued my play by play for Chloe's benefit. "And here's another, 'Oneguy2go'. While I'm not usually a fan of blonds, he's striking and has a really warm smile. He says he's a professional, he plays a few sports, likes dogs, is divorced, no kids and loves to read, travel, cook. And he comes equipped with a tool belt." Him we kept in the favourites list.

"Is that a sexiest man of the year look-a-like with a puppy? Yep, definitely into the faves with you too 'pixelpunk'."

"'Imanuwoman' – ya right, 41, my ass. If you're a day under 55, I'll eat that potato that 'potatoman' was talking about earlier. See ya, wouldn't want to be ya!"

"Your instant message window just flashed open," Chloe piped in from her seat as co-pilot.

Cumsafter68 says:
You are very pretty katontheprowl

Katontheprowl says:
Thx

Cumsafter68 says
You have nice full lips 2.

Katontheprowl says:
Thx again

I smiled, sat up a little straighter, feeling my desirability quotient rising.

Cumsafter68 says:
How would you like to wrap those big lips around my huge hard cock?

"Oh my gawd - Chloe does this say what I think it says?" I almost screamed as the words tossed me and my nice full lips back in my chair.

"EEEW – yes! Get rid of him."

Katontheprowl says:
No thx!

"Can you believe that?" I closed the message window. I was shocked at this pig's directness. This message in no way resembled the highly romanticised version I had concocted in my head of the warm, witty, well written, mannerly and respectful message I'd envisioned receiving as my first. I shook my head.

"I guess his profile name should have been my first clue. Had I honestly expected manners or romance from someone named 'Cumsafter68'? I'm really not sure this online dating stuff is for me. What if they're all like that guy?"

What if this was another big fat dating failure to add to my growing list? My doubtful thoughts had to make an appearance and take a bow. They couldn't sit idly in their seats and watch and applaud as my optimism around finding love took centre stage. They had to inject those tiny little shadows of doubt. They were just cameo appearances, but they were there.

"Give it a chance. They can't all be goofs. And, at least here you don't have to meet them face-to-face unless you want to. The dirtbags will show their stripes early and you do what you just did, delete them and move on."

Chloe was right. When it came to love and matters of the heart, she usually was. It was my own judgment that was somewhat less than reliable.

"Okay who's next?" I sifted through more photos and added more Mr. Maybes to my favourites list. 'Suckerforasmile', 'Dearintheheadlights', 'Allthiscanbyours', 'Firstborn' and 'PHDjock' all got added, bringing my number of favourites up to 17. Not a bad first sort.

"There's Boomer," I called to Chloe as she was stepping out of the bathroom.

"What?" she shrieked. She ran to my side still buttoning her jeans, her eyes wide with a fiery mixture of fear, disbelief and anger. She peered at the screen, scanning the eight photos that were displayed there. "Where?"

"Whoa, calm down girl, he's outside. I just heard him pull up and Dylan has already assumed the position downstairs at the door, tail tapping the floor, ready to greet him."

"I knew that." A calmness then replaced the panic in her voice.

I pondered the reaction I had just witnessed. Not at all what I would have ever expected from Chloe. But I guessed that even the best relationships had their moments when doubt could arise. And given how easy it was to put yourself out there and create a profile on these sites whether you were married or not, I guessed that just added fuel to that doubtful fire.

CHAPTER 3

The door closed behind them and there it was again – the loneliness that always felt the worst in those minutes right after company said their goodbyes. When visitors were there the house hummed with warmth and laughter, activity, stories and fun. It just felt more like a home when others were there within its walls.

The loneliness was one of the main reasons I had adopted Dylan. Others thought I had performed a noble gesture, adopting a rescue dog that had suffered a tough start. I spoiled him and gave him a good home, a place where he was safe. He was loved but it wasn't without its selfish motivations. I needed him as much as he needed me. I was comforted by his presence. It warmed my soul to reach down and burrow my hand in his warm fur or look into his gentle eyes. I felt reassured by his loyalty. He made me chuckle when he pranced proudly from room to room with his squeaky toy hanging from his mouth. I felt protected through the night. At the slightest sound he'd be up at the top of the stairs issuing a warning bark to ensure danger stayed at bay. I felt safer when we ran and went on long walks together. He was good company. Life was better shared with him.

He lay sleeping on his mat near the door. Quiet now. The house hungered for more laughter, more interaction, more life, more love.

Cleaning up the dishes, I thought about Chloe and Boomer. On some level I was jealous of their wonderful relationship and happy, busy home. Staring down at my left hand there appeared a 5-carat sized bubble on my left ring finger. Was it a sign?

I glanced back at the stairs. With a few keystrokes I could end this uncomfortable solitude. There were at least 17 men upstairs I could invite in for a visit. Invigorated by that thought, I fixed myself a lemon chamomile tea and honey in the biggest mug I could find, trotted up the stairs and settled myself into my very own contemporary parlour where I began chatting up the gentlemen callers.

Within seconds of logging on, the instant message window within the site opened up to greet me.

Somebodysprince says:
Hi how are you tonite?

Katontheprowl says:
Great you?

Somebodysprince says:
Excellent! So, beautiful, DYCHO?

Katontheprowl says:
Huh? DYCHO???

Somebodysprince says:
Do you come here often? LOL

Katontheprowl says:
Haha. No, in fact, you're the first person I've talked to, just posted my profile tonight.

Somebodysprince says:
I'm flattered. So I'm your first? LMAO. How often can we say that

when we're in our 30s?

This guy had a sense of humour. But where was his profile? I clicked on the hyperlink of his profile name and that presented me with the details of his online calling card.

> Hello Ladies. I am looking for my new best friend, lover and partner all in one. I am an independent business professional who is not into playing games. I am looking for a woman between the ages of 28-42. She should be confident, honest, professional, likes to dress up and down, affectionate and open minded. I love to live life to the fullest and I'm looking for someone who would like to join me on the ride. I love the outdoors, fine dining, wine tasting and travel. If you're interested, let's chat and see where things go.

He had similar interests too – volleyball, hiking, campfires, dogs, Thai food. He was tall, a little on the young side but definitely cute – full head of thick dark hair, nice build from what I could tell and big hands. I liked a man with big hands and strong forearms.

> **Somebodysprince says:**
> So u play v-ball?

> **Katontheprowl says:**
> Yep, every Thurs.

> **Somebodysprince says:**
> Me too on wed – great game. If I'm lucky maybe U and I can play, get our own game of 2s going and tumble around in the hot sand some time soon.

He followed with a wink. He came out of the gate flirting. I joined in.

> **Katontheprowl says:**
> And when we discover just how well we play together, we'll reign king and queen of the court. After we hit the showers, I could whip us up a tasty Thai dinner to celebrate!

> **Somebodysprince says:**
> Mmm Thai – now that's the spot – give me basil beef or

massaman curry and oh, baby. U do have game. Sign me up – I'll even bring the wine. Do u prefer red or white?

Katontheprowl says:
**I drink both. Just not together! Red relaxes me and white, well…
I'll tell you later!**

I added a wink of my own.

We continued our flirtations and I learned that this prince's name was actually Mike. He was the younger of two boys, did software consulting, his last relationship ended about a year ago, he preferred older women (which was good because I was, by about 6 years) and he appeared very attracted to me, or at least to the picture I had posted.

We chatted online for almost an hour, laughing about past dating adventures and sharing details about our lives. We exchanged email addresses and made plans to meet the next weekend to see how we'd connect in person. A pretty good first encounter – okay, second encounter really, but who was counting.

Not caring about the time or that I had to work in the morning, I cycled through a few more profiles, scanned a few more photos, reacted to a few more corny lines, added a couple more maybes to my burgeoning favourites list and was just about to sign off for the night when I saw an opening line that drew an audible 'oh' from my lips. It wasn't wickedly amusing, predictable or corny but solid, warm, sincere and innocent. Yes, the words that caught my eye must have been written by a decent and playful man.

Attaboy77

Happy, curious, plays well with others, a pleasure in the room, but hates to share his crayons…

His profile was awaiting review so his details hadn't been posted yet. I wondered about the man who wrote them – those few words painted a vivid picture. A picture of a well mannered, well behaved, well adjusted, happy school boy who was sociable and balanced but, even at a tender age, knew where his lines were drawn and grasped tightly to the things he held dear. Yes, I wondered about what kind of man that boy had grown to become. Even though he hadn't posted a picture yet he was quickly added to my list of 'Those I Must Learn More About'.

I retired that night with a smile on my face and a revitalised faith in romance. With Dylan settled on the floor at the foot of my bed, I drifted off easily to the comforting thoughts that maybe, just maybe, this online dating thing held some real promise.

CHAPTER 4

Beep. Beep. Beep. Beep. Beep. The blaring sound of a truck backing up shot me upright from a sound sleep. I had managed to flip the alarm switch from radio to buzzer again. I hated when that happened. It propelled me instantly into the hectic pace of the workday rather than easing me into it gradually. But let's face it, rising at 5:00am is not enjoyable, regardless of how you're woken.

My mind wandered and entertained one possible exception. If at 4:59am a warm strong hand reached out and began gliding its way ever so tenderly from my neck to my shoulder, tracing its fingers across my bicep, down the forearm that framed my side, I wouldn't mind waking up. Then if it snuck around my waist, to rest for just a moment in its curve before reaching around and more firmly clasping my butt and pulling me toward the man to whom it belonged, I'd be okay with rousing from slumber. If that was then followed by one long stroke from this manly hand as it ran down my long leg, tickling the back of my kneecap, then quickly racing up the inside of my thigh to frolic in the warm and welcoming amusement area that had been closed to visitors for too long now, I'd be okay with opening my eyes. If all that were to happen, waking at that hour would be a welcome change.

But that was not to be the case today.

I sleepily stepped over Dylan and into the washroom. From my porcelain perch I looked down at the curled-up clump of golden fur that watched from the hall. I returned his stare, shook my head and said aloud "Dylan, it's been way too long. I really need a date!"

But first, I had to go to work.

"You've got to be kidding! She wants WHAT?" Barb, the senior designer stood up and screeched the question over the grey maze of office dividers that spanned four desks, a production table and a small meeting area, complete with funky chairs, that defined the Marketing den.

"Barb, please keep it down. Everyone, come on let's gather 'round for a team chat." I needed to communicate Beatrice's latest request to the people who would actually be responsible for making it all a reality.

"What's up?" Ravi came around the corner sipping latte number three. He was dressed in black, MacBook under his left arm.

Her perfume arrived before she did. Candace, our Marketing Manager, chirped in with, "Rumour has it, there's some new buzz from the Queen Bea". She plunked herself on the corner of the desk.

"Yes there is. Please, have a seat everyone."

"Can we make it quick? We're on deadline with the first round of ads."

"Yes, I know Barb. Just join us over here. This will only take a few minutes. Everyone knows that we've been toying with the idea of changing the format for our client proposals, making it more brand appropriate, reviving it, giving it a far more contemporary look, layout and feel."

They all nodded.

I continued. "We all agreed that this was necessary… actually we even got excited about the prospect as we could have some fun with it… get creative. We also had this on deck for completion for year end."

"Let me guess, regardless of what the calendar says today, it's now December and we have four weeks to do it all?" Ravi wasn't usually this sarcastic, but the workload of late was stressing him. His daily intake of cres had increased from five to seven over the past few weeks.

"Just under. Beatrice wants the new format to launch alongside the 'Do What You Love' campaign."

"And just who does she expect to do it?" Candace was rolling her eyes. "And if it's us, what huge project are we delaying to make room for it?"

"Well it is us. And unfortunately, nothing else is changing – we are still committed to delivering everything else. I know how hard you've all been working. I know that it's a lot to ask. I know that it's not the desired timing, but I also know that if anyone can pull it off, it's this team. You guys and gals are the best."

"But where does it end?" Barb was scowling. "I was hoping to take some vacation in the next month. It's been seven months since I've had a vacation day, let alone a week off."

"And I'm spending more time with my laptop than I am with my girlfriend and she's not happy about it… not happy at all," Ravi added.

"What is she expecting in that time frame?" Candace was always the first to move forward into taking action. 'Just git 'er done' was her motto. In fact, we bought her a t-shirt that she proudly dons as a testament to her approach.

"Well, the good news is, I've talked Beatrice out of the hard copy versions and we're looking only at a new media format. However, we will need to create some new messaging for the template as well as some regional variations. We will also need to develop options that can accommodate joint venture proposals. But it could be – and was until I spoke to her – much, much worse."

"So we have a month?" Barb asked.

"Just under… and I'll work side by side with you all to 'git 'er done'!"

"Then can we take some vacation?" Barb was almost pleading.

"Definitely." Their faces were not pleased, but they were a great team. They were committed to me and to doing a superior job. I was grateful for their support. "So, are we in? Can I count on you?"

"Ya, ya."

"Of course. But you'll need to buy me the occasional one of these," Ravi said, shaking his latte cup at me.

"Yes, but let's be clear we're doing it for you… not for the Queen Bea." Candace had to add that caveat.

"Thank you all. I'm lucky to have your support and am grateful for it. Now, let's get to work."

7:15pm and I was finally arriving home. This working for a living bites. I would finally arrive home more than twelve hours after I had left. No wonder I hadn't been dating. Even if I made the time for it, I didn't have the energy. Yes, something had to change. Things had gone too far out of balance.

Luckily Dylan had a dog walker come in twice a day. He had hour-long walks, visits to the park and time with the neighbour-hood canines. He spent a day at the doggie spa every couple of months. When it came down to it, he had a more active social life than I did. And far more balance.

For the most part, I enjoyed being Vice President of Marketing at Ardent and was proud of my career successes. But lately, I was growing more and more resentful. Unlike a lot of my friends, my job was more than a way of life for me. It was my life. I commuted every day from the calm lush greenery of the suburbs to the city that sprouted crops of concrete, glass, power and money. I travelled a lot, visiting some airports with a frequency that equalled that of visits to old friends. I worked long hours attending industry functions, working on volunteer committees to build and maintain a profile both for the firm and myself. I wore my mobile phone and laptop as fashion accessories, and rarely had days where the thoughts, problems, frustrations, demands and politics of the job didn't circle around me, swarming like bloodthirsty mosquitoes looking for a fix.

In a way, my career had become my spouse. We had been cohabitating now for almost 15 years. When people asked if I was ever married I often responded jokingly by asking in return, "You mean other than to my career?"

Not that I wasn't grateful. My career had afforded me certain luxuries; a home, furniture, travel when I had the notion, and I could buy a $40 dollar bottle of wine, pick up the tab at dinner, purchase a $700 suit, the vehicle of my choice and another pair of shoes whenever I felt like it.

My job had been a good spouse. But today I wanted a divorce. At Ardent Staffing Inc., there had been growing pressure to perform, produce more in less time, spend less money and see greater returns. Their demanding standards had grown more and more impossible to meet. The past six months had been a pressure cooker, sucking out every creative idea, cost-cutting measure, diplomatic PR recovery and strategic marketing campaign that I had in me and from every member of my team. As VP Marketing, my job was supposed to be tough, demanding, challenging, but not impossible. And now, the CEO was on my back again, pushing, prodding, insisting that the current project be completed three weeks faster at 20% less than the budget projections that everyone had agreed to at the project's inception. Apparently, both magician and miracle worker should have appeared on my resume. My frustration had reached new heights.

I closed the front door, kicked off my shoes, gave the boy a hello pat and went straight upstairs to my home office. 'Leave work at work, and concentrate on home at home.' I chanted my new mantra over and over as I sat down.

I dropped my mail on the desk and was just about to change into Dylan-walking clothes when I was interrupted by The Wolf-man IM-ing me. It was like Roman had ESP and knew exactly when I'd stepped within arms length of my computer. Why he just didn't use the telephone, I'd never know.

K8 says:
Yes?

Bigbadwolf says:
So, how's the online d8ing virgin doing 2day?

K8 says:
Just fine thanks, my first time was a bit awkward, but fun for the most part

Bigbadwolf says:
Yes we've converted another 1

K8 says:
Let's not get carried away, it was fun, I sifted through a bunch of profiles, had a really good online chat with one, and I actually have A DATE!

I added the celebrating smiley with the party hat for effect.

Bigbadwolf says:
Gr8 – YMMD - I'm proud of my student!

K8 says:
YMMD?

Bigbadwolf says:
You made my day.

K8 says:
Thanks oh omnipotent one

Bigbadwolf says:
But b4 u meet this guy, I think u need the benefit of Rule #2 from Roman's Rules of Online Dating

K8 says:
And what might that be?

Bigbadwolf says:
Have at least 2-3 chats b4 meeting this dude. Enough to get a good feel about him – make sure he's not a creepy wacko psycho killer – not 2 many tho, or they might b a waste of time.

K8 says:
Sounds reasonable. But why a waste of time?

Bigbadwolf says:
Ah... I know people who thought they were in love based on their online chats that went on 4 hours nite after nite. Then they met IP/IRL and no spark, not chemistry, nothin', nada, rien, neechochoh.

K8 says:
IP? IRL?

Bigbadwolf says:
In person or IRL = in real life

K8 says:
Good point – thanks – maybe I'll go see if my guy's online now and check to see how many other e-notes were left under my pillow last night- lol.

Bigbadwolf says:
Hope your mailbox is burstin' babe.

K8 says:
Thanks R – Kayte OUT!

CHAPTER 5

I sat down at the desk, opened up my music library, set it to random play and signed on to www.wheresinglesfindslove.com.

I wondered if I had actually received any messages. And if I had, would there be one from 'Attaboy77'? After checking, it was a 'yes' on the first count and a 'no' on the second. But, on a positive note, I had four new men waiting to chat with me. I felt my confidence shine just a little brighter.

All of the notes were similar. "Hi saw your profile, liked your picture, sounds like you know what you want, I could be it, have a look at mine and if you're interested, then get back."

There was, however, one that stood out from the rest, yet not in a good way. It was from 'Mantasy'. It proposed something very different from the other three:

Seems you need a cuckold. You look like the perfect cuckoldress. In case you don't know, this is a relationship where the woman is allowed sexual freedom while the man is not. An agreement where she can have other lovers for sex only (with his knowledge, of course) while remaining in a loving relationship,

and he remains totally faithful to her. You get your cake and eat it too while remaining in a good emotional and sound relationship.

Just what was it from my profile that made Mantasy think that I'd be looking for a cuckold? I thought this sounded absurd. Definitely not what I was looking for. That was one note that wouldn't get a response from me. It made me stop and think about just how many kinds of "relationships" one could have. It's no wonder finding the right guy, who wanted the same kind of relationship you did was such a challenge. I copied and pasted this into an email and sent it to Chloe and Marnie just to see if they'd ever heard of such a thing and give them a little glimpse into the dating pool I had dipped my toes into. Then I blocked him and moved on.

Okay, now where was 'Attaboy77' and his crayons? I sifted through my favourites list and there he was. His profile had been approved. I had a look to see what he had to say for himself.

Hi there. Thanks for having a look.

I'm looking for new experiences, some new friends and eventually, when slapped upside the noggin with it... THE ONE!

Things have to start somewhere, so I figured why not here? Given all the cool kids seem to be doing this I thought I'd give it a try too. Ultimately, we all want someone to grow old with and have fun doing it but I'm not in a hurry to jump into something serious. Some things just shouldn't be rushed. I already have great kids, so I'm not looking for more. If you want 'em, great - go for it. But I'm not your guy.

I love new experiences and am open to pretty much anything (but I do have limits). Being a witty sort, you can bet I'll make you laugh - hopefully so much that it hurts (but in a good way). And if you can return the favour, you get big bonus points.

I'm a man who's pretty easy to please. I'm just as happy at the beach, travelling, motorcycling through winding country roads, dining out for Thai, Italian or just a big ole juicy burger, or staying in and enjoying good food and great wine with the right company. I'll even admit to enjoying shopping, but shhh... you

didn't hear that from me.

So if you're upbeat, fun, fit, attractive and you like new things, drop me a line with a photo please.

Cheers!

I might just be the "new thing" you've been looking for.

T.

Compared to 'Mantasy', 'Attaboy77' sounded so incredibly normal, like someone who could actually fit into my world. I wondered what the T stood for. Ted? Timothy? Terry? Tobias? Todd? Tyrone? And how old were his kids and how many? Oh heavens, what if he had five or six? A couple I could probably handle, but a half dozen? Not in this lifetime.

The speakers caught my attention with an all too familiar and memory laden tune. The song posed the question, "Do you remember?" The melody transported me directly back to The Palace to that one extraordinary Valentine's evening. The Valentine's I'd remember for a lifetime.

How long had it been since I had seen him? The song continued to flood more and more details of that last magical night with Simon into consciousness.

I remember that he was dressed in his crisp white, highly starched Egyptian cotton shirt, jacket long since removed, sleeves rolled up showing his muscular hairy forearms, black and silver tie undone and slung loosely around his neck, black wool dress pants hugging his butt just tightly enough. I recalled him, placing down his freshly mixed scotch and soda, rising from his chair as he heard the first few bars of the song. He extended his left hand, palm up, requesting mine in return. Using both hands, he pulled me to my metallic, t-strap sandaled feet and locked my gaze with his deep sultry cocoa eyes.

Exactly on cue, he began his serenade posing his own question, "Do you remember?" We were all alone in our very own love filled cocoon. Our shyness disappeared. We danced unabashedly, kissing, twirling, laughing, touching and owning those few square feet of dance floor like is was the most prized parcel of land on earth. Simon added his own animated gestures. The air was lightly scented with a hint of the scotch he had been drinking as he continued to serenade me with his deep gravelly voice and I drank in every word.

Dylan appeared, arresting my trek down memory lane. He stood there leash in mouth just as I came to the liberating realisation that I hadn't thought about Si for almost one whole month. Maybe that meant I was finally getting over him. It had been four years. Four years since the man of my dreams, the man I thought I'd dance through eternity with, shattered the fragile twin gifts I had given him, my trust and my heart.

It had been a long time for a lot of things.

The song played me out as I got up and walked to the stairs, ready to go spend some quality time with my loyal little Dylan.

'Attaboy77' would have to wait until I had some time to ponder his profile and consider what I'd say to make the right first impression. There was something to think about while I walked.

CHAPTER 6

By 9:30pm, I had dined on a large bowl of homemade apple curry soup, spent some time online and taken the boy for a quick jog around the big block.

I ran through the community park with its swing sets and slides and open playing fields, then by the large single-family units that dominated my neighbourhood. I smiled acknowledging the neighbours who were toting grocery bags in from their SUVs, the men placing trash cans and recycle bins at the curb, and those sweeping or watering. I passed couples out for their evening stroll, some with dogs, some with children and some with neither.

Dylan and I ran by driveway after driveway of parked cars placed beside well-manicured lawns and inhaled the smell of family life as it wafted out from windows and doors. I wondered how life was lived in those houses, how couples spent their evenings, how it felt to share a space, a closet, a life, spending all your days with a spouse and children. This was the life that Simon and I had planned. Every day my neighbourhood would taunt me with its appeal. Everyday I doubted its viability as a life option for me just that little bit more.

Dylan's mouth was open and smiling, his tongue hung low, panting and dripping. My stride slowed as we turned the last corner, just doors away from our place. I climbed the steps, packed the memories of Simon away, entered the house and bounded up the stairs to the office. Red-faced, sweaty and panting, I sat down with determination. I tapped at the keyboard until I had scheduled another date.

That meant I had two dates in one week, with two different men. I looked forward to meeting Mike on Saturday, but the second date for the week just seemed to be the natural result of that evening's conversations.

When I signed on, 'PASHN81' was the first to instant message me:

PASHN81 says:
Hey beautiful, how are ya? I just ran across your profile and thought I'd give you a shout. I'm sure you must have a lot of men writing to you, so I'll keep this short.

Check out my pics and profile and get back to me if you're interested. Hope to hear from you soon.

Bryan.

'PASHN81''s profile read:

It's pretty hard to sell yourself in general, let alone on the Internet. I'm a man who takes pride in everything he does. I believe in honesty and doing the right thing. I love life and try to live everyday to its fullest. I know only too well that it can be far too short. I have an appreciation of the finer things life has to offer, however, I'm happy with the small things as well. I'm very passionate, seductive, open minded and down to earth.

I've been told I'm the right balance between protector and cheerleader. And I'm always a gentleman. I'm charismatic and take enjoyment in trying to make everybody around me smile. While I've seen enough challenges, I'm not negative and don't sweat the small stuff. My best friend is a furry four-legged lady

so please don't be jealous. Okay, I've babbled enough, if you're interested in finding out more give me a shout. Hope to hear from you soon.

Bryan

His interests included anything active, literature, the arts, traveling, running, fundraising, cooking and he openly admitted he was hopelessly addicted to hot chocolate. He had a dog, had been married once, no kids, six foot, muscular and quite striking.

I responded.

Katontheprowl says:
Hi there. Thanks for the note. I'm keen to learn more about you. Where to now?
Kayte

Within seconds he replied.

PASHN81 says:
Thanks so much for the compliment. How about chatting on IM?
Bryan

It was my turn again.

Katontheprowl says:
Sure. Here's my email address... K8@socialarity.com

I waited for the messenger instant window to appear. It took all of 10 seconds.

Bryan says:
Hi, how are ya?

K8 says:
Great - you?

Bryan says:
Always good thx

K8 says:
Such a positive response – I like that.

Bryan says:

So what brings a sexy and intelligent woman like yourself
online? You must have men banging your door down.

K8 says:
I'm trying to meet men I wouldn't normally meet, casting the net
a little wider – pardon the pun

Bryan says:
Badumpbump!

K8 says:
I liked your profile.

Bryan says:
Yes, I changed it. Originally had a profile that I playfully titled,
"I'm looking for a real dog!"

K8 says:
OK???

Bryan says:
Let me explain. It compared the kind of woman I'm looking for to
all the characteristics of man's best friend.

K8 says:
Being a DP, I get that. Love to read it - do you still have it?

Bryan says:
DP?

K8 says:
Oh sorry, dog person.

Bryan says:
Ah… and yes still have it! You sure you want to read it?

K8 says:
Absolutely!

Bryan says:
Okay. Here you go…

I'm looking for a real dog. People ask me what type of woman
I'd be happy with. My usual response is one who's a lot like my

dog, Wink. I want a woman who'll gladly eat all of my cooking (sometimes right out of my hand, sometimes off the floor). I want a woman who is sociable and gets excited when we have visitors, one who is happy to play catch, go for a walk, lay in the sunshine, go for a swim, accompany me on a long run and get her belly rubbed. I need a woman who isn't caught up in accumulating things but prefers experiences instead.

I'd love a woman who could be happy spending all day every day with me. I'm looking for a woman who doesn't play games, who's upfront, whose behaviour is consistent, a lady who is incredibly loyal and tirelessly affectionate. I'd love a woman who is curious and likes to venture off on her own to explore new things, learn some new tricks, but gladly returns to share them with me. I'd be grateful for a woman who can easily shake things off and bury things, like any past baggage and silly arguments. I'd like a woman who receives affection freely and loves to be made a fuss over. So, I guess, I'm looking for someone who is a lot like my best friend Wink, but hopefully she won't be as hairy or as comfortable relieving herself in public.

K8 says:
LOVE IT!!!

We went on to talk about where we lived, our dogs, our interests, our jobs and our shared hot chocolate addiction. He confided that he had studied criminology and I thought that sounded fascinating. I asked a number of questions about his work, but he politely avoided answering some of them with a commitment to doing so later. We chatted more, he then asked what my schedule was like and if there was any chance we might meet up the following night to build on this great conversation. I thought, heck, why not? If I was going to do this, I might as well do it. And he was so handsome. He was going to be in great demand so I might as well get the jump on my competition.

We agreed to meet at a busy restaurant at 1900 hours (his words, not mine) that was part of an entertainment complex located half way between our respective homes.

He seemed like a good guy, very upbeat and positive. And

did I mention he was handsome? Just how handsome, I looked forward to finding out.

I rushed home from work, had a quick shower and retrieved the date outfit that had been ready and proudly displayed on the bed since 6:30 that morning. The new burgundy long sleeved top was clingy where it should be and gathered where I needed a little help. The dark jeans were the best choice to complete the ensemble as they had a fine caramel coloured stitching that picked up the accent colour in the top. I donned the date underwear. Tonight it was the brown lace underwire bra with the matching Brazilian cut panties – the perfect balance of form and function. Not that anyone was going to see it, but it just made me feel better knowing that they could. I think of it as the female version of the boy scouts 'Be prepared' motto. The combination of pretty panties atop freshly shaved legs was telling evidence that a woman was prepared. I wore the new matching necklace and earrings where all three had a quarter sized creamy yellow stone, the perfect shade to accentuate the lightest colour in my top.

I surveyed myself in the mirror, and was pleased. The hair played along and styled easily. The makeup was just right and the lips, oh, the lips. They looked perfectly kissable.

I had 40 minutes to get there and it was only a 25-minute drive, but I prided myself on rarely being late. Traffic moved along, I parked near the restaurant with 10 minutes to spare. I answered a text message from work and then pulled down the driver's side mirror and applied a final coat of lustre to my lips, a dab of powder on my nose, I removed my driving glasses, and performed the final check with one big wide smile – nothing in the teeth, and the final step in the ritual, a glance up the nose, nope, there were no "bats in the cave". I was good to go. I hopped out of the car to go meet Bryan. Hmm, Kayte and Bryan – that had a nice sound to it. Or, maybe Kathleen and Bryan? Or would it be Bryan and Kayte? The last one sounded best.

What would it be like to be married to a criminologist? What kind of exciting stories might he bring home? What sad tales would he endure? Would it be like what you see on all the crime scene investigation shows? I pondered whether or not our dogs would get along – his was a 40+ kilo Bernese Mountain Dog with only one eye, aptly named Wink and mine was an 30 kilo Golden, so I hoped that our hairy kids would at least like each other, 'cause I wasn't strong enough to control them if they didn't. I thought about what it might be like to kiss him. He's so handsome and looks like he has big soft lips. Would he try to kiss me that night in the restaurant? If we went for a walk? As he left me at my car?

I had a couple of minor butterflies, but they were flying in formation. I felt good about this one for he was the one who messaged me, he sounded very interested, wanted to meet sooner rather than later, so nothing to worry about. It was good practice for meeting Mike on Friday too.

Ten minutes of waiting grew to 15, which grew to 20, which grew to 25. I checked my mobile. No missed calls. Tables of twos announced themselves then were ushered off to various parts of the busy establishment. There was a group of 20-somethings meeting, then exploding, all over their newly engaged girlfriend. The ring was glistening, gorgeous and jealousy inducing. There was a team of co-workers who, judging by the balloons that bobbed above them, were celebrating a 50th birthday, and a variety of couples looking to grab a bite before crossing the street to snuggle up and take in the latest big screen flick.

But there was no Bryan. No call, no text message and no way I was waiting much longer.

25 minutes grew to 30, then to 35. Every time the door opened I'd feign a warm and welcoming smile in the hopes it would be him and that I'd make a stellar, unruffled, cheerful first impression. Shoving my hands in my pocket, I found the doggie cookies

I had brought for him to take home for Wink. That was okay, more for Dylan. I found my phone in the other pocket, checked it and no calls. He was now more than 40 minutes late. I decided to leave, albeit with my head hung a little lower, my step a little slower, my smile a little more forced and a heavier heart than when I had entered through those same doors. I went back to my car, deflated, disappointed and frustrated – not the feelings I had imagined this man was going to evoke.

I wondered what happened. The logical adult part of my brain said he'd forgotten, or something urgent or important came up. An accident, a death in the family, a fire, and he didn't have my number with him. Or that there had been some big break in a case he'd been working on, so he'd had to stay late at work and solve the case – him being a criminologist and all.

The self-conscious fat 13-year-old girl inside, however, had a very different version of the evening's events. She claimed he'd found someone prettier or nicer just that afternoon, or that the date had been nothing more that a cruel trick resulting from a bet with his buddies to see how fast I would agree to meet him. Worst of all, she teased that maybe he had actually been there, somewhere out of sight, watching, assessing, judging as I entered the restaurant and didn't like what he saw. He found me too tall, too old, too fat, or not pretty enough, not dressed well enough, just not his type.

I tried to quiet the screaming pubescent voice in my head, but we all know how loud teenagers can be.

The adult in me reached the car and took the driver's seat. I took out my phone, called his mobile, which I had packed in my purse, and surprise of surprises, I got his voicemail. "Hi Bryan. It's Kayte. It's after 7:40 now. I thought we were supposed to meet at 1900 hours. That is 7PM isn't it? There's no sign of you, so I don't know what's happened, but I'm going to head out as it looks like you're not showing. So maybe we'll talk again. Bye."

I thought that sounded very mature, very diplomatic because

what I really wanted to do was text him with a single word…
DICK! But I refrained.

Yes, this was a great first experience with dating in my newly
adopted online dating community. Hopefully, this wasn't the
M.O. of all the men online. While I drove home, my aggravation
grew, so I phoned Roman for some reassurance.

"Hey girl, great timing, I was just gonna call you. We're short a
gal for v-ball tonight. Wanna play?"

"I'm a little overdressed."

"Then take off a little sumpin' and get your cute butt out here.
We could sure use you."

"It's so nice to be wanted." I didn't feel much like playing, but I
did have my gym bag in the back and I was sure I could channel
my new found frustration into a few good hard hits. The reality
was that I had no competing plans and a whole lot of frustration
to unload.

The gym air was humid. It smelled of old wood, new shoes,
mold, dank leather and fresh sweat. Runners squeaked across the
polished floorboards. The sounds of whistles and bouncing balls
and player calls punctuated the constant hum of movement and
conversation.

We were up 24–17, game point. It was my serve. I bounced
it my signature five times, tossed it high with my left, jumped,
reached high and connected full right palm with the ball with
deft precision sending it hurling across the net. Its target was the
hole located about a foot and a half from the back line. Three of
our opponents moved toward it, one called "mine", extended her
arms, reached for the bump and missed, the other two dove to
either side of it narrowly missing each other and the ball. It was
the perfect ace. It curved and landed hard. The point was ours:
the game was too.

"Good game, good game." The two teams lined up for the ceremonial greetings and handshakes that signified the end of the game. Roman was booming behind me, "no way, he actually stood you up?"

"Could you keep it down, please?" I didn't want others to know my shame.

"The nerve."

"I couldn't believe it. Maybe this online thing isn't for me. Maybe these guys are all talk and no action."

Back at the bench, a perspiring Roman chugged from his water bottle. "Kayte, you just learned, albeit painfully, lesson #3 from Roman's Book of Rules for Online Dating. Never break the first date because you're apt not to get a second chance. There are tons of guys or gals swimming around in these online dating pools. If you're not prepared to dive in and take your place beside your chosen one, there are many others who will, gladly pushing you aside and claiming your prize."

"I guess it's pretty competitive... like dating on steroids, huh?"

"Exactly girl – you snooze, you lose. But his loss is my gain." He winked. My face obviously showed some discomfort with the suggestion. He quickly added, "because we got to spend the night with you on the courts."

"Exactly. It was just what I needed given the circumstances." I felt much better. I didn't know whether to attribute it to the ace, the two cleansing kill shots, our wins or the talk with Roman, but it had all helped.

Roman asked me to join him for a beer and wings, but I declined. I had a sushi craving. So, I got my sweaty hugs, grabbed my gym bag that now held my crumpled perfect date outfit, said my goodbyes and drove directly to my comfort food fix - one dragon and one kamikaze roll with extra pickled ginger on the side.

CHAPTER 7

I popped into my new hangout. First I checked my email for a note from Bryan explaining his absence. Nothing. I read a few emails, returned a couple, deleted the spam emails that clogged my inbox.

I laughed when I opened one of the few emails where I actually knew the sender. It was from Marnie. She had found herself a wonderful man, and enjoyed a healthy and supportive relationship. Her single days were now behind her but she still could relate to me more than most. She was pleased to hear that I was exploring another dating avenue, especially after the Roger fiasco, and this latest note was evidence of her unending support and encouragement. And of her impeccable timing.

The subject line read: **Fwd: Marriage, Schmarriage**

The body of the email read:

KaytieKat, In your efforts to find love, know that I'm right behind you and praying you find it. While you're looking, this might serve as a great reminder of just how good you've got it girl! Keep it handy.

Love you,

M

The attachment read:

Once upon a time, a guy asked a girl "Will you marry me?"

The girl said, "NO friggin' way!" And, of course, the girl lived happily ever after.

She ate, she shopped, she danced, went camping (AT THE HILTON), drank cosmopolitans, martinis and other girlie drinks, enjoyed a clean house, one with no noxious pull-my-finger smells hanging in the air, but there were gallons of ice cream in the fridge. She didn't cook unless she wanted to, she had sex whenever she pleased, did whatever the heck she wanted, never argued, didn't get fat, or if she did, she didn't care. She travelled more, slept in the centre of the bed, had lots of boyfriends (and maybe some girlfriends) or none at all, if she preferred. She saved more money, spent most of it on herself yet gave the occasional charitable donation to make her feel good inside. She had all the hot water she could ever use and the closet space was all hers.

She watched chick flicks, never football, wasn't forced to wear lacy thongs that crept up her butt or deal with mothers-in-law, crazed ex-wives, or whining children and she enjoyed high self esteem and an organised life if that's what she wanted. She never cried or lost her temper. She asked for directions and she felt and even looked fabulous in any one of the many pairs of sweat pants that filled her closet.

I saved Marnie's email in my 'keep these' folder then signed on to wheresinglesfindlove.com for two reasons. First I wanted to take a closer peek into 'Attaboy77''s profile and second I needed to send 'PASHN81' a note looking for an explanation for his absence last night.

I needed to close one book before opening another so I went to my favourites list, found 'PASHN81''s profile and clicked to send him a message. The subject line read, simply,

Well?

The note that followed wasn't nasty or bitchy or assumptive or judgmental. I typed:

I was there. You weren't. What happened?

I hit send and moved on to more enjoyable pursuits.

The error message popped up.

This email could not be sent. The recipient is no longer active on the system.

"No longer active?" I said out loud. I checked and Bryan's profile was not coming up under any of the search terms it should. I typed in the profile name and the message **No such profile exists.**

That was strange. I wonder what happened. He was probably married. In fact he did say he had been married. Funny, I can't remember him saying that he was no longer married. Great. He did sound a little too good to be true.

A few more keystrokes and I had located 'Attaboy77'. There he was in all his glory. I smiled when I saw his picture had been added. Well he certainly was at least 6'2 – in fact, he was ticking a number of boxes on my list. He was tall and lean from the looks of things, actually leaner than I liked, but that wasn't a deal breaker. Nothing my cooking couldn't rectify. He had a great smile, a pleasant and handsome face and he was slightly tanned. I couldn't make out much more because he was also wearing a baseball cap and sunglasses, looking very 'weekend-at-the-beach' casual. I had hoped I'd see more details, especially the eyes, but at least he was pretty clean-cut looking and probably quite handsome from everything I could tell.

After rereading his profile, I noted he seemed to have good manners as evidenced by the way he began it 'thanks for stopping in'. It sounded as if he was open to meeting, but it was also very apparent that he wanted to take things slow as there were a couple of references to that. I wondered why? Maybe he was hurt, maybe he had just come out of marriage, or maybe he wanted to play the field. Or maybe, like so many of us here, he was just a little suspect of this way of meeting people - curious, but cautious.

His sense of humour was evident and he was looking for someone of a similar ilk. He had a good variety of interests and apparently, judging by the photo, liked the beach. This was a biggie for me: I once dated a man who couldn't stand to be out in the sun, not a fit for this outdoor lover I'm afraid.

I wondered what Attaboy77 meant when he said 'FIT or slim, attractive' as those things are always so subjective. I was relatively fit, but not what I'd call slim, but that was my assessment, not his. What would he think of me? There was one sure way to find out and that was to message him.

The first contact had to sound fun and upbeat (his words) and I wanted it to be casual enough as not to appear to be 'rushing' him, again his words. I wanted it to sound confident and not desperate in any way, but it had to balance a slight aloofness with obvious sincerity.

Subject: I'll share my finger paints, if you share your crayons!

Hi there Attaboy77. Great profile - I especially loved your opening line! Sounds like you have quite the sense of humour and can appreciate the same. Like you, I'm open, optimistic and fun and am looking to meet some new people and figured why not try this avenue – I want to be one of the cool kids too! Have a peek at my profile and if you feel, as I do, that you'd like to learn more, then you know what to do. And, handing over the burnt sienna crayon would go a long way in scoring you some bonus points!

Before announcing my interest through cyberspace, I re-read the note and was pleased. It was playful, somewhat witty, light, and optimistic – and it showed that I actually read his profile and didn't just look at his photo.

I gave myself a well-deserved 'Attagirl!' and hit send.

It's almost as if he knew I had just sent a note to some other man's profile because I was then greeted by an instant message through the dating site's instant message window:

> Hey beautiful, just wanted to say hi and tell you that I can't wait to meet you.

This little ego boost came from 'Somebodysprince' who was currently online too.

Katontheprowl says:
It should be fun. Is it the weekend yet?

Somebodysprince says:
Not soon enough.

Katontheprowl says:
True – with the week I'm having at work, it can't come fast enough.

Somebodysprince says:
Sounds like someone needs a hug.

Katontheprowl says:
That would do nicely.

Somebodysprince says:
Then a hug you shall have.

Katontheprowl says:
Thanks Mike. Looking forward to meeting you too, but now I should head to bed. It's been a long day.

Somebodysprince says:
Goodnight Kayte, sweet dreams beautiful, xoxo.

Ahh. That was sweet. His interest was very reassuring, almost making up for the disappointment of last night.

Off to bed I went. Just before jumping in, I picked up the clock radio and made sure that, unlike today, tomorrow I'd wake to music that would gently glide me into my day, rather than hurl me headlong into it.

CHAPTER 8

It was Friday night and the throngs of commuters around me fell into two distinct categories. There were those who were battered by the week. Their expressions of visible exhaustion pleaded for the weekend to begin. There were also those with faces lit up with anticipation. They had finished the work week and were actively making plans on their mobiles as their faces glowed in hopeful anticipation of the weekend ahead. Like so many Fridays before, I had managed to leave work at the last minute. I packed my briefcase as I ran and wished hurried "have a great weekend" greetings to those last few people scattered around the office. I rushed for the last train where I'd try to squeeze in some needed socialising and venting during the ride home.

"That fucking bitch, I hate that fucking bitch boss of mine. I'm buying some lottery tickets right now, so maybe, just maybe, on Monday I can march into her office and tell that skank to gather up her half-witted lame marketing ideas, toss in her unreasonable expectations and sprinkle in some of her contacts who can do things 'much cheaper', mix them all together in a cocktail shaker and then shove it and her job up her skinny, little, tight, lily white ass and give her head a shake. And as a finishing touch, I'll serve it up with one of her signature smile and thumbs up combos as I say it." Poor Chloe was getting an earful, as were the people I passed as I clutched my phone and rushed for the last train out destined for my suburban refuge.

"Can I watch?" Chloe added.

"Sure. You can video it and put it on YouTube if you'd like."

Work was horrible lately. My boss had been worse than normal for a while now, I was overwhelmed with too many tasks, far too little time, I was stressed, tense and needed an escape and I hadn't had sex in ages. Yes, even oh-so realistic, 'proud to be independent and accomplished' me was having "knight on white horse" fantasies of a man who would not only love me like no other, but who would also whisk me off and away from my misery.

Chloe reminded me, "It's the weekend, time to focus on good things. Like your date tomorrow. So, what are you two doing? What are you gonna to wear? Besides the date panties? 'Cause I know you'll be wearing the date panties."

"That's if I wear panties at all," purposely whispered so the commuters wouldn't blush. "As for the outfit, haven't decided yet. What we're doing? We're going to meet for a coffee so we can talk, get to know each other a bit more. There's a great cosy little place down by the lake called The Snuggle Mug. They serve up a mean mochaccino. We can sit in or take it to go if we want and stroll around the waterfront. Just don't tell Dylan I'm walking without him. After that, who knows? We'll play it by ear. Okay hon, the train's about to pull in and I won't be able to hear you."

"Have fun KitKat, and be careful. Call me the minute you're done. I want to hear all about it. I love you."

"Love you lots too. Bye sweetie."

I put my phone away, plopped myself into my regular seat, let out a heavy sigh, closed my eyes and had a short fantasy of my boss getting her stiletto heel caught in the escalator as she tried to step off, laying there unable to extricate herself as hurrying commuter after commuter strode past her, ignoring her plight and pleading. The faceless strangers strode past her in their self-absorbed hurry to catch the train out of the rat race.

I switched my own train of thought to a more positive track and began mentally sorting through my closet for an appropriate outfit for my date. Coming up empty, the only thing I knew for certain was that I'd be wearing something different than what I had for Tuesday's fiasco and then decided that I'd treat myself with something new. That was the easy solution.

How I was going to find time to complete my weekend work tasks and have some semblance of a social life – now that was a tougher and all too familiar problem to overcome.

"You waited for how long?" Aaron asked as he filled my goblet far too full with Promised Land Shiraz, a deep, full-bodied Australian vintage.

"Over 30 minutes, just standing there in the foyer, head turning every time the door opened. I felt like a desperate puppy waiting to be liberated from the pound. I don't even want to imagine what the restaurant staff must have thought. I must have looked so pathetic." I took a sip and I glanced up with my best puppy dog eyes.

"He didn't even have the decency to call?" Melissa refilled her glass of white and then added an ice cube, a practice I could never quite understand. I preferred my wine, red or white, room temperature; the flavours were more pronounced.

"Nope. No call. No text. No call to the restaurant. No email waiting for me when I got home. Nothing!"

"Asshole," Melissa and Wanda echoed in unison before breaking into laughter.

"Aren't they all?" added Melissa.

"No, that's not fair. There are some good ones out there. Right here we have two of the very best."

"You know it." Aaron knew how to take a compliment.

"Seriously, you've ruined us. Other men will never be able to compete," I said.

"Yes, I'm beginning to think gay men should run courses for straight guys to teach them how to treat a woman right." Darlene, Wanda's sister and regular attendee of our Friday night gatherings, added, "You know what I think? I think we should call the jerk who stood you up and tell him exactly what we think of him. He can't do that to our Kayte and get away with it."

"He's going to have to deal with the likes of us." Aaron was puffing out his chest.

"Yes, let's, but let's have more wine first. Then we can't be held accountable for what we say," added Melissa.

"Or do," added Wanda.

"What happens at Aaron and Andrew's stays at Aaron and Andrew's," announced Andrew as he joined us from the kitchen and leaned into the group presenting us with a huge white oval platter of perfectly placed shrimp served over a bed of crushed ice, complete with cocktail sauce and the requisite lemon wedges. This was always the first course. Andrew was a class act. And this was just the beginning of what would be four to five hours of food, wine, laughter and camaraderie that had become a Friday night tradition. They didn't happen every Friday, and sometimes we'd go for weeks without them, but we knew that there would be another Friday dinner coming soon and we'd be back gathered together for another chance to connect and catch up and share in each other's lives.

The next round of appetisers was served. Smoked Camembert melted on a sesame cracker with a dollop of sundried tomato puree topped off with a lone caper.

'Mmmm… Andrew these are incredible. You're spoiling us. Now, I have to find me a man who is filthy rich, dangerously handsome, fashionable and a master in the kitchen." Melissa was reaching for her third cracker.

"You just need to find you a man, period." We all cheered at once. No one knew for sure, but we estimated that Melissa hadn't been with a man for almost three years.

"Ya ya ya… when I'm ready."

"Melissa, maybe you should try this online dating thing too. Frank and I are moving past dating into the relationship stage, but if we weren't, I might give it a go. It seems everyone is doing it. It's getting so hard to meet quality men these days so the thought of flipping through an online catalogue full of them in the privacy of your own home is rather intriguing… impersonal, but intriguing."

"I'm not sure. I don't think I'd have the guts. Plus, I think it takes so much of the romance out of it. How can you find your heart's desire on a computer? I'm just not sure I buy it. I think I'm more traditional than that, but it does spark my curiosity. Are there many men on this site you're on?"

"Yep. Tons of men. And all different. Lots of them are pretty handsome too."

"Will you show me the site sometime?"

"Of course Mel, just say when."

"When." Aaron just couldn't help himself. "Did someone say tons of men?"

The alluring aromas of coffee, onions and grilled meat made their way into the living area. Andrew was seducing us with another gastronomic masterpiece. He teased us first with fine wine and appetisers. Then he tickled our tastebuds with a menu that included garlic buttered toasted crostinis with grilled figs, melted gorgonzola cheese and caramelised red onions. This was accompanied by a spinach salad with snow pea sprouts, toasted pine nuts tossed in a fig and pomegranate balsamic dressing.

The main event consisted of roasted baby potatoes, a coffee bean encrusted rack of lamb, steamed brocco-flower florets and a julienned mixture of baby carrots and zucchini in a maple butter sauce.

"Dinner is served, ladies."

We all gratefully took our regular seats around the table. We were lucky. We had friends. We had a support system. We had strong bonds. We had each other.

I could always count on our famous Friday night gatherings to make things right with my world. They had become a ritual here in our quaint little community. Aaron and Andrew always hosted. They had, by far, the most handsomely decorated home. They had renovated and upgraded just about everything. The deep burgundy and olive green palette was reminiscent of a formal study. Thankfully, it was minus the cigar smoke and instead was lightly accented with cinnamon and hazelnut scents wafting softly from waxed art forms subtly placed about the house. Creamy soft leather, hardwood floors, thick carpets and rich fabrics co-mingled to provide a variety of tactile experience.

The lighting was the crowning designer touch. A flattering glow hung over us at the table and the use of spot lighting and subdued candle glows made the accents pop. The formal gallery lamps showcased the rich hues that jumped from the jazz inspired artwork hanging on the walls and the interior cabinet lighting did the same with the china and art pieces that glistened atop the shelves of the cherry wood cabinets. Aaron's keen eye for detail and his discerning decorating sense were evident throughout.

Andrew's presence was equally evident. He was strong and stable, a brilliant man, phenomenal chef, amusing conversationalist and an incredibly attentive and tireless host. Aaron and Andrew provided a gathering place for friends to share experiences. We indulged in fabulous food, wine and laughter and in doing so experienced a sense of family and community that supported and reassured us.

It was ironic that four attractive, funny, single women enjoyed every moment of these evenings with our two perfect male hosts, yet they were the only couple among us. Aaron and Andrew treated us royally, offering us a reprieve, a friendly hideaway, our indulgence for the week. It recharged and reconnected us. We had men who loved and pampered us, even if for only one night every few weeks.

Sporting a ponytail and sweats, I sipped through my Saturday morning java. I sat at the computer poised for another journey into man-land in the hopes of finding my mailbox bursting with "man-mail".

I was about to open my one new message when the dating site's online chat window opened. I was greeted by a relatively handsome guy whose demographics fit those on my wish list. Not wanting to limit my options, I embarked upon another hopeful dialogue with 'Fishin4Love'. It was great that the dating site provided a chat forum for members. That way, you didn't have to disclose any of your personal information to have a chat. When and if you wanted to connect outside of the safety of the site, you could.

Fishin4Love says:
Meeeeeoooooooooooooowwwwwwwww!

Katontheprowl says:
Hello?

Fishin4Love says:
Hi there beautiful

Katontheprowl says:
Hi

Fishin4Love says:
What's you're name?

Katontheprowl says:
Kayte & you?

Fishin4Love says:
I'm Ben

Katontheprowl says:
Nice to e-meet you.

Katontheprowl says:
Have you been online long? LOL

Fishin4Love says:
Ha! Ya 'bout 8 mos

Katontheprowl says:
Still haven't found the woman of your dreams huh?

Fishin4Love says:
No most women on here are liars or bitches or both

Katontheprowl says:
Really? Thems pretty strong adjectives for this time of the morning!

Fishin4Love says:
Yep they say they want a nice guy. They meet me. I'm a nice guy and then they get bitchy or make some lame excuse that I know is a lie and cut the date short.

Katontheprowl says:
Sounds like you're not having the best of luck

Fishin4Love says:
I think this site just attracts the wrong chicks

Katontheprowl says:
Ouch said the wrong chick.

Fishin4Love says:
They all want it all - handsome - rich - nice - smart - funny - etc.

Fishin4Love says:
When reality hits they give some serious attitude maybe 'cause

they think there are just tons more dudes to choose from

Katontheprowl says:
Maybe - but you can't say that applies to ALL of us

Fishin4Love says:
I sure can. Maybe you're an exception but you'd have to prove me wrong.

Katontheprowl says:
I don't make a habit of lying. I'm not usually referred to as a bitch unless I'm fighting for the last pair of Manolos in my size on the last day of a sale! LOL

Fishin4Love says:
You sound like you're just as fake as the other bitches on here.

Katontheprowl says:
Thems not the kind of words that will be getting you a date there buddy. Why would you say that?

Fishin4Love says:
Your shopping reference.

Katontheprowl says:
Geesh. It was just a joke. Lighten up - besides, shoe addictions are just part of the female DNA

Fishin4Love says:
I'm light - maybe time for a change in topic

Katontheprowl says:
Great idea - so what kind of woman are you looking for on here?

Fishin4Love says:
A babe that will make my friends jealous and who says what she means, doesn't play head games, lets me hang with the guys and go on my hunting and fishing trips... and most importantly... someone who actually likes sex... lots of sex.

Katontheprowl says:
Sounds like you know what you want.

Fishin4Love says:

Yep. Does it sound like you?

Katontheprowl says:
The "says what she means" part definitely does.

Fishin4Love says:
Maybe we should meet then. What are you doing tonite? You could come over and if we hit it off, you could stay over.

Katontheprowl says:
I'm flattered, but I don't think so.

Fishin4Love says:
Why not?

Katontheprowl says:
I just get the feeling that you're not my type.

Fishin4Love says:
Why?

Katontheprowl says:
Just a feeling - call it women's intuition.

Fishin4Love says:
You're just like all the others - lead me on and then change your mind.

Katontheprowl says:
Whoa there big fella. Back that big truck up. I NEVER lead you on. We were just having a brief chat.

Fishin4Love says:
Why talk if you don't want to meet?

Katontheprowl says:
To find out IF you want to meet - IF you have anything in common, IF there's a possibility of a connection.

Fishin4Love says:
You're just a fucking cock tease

Katontheprowl says:
Excuse me. I am nothing of the sort. You just have a warped way

of interpreting things.

Fishin4Love says:
I see things just as they are - you're just like all the other online bitches - YOU are the problem.

Katontheprowl says:
Excuse me Buster, but the problem is not with ME, but with YOU. Maybe the reason you've been on here so long is your attitude.

Katontheprowl says:
You might want to go fishing for a new personality on your next boys' weekend.

Katontheprowl says:
This conversation is OVER. Good luck on here Buddy. You're going to need it!

I blocked him and then reported him to the site's security. 'Fishin4Love' sounded like he was a few lures short of a full tackle box!

I shook my head all the way downstairs to the coffee maker, filled my cup, returned to the computer, signed off the site and then sorted through the 34 messages sitting in my personal email box. There was some obvious spam, a joke forwarded from Chloe, an email from Marnie, and a note from my boss. My first thought was why was she sending this to my home instead of my work email. My second was didn't she have a life? I guess everyone has different priorities.

The message must have arrived last night around about the time we had opened the last bottle of wine over at Aaron and Andrew's place. Remembering my indulgences from the previous evening, I knew that I needed a run – a long one.

It was the weekend so my priority was life first, work later. In order, my plan was coffee, run, shower, check the dating site for any new 'man-mail' and then maybe read the email from my boss. Maybe.

CHAPTER 9

Still puffing and definitely still perspiring from my 8K run I filled Dylan's bowl and then ran upstairs. I had promised to send Mike my mobile number just in case we had any difficulties meeting up, so I popped into my office and signed on the computer.

I shot a quick note to Mike with 'my digits' as the saying goes. What was happening to our language?

Before I could log off, I was sidetracked by Roman calling out through IM.

Bigbadwolf says:
Hey woman – wassup?

K8 says:
Just about to jump in the shower and get ready for my date

Bigbadwolf says:
Need someone to wash your back?

K8 says:
I'll pass – one man at a time - thx

Bigbadwolf says:
That's okay, U know how I prefer my girls dirty!

Bigbadwolf says:
but really Kayte there's nuthin wrong with 2 @ a time.

K8 says:
You know that's not my style.

Bigbadwolf says:
Yes, U R a good girl, but I'm a BAD boy – and I need 2 B
punished - I double dipped yesterday and I deserve a spanking.

K8 says:
Double dipped what?

Bigbadwolf says:
I had drinks with this chick from work and she invited me to her
place to burn some music CDs I'd been wanting

Bigbadwolf says:
After a couple of drinks, we ended up naked & making our own
music.

K8 says:
You dawg!

Bigbadwolf says:
It gets better.

K8 says:
How so? Did she invite a friend over?

Bigbadwolf says:
I WISH, but no. She knew I had plans for later.

Bigbadwolf says:
So I left her place around 9.

Bigbadwolf says:
Went home

Bigbadwolf says:
Showered

Bigbadwolf says:
Then went out with the dudes

K8 says:
You didn't do what I think you did

Bigbadwolf says:
& I picked up – brought her back to my place and had 2nd and 3rd helpings

K8 says:
Glutton! I hope all guys aren't like you.

Bigbadwolf says:
Not the ugly ones – LMAO!

K8 says:
If I didn't have to shower before this conversation, I sure do now. Gotta get ready for my date

Bigbadwolf says:
Have fun, but B4 I sign off, I want U 2 know Roman's Rule #4

K8 says:
Which is?

Bigbadwolf says:
make sure someone knows who U R meeting, any contact information you have about them, where UR meeting and when, just in case.

K8 says:
If I give this to you will you promise not to come and spy on me?

Bigbadwolf says:
Maybe

K8 says:
Glad I get such straight answers. I'll send you an email with the "deets"

Bigbadwolf says:
K

K8 says:
Gotta fly - Kayte-out!

Roman was a lot of things and horny topped the list. He was rough around the edges and narcissistic by nature, but he was a good friend to me. We did a lot together, played sports, had drinks and dinner occasionally and took in some cultural events. Underneath his sometimes inappropriate and often perverted exterior, he was an intellectual and had a depth many didn't see. I could always rely on him to be there if I needed help or advice, in a chosen few areas, especially when it came to household improvements that had anything to do with plumbing or electricity. I knew my limits and his skills.

He was pretty much a 'dawg' when it came to other women. This was something I just barely tolerated, but did so because I sensed it was born out of a deep need for acceptance and lack of confidence, rather than downright disregard for women; that and the fact that I wasn't dating him. He was one of those guys who I'd be friends with, but wouldn't date. I hoped Mike would be very different from Roman when it came to how he treated women. I had a feeling that he would. He seemed much gentler, much more perceptive and in tune with the female psyche.

I received an notice while chatting with Roman. **You have new mail on wheresinglesfindlove.com. To access it, click here.**

Woo hoo. More man-mail! I liked this online dating gig. I had man-mail, I had man-mail, nah nah nah nah nah nah!

Double woo hoo. It was from Attaboy77.

Subject: RE: I'll share my paints, if you share your crayons!

Hi Katontheprowl:

Thanks for the message. You made me laugh. Nice first impression. And your profile? WOW. You sound terrific – lots to offer, which is great 'cause so do I. And I know who to call if I ever need an adjective – you a writer?

I'm intrigued and would love to know more, so here's my email

addy - tomtom@socialarity.com. Now, as for handing over the crayon, burnt sienna or otherwise, not so fast, girlie. What do I get in return? Negotiations start now!

Thomas

P.S. I'm not my father yet, however am seeing the first signs, but no biggie, he's a pretty good guy.

Very cool indeed. Thomas, his name was Thomas. Well if he was Thomas, I'd be Kathleen.

My text message indicator blared from my mobile. I picked it up and reading it brought a smile, **Can't wait 2 meet U**. It was from Mike.

I was feeling very desired - very desired indeed. Perhaps this online dating thing was just what I needed. Thanks Chloe!

CHAPTER 10

I was about 10 minutes away. Some upbeat salsa music accompanied me on the ride. Still driving, I reached down for my purse, opened the zipper and found my makeup bag. I zipped it open, grabbed my gloss and applied a fresh coating of frosted mocha ice, then traded the gloss for powder and patted my nose. A quick check in the mirror and I was date-ready.

Just past the next lights, I found the parking lot for the Snuggle Mug. It was one of the only independent coffee houses that still remained. Family-run by locals, it truly did serve the best beverages anywhere.

I gathered my things, did another quick teeth and nostril check and I headed for a place where I knew I felt comfy. I had forgotten to ask Mike what he drove, so I couldn't even look for his vehicle as I walked through the parking lot my tummy aflutter. With each step I chanted silently 'please don't stand me up, please don't stand me up'.

I opened the door and absorbed the deep rich coffee aromas through every pore. They leapt right into my nostrils and lodged themselves there. I scanned the room from left to right. Something sparkling stopped my gaze mid way through the room. There he was. Mike, more handsome than his photos suggested and larger too, was wearing a chocolate brown, slightly worn, leather jacket, a loosely knit ivory cable knit cardigan over a t-shirt the same colour. His thick dark hair was curly and gelled, but the piece de resistance was that there he was, in public, people all around, proudly wearing a golden burger joint's giveaway cardboard crown.

His sparkling-eyed smile assured me that he was just fine with the stares he'd been getting as he'd immersed himself in the identity of his online profile name. Yes, he truly was 'somebody-sprince'. But was he my prince? I was about to find out.

"Priceless, absolutely priceless. I love the crown. I can safely say that this is yet another first in my dating history." The prop had not only made me smile, but it went a long way in dispelling the nervousness I had been feeling. It definitely broke the ice. Mike and I had really connected online and I was a little nervous about meeting face to face, because I was unsure as to whether or not the connection would carry over into real life.

"So, the royal thing wasn't too much?"

"No. Not at all… Your Highness," I giggled.

"Because I almost didn't wear it. But, I got the feeling that your sense of humour would appreciate the gesture."

"And you were right Your Excellency!" I was smiling now.

"Good. Won't you please have a seat." He had moved in behind me and had his hand on the back of my chair ready to glide it in after I sat." Ah. He was a gentleman – a gentleman with a sense of humour. In fact, he was a gentleman with a sense of humour who was a sharply dressed, gorgeous man with warm eyes, who smelled nice and had a deep, sexy but gentle voice.

We both ordered mochaccinos and found the conversation between the sips came easily. While we talked, we kept looking at each other and smiling those goofy, childlike, nervous little smiles. Not staring a constant gaze, but down at our cups, then at each other, around the room, then back at each other. It was almost like we had to keep checking to see if the other person was actually real. It was a strange feeling indeed, very reminiscent of high school.

There was something very young and vulnerable about Mike. He was certainly masculine and strong and handsome. He appeared younger than his age and came across as both playful and mischievous. His pictures had not done him justice. Mike had a full head of dark, loose curly locks that framed a very pleasant face, a broad and high strong forehead, with nicely shaped ears with thick lobes, big brown slightly sleeping looking eyes, a broad nose, that may or may not have been broken before, and a full mouth with large soft lips covering nice but somewhat small, white teeth. His complexion was clear and pale, but not pasty and there was a trace of dark facial hair beginning to show itself just beneath the skin's surface. It was obvious, that if left to grow, the dark hair would hide a very attractive face.

We talked more about our lives, our jobs, our volleyball experiences, our friends, our favourite movies, the restaurants we frequented, the places we'd travelled and those we'd still like to see. We sat across the table from each other, but the distance between us lessened as the conversation expanded. There was a moment as we were sharing a laugh over a story where Mike had been the butt of a well-orchestrated practical joke when I looked up and we locked eyes and I honestly thought he was going to kiss me. And oh, I wanted him to kiss me. And do many other things to me for that matter. However, he remained a perfect gentleman.

The afternoon was sunny but crisp. There was little or no wind, so we took our date outside, for a stroll along the lakeshore. We walked side by side. Two things struck me. His height was a welcome change. It was nice to be alongside a man who had four inches on me. I felt more feminine in the presence of a taller man.

Being in the fresh air, outside the aromas of the coffee house, I could now smell his cologne. It was masculine, spicy and seductive. It suited him. And I was drawn to its suggestions of citrus, sage, cedar and tobacco. I walked slightly down wind of him so that I could indulge fully in its intoxication.

Mike turned to me and asked, "Kayte, do you swing?"

This question might have been premature for a first date, if we hadn't just rounded a corner and reached the children's playground that overlooked the shore. We were greeted by a rainbow of red climbing bars, yellow slides, green swings, and blue climbing cages.

I smiled widely, "Only if you push me," was my response. It was refreshing to find a sexy man who also had a childlike personality and playful side.

Mike grabbed my hand, ran me over to the swing set and gestured for me to sit. "Now you're my kind of woman! And just so you know, I'll only push when absolutely necessary."

First we swung side by side, competing to see who could get the highest fastest. Once he was solidly declared the winner he descended his mount and began pushing me on mine. This was our first physical contact. Mike's strong hands were placed high on my back at first. They worked their way down to my waist as I achieved greater height with each push. I felt the heat from his fingertips penetrate through my jacket.

On the last push I went so high I caught some air, my bum actually lifted from the seat and I had to cling tightly to the chains that held me there. I guess he saw my clenched fists and let me pass a couple of times giving no additional pushes. Then he moved around to the front of my swing and extended his long arms, grabbed the chains on either side, bringing me to a slow but determined stop.

Mike reached down with his left hand. He placed a softly formed fist led by a slightly extended forefinger under my chin and with his thumb lightly caressing my bottom lip, he lifted my chin upward. His eyes focused on mine and his face came closer, his mouth locating my lips with incredible accuracy. I inhaled his cologne as he kissed me with a balance of strength and softness. His lips were soft and warm and very much in control. They remained there blanketing mine for as many seconds as it took me to realise that even though this was our first kiss, Mike had just planted a distinct promise of more.

He instinctively reached for my hand and I gladly gave it to him as I stood up. We walked back to the Snuggle Mug's parking lot.

"This has been a great first date," I offered as we got close to my vehicle.

"Yes, I agree. But I knew it would be."

"How so?"

"There was something about you that I knew I liked right away."

"Really?"

"Yes, a confidence, but also a playful side. It's a sexy combination."

I smiled and winked, "Yes, I can do playful."

"I'm counting on that." Mike returned the wink. "Can I admit something?" Then I saw it again – that boyish, slightly shy look.

"Sure."

"I don't want our date to end."

"Really? Well, maybe it doesn't have to. What did you have in mind?"

"Would you like to join me for a movie? I've been waiting weeks for one that just opened yesterday."

"I'd love to, but only if you promise that we'll get a big bucket of popcorn with lots of butter. All this fresh air's made me hungry."

"I wouldn't have it any other way."

Mike was off getting popcorn and my mobile indicated that I had a text message. I had neglected to turn the sound notification off, so while I was doing so I took a peek. It was from Roman.

How was your d8 - did u get any?

Great date & I'm STILL on it so maybe I will!

I hit send, turned off the phone and placed it back in my purse. I licked my lips, brushed my hair from my face and adjusted "the girls" to showcase just the right amount of cleavage, all before Mike returned.

CHAPTER 11

"You're going where? When?" I could hear the hints of jealousy in my own voice as it travelled across the phone lines. I hoped Chloe hadn't picked up on it.

"Barbados. Boomer's had to travel so much for work lately so he thought he'd surprise me and the kids and take us with him this time. While he's working, we'll be enjoying sun and fun for four fabulous days. We leave next Wednesday."

"You lucky little wench. Tough life you've got. Where do I find me a Boomer?"

"Hopefully on that dating site we've got you on. Speaking of which, girl, how was your date with Mike? Don't leave out a single juicy detail." I could hear Chloe chopping vegetables in the background.

"It was wonderful. He is just like a great cup of cocoa – so hot and so sweet. We had a fabulous time." I regaled her with the details from start to finish. I told her about the crown, the conversation, the walk, our swing and our time at the movies. "Once we were done eating the popcorn, occasionally feeding each other, we held hands. We sat so close that I could feel the heat radiating from him. At one point, he leaned right over and with his mouth almost in my ear, and whispered, 'You're making me crazy, can I please kiss you?' So we did."

"Hope you were sitting in the back row."

"Nope, right up front for everyone to see. But I didn't care. Now there was a kiss. Man, I'm getting all flustered just thinking about it. And this has been, oh, about the 100th time I've re-lived that moment already today. Mmmm, he's yummy."

"You're smiling that goofy smile aren't you?"

"Uh-huh. But that wasn't the best part."

"Oh?"

"We sat and shared the popcorn and were about a third of the way through. I was licking the excess butter from my fingers, when he stopped me, grabbed my hand and placed my fingers between his lips and sucked away every drop of butter."

"He sounds hot, smokin' even! Are you seeing him again?"

"Absolutely. He'll be here in about an hour. We're taking Dylan for a nice long hike."

"Good going girl. I'll want to hear all about it."

"You will, but if we don't connect before you go, have a great time, you lucky duck. Love you."

"Love you too, hon."

I put the phone down and signed on to check emails, the IM automatic window opened and my status changed to 'online'. My online address book was certainly growing. Mike was showing as 'offline', Roman was 'busy', Chloe was 'online but away' as she was obviously just on the phone with me, and Tomtom's status indicated that he would apparently 'be right back'.

I went to email and sorted through the 45 emails I had received since yesterday morning. The spam had definitely increased.

There was another note from my boss marked Urgent – Read IMMEDIATELY. This ought to be good.

It was addressed to me, the VP Sales, the head of HR, The VP Operations, the CFO and all the Regional Managers, essentially the entire senior management team. It had arrived at 9:30am.

Hello all,

Due to sagging market share numbers and a weaker than expected pipeline of potential new business, I need all of your support in pushing ahead the launch of Project 'Do What You Love'. I want us to be ready for market launch four weeks earlier than we had initially agreed. I realise this will add some new challenges, but I know that you won't let me down, and that you will all work together to get this done.

Thanks in advance for your continued support in making Ardent Staffing the very best it can be.

P.S. I will be out of the office until Wednesday, but as always, reachable by phone or email.

Best,
Beatrice

Four weeks earlier? Was she fucking mad? Four weeks earlier on a project that was only meant to be 12. She had finally lost it. In other companies this would have been at least a six-month initiative. Not 12 weeks, and certainly not eight. I knew how the team would react to this. This wasn't going to be pretty.

What bothered me most was that it was a fantastic campaign concept. The creative was brilliant and would really resonate in the marketplace. It had great legs. But now its ultimate success was being jeopardised by artificially imposed deadlines. Boss-Lady was, yet again, shoving another short-sighted approach down our throats.

Her management skills had us all at breaking point. The entire senior management team was losing patience with her rampant incompetence. Turnover was at an all time high. Lately management was being referred to not as the leadership team but rather the 'Leave the Ship' team. But who could blame them.

My heart was beating way too fast for a Sunday morning. Now that bitch was even ruining my weekends. Why did I have to open the email? Why? I began to chant out loud 'Leave work at work, and concentrate on home at home'.

On my fifth mantra chant, the conversation IM window opened and it was Roman.

Roman says:
So how was your date?

K8 says:
Great thanks.

Roman says:
Did you get any?

K8 says:
A lady never tells!

Roman says:
U c-ing him again?

K8 says:
Yep, later today

Roman says:
Whoa – this guy moves fast. Sounds like it might be time for emergency measures. You must learn Rule #5 immediately my star student.

K8 says:
And that is?

Roman says:
After a good date, make sure to schedule another date with someone else ASAP.

K8 says:
HUH? That doesn't make sense.

Roman says:
Hear me out. If U make a date with someone else, and U go, it distracts U. Takes the pressure off waiting for the guy U really like to call.

K8 says:
I guess that makes some sense. That way you don't obsess.

Roman says:
Exactly. Trust me. Women do some serious whacked shit when they're waiting 4 the guy they like to call. Ruining some potentially great relationships that could have happened if they had just gone a little slower and dialled back the crazy!

Roman says:
Makes some of us dudes want to run for the hills even if she's hotter than hell. But then again, there are some of us who like the crazy ladies!!!

Of course this was followed by the smiley with his tongue hanging out.

K8 says:
Well I'll take it under advisement.

Roman says:
K8 do it – U'll thank me. And who knows, "distraction man' might turn into someone U like even more. I could volunteer – give U a little bite of the Wolfman.

K8 says:
I'll politely decline the bite. On the other, no promises, but thx for the suggestion - gotta go get ready for date #2
– Kayte out.

Roman says:
Later Gorgeous

Tomtom's IM status just changed to online. *Wait for it. Don't initiate contact, Kayte. Let him do that. Patience, girl, patience. You don't want to be the crazy lady Roman was referring to. Open and read another email. Fight the urge. Fight it. He'll say hi, just let him start.*

Din din din. The IM flashing orange bar was calling me. *YES! Bingo. Now, take it slow. Don't respond too quickly. Dum de dum, la la la. Count to 20 then you can reply.*

I got my first online message from Thomas. As I opened the message window, I sat a little taller in my chair and felt my excitement rise.

Tomtom says:
Hey Kayte

K8 says:
Hello Thomas – nice to e-meet you.

Tomtom says:
Likewise, the pleasure is all mine.

K8 says:
So what are you up to on this fine Sunday morning?

Tomtom says:
Just catching up on some work, reading the paper, having an extra cup of coffee – Sunday morning stuff. And you?

K8 says:
About the same and trying to avoid the dog's "when are we going for our walk?" pleading stares.

Tomtom says:
LOL – ya, they're like kids eh.

K8 says:
Yes, but much hairier.

Tomtom says:
LOL – but far more obedient. So what are you up to today?

K8 says:
Actually just getting ready to take the pup on a nice long hike.

Tomtom says:
Well don't let me keep you.

K8 says:

I should go, but will you be online later?

Tomtom says:
Should be

K8 says:
Well I look forward to chatting more then. Enjoy the day and thanks for saying hi.

Tomtom says:
U 2 – looking forward to our next chat. BFN

K8 says:
Me too! Kayte-out

K8 says:
Sorry, force of habit, I meant to say, bye.

Tomtom says:
LOL – no worries – I liked it. In fact, I might use it, Thomas-out!

He followed that with a wink and then his status changed to offline.

I anticipated the next conversation with Tommy. What interesting tidbits would I learn about him? More importantly, what should I reveal about myself? Would it be flirtatious? Funny? Would it lead to a date? To more? To marriage?

I needed to focus. First I had to get ready for date number two with Mike.

He appeared at the door right on time, wearing relaxed denims, a white t-shirt beneath a red fleece top and tan hiking boots. I had chosen the same outfit.

"Great outfit!" was his first words out of his mouth.

We both laughed. "I guess we both have good taste. Dylan, I guess you're going to be odd man out. Tell you what, we'll use your red leash today."

He ran around our legs excitedly wagging his tail and letting out little squeals

Mike kissed me a light kiss hello and gave Dylan a big scratch behind both ears.

"Everyone ready?"

We piled into Mike's Black SUV and drove to a nearby conservation area. We hiked and played catch with Dylan, tossing newly fallen sticks and branches and his favourite bright orange super eight tug toy. He obediently chased each one, retrieving it, bringing it back, and looking at us eagerly ready for the next throw.

Mike and I chatted easily as we walked the trails cut through the dense forest. He confided that he had worked hard to overcome the impressions left by his highly judgmental father and that he still gave too much regard to others' opinions, but was committed to changing that. He took advantage of the opportunity to tell me that he sincerely cared about what I thought of him though because he sensed that there was real possibility with us.

We laughed about our respective dating disasters of the past and I shared the recent Roger story. This made us erupt with laughter strong enough to challenge our footing and send us tumbling down the hill where Dylan bounded down after us barking his concern or 'dog laughing' at us. We weren't sure which.

We chased each other through the woods. Mike would catch me, grab me around the waist, then with one gloved hand would reach for my face and kiss me. The cool crisp air seemed to warm instantly when his lips met mine, sending warm and welcome waves through my body. It was a simple date. It was a comfortable date. It was a romantic date. I felt myself connecting easily with him on a number of levels.

On the way home we stopped into a small town to check out some local artists' studios. He insisted on buying Dylan a custom painted water dish as a memento of the day. We had a late lunch in a cosy little bistro bakery that smelled of the sweetness and love I recall from my grandmother's kitchen. We warmed ourselves on hearty homemade beef and lentil soup with a generous slice of still warm rosemary bread. Even though we needed jackets and gloves, we sat outside at our own little table where Dylan could join us rather than leaving him in the car. He scored a couple of big chunks of beef and a full slice of bread when Mike 'accidentally' knocked it off the table.

"Kayte, this has been an incredible afternoon."

"Apparently we not only dress alike, we think alike too! I agree."

"Does it have to end? I hope you don't think I'm being too forward, but what would you say to us continuing this date? Maybe we could create our own masterpiece of the culinary kind? I'm feeling inspired by the artists we saw today."

"Not too forward at all. I have no plans and I think that's a spectacular idea. There's another town about 15 minutes from here we could stop and get groceries"

"Perfect. This will be a team effort though, deal?"

"Deal. We'll see if you can keep up with me in the kitchen."

"You're sounding pretty sure of yourself, Kayte. I like that. I might just surprise you."

We arrived home and I realised there was no wine so Mike offered to make another trip to the store and go get some. He reappeared about a half hour later with a lovely bottle of South African Shiraz and a huge bouquet of white daisies, my favourite. I had mentioned them only fleetingly during our hike and apparently he had listened. I was touched by the gesture, but mostly by the fact that he actually listened. He was certainly making a wonderful impression, but maybe just a little too perfect. I quelled my inner sceptic while I grabbed a vase to prominently display the lovely flowers.

We shared the kitchen well. Mike washed and chopped as I sautéed and mixed. He fed me slices of red pepper and he taste-tested the sauce as I held the spoon to his lips, both of us teasing each other with a gaze that lasted that little bit longer than necessary.

We dined on a fine combination of grilled chicken breast blanketed with a balsamic vinegar and asiago cheese sauce, accompanied by grilled asparagus and red and yellow pepper strips, served alongside rosemary, onion and garlic roasted red potatoes.

With bellies full we moved to the couch and folded into each other so that we could just relax, kiss, sip our wine, talk, kiss, touch and kiss some more. The connection between us felt far more like we had been a couple for months than that of two people who had met so recently.

I don't know if it was the exercise, the fresh air, the great food, the candlelight, the sexy man who sat next to me, or some combination of these, but I felt happy, peaceful and connected. So much so that we nodded off in each other's arms with Dylan dreaming away on the floor beside us.

We awoke a few times, smiled, kissed, changed positions, held each other a little tighter and smiled some more both feeling the strength of our newly formed connection. It was easy. It was unpretentious. It was passionate yet gentle – so unlike many other dates. The peacefulness that existed between us was so contrary to my hectic daily grind. I soaked in every replenishing moment of it.

CHAPTER 12

"Good Morning!"

"Hey, Kayte. How was the weekend? Any hot dates we should know about?"

"As a matter of fact…"

My regular seat was waiting for me, so I settled in for the 45-minute ride with my commuter crew. I rode the train with the same group almost daily. The fact was that I spent more time with them than I did with most of my friends, so of course friendships developed.

Most of the group was older than me. Those who weren't were married and happily settled into their family lives. They enjoyed living vicariously through the single girl. They hungered to be regaled with the details of my search for Mr. Right. Some occasionally even offered introductions. From where they sat, they found my freedom fascinating. At times they appeared somewhat envious of the perceived excitement that my life apparently provided. They saw the romance, they were eager to relive the highlights with me, especially on Monday mornings.

I would rather talk about something, anything else.

My mobile rang, interrupting the chatter of the regular train gang. Maybe it was Mike. I checked the number; it was Chloe.

"Good morning."

"Hey darling, I know you're probably on the train."

"I am."

"But I just heard a news story that I had to tell you about immediately."

"Okay, what's so urgent?" I heard the blender in the background, probably making smoothies for the kids.

'Well it appears that there can be some pretty seedy characters using these online dating websites. Given that I pretty much twisted your arm to do it, I thought I'd better bring this to your attention."

"Bring what to my attention?"

Dishes were clanking loudly, but I could hear Chloe over the distraction, "Well this story mentions that hours after they featured this murderer on America's Most Wanted, they arrested him because some women recognised his photo, linking it back to his online dating profile. This guy has murdered two, possibly three people, yet he's online looking for love. Apparently, according to his profile, he likes to spoon."

"Wow. You just gave me shivers. It's a bit of an eye-opener isn't it?"

"Yes, and I'd never forgive myself if you were to meet some crazy on there that would even think about hurting my KitKat."

"Don't worry honey, I'll be careful. And just to be sure, I'll focus on the guys who like to fork!"

"Good!" I could hear Chloe's dog barking playfully.

"Plus, not that I want to jinx it or anything, but this guy Mike has some real promise, he's fabulous. He's so sexy, so romantic, so perfect. We had a magical day yesterday."

"Oh, good. I'm so happy. You deserve it. You know that. Okay, I've got to get the kids off to school, the dog for his walk and then go buy me a new bathing suit. Barbados, here I come."

"Bye Sweetie and thanks."

"You're welcome. Bye."

"Urgent meeting in the boardroom in 10 minutes." Mike MacPherson, our VP of Sales, popped his head into my office, and alerted me to the impending fireworks.

I was ready. I had met with my team, explained the new timetable, reorganised our priorities, cut some components of the campaign that just couldn't be completed within Beatrice's new time frame. I had also put in calls to the PR people, advertising sales reps and assorted support resources. I had one of our best recruiters searching out two additional designers to assist us. This was all done before my second cup of coffee.

I checked my mobile for messages. There was a voicemail from Andrew, wondering who the hot guy carrying flowers into my place was yesterday and when was I sending him over to say hello. While my little community was a wonderfully friendly place, there were certainly no secrets.

Then came the message from my Mike. My mobile phone was getting a workout that morning.

Had a wonderful day yesterday. I'm so lucky to have met you. I can still taste both you and that fabulous meal, mmm. See you soon, xxxx, Mike

Oh how sweet!! My battery died just as I finished reading his message, but I wanted to respond. With only a few minutes before our meeting I shot him a quick email from my work computer:

Hi sexy, I have a riddle for you. You, balsamic chicken or choco-late mousse cake, which do I have a craving for right now? My choice could end up being terribly addictive. Can't wait to kiss those soft lips and feel those long strong arms around me again. I really enjoyed yesterday too.

Kisses,
Kayte

Kayte Wexford, VP Marketing
Ardent Staffing Inc.

Okay it was a little sappy, but he was so sweet. He'd appreciate it.

I hit send, grabbed my files and proceeded to join the others in the corporate boxing ring.

Beatrice was calling in remotely. She was out of town, but needed to ensure that the management team was on board with her 'management by email' tactics and aware of the associated timing change that she communicated over the weekend.

I was the last to enter the conference room. Scanning around the table, there was not one happy face. In fact, the frustration level would have registered a 9.5 on the Irritation Scale if one existed. The infuriation was palpable.

I looked over at Percy, one of our Regional Managers. His brow was furrowed and his lips had disappeared in their terseness. He was blatantly flipping through the Careers section of today's paper. Given that we were a staffing company, the practice was not out of the ordinary, but something in his manner suggested this time it was personal.

Harold, our Director of Human Resources was nodding his increasingly crimson cheeks in agreement and saying, "I know this is unreasonable. I know you're all frustrated, but what can I do?" He was taking the brunt of it as the entire table voiced their concern and displeasure with these recent developments. He was boiling beneath the heat of our displeasure. But we all knew he could do nothing. None of us could. Beatrice was a dictator.

Thankfully the residual effects of my date with Mike still had me in a somewhat positive mood.

The Beast hadn't called in yet.

"Is what she's proposing actually possible, Kayte?" MacPherson asked me.

"Honestly, Mike, I'm not sure. My team and I would do our best, but we'd be testing our supplier relationships. And our own skills and composure would be stretched to capacity. And that's assuming no one cracks. We'd have to pare back the campaign to meet the deadlines. And the associated revenues will also diminish as a result. But Beatrice knows that. At least I hope she knows that."

The speaker in the centre of the table erupted with a bark from our west coast office. Alex, Percy's west coast equivalent, asked "Does anyone even know why the hell she's doing this?"

"Cause she's gone mad," I responded, with eyes opened wide in a crazed look and mouth equally gaping with my tongue hanging out.

"She has a sick and twisted sense of humour," Harold added.

Percy put it best, "Because she's fucked!"

"Feels more like she's fucking all of us," Alex's anger was unmistakeable.

Mike's eyes shifted uncharacteristically. He shook his head and said only, "Let's get her on the line. Maybe she'll tell us her rationale."

Was he defending her?

He pulled out his mobile, dialled her number. "It's me. I'm with the team. We're all waiting for you to dial in."

We heard the line connect, then, "I'm assuming you've all read my email. So, we all on board with this?" No hello, no niceties, just right to it.

No one spoke. I looked from face to face, waiting for someone to speak. Percy was quiet, Harold was looking down rearranging papers and Mike was looking at me.

I had one chance to speak up. Feeling stronger and more in control than I had in ages, refreshed from my great weekend and all the attention lavished upon me, I said, "No - I'm definitely not!" I was louder than I expected, but the more I thought about it, the more I realised how unreasonable her request was.

"Beatrice, this change will sacrifice the very core of the campaign. This decision could easily backfire and our investment to date could be completely lost." I went on, "This will not bode well for our relationships with our suppliers, my team is already burnt out and this new timeline is expecting way too much from them. I don't think we'll be able to change our media buy at this late notice. In short, I just think it's the wrong way to go. I say we stay with the original plan."

"Kayte, no offence, but I disagree on pretty much all counts. The campaign concept is solid. It will sustain these changes. Our suppliers will supply us or we'll go elsewhere. And if you or your team are not up for the job, I'm sure we can find others who are."

Her words threw me back in my chair. She clearly had made up her mind. I was furious. "What does everyone else think?" her voice was barely above a whisper now.

Percy actually stood up, moved in as close as he could to the microphone in the centre of the table and said simply, "I've had enough. I can't do it and I won't do it." He tossed the newspaper on the table and left the meeting room.

Mike added commentary for Beatrice and Alex's benefit.

Frank was the next to vent. "Bea, we just can't change this thing mid-course. A great deal of research, planning, resource allocation and project management has gone into the plan to date. It's solid the way it is. Why do you want to make this change so late in the game?

"I have my reasons," was her only response.

This seemed to ignite a series of fiery responses from those in the room. Everyone had their turn to come down on her... and hard. Mike was the only exception. He remained quiet.

Maybe the mutiny was due in part to her not being physically present. Maybe because it truly was a bonehead decision that was short sighted and put too much at risk. Maybe because we had all been in this position too many times, floating in this badly managed boat for far too long.

Whatever the reason, we all had our say and it was liberating. However, it just made my job harder. For now, she was running some more numbers, reconsidering the date change, yet again. So all the calls, all the changes, all the plans that my team and I had initiated might have been for naught.

I went back to my office, exhausted and it was only just before noon. I took a moment to escape to more pleasant things. My mind wandered back to the day before when I cuddled up in Mike's arms.

An hour later I left to go grab some lunch and was sharing the elevator down with Mike, our Sales VP. He appeared very subdued. Confused even. The elevator doors were closing and he was just about to say something to me, when Jackson, our lead graphic designer thrust his hand between the nearly closed doors. The doors reopened and he joined us for what was then a silent ride.

The following day was much the same, still uncertain deadlines, yet we needed to continue to push things ahead. Long days were definitely in store for the team.

Beatrice was obviously affected by yesterday's backlash as she flew into town a day early. I hadn't managed an audience with her yet, but would try after lunch.

I had a lunch meeting scheduled with our PR Consultant, Liz, to brainstorm a few new options we could invoke should we need them for some quick hits within this new abbreviated campaign.

We met at the newest and most sought-after sushi restaurant in town. Many couldn't recall its name, but its location, right in the centre of the financial district, was its calling card. It was huge, but surprisingly intimate. It spun a web of curtains and mesh hangings, frosted glass walls, fountains and other unique architectural features that gave its patrons privacy and a cloak of anonymity not experienced in many other establishments.

As we enjoyed our first course of edamame, miso soup and green tea, I heard a familiar voice at the next table. It was the newly arrived Beatrice and she was obviously not happy with her luncheon companion. He spoke next. I recognised the voice of Mike MacPherson. They were seated just around the corner to our right, out of sight, but not out of earshot. I purposely adjusted my volume when speaking across the table to Liz and did my best to follow two conversations at once. This lunch had suddenly become more enjoyable than I expected.

Mike sounded far more defensive and passive than usual. He kept repeating the same thing over and over, "I'm telling you the truth. No, there isn't, nor ever has there been anything between us."

She obviously didn't believe him. Her tone was undeniably sceptical and accusatory. She shot question after question at him as if trying to catch him in a lie. At first I thought that she might have been accusing him of entertaining a role with our biggest competitor. What else could it be? I thought it rather strange that his boss would care that much about what appeared to be his personal life, but then it hit me. Maybe they were one and the same. Around about the time we were finishing the last bites of our spider roll, unagi and sushi pizza the surprising truth about Mike and Beatrice was served up as an indulgent and very decadent dessert.

Mike pleaded with her to stop her unwarranted accusations. In a final plea he offered up those cherished three little words, albeit delivered with subservience and desperation. "I love you." This was followed by a long pause, then a reiteration, "There is no one else, not at work, nowhere, just you. I love you – just you – only you." She repeated them back to him in her practised firm, unemotional and controlled tone. "Mike, and I you."

They were powerful words indeed. Especially the "just you – only you" part, given they were both married. I wondered when the last time might have been that either of them had uttered that phrase to their spouses.

I was bursting. This was huge.

Back in the office, I could barely stand it. I couldn't look at either of them. One thing I couldn't understand was cheating. How greedy do people get? Here I am trying so hard just to find one person to love and these two both have mates and they're being gluttons. More importantly, they are breaking solemn vows. Maybe I was just too traditional. I didn't understand how people cheated.

I returned to my desk to various emails, a meeting request from her highness for 3:00 pm, a couple of phone messages, a text message from my Mike that read "I'm thinking about U. I can picture you reading this. U R probably smiling that sexy smile of yours." I was. I sat for just a moment to enjoy it.

I had a 2:30 with the "cheating with the boss" Mr. MacPherson to determine the new priority for the collateral pieces that would be supplied to his sales team. It was indeed the strangest meeting I had experienced throughout my career.

I thought I was doing a great job of hiding my newfound knowledge even though the mental pictures of the two of them entangled in each other continued looping through my brain. I focused on the work, the task at hand. Every time I leaned in or got closer to point out a component of the brochure, he'd back away like a beaten puppy. He couldn't look me straight in the eye. He was not his usual puffed up, confident take-charge self. I guess his lunchtime discussion had affected him.

Boss lady walked by and saw us in his office, stopped abruptly at the door, looked at him, then me and said, "Kathleen, let's meet now rather than at three, I've finished up earlier than expected." Then she shot an icy and commanding stare that landed with the precision of a well-aimed arrow, smack dab between Mike's eyes. He reeled. She turned on her Jimmy Choos and marched to her office. I grabbed my things and followed.

After I sat down she got up and closed the door, which in itself was strange.

I had the revised schedules, work plans, three versions of a full campaign based on three possible dates. I had a list of calls, emails and requests that had been made to accommodate her latest scheduling change. Everything was well in hand. It would be far more work in far less time, but the team was up for it. We had a plan. Even though I was stressed and frustrated by the changing deadlines, I was confident that we could deliver a great campaign. There were two important details that I didn't know: when the actual launch date would be and that I was about to get fired.

"I just don't think things are working out here."

I could hear the words, see her precious peach glossed lips mouthing them, her eyes darting awkwardly, anywhere but meeting mine.

"I'm sorry, what? You've got to be kidding. Beatrice, are you messing with me? *She couldn't be serious.*

"Kathleen, no I'm not. I just don't think we're a match. You know how in our campaign we liken finding the right job to finding the right mate and having a great marriage? It's all about the chemistry, the connection, the common ground. I just don't think we have that."

"Hold on a minute. You mean that you aren't getting enough 'love' from me? You mean the campaign that I created, the concept I expanded, the one I've rallied the whole sales and marketing groups around is not working for you?"

I was furious. "You mean the one that is absolutely brilliant and so far beyond anything this company has done before? Would this be the same campaign that motivates the team, even when every drop is being squeezed out of them? The one that has them so jazzed, excited and proud that they have daily competitions to create new ideas to expand upon it?"

The more I thought about the brilliant work I had done, the more I was convinced that she had lost it. My interrogation continued, "Do you mean that I, the creator of the campaign that is guaranteed to get us premier media coverage and buy us at least five solid market share points within the next three months, don't share a common vision? When I can work with everyone here and create these kinds of results, you can't seriously say that you don't think we have that the right connection?"

"No, we just don't have a fit. I don't think we're kindred spirits. I think it's better that we end things now so that we can find someone who is. I'll have a letter drawn up that will outline your package. I just don't think we have priorities and loyalties that are simpatico."

Okay, she had gone and done it. I wasn't going to say anything about her and Mike. I was truly going to keep my nose out of it, but she had gone and insulted me, demeaned my great work, and that of my team. She brought up the subject of loyalties and to top it all off, she actually used both the words 'kindred' and 'simpatico' in a sentence. I couldn't slap her, but a verbal sparring was definitely in order.

That was it. The gloves were off. "What the hell do you even know about a good connection or a good fit, and *especially* about loyalties?"

She had no idea where I was going with this. I knew there

would be no turning back, yet I didn't care. It had to be said.

"Nothing. That's what you know. Nothing! You wouldn't know a good campaign, a strategic marketer, or a moral for that matter, if it jumped up and slapped you on the ass. Loyalties? You don't have a clue about how many people within the company are on their way out, with one exception and I'm sure you know who he is. Your leadership team is all looking for other work; in fact we refer to ourselves as your 'leave-the-ship' team. And on the topic of forming loyalties and 'kindred' connections, I'm curious, just who do you think is more loyal to you - your husband or Mike? And while we're comparing them, whose spirit do you find more kindred, Mike's or your husband's?"

I continued with my freedom tirade. I was standing now, both hands on her desk, leaning in close enough to smell the fear on her breath, staring straight into her hollow eyes. "And, Beatrice, just so there is absolutely no confusion, I just have one final question for you. Did you enjoy your sushi today? I know I certainly did. That restaurant is all the rage for a reason. I know my lunch meeting certainly provided me with a great deal to chew on."

There it was, that one decisive moment. I'd done it. There was no going back.

Strangely I wasn't sad. I wasn't hurt. I was still angry and astonished, but I felt so free. I was bursting. I swear I felt like I could almost take flight.

I adjusted my tone to barely a whisper and said, "You'll hear from my lawyer." I smiled and winked and turned and walked away from Ardent Staffing, my fabulous team and my baby - my coveted campaign of a lifetime.

CHAPTER 13

"Hello."

"Hi. You're home? I was just going to leave you a message so you'd have a nice surprise after a long day at the office. I thought you wouldn't be home until at least eight."

"That, sir, would be accurate if I still had a job."

"What?"

"I got fired today."

"No. You aren't serious?"

"Oh, yes, very!"

"Hon, I'm so sorry. Can I come over? Or would you prefer to be alone?"

"I think I'd like the company, thanks." My admission caused me to tear up. The harsh reality was that when big things happen, good or bad, that's when you feel the loneliness the most. When you're bursting with wonderful news and you just need to share it with someone for validation and to ensure its real, or when you have something unexpected and life-jarring happen like today's events, and you simply need a person in your corner to give you a hug. It's in these moments that the pain of living along hurts the most.

Dylan was certainly a comfort but the big hairball could only do so much.

An hour later, there was Mike, more flowers, a DVD, a comedy of course, and Chinese take-out. As he came in the door and made it through Dylan's enthusiastic greeting, he placed the food on the counter, looked into my eyes and put his big arms around me, giving me the strongest, longest hug I had had in... forever. Then it was time to actually let a tear or two fall from my eyes. Because I was sad, I was deflated, I felt like I had worked so hard and sacrificed so much to have it just disappear on what seemed like a whim. In my book, that's not the way things were supposed to happen. Honesty, integrity, hard work and creativity were supposed to matter. They were supposed to be rewarded. Maybe there was some reward in this that I just didn't see yet. All I saw was that in one short meeting, my life was changed dramatically. All that I had focused on, all that filled my day, all that I was so proud of was snatched away from me. I didn't know how to deal with that.

The next few days felt surreal. I felt awkward not having to adhere to a strict schedule. I enjoyed sleeping in, watching daytime television and catching up on a few outstanding chores around the house.

I immediately met with a lawyer recommended by a friend of mine. He was helpful and explained it to me bluntly. He said that no matter what, just about any company can fire any one, at any time, for any reason. It just comes down to how much they're willing to pay to do it.

He asked for files, contact numbers etc. and agreed to investigate my options a little further.

While I was downtown, I managed a clandestine coffee meeting with Mike MacPherson. It took a great deal of convincing, but it was ultimately for his benefit. Beside my team, he was the person most affected by my departure, not only because we were a wonderful complement and we actually got along without the usual Marketing versus Sales animosities, but because he was going to have to fill the void. I did not envy him… for many reasons.

Our meeting was somewhat self-serving on his part because he wanted some advice, but he also had something else on his mind.

"Now that we're not working together anymore it won't be an issue, but Kathleen, just what did you mean by that email you sent the other day?"

"Which one in particular might you be referring to? I send about 250 a day Mike."

He was becoming more and more uncomfortable, like that day in his office.

"This one." He handed me a printed piece of paper. I began reading the mushy words I had sent to Mike, my Mike. I was smiling but confused. How did he get this? Where did he find the note that I sent to Mike? Then it hit me. I was reading an email addressed to *this* Mike, but containing a message meant for 'Somebodysprince' Mike.

My laughter shocked him. And while I felt bad, it was funny. "Mike, this email was meant for the man I'm dating. His name just happens to be Mike too. I'm so sorry. I guess I was in a rush. It was just before our big emergency meeting. I guess when the 'to' line was populating, I just must have highlighted the wrong Mike. No wonder you've been uncomfortable around me lately!" I was feeling a little sheepish, "I'm sorry for any discomfort this may have caused you."

While Mike was relieved, I saw an expression that hinted at

more. My mind shot right back to the sushi restaurant where I had overheard him and Beatrice arguing. Could it have been? No. Surely not. But it certainly would explain a great deal.

"Mike, can I ask you just one question? Will you answer it honestly?"

"I'll try."

Shaking the paper in my hand, "Does Beatrice know about this email?"

I handed it to him. I could see the recognition flash across his face as I'm sure he could mine.

It was that moment when it became clear as to why I was no longer with Ardent Staffing.

Mike didn't have to say anything, but he whispered, "Yes, Kayte, I believe she does." Then he wiped his mouth with the napkin, placed it and the paper down on the table and walked away.

I grabbed the email and tucked it in my purse.

I had to share this new information with the only person who could do something with it.

"This changes things a great deal," said Harrison, my lawyer. "Not in the eyes of the law of course, but certainly it gives us a far greater point of leverage for a settlement. I think I could probably get you a year. Would you be happy with that? Or would you like your job back?"

A year where I could forget about work? A year where I could focus on me? A year where I could get in shape, rest, relax do the things, see the people, go to all the places I never had time to with the schedule I kept working at Ardent?

Or would going back be the better choice? Would facing all the questions and going back to working for Beatrice be balanced out by seeing my campaign through to the end and being there for my team? I wasn't sure. The way I spoke to Beatrice, I was pretty sure she'd never invite me back.

The choice was clear.

"I'd be ecstatic."

"I'll adjust my approach to include this new information and let you know how it all plays out. In the meantime, do not talk to anyone from there. Don't discuss it with anyone. I am the only one you discuss this matter with. Are we clear?"

"Yes. Thanks Harrison. I'll wait to hear from you."

How am I going to not talk about this?

I was bored and I couldn't really start emailing all my friends and business network because that would beg all kinds of questions. I figured, why not go online and see what's happening on 'wheres-inglesfindlove.com' and see if I had any new mail from any new males.

There were a couple of them waiting, but none that made any lasting impressions. I probably wasn't in the right frame of mind to be looking. Besides, things were going very well with Mike. He was attentive, romantic, sexy, and affectionate. Things were moving at a good pace, not too fast, not too slow.

Din, din, din. The IM window was calling. I expected Roman to be questioning why I was online in the middle of the day. But when I looked down it wasn't Roman at all. It was Thomas.

Tomtom says:
Hello Kathleen

K8 says:
Hi Thomas

Tomtom says:
Tough day at the office?

K8 says:
The toughest! LOL.

Don't talk about this with anyone. Harrison said not to mention it.

Tomtom says:
I'm actually working from home today. Just moving into a new place so I had to be here to get everything delivered and hooked up etc.

K8 says:
Congratulations. When's the housewarming?

Tomtom says:
When I get some furniture! This divorce thing is tough.

K8 says:
I can only imagine. But it must feel good to have your own place though.

Tomtom says:
It certainly does. This is the first time ever living alone. Was married for 15 years and went from my parent's home directly into the marital one.

K8 says:
Well then you're due. Time to decorate however you want, including posters on the walls, stay up all night, crank up the stereo and eat mac & cheese straight outta the pot.

Tomtom says:
You don't know how accurate a description that is, except for the stereo part on account of I have neighbours. But you can bet your behind the TV is tuned to the sports channel and I maintain sole control of the remote.

K8 says:
Sounds like you're officially a citizen of a great little country we'll call 'Manland'!

Tomtom says:
You betcha. Did you know our national symbol is the beer bottle and our 'manthem' is "Don't Stop Believing"? Our national dish

is really spicy chilli and the national flower is... ah who the f@#% am I kidding, there's no damn national flower!"

K8 says:
LMAO. You ARE funny!

Tomtom says:
Thanks for noticing. That's one thing the ex can't claim in the divorce. My sense of humour is mine, mine, mine, all mine!

K8 says:
I guess it's helped in getting through it all.

Tomtom says:
Yes. That and family and good friends. You sure find out who's in your corner.

K8 says:
That's for sure. So tell me about these new digs.

Tomtom says:
I'd love to, but they've just arrived with the appliances and I'll need to jump off for now. Can we chat later?

K8 says:
Of course. I'd like that. Congrats again. Enjoy your time in 'Manland'.

CHAPTER 14

"That's fantastic news, and so fast too. Thanks so much Harrison, you've certainly made my day. Matter of fact, you've made my year!"

Ardent Staffing had agreed to a settlement that was generous. It took the pressure off that was for sure. I would have been satisfied with six months salary. Thanks to being in the right place at the right time and an aggressive lawyer who wasn't afraid to leverage such politically volatile information, I was going to receive a settlement equivalent to one year's salary. I would receive a cheque within a week and that chapter of my life was over.

I felt myself smile as I entertained the possibilities of how I might indulge myself. I was worth it. I had just gone through hell and needed a little pampering. Maybe I should grab a flight to Barbados and join Chloe, but no, they were only there for two more days. And, that would be a little too frivolous. I could think of better ways to spend some of this money. For the practical part of me, knew that the majority of it was to go into savings, but I could have some fun. I'd worked hard for this and made a lot of sacrifices, so it was payback time.

I had always wanted a personal trainer. It would be a change to have someone to crack the whip at me instead of the other way round. Seeing as my schedule was as open as it could be, this was a great time to do it. Right after I went out to buy some new workout clothes, I went to the gym and found myself my new taskmaster. We scheduled a fitness test for the very next day.

Mike and I agreed that he'd come by Friday night and take me out for a celebration dinner. It's not often a girl makes a year's worth of wages in a week. We both knew that if I played my cards right and began my job hunt quickly this could be the most lucrative year of my life. But more importantly, I was convinced that we were finally going to sleep together that night or at some point that weekend. That, too, was worthy of a celebration.

But it was also scary. Everything had been wonderful until that point. I hoped that we could find the same compatibility sexually as we had everywhere else. But I was haunted by the prospect that it could be disastrous. Even though there was the possibility, I was sure that sex with Mike would be as magical as everything else had been.

But what if it wasn't? What if we were both so concerned about it being as great as everything else had been and we put too much pressure on ourselves or on each other?

I then considered waiting. Perhaps it was still too soon. But I knew I wanted to. I knew I needed to. I needed to know that part of Mike. More importantly, I needed to reconnect with that part of me.

In preparation, or just to put it all out my mind, I treated myself to an afternoon at the spa – manicure, pedicure, wax, massage – the works. As I lay on the massage table, my thoughts drifted to that now far away land of rush, anxiety and hustle and for the first time since losing my job, I felt at peace with it. Somewhere deep inside, I knew it was something that was meant to happen. The reasons why still remained a mystery, but I knew without a doubt that it was part of my destiny.

Then the fingers did their magic and I became this gelatinous ball of flesh that surrendered to the two powerful hands that kneaded and stroked away every ounce of stress from my body. That feeling of submission felt unfamiliar but wonderful. I had been liberated on so many levels.

Mike arrived and in typical romantic fashion had a single rose for me and a bone for Dylan. This guy was so thoughtful and he looked especially fine tonight. His cologne entered first, greeting me with its seductive tones. Maybe he was thinking exactly what I had been thinking.

We went out for a lovely dinner at a Moroccan restaurant where the meal included belly dancers gliding from table to table, infusing authenticity into the experience. Maybe after a few sessions with my new trainer, I'd recreate a dance for Mike. He seemed to enjoy the show. I had almost forgotten what visual creatures most men were. Good thing I was wearing the sexy crimson matching lace bra and panty set. Mike HAD said his favourite colour was red, so that was the colour I wore. I think I even caught him taking an approving glimpse when I reached over, slightly exposing myself as I hand fed him some couscous and raisins.

With a full tummy, a couple of glasses of wine, a strong arm around me and no work stress I didn't think I could be any more relaxed. Boy was I wrong!

Now I remembered what great sex was like. What a night. I woke up to find Mike's protective arms wrapped around me. I could smell the spicy mixture of citrus, sage, cedar and tobacco now absorbed in my sheets. I inhaled deeply and revelled in the intimate moment. Sex is great, but beyond it were the moments like this that I had missed the most. It was that emotional connection in the simplest of situations, curled around each other on the couch in front of the TV, or lying in bed late on Sunday morning or just driving together in the car that was what I truly craved. In a good relationship even the basic things become special moments simply by virtue of the company you're sharing them with.

It appeared that Mike and I had in fact both been on the same sexual timeline. Last night was the right time. It was a natural progression, a comfortable extension of the feelings we had shown so far. It felt right. There were no doubts. It felt physical and emotional. It wasn't two people just taking advantage of a comfortable opportunity to satisfy a natural urge. We were surprisingly compatible. He was a respectful and gentle lover. He was patient and didn't rush the process. We both seemed to sense when we needed to escalate our interaction and we found a rhythm that allowed us each to equally express our need to lead and our need to follow.

His lips ensured that no part of my body felt abandoned and when he was inside me the connection was both complete and compelling. There was no awkwardness that night and there was none that following morning. For when we woke, we began again. Then more sleep, then, again. Then some sustenance and then, again. At the end of the sexual marathon with Stamina-Man, I was truly the most relaxed and peaceful that I could ever remember being. I was very fond of Mike and could see the possibility of that growing into love. I knew I was smiling at the thought. I'd be sure to thank Chloe for suggesting this online thing. I remembered thinking this as I drifted off to sleep again, this time sprawled across Mike's broad chest with my face resting comfortably on a bed of chest hair and muscle as he lay on his back claiming the very centre of the bed.

CHAPTER 15

"You want me to do what?" I just about spit my Sunday morning coffee into the paper when I heard his question.

"C'mon Kayte, it will be fun. I was a little wary at first too, but it's not what you think."

Mike was trying his best to sell me on this one, but I wasn't buying.

It wasn't that he had just asked me to join him in full costume at a week-long Star Trek convention, or to eat a bucket of live crickets or go bobbing for leeches or anything you'd see on a 'Face Your Fears' type reality television show. He didn't want me to surrender my new found settlement money, shave my head and run off to join some sort of religious cult, but it might as well have been any of those. All those options, Mike's included, were equally outside of the Kayte Wexford comfort zone.

"What is it about me that makes you think I'd be interested in something like that?" I asked.

"You're very sexual and I think you'd enjoy it. And I'd like to think that even if you're not completely convinced that it's for you, that you might try it for me. It would make me happy if you'd consider it."

He continued, "It's not as seedy as people think. It's more like a social or sports club where like-minded people gather to share a common interest. There are people from all walks of life, all levels of attractiveness, all levels of, umm, "involvement" and some really nice people. It's not all about the sex, there are events and activities and we could even make some new good friends."

My immediate reaction was no… no way… never, I had enough friends, thanks, and I think I prefer not sleeping with them. That said, I felt like I still needed to play this one through. I had to learn what was behind the question. Was this something that Mike did a lot? Was it just for fun? Was it instead of a relationship? Would it change if he were in a loving relationship? Or was it more? Was it a lifestyle? Or was he testing me? Yes, this required delicate handling indeed and some post breakfast pondering.

To buy some time I took another sip of coffee and another mouthful of eggs, looked into those huge sexy eyes and then smiled, "Okay, I'll tell you what. I'll think about it. I'm not promising anything, but I will think about it. That's all. Think. Do you hear me? I'm saying 'think' not 'do'. That's not a 'no' but it's not a 'yes' either. We'll just have to see about this, but absolutely no promises. None."

"You are too adorable," he got up from his chair and pulled me from mine, put his arms around my waist and undid the tie from my bathrobe. The kiss he gave me was hard. And it wasn't the only thing.

CHAPTER 16

"We had a fabulous time." I could hear the thud of cupboard door after cupboard door closing and the rustle of the plastic grocery bags and assumed Chloe had been shopping and was re-stocking her kitchen.

"I'm so happy for you – and the kids, did they enjoy it?"

"Yes, and that added to Mommy's enjoyment. They had a children's program and I barely saw them until we all got together for dinner in the evening. I read, ran on the beach, had a couple of leisurely lunches, got a massage and read a few books and people watched like crazy. And just what have you been up to over the past two weeks?"

"Good for you my dear, you deserve it. As for me, I was fired, got a year's severance and had a marathon sex weekend with Mike only to find out at the end of it all that he wants me to go to a swinging party with him."

"Always the comedian. Now seriously, how's the campaign going? And did you honestly sleep with Mike? Details KatieKat, details?"

"Chloe, listen to me. I'm serious. I came into some vital office gossip that went straight to the top, got fired, got connected with a fabulous lawyer who I am convinced is part magician. The Mike stuff? All true."

There was silence on the other end of the phone. "Oh dear. Sounds like we're in urgent need of an emergency girlfriend day. Why don't you come by tomorrow?"

"Perfect. I'll do that, say around ten. So glad you're home."

"Me too. Love you sweetie and I'll see you tomorrow."

I grabbed a hot chocolate and went upstairs to the computer to send a few messages to those great friends I have that live in different cities. Thank heavens for email, sms and social networks. It certainly does make keeping in touch easier. I guess you can be in contact more often and more easily but the quality of the contact is nowhere near voice to voice or in person contact. Truth be told I'd been lousy about initiating any kind of contact lately as work had been so all consuming. I was determined to change that.

I logged in and my status on various platforms magically changed to online.

I sent a message to Marnie asking if she'd like to join Dylan and I on one of our long hikes soon. Given we were in the same line of work, it would be good to update her on my recent career status change as well. She was very well connected and while she hadn't succeeded in introducing me to my dream guy, connecting me with a dream job wasn't out of the realm of possibility.

Roman's status showed he was online. It had been a while since we had seen each other, so I sent him a message too.

K8 says:
Hey Wolfman, we need to get together for dinner soon. I have some news.

Bigbadwolf says:
U pregnant?

K8 says:
NO! Bite your tongue.

Bigbadwolf says:
Engaged?

K8 says:
Maybe, but you'll just have to wait 'til dinner to find out.

Bigbadwolf says:
OK - how 'bout Friday?

K8 says:
Perfect. Where should we go?

Bigbadwolf says:
Why don't you meet me at the Bear and Beaver?

K8 says:
K – 8pm okay?

Bigbadwolf says:
Looking 4ward 2 c-ing U girl!

K8 says:
Back atchya – Kayte out!

Bigbadwolf says:
Later.

Tomtom's status was still offline. I was disappointed that he wasn't available for a chat. But those feelings confused me. Why should I even want to talk to other guys when I had Mike? I guess I wasn't feeling completely sure about the relationship with Mike. I suspected that it came down to the whole swinging thing. I was still a little shell-shocked by his request. But in every other way he seemed so perfect. I definitely had more thinking to do on that subject as I found myself thinking more about Thomas.

I had enjoyed our brief but entertaining conversation the other day. He was funny. I had hoped he'd be online tonight. But I guess moving into a new place there are lots of things to be done.

I couldn't imagine his situation though, living on his own for the first time in his life in his thirties. Divorce must really suck. Just when you think your life is all sorted out and your future is laid out for you, wham, it all gets tossed about and you're forced to start over. That couldn't be anything remotely close to easy, especially after being a couple for so long.

I felt for the guy. Here he was thrust into the dating world with no experience for the last 15 or so years. And boy had it changed. This whole online dating thing was so different than dating 20 years ago. The poor guy must feel like he'd landed in a new country and didn't speak the language, but kudos to him for putting himself out there. That takes courage.

I opened a few emails. There was one from Marnie. Her timing and sentiments were always bang on. The subject line read:

Things we should always remember.

She introduced the body with:

Enjoy the sentiment... M.

Things that we should all remember:

Always try to help a friend in need.

It's ok to be afraid sometimes.

Give lots of kisses.

Meet new people.

Take a nap if you need one.

Love your friends, no matter who they are.

Don't waste food.

RELAX... EVEN, ON THOSE STRESSFUL DAYS!!

Try to have a little fun each day...

Share a joke with your friends and neighbours,

Fall in love with someone special...

Say, "I love you" often.

Express yourself creatively.

Remember the saying, "good things happen to good people!"

There is always someone who loves you more than you know.

Exercise a little each day!

Live up to your name.

Hold on to good friends; they are few and far between!

And remember, this friend is thinking about you.

It made me stop and think - a short email that so aptly captured the priorities of life. I wondered how this little reminder might affect the myriad of readers it would eventually touch. I wondered if it had the power to motivate a reader to do something that would change their destiny. And, selfishly, what might it inspire me to do.

Din, din, din. The chat window beckoned. It was Thomas.

Tomtom says:
Hello Kathleen

K8 says:
Good evening Thomas, how's life in Manland?

Tomtom says:
LOL - perfect - it's estrogen free and all about me!

K8 says:
Glad you are enjoying it. Sounds like you've just created Manland's tagline!

Tomtom says:
And what is new in your world?

K8 says:

Lots – the biggest of which is a career change.

Tomtom says:
I'm listening. OK, to be technical, I'm reading actually, but please tell me more.

K8 says:
It's a long story, but the short of it is that I got fired through no fault of my own, had a great lawyer who secured me a very good settlement. Now I need to figure out what's next.

Tomtom says:
Wow. I'm so sorry. Good on the settlement, but horrible on losing your job. What do/did you do?

K8 says:
I was head of marketing for a staffing firm.

Tomtom says:
Wow I'm impressed.

K8 says:
Don't be too impressed, now I'm unemployed.

Tomtom says:
I'm sure you'll find something soon, what little I know of you sounds pretty intelligent and judging from your profile you're a great communicator, so they'll be banging down your doors in no time.

K8 says:
Thanks for the vote of confidence. To be honest, I'm almost grateful for the break. I'd been spending too much time working and not enough time on the important things in life so now I might be able to explore the possibility of turning work life balance into a reality rather than some elusive concept.

Tomtom says:
Sounds like we're both dealing with some big changes and challenges. But remember, where there's challenge, there's opportunity.

K8 says:
Agreed!

Tomtom says:
There's something better ahead for both of us.

K8 says:
I believe that too. So how'd you get so smart?

Tomtom says:
My folks learned me good and I done readed as much books as I could whened I was a wee feller.

K8 says:
Is that so?

Tomtom says:
Yes ma'am.

K8 says:
Hate to do this, but I have to say goodnight to Manland's smartest resident as I have an early date with my best friend tomorrow and I must get my other best friend, the dog, out for a walk before bed. I really enjoyed our chat though.

Tomtom says:
Thanks Kayte I really did too. You enjoy your walk. I gots me some meat and some beans and I gots to go makes me some chilli!

K8 says:
Great - enjoy - sounds like perfect food for Manland. Good night Thomas.

Tomtom says:
Good night Kayte

I wondered if Thomas was the swinging kind. I hoped not. And DAMN IT, why did Mike have to be?

CHAPTER 17

"I'm not sure whether it's a deal-breaker or not," I was saying to Chloe as we took one of our marathon power walks through her densely packed downtown neighbourhood.

"Is it something you'd like to try? Are you curious about it?"

"I've never really thought about it to be honest. But my gut says that I just couldn't be a swinger and if Mike is, then he's probably not the guy for me."

Chloe, being the true diplomat and taking a balanced look at things, asked, "Even with all the wonderful qualities you say he has, like romantic, thoughtful, open, communicative and handsome? You wouldn't overlook the swinging thing for all that?"

"That's what makes it so tough. If the swinging thing hadn't come up, I would have thought that he was the perfect man for me. I'd be picking out china patterns next month. We connect on all levels. We have fun. We talk about everything. He's so sweet and so good with Dylan. He's established and likes to do things from all ends of the spectrum. He hikes, plays volleyball, likes to dress up and go out to dine in nice restaurants and he loves to cuddle in bed for hours on end. But there's still this swinging thing and I don't quite know what to do with that."

"I feel for you honey. Sounds like you need to think on this some more. With everything you've been through in the past little while, don't rush anything. Give yourself some time to wrap your head around it. You'll come to the right conclusion."

"You're right, but then again, you always are."

"Now, tell me, word for word, how you stuck it to that Beatrice-bitch back at Ardent. She must hate you now. First she thinks you're doing the nasty with her man, okay, correction, her man-on-the-side. Then she fires you and you end up having the last laugh by letting her know that you know about her affair. Then you go that extra mile and stick it to her for a year's salary that is negotiated by someone else who now knows about her infidelities. Man, she's getting fucked by everyone, isn't she? Poor, poor little Queen Bea."

We both erupted in laughter.

It was nice to spend a weekday with my best friend. We walked, went for a nice Thai lunch, and popped in and out of the eclectic mix of street front shops, looking but not buying. Then we lounged in big comfy chairs near the window in our favourite little coffee house and just chit chatted about everything and nothing. This was in sharp contrast to how I had been spending my days of late. The liberating thing was that I was almost certain that I could grow to like this lifestyle. I was becoming more and more accepting of my new reality and on the verge of actually embracing it.

The Bear and Beaver, besides being interestingly named, was a very comfortable little pub. When you entered it was different from most pubs. Although it had the requisite casual feel, it was just that little bit classier. The lighting was dim but the traditional black painted trim was upgraded to deep mahogany. The walls weren't cream or white; they were a warm sand, punctuated with pops of burgundy, brass and deep mossy green, adding a sense of sophistication and warmth. It was more like pub meets library. The most important part was that it was clean. The new owners had just celebrated a grand re-opening two months earlier. They had the best meatloaf, bacon-wrapped scallops and fish and chips for miles. It was a slice of comfort food heaven.

Roman was late, as usual. So I ordered a merlot, found a comfy booth and waited. Traditionally this would be a time where I'd take advantage of the found time and return some work emails, send a text or two or make a list of things that needed to be done over the weekend. But I didn't have to do any of that. It felt awkward. I felt like I was forgetting something. I guess it would take a bit of time to adjust to my new reality. So while I waited, I watched the patrons and the staff interact, going about their rounds. The odd whiff of new paint and new carpet wafted through the air as the servers created a slight breeze as they passed my table. As I reflected on my own recent changes, I wondered what life events might be happening in these people's worlds.

There was a 50-ish red haired woman, with a long oval face, huge eyes, slightly overdone makeup and long well manicured nails. She was probably a smoker. She had the telltale deep lip wrinkles and her nails tap, tap, tapped on the table as she spoke. She fidgeted and moved her glass first, then the salt and pepper shakers, then the coaster, then back to the glass. It was intriguing to watch her play this solitary game of tabletop chess.

Her companion on the other hand, a barrel-chested greying man with a hint of a moustache appeared stolid. He wrapped his hulking paws around a half-drunk pint of dark malt, sitting and listening ever so attentively to her as she spoke. Expressionless and passive, his only movements were raising the glass to his thin, slightly pursed lips to take sip after sip.

It was 8:20 when I received a text from Roman.

Sorry K8, running behind, see you in 10.

When will I learn? If I say eight with Roman, I should show for 8:30. Maybe make him wait for a change. I was obviously wearing my angry face and shaking my head as I returned my phone to my bag, for Roman was right there to catch me mid frustration.

"Gotcha!" he beamed with boyish mischief.

"Goof!" I swatted him playfully on the shoulder as I got up to give him a big hug. One thing about Roman, he gave the best hugs. They were strong and sincere and just that little bit longer than everyone else's. Hugs were one of the highly effective tools found in Roman's romantic arsenal.

"Look at you girl. You look different. You look so relaxed. That's it, relaxed. Don't know that I've ever met Relaxed-Kayte. Hi there. Allow me to introduce myself. I'm Roman Wolfsky, Wolf, for short. Pleased to meet you." He was now grabbing my hand and placing a delicate kiss upon it.

"You know that crap doesn't work on me, right? And just to be sure, I took a dose of Roman anti-venom before coming to meet you. So I am completely immune even if you bite!"

"Oh don't kid yourself Kayte. No woman alive is totally immune to the ways of The Big Bad Wolf."

"If I thought you were serious, I'd hurl."

He laughed. He knew it was all in fun with me. We had a different relationship than he had with most women. Maybe because we met as sports friends and I knew from the beginning that I had no romantic interest in him. I'm not sure I would have bet on the same from him, but we managed to maintain a good, but very platonic friendship. We learned from each other. We enjoyed some of the same pursuits, movies, plays, sports, and food. And we shared our singledom. We could share dating stories with someone who could relate. We usually had a good laugh when we were together, so it was nice to see him face to face. Too many of my friendship interactions these days took place online. It was nice to be face-to- face, person-to-person for a change. Roman looked out for me. He always had my back, included me when there was a new volleyball team being formed or a tournament happening.

"So catch me up girl. What's been happening? How's the online dating thing going? Are you breaking some hearts?" Roman ordered an ale and we settled into one of those great, heart to heart, no holds barred, down and dirty, nothing's off limits, 'catch me up to the minute before you sit down' kinda chats.

First I told him about meeting 'Somebodysprince', AKA Mike. I gushed about how wonderful he was. I could feel my smile widen and my eyes sparkle brighter as I spoke about him. I half-bragged about how attentive he was, how romantic, how demonstrative. I confessed to seeing, talking, emailing, online chatting with him every day and that's where Roman stopped me.

"You're still chatting with other guys online though right?"

"Well to be honest, no, not really. I haven't been on the site much lately."

"Okay girl, time to teach you Roman's Rule #6. Listen closely. Even if you think you're getting serious about a man that you've met on the dating site, you still must spend time on the dating site."

Sceptical but curious, "Okay. I'll bite. Why?"

"I'm so glad you asked. And I'll take you up on that bite offer later sunshine! You still need to be online for two reasons. First, if men see that you're not online for periods of time, they may think that you're not serious about actually dating. They may think that you just pop in to get your ego stroked when you're feeling lonely or have some time to kill. Lots of people do this – both men and women – they're not serious about ever meeting and they waste the time of those of us who are. Secondly, and more importantly, if you like this guy, don't let him think you're "all in" too soon. If he sees that you haven't been on there, he might just think that you've figured you've found Mr. Right and he might just get a little spooked by that. Or, he might get a little too cocky - been guilty of this one myself. Make him think he's got some competition. It makes us blokes work a little harder."

Rule number six of Roman's Rules of Online Dating was very enlightening. "You make some good points. To rule number six." I clinked his glass and looked him straight in the eye. "Cheers."

I also learned that Roman had dated 10 women in the last three weeks. I was exhausted just hearing about it. I compared that to Mike. He was so different. With all the time we had spent together, there was no way he could have been cycling through a dating marathon that even came close to Roman's. I wondered if he was on a date tonight. I had just told him I was seeing Roman and never even asked what he was doing.

The man sitting across from me had stamina that was for sure. And a steel trap for a memory for he could keep every detail about every woman straight for as long as he needed to. Then, if the opportunity arose months later, say running into one of these women in a bar, or on the street, he could retrieve the necessary, as well as the trivial, details at whim. Truly remarkable.

"So aren't you bursting to know my news?"

"I thought the Mike relationship was the news."

"Nope."

"Well what then? You're not pregnant are you?"

I held up what was the end of my second glass of wine and said, "I sure as hell hope not!"

"Spill it girl."

"I got fired."

"What. No way. Are they mad? You did the work of three men. Oops, I mean people."

"Yep. I'm unemployed. That's the bad news. The good news is that I received almost a year's salary as a lovely parting gift."

"No way. Man, then you're buying."

So I told Roman the whole sordid soap opera story and as I told it, I felt detached. I was amazed at how I had been able to distance myself so far so fast. But I had.

"Think of it this way Kayte, it gives you so much more time to date."

Another good point.

"So have you been getting many messages? I always wondered about the volume of messages women received versus men."

"To be honest, no, not too many lately."

"Well then, it might be time to invoke rule #7. While I don't usually give away two of my online teachings in one sitting, I'll make an exception for the unemployed gal."

"Ah shucks. Thanks Wolf."

"So you might be at the point where you need to refresh your profile. Kayte, just like in marketing, you gotta keep it new and interesting. Maybe just edit your opening line rather than re-doing your whole profile. Which is very good by the way – I had to read it. If you do this, you keep cycling your profile through with the other new ones. It's a good practice because many people just choose to view the new ones, using that as their primary sort. So you want to be with the new profiles. It's all about visibility babe."

Again, he had a point.

"Thanks. I'll do that. Even though I'll probably run off next month and marry Mike. I'd dote on him hand and foot, a happy housewife, keeping a lovely home, greeting him at the door after a hard day's work with a martini followed by a scrumptious dinner, full control of the remote and sexual favours every night. I could do this easily now that I have all this time on my hands."

"You? Ya, right!"

We both laughed. Traditional 50's housewife I was not and

would never be. But, I knew that when I found the right man, I would probably embrace it more than others might think. No one needed to know that just yet.

I felt my phone vibrate through my purse onto my leg. I grabbed it and read the text message.

Hey sexy. I can't get you out of my mind. I'm thinking about U. About kissing U, touching U, holding you & being inside U. I can't wait to see you again.

The text message from Mike instantly delivered a smirk and that stirring feeling down there. He was so sexy.

Mmm. I like the way you think. But, you'll just have to wait until tomorrow though handsome.

If I have to. But I'll call you later.

Look forward to it, xxx.

"Mike I assume?" Roman asked.

"Yes sir. Did I mention he was attentive? And so very sexy and sensual - so in tune with me."

"Stop it! Enough! I can't take it anymore. He sounds like a big girl!"

CHAPTER 18

"So. What's. The. Surprise?" I punctuated each word with another kiss.

Mike was still standing, taking up the majority of the front door frame. He hadn't even entered the house and he had reached his long arms out, grabbed me and pulled me to him. My chest met his, my lips connected with his lips, and my body arched as he ran his hands up my back.

"It won't be a surprise if I tell you hon."

"You don't have to tell me where, but you do have to tell me if I'm dressed okay."

"You're perfect." He looked me in the eyes and delivered those two words with a pride and certainty that erased any doubt or uncertainty I had about anything. At that moment, in his arms, I believed I was.

We gave Dylan a cookie, a pat good night, then closed the door and made our way to Mike's car to begin our mysterious adventure.

"Are we going to a play?"

"Negative."

"Are we going to a basketball game?"

"Not this time."

"I know. We're going to eat at that new total darkness restaurant. Now there's an inventive way to save a bundle on the interior design budget. And you don't have to pay big electrical bills or worry about food presentation. Man. I wish I'd thought of that. I'm guessing it would also be a great place to take your mistress out for dinner – no one would ever see your cheating ass!"

"Good point babe but no, we're not going to plunge ourselves into total darkness. Besides I want to see your pretty face."

I reached over and kissed him on the cheek for that one.

"Are we going to the new exhibit at the Art Gallery?"

"Nuhuh."

"To the airport to jump on a plane to Vegas?"

"Sadly, sweetie, no."

"To sort food at the food bank?"

"Not tonight, but that would be a nice thing to do."

"Salsa lessons?"

"Non, Senorita."

"A book launch?"

"No."

"A lecture?"

"Close." There was my first hint.

"Well I hope they have vending machines there, 'cause I'm starved."

"You won't go hungry."

"Good." Hint number two. I was even more intrigued.

We were in the city now, not too far from my old office. I didn't realise how much I missed it. Perhaps the full magnitude of the change hadn't sunk in yet. I just felt like I was on a break, a mini-vacation of sorts. While I didn't miss racing for the train or not getting home until after 8pm, I certainly missed my team. I had gone from spending 10-12 hours a day with them to nothing, no contact. I hadn't spoken with any of them since this all transpired. Harrison directed me that until I had the cheque in hand, or better yet, cashed and cleared, that it would not be advisable to speak with anyone from there. I was paying for his expertise and guidance so I should listen to it and abide by it.

"Okay, my dear, we're about five minutes away. I'd like you to reach in the glove compartment and pull out the envelope and it will explain everything."

"Yippee."

Thank you for choosing "Sous Chef Supreme – The Battle of the Rising Chefs", taking place at the La Truffe Culinary Academy. Your evening will have you interacting with three of this city's finest sous chefs. In addition to sampling their masterpieces, you'll observe preparation techniques, learn how and why each dish was chosen, have an opportunity for questions and, ultimately, have the power to affect their fate by scoring their culinary creations. This is a competition for gastronomic superiority where you and your tastebuds are the judge.

You'll also sample a variety of wines, each one expertly chosen to complement each course. There will be an onsite sommelier who will provide background on the wine choices, details about each vintage and he'll share general wine matching tips and hints. As he strolls from table to table, he'll answer your wine questions and gather your feedback on the evening's choices.

"Really? Wow Mike. I'm stunned and salivating! This is fabulous. You are too good to me." I was beaming.

"I thought this would be a perfect Kayte-date."

"How right you are." I reached up and grabbed his face turning it toward me and gave him a huge kiss, tongue and all.

Later that evening we enjoyed the best course of all, each other. We arrived home full and happy. I even had some new recipe ideas. Dylan greeted us sleepily but enthusiastically. He was asking for a walk. Mike and I gladly complied as we needed to wear off some of the evening's indulgences.

As we walked through the neighbourhood I offered, "I think my favourite was the lobster salad with the fennel and red pepper strips in that butter and bourbon reduction."

"Mine too. You could really taste the lobster. But I also liked that dessert – the custard thing."

"The rosemary lemon pannacotta drizzled with olive oil?"

"Yes. Yum."

"I would have never thought to do that for dessert – rosemary in a dessert? That was a first. But it worked."

"Speaking of firsts, "have you thought any more about what I asked you?" We had entered the park by my house and were passing the swing set.

I was pleased that he hadn't brought this up earlier, that we could focus on the food and the wine and the indulgence of a truly wonderful "foodie" evening.

"Yes I have and I've got some questions. How does this swing-ing stuff all work? Are there special bars, clubs? Do you go to someone's home? Is there a website where you find people and events? Do you have to be a card-carrying member of 'Swingers-R-Us'?"

"Well Kayte, just about all of the above – minus the club card. Many people start with going to the clubs and bars that are specifically known as swinging clubs. Websites will list events and parties, but most people attend through referral or invitation. The clubs give you the chance to sort of ease into things gradually."

"How so?"

"Well, there are public areas and then there are rooms for specific purposes, like an orgy room for example. Some have levels or rooms that are for people in varying degrees of undress. In the clubs you'll see lots of provocative dancing, and alluring clothing, albeit sometimes not much of it. You can pretty much drink and dance as in any regular club, but if you're attracted to someone, let's just say they are more likely to be open to your advances."

"Really? This is all fascinating. Not saying that I'm doing it, but it is fascinating – a completely different world than I'm used to."

"One I hope you'll experience with me." Before I could respond, Mike turned, faced me, drew me to him and kissed me hard, almost forcefully, right there in the park, standing next to the swing set, where only a hint of light from the far off crescent moon and the subdued glow of the lone lamppost cast away the imminent darkness.

We kissed and walked and walked and kissed the rest of the way home. Once inside, the intensity grew. His hands explored my body with a balance of eagerness and appreciation. Our tongues entangled and wrestled for superiority, each taking its turn in the lead. The intensity of our hunger for each other was in sharp contrast to the slow and deliberate way in which we undressed each other. Never breaking our gaze, clothing came off item by item. Standing in my bedroom face to face, body to body, first he removed my blouse, button by button, ever so slowly. Once removed, he ran his hands over the bare skin that had just been exposed as if to welcome it gradually to its new naked reality.

In turn, I removed his tie first, then his crisp shirt, freeing him from the constrictions of his daily uniform. Once the shirt was off I planted light soft kisses on his shoulders, his biceps and then upon each fingertip, taking the index finger into my mouth and encircling it with my hot, wet and welcoming tongue.

Our lovemaking was slow and deliberate and by reaching for ever-increasing levels of anticipation, it ensured we were both moved by the experience.

"Kayte," he brushed the hair from my ear with his fingers and whispered ever so softly, "I want you to know that I feel incredible here with you. I'm so happy, so lucky to have met you. I think we're on to something good here."

"I feel pretty incredible here with you too." I nuzzled my head under his chin, he held me tightly and we fell asleep connected to each other on all levels. We were linked so closely that I half expected that we'd share in each other's dreams.

I woke up before him. I lay there listening to him breathing, wide awake, pondering my decision on the swinging thing. As he inhaled, I found myself saying "yes". On the exhale, "no". I went back and forth. Inhale, "yes". Exhale, "no". Inhale "yes". Exhale "no"… until I finally deferred my decision by drifting back to sleep.

Over strong coffee, fluffy scrambled eggs with a hint of dill and lightly buttered ancient grain toast, all lovingly prepared by the handsome tousled and tender man standing in my kitchen, Mike provided me with even more insights into the swinging world.

His large strong hand wrapped itself fully around his coffee cup. He took a sip, swallowed and then spoke very matter-of-factly.

"Often the clubs are a meeting ground but because laws are different for public places than for private ones, much of the swinging socialising is done in people's homes."

He explained that not just anyone can show up and be welcomed in, or as he put it, "a single horny dude looking to get a little can't just knock on the door, walk in, look around and shout 'okay, so where are da hoes at?'" At this, I literally spat my eggs out on the floor from my laughter. In a split second, Dylan raced to inhale the rare treat.

Mike explained further that to gain entry, you had to be invited and you would most likely have to go through a screening process, especially if you had never been to a swinger party before. The hosts were responsible for explaining how things worked, determining whether they thought you could handle the emotions brought about by actually seeing people having sex right there in front of you, the jealously that might arise if your partner is involved with another, or even personally dealing with the numerous advances you may receive in a very short period of time.

Truly fascinated by a world I'd never known, I was agog as I sat cradling my second coffee listening to Mike tell me about the various dress; everything from lingerie to leather was acceptable and encouraged. The demographics could span from decidedly average to higher than average intelligence, good income earners, mostly married couples, but with an infusion of a few singles and dating couples tossed in to mix things up a bit. It hadn't evolved to what he'd call an ethnically diverse group yet, or at least that had been his experience.

Many people made their living or supplemented it handsomely by hosting these parties. Everyone was charged an entry fee and depending upon the turnout, the evening could be quite lucrative.

I think my jaw was tired from my mouth hanging open through the entire "Swinging 101" lesson, but it certainly had been informative. I was definitely curious, but certainly nowhere near committed to trying this yet, but I had to admit it was truly fascinating.

One thing was for sure; this wasn't usual breakfast conversation. It was a topic that probably would be better discussed later in the day, preferably wine in hand!

CHAPTER 19

After Mike left I was more confused than ever. So I took Roman's advice and logged onto the dating site for a bit, to give myself some exposure. I actually did what I had referred to as 'trolling'. I logged on then reduced the site window and appeared online as I did other online things like chats, surfing, banking and sorting through my emails.

My chat window rang out and called for my attention. It was Thomas.

Tomtom says:
Well hello Miss Kayte

K8 says:
Hello Tomtom! Love that handle btw - it's not lost on me!

Tomtom says:
Thx - so how's unemployed life treating you.

K8 says:
Wonderfully. Sleeping in, watching the soaps, staying in my pjs all day. You know the drill. LOL. It's work, damn it, hard, hard

labour.

Tomtom says:
No, my dear, work is that thing that the rest of us have to do for 8-9 hours a day.

K8 says:
So what do you do?

Tomtom says:
I'm a mechanical engineer for an international supplier of manufacturing equipment.

K8 says:
Sounds very "machiney"

Tomtom says:
I design, oversee installation, troubleshoot and manage the training needs of clients for the machines we build and install.

K8 says:
I guess you have to be very mechanically minded.

Tomtom says:
Yes, I'm that way. And I'm not afraid to say, I have tools and I know how to use them!

K8 says:
I might just have to ask for some help in that dep't some day. I can do a lot, but I don't have many tools and me and plumbing or electrical, just will never get along.

Tomtom says:
You're such a girl!!!

K8 says:
Thanks for noticing.

Tomtom says:
I couldn't miss them (oops I mean it!) Especially in that photo you're using as your display photo, the one with the pink sweater. Very girlie. Nice, hmm, ah… sweater! He added a winking smiley for effect.

K8 says:
Thanks. Yes, one of the first things men usually notice about me is my, hmm, ah, sweater! LOL

Tomtom says:
Touché - hope I wasn't being 2 forward.

K8 says:
Heck no. But now I feel free to mention my handyman a la tool belt fantasy. LOL. Plus I liked it! I added the blushing smiley.

Tomtom says:
Oh someone's a flirty girl!

K8 says:
Guilty, so sue me.

Tomtom says:
From what I understand, isn't suing your dep't?

K8 says:
OUCH! Mr. Smarty Pants!

Tomtom says:
Seriously, Kayte, how are you adjusting to things? It must be a huge change for you?

K8 says:
I feel like I'm on vacation. I don't think it's hit me yet. But things will be fine. I can always start up my consulting company again.

Tomtom says:
Woo hoo the lady has her own company. Now who's wearing the smarty pants?

K8 says:
LOL – you're funny – quick too.

Tomtom says:
Not in all things, but I try.

K8 says:
So how goes life in Manland?

Tomtom says:
Good - settling in - getting things set up - now that the bedroom is set up the kids are welcome to visit Dad in his new digs.

K8 says:
I'm sure they'll love that. They must miss you.

Tomtom says:
Not nearly as much as I miss them I'm afraid. But this should be a nice balance. Give me some me-time.

K8 says:
Yes, you've probably never had that.

Tomtom says:
Nope.

K8 says:
I am just figuring out how important that is too.

I've enjoyed this time off. I'm sure I'll tire of it eventually, but it's been nice to be able to make myself first priority for a change.

Tomtom says:
You know I can't remember ever doing that. So it's a new one for me. But selfishly, I think I'm going to like it. I think I'll like it a lot!

K8 says:
You just might grow to love it!

Tomtom says:
If I get to spend time with great people like you – I just might.

K8 says:
Aw shucks Thomas, you say the darnedest thangs (southern accent intended)

Tomtom says:
Am I making my-lady blush?

K8 says:
Yes and smile too.

Tomtom says:

I have an idea. We seem to get along pretty well. Would you
be interested in meeting for a coffee or a drink or something?
It might be nice to compare notes on being incredibly self-
indulgent and offer each other tips on making ourselves priority
one.

K8 says:
Thomas, I thought you'd never ask! (Southern drawl still
evident). I do declare that I think I just might fancy that.

Tomtom says:
I can just see you fanning yourself! LMAO. So Scarlett, is that a
yes?

K8 says:
Why sir, I do believe that it is!

Tomtom says:
Great - is it okay if I get back to you with a couple of options for
where/when?

K8 says:
Of course. BFN.

Tomtom:
Ciao.

Why not? I wasn't going to sleep with him. It was just meeting
and that was the reason I went online in the first place, so that
I could meet men, not just one man. While I'm ultimately after
Mr. Right, making some new friends along the way was good too.
Things were great with Mike, but we hadn't even begun to have
the conversation about being exclusive. Neither of us had said "I
love you." And Thomas piqued my interest from the very beginning. He seemed like a truly nice man, amusing and playful and
smart, so I felt like I was right to do this. The more men I met, the
more chances I'd have of finding true love, lasting love. The more
I learned about what I did and didn't want in a mate, the better.
And I certainly had the time these days to do it.

So that was it. Settled. I was going to meet Thomas. And I was
excited about it. And that was okay. I immediately went online to

read his profile again and take another look at his photo.

Then I perused my wardrobe to choose the right outfit and think about whether or not I would mention meeting Thomas to Mike. I most likely would but I'd be wise to give some thought on how best to say it.

CHAPTER 20

"If you're uncomfortable and you want to leave at any time, just say the word, Kayte, and we're out of here."

"That makes me feel a little better, Mike. Thanks."

Who the hell was I kidding? While I was still very curious about this netherworld of hedonistic pleasures, I was almost sure it wasn't for me. I couldn't believe that I had actually agreed to accompany Mike to a swinging club.

I just felt like I had to try this for him – he was so perfect in every other way. He was a gentle yet passionate lover and I felt wonderful when I was with him. He had a good job, a solid relationship with his family, a few close friends, hopes and dreams for the future that would mesh with mine. But he was a swinger. We discussed it and it had become part of his lifestyle now for over five years. He knew it limited his chances with some great women, but it was who he was. He didn't think that he could give it up.

So here I was, just minutes away from entering my very first swinging club. Mike had got us on the guest list for one of the hottest clubs in the city. The Naughty & Nice Klub, the city's hotspot where 'naughty was the new nice', or at least that was what their advertising had promised. It went on to describe itself as a place to drink, flirt, dance, socialise, get acquainted and make nice with others just like you. Entry was at the sole discretion of the door people and the selection for entry was based on attractiveness, appropriateness, dress, and sophistication. I highly doubted the latter but all told, if this didn't bring back teenage horrors of fitting in and being cool enough, pretty enough, dressed well enough, sexy enough, well endowed enough, I don't know what would. This swinging thing was certainly not for the faint of heart.

Just to make us first-timers feel welcome, the Klub encouraged us to tell them at the door that we were 'naughty-virgins'. This way the hosts could make a point of welcoming us and greeting every new guest. I had half hoped it would be with a shot or two of vodka because that might be the only way I would get through the experience.

Once inside, the place was certainly decked out in the finest of naughty and nice features. There was champagne service, VIP booths, bed booths and their Nice & Naughty show-off cages. Their most recent addition was the N&N eight-person, transparent shower stall. This was all overwhelmingly foreign to me and I really had no idea what to expect.

Apparently the big payoff came if you were deemed really naughty or really nice, for you just might be invited to the after party that takes place in someone's private residence after 1am. Here you would join a group of handpicked naughty and nice friends and friends of friends for another level of pleasure exchange.

We had made our way to the door. The two doormen and one doorwoman greeted us with smiles, looking us up and down. The woman gave an appreciative glance to Mike as her eyes passed the generous bulge in his tight clean-line trousers. The larger of the men, the penguin-chested balding man with a fine moustache and goatee and three earrings asked me to open my coat. I automatically obliged, much as I would if a police officer had demanded my ownership and insurance. He apparently thought the shortness of my skirt, the length of my legs, the sheerness of my stockings or the ampleness of my bosom, blossoming uncharacteristically out of my red silk halter top, was Naughty & Nice-worthy, because he then waved us in with their trademark phrase, "Go ahead. Be naughty," as if he was some moralistic judge granting us permission to indulge in the hedonist behaviours of the evening. If you were refused entry, you heard the words, "Sorry you're too nice."

The club was about half full when we arrived. Appropriately the music thundered out "Let's get this party started". Most people were just milling about, sauntering up to the bar, some small groups were chatting and laughing, over by the cage a tall blonde snuck up behind a man who had just stepped off the cover of GQ and without a word, turned him around and placed the biggest kiss on him and he, in return, reached round and grabbed her butt with both hands, lifting her skirt as he did so.

I don't know what hung more noticeably in the room: the concoction of various perfumes melding into one that cloaked the air in its heavy seductive scents or the brazen splashes of red that were strewn throughout. The bar was red, the stages and cages, the lounges, the shining glossed lips of the women, the four, sometimes five-inch stilettos that clicked across the floor, the polished claws that adorned the long talons of the females on the hunt, the bustiers, thongs and bras that peeked through the sheer white layers of blouse and skirt fabric, the balloons, the drinks, the dancing pole, bathroom doors and even the speakers were all red. And I'm sure my face donned a crimson hue too.

Mike surveyed the room with a much greater confidence than I could. He kept checking with me, asking "Are you alright?" I was thankful for that. He truly was trying to make this as enjoyable as possible for me, or the least traumatic it could be.

We stepped up to the bar. It was busy, not 'push your way through, three people deep busy' but busy enough that there may just be contact as you made your way to order. I stuck close to Mike. He was my life preserver here. As we stood at the bar, I watched some more. It was like most other bars, but the people, both men and women, were much prettier. The interactions were more physical, more touching, more hugging, more kissing.

My survey of the room was interrupted by a tall, shapely brunette in a tight red plaid mini and black halter-top approaching on the other side of Mike. He smiled approvingly. She smiled back and winked. I think I detected a slight purse of the lips too. She slid in beside Mike, close enough to have her breasts brush against his propped up hand holding the $20 to pay for our drinks. He smiled at this. I was fuming inside. This was the first time I had felt jealous with Mike. He was a great looking man and women acknowledged this all the time, but here he seemed to be enjoying it a little too much.

Just as I was about to climb atop my jealous peak, she was joined by her equally handsome date. He was chiselled and muscular, with a mouth full of brilliant white teeth that reminded me of piano keys. He put one arm around her small waist and the other extended to Mike as his eyes were directly aimed at me.

"I'm Lloyd and this is Shawna. Nice to meet you."

"Hi. This is Kayte and I'm Mike. Our pleasure."

She shook my hand and he kissed it very gallantly.

Did we just get picked up? Were they interested in us? Had they already decided on this before they even approached the bar? Did she spot us first? Or was it him? Who was more attracted to whom? Was Mike the lure or had it been me?

I had to consider all these questions I've never had to ask before. This was certainly different than anything I had experienced until now.

We chatted some more and it turned out that Lloyd was an

Investment Broker and Shawna was in Public Relations for one of the largest firms in the city. I had used them about 10 years ago for a CEO profiling assignment and we knew a few of the same people, at least on a cursory level. She volunteered to introduce me to a few people and maybe help find me my next job. They seemed pretty normal. They had been married for two years. Their wedding was a small affair in the Caribbean. Shawna confided that they used the money they would have spent on the big over-the-top wedding her friends expected from her and put a nice sized down payment on a lovely house in the city instead. They had two beagles named Hugo and Boss. They were both into running. Lloyd loved scuba diving, Shawna was a retired Pilates instructor and they were planning a trip to Tuscany in a few months.

Even against my urging, Mike admitted to them that it was my first time in a swinging club. At this, Shawna reached out and placed a gentle touch on my forearm, sliding her fingertips across it and along my hand and whispered, "Don't worry, we'll be gentle." Everyone roared with laughter – everyone but me.

They were 'regulars' but went on to say how happy they were to see new people adopting the lifestyle as they felt that's what kept it interesting.

Wait a minute! I'm not adopting anything. I'm curious. I was doing this for Mike. Just to learn more about it. I wasn't even close to adoption.

I kept these thoughts to myself.

The evening had been surreal. It felt different, but it really wasn't all that different than other evenings in clubs. But as the place filled up, people got closer and louder and it seemed like the alcohol clicked in all at once. For when I left to visit the ladies room, things were normal, when I came out, there were women with women dancing in the cages, the dance floor was full of men and women gyrating. Like the song said, "it was getting hot in here." On the dance floor, the display of teasing and taunting included the lifting of tops and skirts and tongues popping out to lick and explore their neighbours. There was a couple making out in the backseat of the classic ragtop that was parked behind the dance floor and there was a conga line led by one very well endowed man who looked to be Spanish. He carried the champagne as five ladies followed in line, each reaching forward with their hands on each the next woman's breasts. They followed him to what I assumed was a private room. I didn't want or need to see anymore of that.

I rejoined Mike, Lloyd and Shawna just as Lloyd was motioning to a friend to join us. Mike reached out and pulled me to him, giving me a soft, full-mouthed kiss. He whispered, "You're doing great Hon. Thank you for this." I could tell he was truly appreciative of my efforts and although it was a little strange, it hadn't been that bad.

Shawna asked, "Can I have one too?"

There it was.

I looked at Mike, "Well, can she?"

The words were barely off my lips before Shawna's glossy curious lips were on them. Her mouth met mine and delivered the slightest tease from the tip of her sweet tasting tongue.

Eyes wide, I turned around just as Lloyd was making more introductions. "Sheila, Simon, this is Kayte and Mike."

There I was, staring face to face, less than two feet away from my past. I was looking into the eyes of the most powerful and passionate man I had ever loved. He had made my heart sing louder and more melodically than it ever had before. Yet he was the same man who had silenced its voice, the same voice that had only recently returned to something that could be heard above a whisper.

The Naughty and Nice Klub disappeared. I was immediately

transported back to that evening four years before when I walked in to see Simon, my boyfriend, my love, my kindred heart, the man I thought I'd marry, naked and thrusting himself into Sheri, my supposed friend from work. My world had crashed. My dreams for a life with Simon disappeared. My gut wrenched. I was stupefied. I was astounded that these two people who had both claimed to care for me had been so reckless with my emotions. There they were in my bed, in my home, spreading themselves and their selfish indulgence all over my sheets.

In the following days, I had found the hardest thing to get over was that it had been an illusion that I had had Simon all to myself. To think that he was saying the things he said to me, touching me in the same way, sharing the same acts with me with another woman was devastating. And the other woman was not some stranger, but someone that had claimed to be my friend. She was a woman I saw everyday at work. We shopped together and tried new restaurants at lunchtime. We had attended parties together. We had even run a 5K side by side. But at that moment at 8:14pm on a Tuesday, I was served a double dose of betrayal. Standing here in this Klub years later, I could still feel its sting.

"Kayte, are you okay?" Mike asked. Everyone was staring at me. Of course they were. My mouth was hanging open, I was just staring at Simon, not moving, not breathing. Thankfully my hand had held my glass just inches above the bar where I let it go and it landed safely atop the glowing cherry of the underlit glass top bar.

I searched for whatever scraps of composure I could muster as I grabbed my bag and mumbled to Mike, "I have to leave." He was dumbfounded by my behaviour.

"Kayte, what's wrong? Please stay."

"I have to leave," I almost screamed. I turned and bolted in the direction of my gateway back to reality. Fumbling through my purse for the coat-check tags, I felt the wave of tears building with the rage of a tsunami. I needed air. I snatched my coat out of the attendant's hands. I didn't care if people were staring at me. I just needed to get as far away from Simon as fast as I possibly could. I needed to get outside, into a world where I fit. I needed to shake that image of Simon and Sheri. I needed a shower. But not in a stall big enough to be joined by seven other patrons of the Naughty and Nice Klub. I needed to un-see Simon. I needed to turn the clock back one hour and to have never been here in this Klub in the first place. I needed to get out of Naughty and Nice. I needed to be alone. I needed to be nice. Naughty was not me.

Mike ran after me. He caught up because he wasn't the one wearing the three-inch pumps. He was so confused. "Kayte what's going on?"

I offered some rationale, "I'm leaving Mike. I'm taking a cab. That's my old boyfriend, Simon – the one who cheated on me with one of my best friends. I need to be alone. Sorry, will explain more later."

I flagged a cab, got in, and spat out my address. Then the tsunami of emotions hit in one huge violent wave. Its force overtook me and then its sheer unrestrained power washed over every negative emotion that had been unleashed just moments before. The anger, hurt, disappointment, the fear, distrust, disgust, and the disdain were no match. Even collectively they could not withstand its strength and all were devastated by its path. While painful, it was also liberating and cleansing. When the wave subsided and a hint of normality returned, the surreal experience at the Naughty and Nice Klub, and the pain of seeing Simon and the memories he evoked, were those of my past.

I felt surprisingly strong as I tucked them into their rightful place. They no longer existed in my present and they had no place in my future.

"Oh Chloe, it was a terrible, horrible, no good, very awful night. I shouldn't have gone. And what's worse? Simon was there."

"Your Simon? I mean your old Simon?"

"Yes."

"Oh hon, I'm so sorry."

"I'm okay. It's weird. As horrible an experience as it was, I think it did teach me a few things."

"Like what?"

"I'm definitely not swinging material. I want one man and I want him all to myself. I am over Simon because I know he represents what I don't want. Unfortunately I think Mike is also in that boat. Even with all his wonderful qualities I think he's not the man I need him to be on one fundamental issue."

"I'm sorry sweetie, but it's good you find out now. And you should be proud of yourself for being so brave and trying. I could never have that kind of courage."

"Thanks Chloe."

"So Boomer's out of town this week. Care to join the kids and me for a dinner out and a movie? It won't be all candles and wine and romantic gestures, and I won't suck butter from your fingers, but its always entertaining and it will be bursting with love and support."

"Thanks, I'd like that."

Mike had been calling all morning. I had sent him a text to tell him I was all right so he wouldn't worry, but I still wasn't ready to talk with him about last night. I was unsure of what I was going to say. I knew he deserved an explanation, but I deserved to know what I was going to say before I said it. There were four messages from him on my voicemail. I wasn't sure I was prepared to say goodbye to him just yet, but I knew that I had to. I had so enjoyed our time together, but the swinging thing was huge. Maybe it was fate running into Simon last night. Maybe that was the fastest way

I'd be able to connect with the emotions and the challenge that would ultimately arise in me having a relationship with someone who chooses that lifestyle. While I wasn't about to send Simon a thank you bouquet, I was able to see the upside of the past evening's events. My decision was clear. All that was left to do was to share it with Mike.

I finally answered the phone the fifth time Mike rang.

I plunked down on the bed. "Hi Mike."

"Kayte, you okay? I've been really worried about you."

I adjusted the pillows, placing the thickest one behind me to keep me seated but comfortably cushioned. "Ya, I'm okay thanks. Sorry to have worried you, but I just needed time to process some things… some feelings… try to come up with some answers."

"I thought so. And have you?"

"I know that it must appear that I've waffled back and forth on this Mike, but I wanted to give this swinging thing a fair chance."

"And I appreciate that, hon."

"I know you do and that's one of the reasons I did it in the first place. I'm sure you know how taken with you I am. I can't believe how well we connect. You're gentle and sweet and supportive and patient and sexy and passionate and curious and interesting. And I love being with you… whether it's out for a hike, curled up in front of the TV or entwined together eagerly exploring each other."

"I feel the same way."

"With all that, I still can't see my way to embrace this swinging thing. Just seeing Simon at the club the other night caused my issues and expectations around relationships to come bubbling up to the surface. I couldn't deal with him cheating on me. His presence brought back the pain, the devastation that I had felt when he broke my trust. Because he didn't break only my trust, he broke me. It took a long time to recuperate from that. But I have, and I know now that I'm not good at sharing some things

- not my toothbrush, not my underwear and certainly not my partner."

"Kayte I understand. I hate it, but I understand."

"Mike, I know you hate it. But, if I were to accept your swinging lifestyle there would always be times when I felt that I wasn't enough, that I couldn't provide enough interest, enough variety and when it came right down to it, I, alone, wouldn't be able to keep your attention. That would not be healthy for me, for you or for a relationship. When we bumped into Simon the other night, what you didn't know was that he was an old boyfriend. A very serious one. Until I caught him cheating on me with a girlfriend. Seeing him brought all that back."

"Hon, I'm so sorry you had to experience that. I had no idea. I thought it might have been just an ex, but didn't know the details. As far as you and I go, I guess I had hoped that I had finally found someone who might embrace my choices. These are choices I'm comfortable with, choices I want to maintain, but I understood and respect your honesty if they are not choices that appeal to you. Most importantly, I am thankful that you were willing to try."

"I wanted to try for you, for me, for us. I guess that somewhere deep down, when it comes to relationships I just have to know that I've done everything I could, to give us every chance of success. That's why I tried. But I can't deny how this makes me feel. The feelings I've been having aren't the feelings that would make for a healthy relationship."

"Kayte, I just want you to know how much I care for you, how much I enjoyed our time together. How excited I was about a future with a wonderful woman like you... with you. I thought I had hit the jackpot!"

"Mike, I wouldn't trade our time together for anything. Okay, maybe for a non-swinging version of you. We had a great con-nection. So much so that I opened myself to exploring something new, something I never thought I'd try. I didn't judge you. I didn't rule things out immediately on impulse, but remained open and took a step into completely unfamiliar territory. And when I felt I couldn't go further, felt it wasn't a fit, I had the courage to stand true to my convictions and step away. I've grown through being with you. So, thank you for that."

"You are so very welcome. I wish I could have done more for you my dear Kayte."

"Mike, I wish nothing but wonderful things for you. You are a sweet soul and I know you'll find happiness."

"And you, my cute Kayte, I know you'll find love. You are so very worthy of it… so easy to be with. You are a rare woman with such a bright and sincere spark. Someone deserving will see that and the flames of true love will be ignited. And my wish for you, my dear, is that the flame is an eternal one."

My eyes had welled; my voice was wavering. I tried to hide my crying. "Thanks Mike, as you've been from the very beginning… you are so very sweet."

"Ah, yes, very sweet… but absolutely no calories!"

"And only slightly addictive!"

We both laughed a little.

"Goodbye Kayte"

"Goodbye Mike."

"Oh, and Kayte… "

"Yes…"

"Give the boy a pat for me."

"Already on it… doing that right now."

Dylan had been seated on my right, head resting on my leg. As I placed the receiver down, I picked the retriever up (his head anyway). He looked up at me with his big bright comforting eyes. With his hairy yellow head in both my hands, I scratched behind his ears and we exchanged a knowing gaze.

"It was a sad conversation but a necessary one because, Dylan, it was the only decision I could live with."

I removed the pillow that had kept me upright, tossed it past Dylan and onto the floor. First I lay on my back, turned sideways, then put my hands between my knees and curled into the comfort of the fetal position. The tears came. I was so tired of the false starts, weary from the search for Mr. Right, emotionally drained from the high expectations falling short and crashing to the ground time after time. I hoped that maybe, just maybe, the next man would be "the one".

CHAPTER 21

Even though I felt my romantic dreams been stomped on yet again, I awoke the next day comfortable with my decision regarding Mike. It was the only one that I could truly live with.

There were other men out there for me – around 337 if I recalled correctly. While I'd had two false starts with this online dating thing, I did feel that it was providing some value. First, it was reassuring that there were so many people who were also seeking love. Secondly, sifting through all the profiles, it helped me to define and crystallise what I was seeking in a mate. And lastly, it was getting me out of the house – it got me dating again. That in itself was worth it.

I'd give it some more time, I'd continue to put myself out there and scary as it might sound, I'd listen to Roman's advice on how to make it best work for me.

Before I had even had a chance to sign in to wheresinglesfind-love.com, I was greeted by an IM from Thomas.

Tomtom says:
Good mornin' - about time you showed up.

K8 says:
It's only 8:48 - geesh. Pretty early for the unemployed. And what are you doing on here when you are supposed to be working?

Tomtom says:
I have a good job and I'm a great juggler.

K8 says:
Don't get caught. Or I might not be the only one who's unemployed here!

Tomtom says:
I won't.

K8 says:
Good. Cause a date where we have to dine and dash isn't what I'd call a great start.

Tomtom says:
Speaking of that, U know Kayte, if our e-connection translates to a physical one, then we might just have ourselves something here

K8 says:
Agreed, and there's only one way to find out. Face to face, person to person, so where and when?

Tomtom says:
How's 7:00pm at Murmur?

K8 says:
Today?

Tomtom says:
Why wait? Plus I have no food in the house

K8 says:
Ha. Okay, sounds good.

Tomtom says:
I'll meet U in the lobby.

K8 says:
I'll be there with bells on.

I pondered borrowing a trick from Mike and actually adding bells to my outfit. With great expectations poised again, I entertained my romantic notions. There was something different about this Tommy Kessler character. He just seemed 'normal'. I had learned that we had similar upbringings, shared many values and had a similar education. There was an affinity there. But would there be sparks? I entertained the potential for skyrockets, butterflies and that tingly-in-the-pants feeling. But I was also learning that with this online dating thing, I might just have to adjust my expectations because you never know what you'll get when the galaxies of reality and cyber meet for the very first time.

It was those last few minutes of the drive, the five to ten minutes before the actual meeting time that were the most nerve-wracking.

Was I wearing the right outfit? Did my makeup look all right? Would I be witty, funny and interesting? Would he look like his pictures? Would he like what he saw? Would he have some annoying mannerism or be rude to the wait staff? Would we find a way to connect in person with the same level of flirtation and openness that came across so freely when we spoke online? Or would it be uncomfortable or awkward?

My heart was beating a little faster. I found a parking space, pulled in and parked. I got out my makeup bag and applied a fresh coat of gloss, a light pat of powder, did the teeth, nose, eye check in the rear view mirror and then I was ready to make the in person acquaintance of one Mr. Thomas Kessler. I was still five minutes early. I hoped he wasn't tardy. I had never been very good at waiting.

The restaurant had both a dining area and a bar/lounge area. I wasn't expecting dinner, but it was 7:00pm so I wasn't sure what Thomas was thinking. Come to think of it, he probably was expecting to have dinner given his earlier "no food in the house" comment – men! I stood in the lobby surveying the dark interior. The walls were deep gold, the chairs and booths a blend of either chocolate brown leather or rich gold, brown and red striped thick upholstery fabric. It felt warm and inviting and the hum of the crowd didn't play too loudly. We wouldn't have to scream questions like, "Do you have any sexual fetishes?" across the table. I was sure the other patrons would be thankful for that. It was a good pick for a first meeting.

That was exactly how Roman described the first meeting. It was as a meeting, not a date. That was why he swore by Roman's Rules of Online Dating, Rule #8. "The female should always offer to pay her share of the tab for the first meeting." He went on to explain that meeting this way, through online dating, you're still not sure if there's a connection so the man shouldn't have to bear the cost of finding that out on all the dates. If you find there is a connection and you make an actual date, then whatever standard dating etiquette you're comfortable with applies, but here you're both still determining whether or not you want to date, so the cost should be shared. I could see his point and always gladly offered to split the check.

I peeked out the window for the fourth time and then I saw him just as he stepped out of his metallic beige SUV. I thought he might be the type of man who drove an SUV. I found that I was more attracted to men who were SUV drivers than those who drove sporty or very practical cars. Minivans would probably be the worst – nothing screams family man more than a minivan. SUV drivers were down-to-earth types, sporty, adventurous and just a little more rugged. A man's vehicle choice said something about him. In Tommy's case, I think mainly it said he was tall. As he unfolded himself from the driver's seat, he rose up and stood to an impressive height. I think his profile said around 6'2". He was a few inches taller than me. Wow, I could wear any heel I wanted and still have to reach up to kiss him.

He was pleasant looking, handsome when he smiled, but serious, almost brooding, or maybe scared, when he didn't. His outfit screamed casual and was big on him. He wore hemp-coloured suede lace-up shoes and slightly rumpled beige khakis. His black leather belt was pulled back two holes from its most worn opening. He wore a black golf shirt that donned his company's brand name and a black baseball cap. You could tell Tommy was comfortable with comfortable. As he got closer, I noted that he smelled clean but a little peppery. His limbs were long and proportionate to his height. I wondered how those long arms might feel wrapped around me.

What struck me was that he was much thinner than I had imagined. I had seen only three pictures, but they all suggested a thicker, more substantial, more muscular man than the one who now stood beside me.

His smile was broad and full of large very white teeth. His lips were full, soft, pink and just slightly chapped. His skin was a reddish tan with obvious lines spreading down and outward from around his slightly droopy eyes. There was just the hint of salt and pepper stubble forming fully over his face. Every face has its showcase feature and for Tommy, it was the eyes that struck me most. They were icy blue. They were smaller than his large face demanded. While cool and somewhat critical, they were also gentle, sincere and seductive at the same time. They darted around a little though, suggesting that Thomas was out of his comfort zone. Hopefully once we were seated the repartee we experienced in our online discussions would replace his obvious nervousness and we could settle into an enjoyable exchange.

"Kayte?" Tommy asked.

I felt kind of awkward. In this situation do you just smile? Shake hands? Hug? I just smiled and said "Great to meet you!"

"You too, shall we grab a seat?"

"Sure."

I tried to be nonchalant as he was obviously checking me out. I could feel his gaze move up and down me. Of course that was when the insecurities made their cameo. This was maybe the hardest part about online dating. Those first few minutes of actually seeing someone in the flesh after chatting online had a tremendous amount of pressure attached to them. I saw why Roman's Rule #2 was so important. You wouldn't want to have dozens of chats, think you have this unbelievable connection, only to have absolutely none when meeting in person.

We were led to a booth and as we were sliding ourselves into the large booths, Tommy, being the mannerly gentleman that he was, self-consciously removed his baseball cap at the table.

Oh my, he did have quite a pronounced receding hairline didn't he? Stop staring, say something, anything. Look somewhere else.

Hopefully I didn't have a shocked expression leaping from my face, because I didn't want to be rude or judgmental. I was just shocked. I guess I had just assumed he had a full head of hair. This certainly explained the ball cap in all the pictures. He was still a handsome man, but I wasn't expecting him to have a 'five-head', the expression my friend Michelle used to describe men whose foreheads had started the inevitable ageing creep backwards.

Thankfully, a cheery little waitress named Brianne showed up right then to take our drink order and explain the specials. We both ordered Coronas with lime; something in common. That was a good start.

We chatted about Mexico, how much we loved the Spanish language and Latin music, especially flamenco guitar. We talked about his new apartment and all the plans he had for making it his own. With great technical precision, he drew me a diagram showing exactly where this new apartment was located. I filed the address for future reference – just in case. He was so proud and excited about this apartment and I had to remind myself that this living-on-his-own stuff was so new for him.

It also helped me realise how lucky I had been to be as independent as I had. Although I was as ready as one could be to surrender my independence and share my life and my space with someone, I could do so trusting in the knowledge that if I had to live on my own, I could and I could do it well.

Tommy was articulate and, once he relaxed, the sense of humour I had experienced during our online exchanges seemed to make an, albeit too brief, appearance. It got me to questioning whether or not people actually present themselves honestly through their online chats. Or did this distanced way of communicating provide certain liberties or higher levels of confidence that we wouldn't or couldn't necessarily demonstrate in person?

Did we become braver, did we border on brazen even, when shielded by the technological curtain of a computer screen that hangs before us? Communicating this way we lacked the visual cues that provide the nuances associated with our words. All we were left with were the words themselves, or what was left of actual words once every acronym imaginable has been exploited and phonetics over spelling has been used at every opportunity.

I wondered if this form of communication, by its very nature, was flawed. And then my brain concocted the scariest hypothesis of all. If the communication channel was suspect and couldn't facilitate effective communication, didn't it also stand to reason that it was highly improbable that it could actually help in creating any kind of meaningful relationship?

"Kayte, hellloooo, Kayte. Come in Kayte - are you there?"

"Oh, sorry, got lost in thought. Hey, I have a question for you."

"Shoot."

"Do I appear to be the same in person as I did during our chats online?"

"Hmm… you don't ask the easy ones do you?"

"Nope."

"I think so. You're as funny. You still ask good questions. You seem as confident and assured, but something doesn't feel the same."

"Do you feel like there's the same connection?" I already knew the answer.

"I'm thinking there's not the same chemistry in person. Sorry. I don't mean to offend you, I like you, but when it comes to physical chemistry it's either there or it isn't. Not that I've had much practice at it though."

"Oh, no offence taken. I was actually thinking the same thing. And with this online dating stuff, you don't know until you meet face to face whether the chemistry is there or not." It plainly wasn't.

So Thomas and I had a pleasant conversation, but it quickly moved away from date talk. I was happy for the eating diversion. But when we finished our dinners, it was obvious that there was no match made in heaven here so we were cordial, respectful and we kept it short.

We didn't make any promises to call or get together or make any commitments that neither of us intended on keeping. We did agree though that it was nice to meet and we were happy we had done so. We gave it a shot. No love connection. We wished each other well and then said goodbye. I paid my half of the bill.

On the drive home, I addressed my disappointment. I had thought Attaboy77 and I might have a great connection. Maybe it was timing. Maybe being so soon after Mike, I wasn't truly into it. Maybe I had higher expectations for the physical presence of this man. Maybe he wanted someone, younger, thinner, prettier.

Whatever the reason. He was not my Mr. Right, so the only thing I could think to say to myself in consolation was "Next!"

CHAPTER 22

"I'm actually paying you to make me feel this much pain?"

"Yes, and you're going to thank me for it. In fact, you might even want to give me a big fat tip once you've seen where we can go together."

"I doubt it, but never say never." I huffed out as my legs shook as I did my last leg press.

"Now it's time for leg extensions. We'll adjust the weight up by 2 kilos and you're still doing 20. Let's go... 20, 19, 18..."

It was session number five with Kevin, my personal trainer. This was the biggest indulgence I had afforded myself from the severance package I had received. I had always wanted to work with a trainer, develop a balanced and aggressive weight and cardio program and this had been the perfect time to realise that dream. I hadn't had much time for working out while I was working, so now that I had the time I was taking advantage of it and none too soon. The results from my fitness test were not pretty.

Kevin was great. He was about 25, tall handsome and fit.

He was about 5'11' and muscular, probably weighed about 80–90 kilos. He had a great body – broad shoulders, firm pecs, washboard abs, long muscular arms, large defined hands, a thin waist, a high tight butt and strong shapely legs all covered in smooth chocolate skin. He wasn't muscle-bound like some of the guys I saw here at the gym, but his body was more that of a track athlete than a football player or weightlifter. He was gentle in nature, funny when he wanted to be, pushed when he should, encouraging whenever I needed it, and he congratulated me for every milestone I achieved along the way.

It's an interesting connection that you have with your trainer. There was a love hate relationship. But, like any relationship, it worked best when it was based on a core of respect and when you could really connect. I remember the moment when Kevin and I first cemented our bond. It was the end of the first training session and I was spent. He hadn't held back just because it was our first time together. I hauled my sorry butt off the floor, every muscle throbbing almost as they were applauding the fact that we had stopped. Grabbing my soaking wet towel and empty water bottle, I remembered saying, "Thank you, I think. I'll see you in three days."

He responded without missing a beat. "It might be three days until we actually see each other Miss Kayte, but I can guarantee you that I'll be the very first man you think about tomorrow morning!" He winked and I broke into laughter.

Boy was he right. Every muscle screamed as I tried to manoeuver my crumpled aching body out of bed. It felt like it was drowning in a sea of lactic acid. The muscles burnt with sheer agony. I thought about him. First I cursed him aloud making Dylan jump. Then I cursed my own out-of-shape throbbing body and the fact that I had let myself get to that point.

The more I thought about it, the more I was happy to have been fired. Things had swung too far out of balance. And now I had taken the first step in getting back into shape and was doing something about it. Kevin had assured me the pain would be temporary. I prayed he was right.

The next few weeks fell into a routine. I'd sleep until I woke up without an alarm, get up, have a leisurely breakfast while I checked into wheresinglesfindlove.com read a few messages and send a couple, but there were no men that caught my attention. So I turned to taking Dylan to various parks for walks, and after coming home I'd grab my gym bag and head there for a workout. I had started enjoying the almost daily visits to the gym and the focus solely on myself.

Marnie would accompany one day on the weekends and we'd alternate going out for lunch with dog park walks with Dylan. We discussed some potential work options and some networking groups I might want to join. She was very connected and as soon as I'd let her, she'd have me that way too.

I had dusted off my resume and updated it, but hadn't begun looking for work. It was heading into summer and I had convinced myself that I'd maybe do some freelance work over the slow period, but I'd start after that with the real job search. By then I'd be rested and ready to take on the next challenge come autumn.

While I spent a great deal of time re-connecting with some old friends and acquaintances, playing volleyball, puttering around the house, I also began working at achieving a lifelong goal. I had always wanted to run a 10K. I had run three, four, even five km runs while out with Dylan or Chloe but could never seem to get past that. A 10K had always been in my sights. I didn't care about my finishing time. I just wanted to finish. So I joined a local running clinic and learned about running. With a built-in network of fellow runners, I was running two or three times each week. We made progress together and the social aspect was what kept me with it. It took the focus off not dating (which I hadn't done since meeting Tommy) and gave me a worthy goal.

I won't lie; it was hard. I had never been very athletic and starting a sport like running just a few months before my 40th birthday, when I was still overweight, was challenging. The knees were already feeling the years working hard retail floors though my teenage years, and years of volleyball. At first the running was tough on them, on my feet, and on my hips, but it was something I had always wanted to try. This was the time to do it. I couldn't wait any longer. Funny, I was finding that this was the time to do a lot of things.

After about six weeks of regular visits to the gym, every visit had me logging 20 minutes on the bike, twenty on the cross-trainer, doing either a full upper or lower body and ab workout and I was doing a slow 2K run on the track as my cool down. I was relaxed and felt physically stronger than I had in years. I wondered how I could have ever maintained the work pace that I had, the stress, the lack of exercise, the politics and the bullshit.

CHAPTER 23

I was online one evening paying my bills and I heard the chime as the IM window called out. I looked down to the right of the screen to see that it was Thomas. I hadn't seen him on there for almost two months. *It would be rude not to say hi, right?*

K8 says:
Hey stranger – how's tricks?

Tomtom says:
Hey yourself

Tomtom says:
BRB – cookin' some ZA

K8 says:
ZA? What's ZA?

It was a few minutes before Tommy returned and I got a reply.

Tomtom says:
Piz-ZA! Sorry, my kids use these terms I just assume everyone knows them – how you been?

K8 says:
Excellent thx – you settled into that new apt now?

Tomtom says:
Yep it's taken a bit of time, but I'm really enjoying my freedom.

K8 says:
Having some 'you time' are you?

Tomtom says:
Yes – and loving it!

You look good in your new profile picture btw. Must be getting some man attention with that. Any new men 4 ya?

K8 says:
Yep, a couple.

Tomtom says:
A couple? You hussy! LOL

K8 says:
Takes one to know one.

Tomtom says:
Touché!

K8 says:
So how goes thangs in the romance dep't for you? Keeping busy?

Tomtom says:
Taking a break actually, took my profile off the site. But I still take a look in there once in a while.

K8 says:
Oh how come?

Tomtom says:
I moved, got really busy, had a few dates, but felt I just wanted to hang by myself

K8 says:
Might be the best thing for you

Tomtom says:
I know a few women if I want company, but I'm not sure I'm ready for dating from everything I've seen so far.

K8 says:
Good for you - that's a mature decision. You seem like a really decent guy, I'd hate to see you tarnished by today's dating scene

Tomtom says:
No shit! It's really WEIRD out there.

K8 says:
Yep, I'm not lovin' it – necessary evil though, but I'm not dating much these days either

Tomtom says:
Breaks are good

K8 says:
Agreed, gives us time for other things

Tomtom says:
Yes, like PIZZA… MMM!!!

K8 says:
So how is it?

Tomtom says:
MMMMMMM - It's hot and gooey and messy – goes good with this nice Chilean white wine

K8 says:
I'm enjoying some white wine too, I prefer Australian though, and ricotta cheese bites and spring rolls… double mmm…

Tomtom says:
Funny, I was going to do spring rolls

K8 says:
Great minds

Tomtom says:
Great m … hey you type faster than me… no fair!

K8 says:
LOL it's all this grease on my fingers they're just sliding around the keyboard!

Tomtom says:
So what are you up to this weekend?

K8 says:
Hosting my best friend, Chloe, her hubby and 2 kids away for the weekend

Tomtom says:
Sounds like fun

K8 says:
Yep it'll be a blast – this couple is a hoot – I just wish I was part of a couple so we could do more things together

Tomtom says:
Like swinging?

K8 says:
WHAT? OMG what is it with you men & swinging?

Tomtom says:
Kidding. Not my style, but interesting reaction… do I detect a bad experience?

K8 says:
I'll plead the fifth on that. Moving on.

Tomtom says:
OK forget the swinging, but hey, kids in bed, some wine, maybe a threesome?

K8 says:
I've said it before and I'll say it again, there are 3 things I won't share: 1- my toothbrush, 2 - my underwear and 3 - my men!

Tomtom says:
Damn, I was going to ask to borrow your light blue thong – it goes so well with my eyes.

K8 says:

How do you know I have a light (I prefer to call it ice) blue thong?

And if you really want to set off your eyes, you must also borrow the matching bra - LMAO!

Tomtom says:
Yes, back to you and your friends, I agree a lot of things are certainly better as a couple... so met any new men?

K8 says:
One in particular I spend time with every few days

Tomtom says:
Oh really you never told me about him the last time we spoke.

K8 says:
Guess maybe I just didn't want to close any doors even though I knew you weren't really interested

Tomtom says:
Ya... well... that's flattering... sorry

K8 says:
No worries. It's either there or it isn't

Tomtom says:
Ah I wasn't really ready to date anyway, but I really do enjoy our chats and that new pic of you is AWESOME!

K8 says:
I really enjoy our chats too – you have a refreshing sense of humour and seem like a really decent guy

Tomtom says:
Ah shucks Kayte (feet kicking floor)

K8 says:
Thx. I'm working really hard on awesome – I've been seeing a trainer and started running again, so I'm half way to my goal in just over 2 months

Tomtom says:
WOW good for you, I'm actually trying to add muscle, almost harder than trying to lose weight

K8 says:
Maybe for you – not me though. I've lost 8 kilos of fat and gained 3 of muscle though

Tomtom says:
Holy moley… hmmm… you're going to make me reconsider here.

K8 says:
I'm running 4-5K now every day with the dog, mainly so I can continue to enjoy some wine from time to time

Tomtom says:
You GOTTA have the wine

K8 says:
Agreed

Tomtom says:
Can I ask your opinion on my new pic? You're honest

K8 says:
Sure

I accepted the file Thomas sent and opened it to find a stunning picture of him splayed out on his couch in black jeans, no top and a full hairy chest that had gained some noticable muscle definition since I last saw him. His face was fuller and appeared calmer and friendly and out jumped the most incredible ice blue eyes I had ever seen. Maybe it was just the photo or the reflection of the blue from the couch, but they seemed so much more intense than I remembered them from when we met.

K8 says:
Thanks it's very nice and your eyes look STUNNING!

Tomtom says:
Aw shucks again, Kaytey! You's makin' me blush.

K8 says:
But if you're using this on the site, just a wee red flag, even though this is just one woman's opinion. I find that if guys are using pics where they're not wearing their shirts, I think they may be trying to be too sexy, or too showy. I figure usually when

you first meet someone in person, it's with clothes on. Should be the same in the photos you use on the dating sites, no?

Tomtom says:
Hehehe – yes, good point thanks. Well if I go back to it I'll just have to take some new pics.

K8 says:
I have a friend, Roman, who's been doing this online dating thing for a while and considers himself a bit of an expert. One of the rules he quotes, Rule #9, I believe, is to limit the use of nudity, unless that's really the impression you want to send loud and clear. He goes on to say that we should really look at the photos people use. They tell you a lot about the person. He has a point I think.

Tomtom says:
Oh really... how interesting...

K8 says:
Well I have a brand new camera and a photographer's eye, so perhaps I could help.

Tomtom says:
Okay I have no money, damn divorce, so how could I pay you?

K8 says:
I work for white wine and pizza – LOL - an appreciation for my art form is payment enough

Tomtom says:
...of your art form or simply your form? Woo hoo!

K8 says:
Woo hoo?

Tomtom says:
Okay, 2 big glasses of wine and little food, forgive me!

K8 says:
So dinner's on you?

Tomtom says:
Literally! woo hoo again!

K8 says:
BRB

Tomtom says:
What R U going to do?

K8 says:
NOT YOU, apparently – LOL – actually refill my wine – I'm a glass
behind!

Tomtom says:
Hey if you were here now, not so sure, me sooo horny!

K8 says:
Oh really?

Tomtom says:
Yep, I'm a little tipsy… any "nekkid" shots of you yet?

K8 says:
Hold on, I'll send you something.

I searched through my files for a photo that Roman had taken
of me last summer. I had been enjoying a cool popsicle in the
searing heat, all very innocently. He saw the opportunity as only
he, and half the male population, would and snapped a picture.
The photo in itself was fine, a full face shot, nothing memorable.
Then Roman, through the wonders of digital photography, had
his way with it. He cropped it down to just my lips wrapped
around a very phallic looking cherry/lemon swirl popsicle that
was suitably just the right shade of pink for the effect he was
going for. The end result was a very erotic photo. While it wasn't
a picture of me 'nekkid', I sent this to Tommy anyway knowing
it would certainly go a ways in keeping this newfound flirtation
going. At that point I felt it was harmless, but had no idea where
it might lead.

Tomtom says:
OH MAN! Lucky popsicle.

I sent back a blushing smiley emoticon.

Tomtom says:
Colour me red and freeze my weeney!

K8 says:
Thought you might have some fun with that one.

Tomtom says:
Here I'm sending you one now

I accepted and opened the file to see yet another very recent photo of him, this time minus the jeans and only in a very brief pair of black underwear. Yes, he certainly had been going to the gym. I didn't know whether it was the wine, the conversation, his evolving physique or the combination, but I was feeling a growing attraction to this Tommy person and that surprised me given my previous in-person response.

K8 says:
Now what do we have here?

Tomtom says:
Me!!! I know, bad undies, I wear them mostly with my jeans.

K8 says:
WOW – you look great!

Tomtom says:
Awwww… you're just saying that… have a lot of work to do yet.

K8 says:
Nah you don't – in fact, I think I just got that tingly in my pants feeling

Tomtom says:
Well thanks Kayte, you're the first one to see it, not sure why I took it, mainly just to see how things were coming along

K8 says:
Most people would just look in the mirror but since you asked I'd say things were coming along nicely, nicely indeed!

Tomtom says:
Stop it… I'm all aflutter!!!

K8 says:
You deserve it.

Tomtom says:
I'm looking at your popsicle pic... wow... those lips... what you could do with those lips eh?

I purposely turned it up a notch here

K8 says:
You mean, what I *do* do with those lips - and a tongue to match!

Tomtom says:
Ahhh... getting that tingly in my pants feeling myself.

K8 says:
Hey that's my line – you're going to have to start paying royalties

Tomtom says:
Yep, it's a good one, I'll gladly plageurise

Tomtom says:
plagerise

Tomtom says:
plagurise

K8 says:
steal

Tomtom says:
copy

Tomtom says:
We think alike

K8 says:
Scary huh

Tomtom says:
it isn't scary... I think it's cool we click this way

K8 says:
Me too

Tomtom says:
Wow, 2 glasses of wine, an online conversation with you and I'm giddy and horny like a wee school boy

K8 says:
Giddy I can see, but where the heck did you go to school? Horny high?

Tomtom says:
LOL – from what I remember, yes!

Tomtom says:
Hey you have a digital camera right – take a pic of your boobs... me likey your boobies

K8 says:
What do you think this is SOD?

Tomtom says:
SOD?

K8 says:
Skin on demand!

Tomtom says:
I'm soooo kidding, but thought I'd call you out... one mustn't drink and chat by the looks of things

K8 says:
Could get you in trouble

Tomtom says:
What else am I gonna do? I don't have cable!

BRB – the landlord is here – buzz kill!

K8 says:
K

Tomtom says:
Landlord is coming to see my bathroom sink... getting a new one woo hoo!

K8 says:

And a whirlpool tub for two?

Tomtom says:
That would be awesome! You'd be invited

K8 says:
Would I?

Tomtom says:
Yeah… but I'm not telling you how to get here

Tomtom says:
You don't remember where I'm at

K8 says:
Oh yes I do, you drew a great map when we met and I have a photographic memory.

Tomtom says:
Yikes, you know where I live?

K8 says:
No worries, I don't go anywhere I'm not invited

Tomtom says:
I was by your place or close to it the other day.

K8 says:
Why didn't you stop in and say hello?

Tomtom says:
Time schedule with the kids, but maybe some other time.

K8 says:
Seriously, we might not be interested in each other sexually, but if you'd like to hang out as friends, I'd be up for that – it's rare to meet quality people and you seem like you's good people

Tomtom says:
Wow… seriously huh? Well thanks… and maybe you can get me drunk and take advantage of my schoolboy horniness!

K8 says:
Thx – but that's not nearly enough anymore – I NEED so much

more!!!

Tomtom says

I understand completely... and sorry if I offended... I was playing... I really was!!!

K8 says:
No offence --- seriously!

Tomtom says:
cool – you's the shiznet baby... what the hell is that anyway?

K8 says:
You got me.

Tomtom says:
Now what am I going to do with you?

K8 says:
Hmmm - you never know!

Tomtom says:
OK... the landlord's back

K8 says:
Tell him to keep his hands off your plumbing!

Tomtom says:
eeeeewwwwwwww!

K8 says:
Nite Thomas

Tomtom says:
Good night Kathleen, I had fun... chat soon!

K8 says:
Kayte out!

Well that was interesting. I do believe that Thomas Kessler was flirting with me. And what was even more surprising was that it was not nearly as unpalatable an idea as it had been a few months earlier. Hmmm. What had changed?

CHAPTER 24

"So let's talk about this party of yours", Chloe began, neglecting to even say hello when I answered on the second ring.

"...oh, I'm fine thanks and you?" I added with a sarcastic yet playful tone. "Geesh, can't a girl get a little verbal foreplay? Or now that we've been together for so long, is it just jump right into the main event?"

We were both giggling now.

"I just thought I'd use this time while Boomer was away to take the next step and get this party planning going, even if you don't want to have it for a few months."

I had decided it was high time to bring my friends together. I regretted not spending more time with them while I was caught up on the career carousel. Being blessed with an eclectic group of people who added greatly to my life, I wanted to celebrate them. So I was throwing a party to celebrate their friendship.

"Great idea, why don't we do this in person? I can make you dinner for a change. Maybe you can even help me search for Mr.

Right. Could always use a second opinion."

"Sounds like fun. I'll be over around four with ideas galore, an appetite and my handy dandy Mr. Right locating device."

"Speaking of that, do you remember that night about fifteen years ago when we went to Sparky's? It was packed with men for some big hockey game. We show up, looking hot and carrying the stud sensor you stole from your brother's toolbox. We were the talk of the bar that night. What a conversation starter that was. I don't think we bought a drink all night!"

"Of course I remember silly, that's when I first met Boomer. And it was 16 years and three months ago. Shall I bring the stud sensor?"

"Yes, one that works online please. I almost forgot that was the night you met Boomer." Wow, they sure had been together a long time. And I had been looking for my "Boomer" for even longer. I sure hoped it wasn't going to take much longer.

"These are the latest in Kayte's Possible Mr. Right Hit List."

Chloe had arrived about an hour before and we had taken our man perch in front of the computer. She was excited to peruse my latest list. First, I wanted to send a note to Thomas, just a short one, to touch base and keep me top of mind.

To: tomtom@socialarity.com
From: k8@socialarity.com
Subject: U R 2 FUNNY

Man, get a couple of drinks in you and you are HILARIOUS –
thanks for the entertaining chat the other night

PS - You were great!

That done, I showed Chloe Thomas' profile that I had copied from the first time I had read it.

"He's tall dark and handsome from what I can see. And it sounds like he's nice and normal and has a sense of humour. If he's going to be with you, he'll need one." Chloe had picked up my nail file and was shaping her long nails as she read. "I approve. When do we meet him? When's the wedding? I better be your matron of honour. And get to help you plan the whole day."

"Of course. I wouldn't trust those jobs to anyone else. But let's not walk me down the aisle quite yet. There are more to choose from."

I then opened up my preferred bachelor list. I showed Chloe five different profiles - Troy, Ben, Scott, Greg and Joey's. She was captivated by the differences in these men and the mischievous smile on her face was telling of her enjoyment. We waded through the profiles learning a little more about these men.

Then she stopped. Her face got serious, which in itself was a rarity for Chloe. "Go back to that last photo," she demanded.

It was the profile of none other than "Chief Love Officer". Albeit a cheesy name, the profile was well written, articulate, detailed and introspective. I noticed him because his words had a certain depth that most on here did not display. Also he was the right demographic and he was attractive, not necessarily handsome, but well groomed, had a full head of hair and donned a sharp suit and a beguiling smile.

"You haven't talked to this guy yet, have you?" Chloe's tone was almost accusatory.

"Yes, online, briefly, a couple of nights ago. Why?"

"What's his name?" She was obviously agitated.

"Scott. I'll ask again, WHY?"

"I'll tell you why. This is Patricia's husband. You've heard me talk about Jocelyn and Joanna, the eight-year-old twins I have in my school program? Well this is their Dad. He's married. And I thought happily so until I saw this."

"No way! Really? Are you sure?"

"Are there any more photos?"

"Yes, he gave me access to his other ones. Hang on."

I clicked the button on his profile that granted me preferred access to his full gallery of photos. This had to be given to you by the profile owner.

"Yep, that's him. I'm sure of it. Did he list running as one of his interests?"

"Uh huh, marathons specifically. I guess he has had a great deal of experience with running. Apparently, around on his wife. I'll never understand what makes men, or women, for that matter, do this. How do they rationalise cheating as part of a loving committed relationship? And if they're not happy in their relationship, then why can't they be honest and find the balls to end it? Or are they just gluttons? Do they just want it all?"

"I don't know, but I'll tell you this is shocking. I don't know what to do with this information now."

"Yes, I guess this puts you in a bit of a moral quandary huh? I, on the other hand, know exactly what I'll do. He's outta here. On to the 'Dick List'!"

"Where do these guys get off?"

"With as many women as possible I'm betting!"

The instant message window interrupted our conversation. I expected it to be Roman, but it wasn't.

MrktgMarnie says:
"Well hello stranger!"

K8 says:
"Hello yourself. It's so good to hear from you. It's been too long!"

Chloe asked, "Who is it?

"It's Marnie."

"Say hi for me."

K8 says:
Chloe's here and she says hello.

MrktgMarnie says:
Ditto. I won't keep you, but thought it's been way to long since I've seen you and the hairy one. You heading out for one of your long walks tomorrow? And would you like some company? I've been chained to my desk far too much this week and I need some exercise.

K8 says:
We are and we'd love for you to join us.

MrktgMarnie says:
Ok. Great. Plus there's something else I'd like to speak with you about. I'll see you around 1pm?

K8 says:
1 it is. It's not another blind date is it?

MrktgMarnie says:
No. Definitely not. I've learned my lesson!

CHAPTER 25

After a lazy start to the day, I dressed, grabbed a big cup of coffee and checked in online with the man bank. There were a couple of new messages. The first was from a man that was closer to my father's age than to mine so it was deleted before I could say "sugar daddy". The second was from a man who had five cats and he had wanted to make it an even six.

Sorry, 'I Fancy Felines', 'Katontheprowl' was staying on the prowl rather than replying to you. She's more of a dog person.

I looked down at Dylan. He was sprawled out like a golden throw rug between me and the stairs. "It's like this Dylan, we're dog people and once a dog person, always a dog person". I deleted the message.

In my inbox I found a response to the email I had flirtatiously sent to Tommy after our conversation the other night.

To k8@socialarity.com
From: tomtom@socialarity.com
Subject: Re:U R 2 FUNNY

Wow... really? I was afraid I offended you. Asking to see your boobies... what the hell? I'm glad you have a great sense of humour. You too are a very funny lady... well not that I'm a lady and funny and... aw forget it, you get what I mean.

Hope all is well with you... checked out that popsicle pic a couple of times!!!! Woo, hoo hoo... why don't you just call me popsicle Pete?

"Dylan, Tommy was flirting back." This was a good sign. I was smiling and went over and gave Dylan a two-handed scratch behind his furry ears. "There was something about our connection that made me smile. He makes me feel almost as good as you do!"

Dylan rolled from his side to his belly and looked up at me with his huge chocolate eyes moving his eyebrows from side to side as if actually considering what I had just said.

The ding-dong of the doorbell, followed by a cheery "Hello, hello, hello" got our attention.

"C'mon boy. You ready? Let's go. You wanna go to the park? You wanna go to the park?"

This had Dylan running down the stairs where he danced around in circles while I tried to give Marnie a hello hug.

"Someone's a happy boy!" Marnie was making a fuss that only fuelled his enthusiasm.

His little doggy life was so simple; his pleasures so basic. He loved his walks, he loved the park, he would never pass up a cookie or a belly rub and he was always happy to greet a visitor.

I shook my head, "Dogs were so easy to please. I wish I was."

It was a beautiful afternoon and I thought we'd explore a new leash-free park I had heard about. I grabbed a couple of Dylan's favourite toys and we jumped into the car and made our way to a place where dogs were free to run and jump and play without leashes in the company of other four legged amigos, some small, some large, but all enjoying the rare freedom that came from being off-leash. I remember thinking that it must feel to them like skinny dipping does to us - ultimately liberating.

The park seemed quite a popular place. From what I could count, there were about 30 dogs frolicking about. Some owners were actively playing with their pooches, some just sat at the picnic tables and watched their pets run as far away from them as they could. Others were chatting with one another and the dogs would make an appearance now and then, only to bound off again to continue enjoying their freedom.

I spied mostly big dogs. There were three other golden retrievers. Dylan joined in and all four of them were running pack style at one point. That's the funny thing about their breed; they naturally seem to connect with each other. There were Dalmatians, and Shepherds and some large crosses. There was a Weimaraner, a full sized poodle and what I think was a Bernese Mountain dog who had a pretty handsome master.

"So how's this online dating thing working for you?"

"Actually not too bad. Like anything, there's some good and bad. I've met a few interesting men – as in, I'd like to get to know them better and then there have been the 'interesting' ones who were right into threesomes or star trek, or who have 6 cats or want to go on dates where they bring their mother's along, and…"

"What?"

"Just kidding on that last bit!"

"So have you been on many dates? Anything serious?"

"A few. I was seeing this one guy, Mike, who was so adorable and romantic and boyishly sexy. We had an instant connection and I thought it was leading somewhere until he turned out to be a die-hard swinger!"

"Oh no."

"But I'm talking to this one guy who has some promise. And continuing to look at others. There are enough on the site to give me hope. I'll tell you one thing – I'm meeting men I wouldn't meet any other way. So I guess that makes it worth it."

"You might as well. There's no real barrier to entry."

"True."

"I love that I can use marketing jargon with you and you get it!"

"To tell you the truth - I kinda miss using it."

"Well that's one of things I wanted to speak with you about."

"One? There's more"

"Two actually. I'm thinking of starting a consulting business – running it from my home at first and I was wondering if you wanted to maybe do this together. And secondly, and this depends on my decision whether or not I go ahead with the consulting thing. If I do, I think I'd like to get a dog. So, I'd love to know your thoughts on that too."

"Wow. Going out on your own. That's quite a change. But, yes, I would certainly consider it, especially if I could do it part-time – I want better work/life balance than I've had in the past. And these little guys are also great for that, so I'd highly recommend a dog."

"Where would I find a dog?"

"I'd highly recommend adopting one from a shelter or through a rescue organisation that specialises in the breed you're interested in, over buying one."

"Why's that?"

"There's something about a dog you rescue, one that you give a new lease on life, it's almost like they know that you saved them and they make the best pets. Ask anyone who has."

"Definitely food for thought. Thanks, I will. How 'bout I ask that handsome man with the big dog over there?" Marnie pointed over the next hill.

"Dare ya!"

"You're on." Marnie walked purposely toward the attractive man with the Bernese.

I watched as I walked. Come to think of it, this guy looked kind of familiar. I wasn't all that close to him and I certainly didn't want to be accused of staring so I took a quick glance here and there to see if I actually knew him or just thought that I might want to.

I walked while keeping an eye on my golden flying furball who would whiz by me at lightning speed to chase something else that caught his attention. I still wasn't sure how I knew the handsome man Marnie was now laughing with. His dog came flying by me chasing after Dylan, close enough for me to get a good look at this large but handsome four-legged gal. Then I saw it. The poor thing had only one eye.

That's it! It had to be Wink, the one-eyed Bernese beauty, and that meant that the handsome owner was Bryan. Yes, Bryan, the first man I was excited about meeting online. The guy I had such a great connection with. The guy who was addicted to hot chocolate, made me laugh with his profile looking for a 'real dog' and had adopted his pal from a shelter just like I had. He was the man who saw into my soul almost instantly. But Bryan was also the guy who stood me up with absolutely no explanation.

I didn't know whether to say something or not. If I did, what would I have said? "Hey, thanks for standing me up!"

He'd probably come back with, "And you are?"

There was no good way to make contact, so I just left it. And, besides, Marnie had already beat me to it. As much as I wanted to tell him what I thought of his rudeness, how I deserved so much better, how disappointed I had been because I had high hopes for our date and more. Would I have told him that I had a feeling that there was a real connection, that there had been something in his words, his smile that felt familiar and comforting? In my mind I couldn't come up with a way to say any of it that didn't sound desperate and whining. So I said nothing.

"Kayte he was so nice and easy to talk to. And mmm… so handsome and built! You should have come with me. And guess what? He adopted his dog Wink. He said he wouldn't do it any other way and highly recommended it.

Bryan was handsome. And he had a much nicer body than I had expected. I didn't know whether to tell Marnie about my experience with him standing me up or not, so I refrained. One thing was for sure. He loved his dog Wink. You could tell by the energy he expended when he played with her. He threw the ball further than anyone; he shouted encouragement louder than the other masters. Bryan smiled wider and prouder than any of the two-legged park visitors and he'd get right down to Wink's level, looking her snoot to nose as he patted her. You could see the closeness of their relationship in how Wink, even with her free roam, never ventured too far away from her master. They were close alright. Ah, I figured that maybe he wasn't all bad. He was a dog person, so my instinct told me he couldn't be. Maybe I should have a look for him online again. Or send him an email. Something I knew I'd have to ponder.

CHAPTER 26

My head hurt. My stomach felt almost as bad. I pulled the cover over my head and then the memories from the evening before started flooding in. Oh gawd, what had I done?

Who would have guessed that on that Sunday evening, things would happen as they had? As it often does in the single world, a male/female platonic friendship moved from safe territory, taking a giant leap across the border AND finding its way into sexual land.

This one shocked me. I was just having dinner with my friend. Nothing special. It was a Sunday night. Heck, I hadn't even shaved my legs. But my guest, while amazed that he finally had the opportunity to do what he had fantasised about for months, was not completely surprised by the evening's occurrences. He confessed this to me later.

Apparently before he left his house that evening, freshly showered, bottle of wine in hand, he had hopefully tucked a few condoms in his wallet before heading to my place for our BBQ. He obviously remembered the motto from his boy scout days!

And he had entertained the thought of us taking things beyond our usual hugs and kisses on the cheek. Things were actually premeditated on his part.

There I was oblivious to all of it. I looked for every opportunity to entertain these days and I loved to cook using the BBQ and I was getting better and better at it. It was nice to have the opportunity to share my growing hobby with those people who were important to me.

The evening's menu was chosen to appeal to the man's man with whom I was breaking bread. It consisted of juicy thickly cut sirloin steaks that had soaked in a beer, herb and spice bath all day, baby roasted potatoes, marinated and grilled mushroom caps stuffed with herbs and goat cheese, grilled zucchini and eggplant accompanied by the crunchiest herb bread that was just dripping with melting garlic and herb butter.

And there was wine. We can't forget there was wine. In fact before the evening was done, we had travelled the global vineyards enjoying a total of three bottles between the two of us. We had one from France, a Merlot that was just a hint too dry and definitely too musky for my taste. Then there came the showcase bottle, the one my guest had provided, from Spain, a warm and sturdy Cabernet Sauvignon that was smooth on the palate. And the third, oh yes, the third, was an old favourite from Down Under – a consistent and familiar Merlot.

We should have stopped at two.

Oh why didn't we stop at two?

The evening felt easy. The conversation traversed topics from friends in common, to past travels, to admitting some pretty intimate weaknesses and fears, to sharing secret hopes and dreams. The ambience was comfortable and familiar and simple. There was no pressure to be anyone other than exactly who we were.

It was warm and slightly humid – the perfect summer evening, complete with a fully speckled sky. The food was spectacular. He was astounded at what a wonderful cook I was. He said that he had no idea that I, a woman, this attractive, smart, genuine and funny could also cook. I should have known that with all the compliments he was up to something.

He added, staring very intently into my eyes, "Kayte, I've noticed lately that you are very capable at many things."

Thinking back to that night, I think we would both recall that between just about every mouthful there was laughter. And not just the little snicker, not just a wee chuckle, but full, hearty, unrestrained belly laughs and loud and sincere guffaws complete with knee slapping and the occasional bit of food escaping at the funnier bits. In fact, there may have been a snort or two resonating from me around the end of bottle number two.

But what later transpired was a mistake. It did not sit well with me in the long term. If I had to place blame for it, I would have to share it equally between the wine and the Motown.

It sang from the portable CD player speakers. I was being twirled around the backyard and I didn't care which, if any, of the neighbours were watching. The patio lights cast a warm glow around the perimeter of the yard as they hung atop the fence that surrounded my little plot of land. I was barefoot and the grass was just starting to dew, it was cooling with the chill of the night air. There was a faint film of moisture that tickled my toes as we danced. I was out, then back in again, then out. I lost my balance, and just before the combined force of the last spin and the numerous glasses of wine nearly had me falling on my keester, a burly arm reached around my waist and caught me. With his hand flat on my back, he then pulled me toward him, closer and closer still. My whole torso was now connected to his. The hold was not loosening. He looked at me in a way I had never seen from him before. Then, before I knew it, the other hand, the one that had been twirling me just moments before, had worked its way from my hand up my arm and behind my head. It cupped my head and pulled it towards his wanting eyes and hungry lips.

The kiss was soft, the lips were strangely gentle and the kiss was sensual, slow and sensitive and warmly inviting. Not at all what I might have expected. But I had never expected to be sharing an evening dining, dancing, kissing and then sleeping with... Roman.

I don't know why I did it. It was just stupid, stupid, stupid. I was lonely. We both had too much wine. He initiated it but that was no excuse.

I wished I could turn back the clock. I knew it wasn't the end of the world, but it was wrong. It was uncomfortable. It just shouldn't have happened.

Oh, why did it happen?

The next morning, when the red wine haze lifted and I woke to see Roman lying beside me, I rose and tiptoed out of the room; I would make sure that there were no morning repeats of the mistaken behaviour of the night before. Besides I was nauseous. I knew I was going to vomit – far too much rich food, way too much wine and, truth be told, I was a little sickened by my own behaviour.

It wasn't that Roman repulsed me but I just didn't think of him that way. I didn't want to think of him that way and even after sharing sex I still didn't want us to have that kind of relationship. I hoped we could salvage our friendship and that things wouldn't be too weird between us. But right now that was doubtful and didn't matter because I just wanted him out.

Then I was struck by a question. Was he interested in me? What if he really liked me? What if all this time we were friends he had been secretly wanting me? No. That couldn't be it. I would have seen the signs. Something would have happened before now. He wouldn't have been helping me meet guys online and giving me tips and hints and suggestions for doing so.

What was I going to say to him? What do you say to someone you just slept with and don't ever want to sleep with again? Do I jump in and deal with it upfront and honestly? Do I make a joke? Do I blame it on the wine? Do I just pretend it didn't happen?

My memory was a little foggy, but I knew what happened. While I didn't recall every detail I did remember feeling surprised by it.

Why did that have to happen? Why did there have to be another one added to my list? I wanted the next man that I slept with to be the last man I slept with in my lifetime. And Roman, while a good friend, was not the man I wanted to spend the rest of my life with. I didn't even want to spend the rest of that morning with him. It was just all too uncomfortable. He needed to get up. He needed to leave. He needed to never do that again. Ever.

I needed to find my Mr. Right. I couldn't do this anymore. I wanted more. I deserved more. Damn why did it have to be so damned hard to find?

Right then the phone rang. It was Chloe wanting to discuss some ideas about an event she was planning and catering. I whispered that I needed to talk to her but I'd have to call her back and I'd explain then.

She knew it was something big. And I knew her. She'd be creating all kinds of dramatic scenarios until I called her back with the real scoop. I had to talk to her about this. I had to get Roman up. He had to go to work.

That's when I went downstairs, grabbed the box of biscuits, came back to the bedroom and tossed in two of Dylan's favourite doggy cookies. One landed on top of Roman and one on the bed right beside him. My dutiful Dylan did the rest. Bless his food motivated little hairy soul.

CHAPTER 27

"I don't know how it happened." I was almost whining on the phone to Chloe. I could hear the kettle whistling in the background.

"Well, it did. You can't change it. You can only change what happens from now on." Sage was not just another spice in caterer Chloe's spice rack.

"I know, but I could hardly even look at him this morning. I just said something stupid, cracked a joke, and ushered him out as quickly as I could. There were no offers of coffee. No chitchat. No coy behaviour, no flirtations. I purposely kept a safe physical distance and it was all so very uncomfortable. How am I going to be able to maintain a friendship with this man?"

"You guys will find a way."

"Just before he left, he asked if I wanted to talk about what happened? I just shook my head and told him that I felt like crap and just want to crawl back into bed."

"Alone," Chloe chimed in.

"Yes, alone and, truth be told, I wanted to crawl right back into yesterday and so I could go back and change things."

"If only you could. Kayte, do you think he has feelings for you?" There was chopping in the background now.

"Chloe, I dunno. I guess I'll have to be delicate about this in case he does, but I certainly don't, not beyond friendship, no matter what my actions of last night might have suggested. Damn that bottle number three!"

"You guys drank three bottles of wine?"

"Yep, just the two of us."

"Man, even Dylan might have looked good after three bottles of wine."

"Yes, if you liked blondes!"

We both erupted in laughter, which emphasised the feeling that my brain was three sizes larger than the skull that was supposed to encase it. A huge throbbing boulder sat atop my shoulders. I knew I needed a few painkillers and water, lots and lots of water. I wouldn't be going to the gym today.

How's UR head? My first text message of the day was from Roman, received about 2pm that day.

I thumbed back, **Gone. I cut it off.**

LOL

Well, at least we were talking, sort of.

Thx 4 dinner & DESSERT followed by a wink.

YW 4 dinner – not sure how I feel about sharing dessert, was my feeble attempt at telling him how uncomfortable this all made me feel.

I thought it was S-W-E-E-T!

I tapped back, **Really?**

I think I'm still on a sugar high!

Oh gawd. He was happy we had sex. Of course he was, he was Roman, he was happy to have sex with anyone!

What had I done?

It would be easier to text this than to say it, so I did.

Roman, things shouldn't have gone where they did last night. I value our friendship, but it really shouldn't be any more than that – friends. I really don't want to ruin our friendship, if we haven't already, but we can't go there again. No matter how much wine we drink. Okay?

For the first time in our friendship Roman was silent.

It was a nice day so I decided to take Dylan and do my 6K run outside, soak up the sunshine and just enjoy the cool breeze and fresh air. I loved running because it gave me a chance to get inside my own head. To ponder things as close to home as those that had that happened that day or those that were happening half way 'round the world.

I stuck pretty close to home with my musings. I was troubled by the recent events with Roman and I just couldn't get them off my mind.

I had completed one third of my run for the day when I broke into a smile as I recalled Roman's wicked, albeit often sarcastic, sense of humour. He always made me laugh. Not the kind of feigned chuckle you give some people, but true, sincere, hearty from-the-gut laughs.

He had been a good friend to me and had been a constant male influence in my life. While I didn't need to hear all the details of his sexual pursuits, I can tell you that I learned a lot about men from him. Some things I wished I didn't know.

We had always been good friends. Now we could also add lovers to that list. Perhaps the term sexual partners was more fitting because whatever feelings I had for Roman, I knew they weren't love.

Was I this troubled about what happened with him because I didn't have feelings for Roman, or because I did?

My legs stopped moving at this point. I stood there panting. Dylan raised a leg on the nearby tree and I was dumbfounded by my inability to decisively answer that question.

Why couldn't I answer that question? Could I possibly have romantic feelings for Roman? Roman, of all people?

The answer to that question required far more reflection than the remaining 3K of my run, but it gave me a great start.

CHAPTER 28

Why I had decided to don my pretty blue frilly skirt and powder blue wrap t-shirt for a regular Sunday around the house I don't know. Call it women's intuition, call it a hunch, call it a lucky little coincidence, but whichever you choose, it was definitely a good call.

It was about 4:30 in the afternoon. After my run, I puttered in the garden, first out front, then the back, so most of the day had been spent outdoors. It was the most humid it had been for days so I didn't even attempt the straight style for my hair, opting instead for the softer, curlier, slightly wild style instead. My cheeks and nose were rosy and glowing without the aid of even a dusting of makeup. I had applied a shimmering, soft pink coat of gloss to my dry somewhat sunburnt, and slightly puffy lips. As I passed the image in the mirror, I was pleased with what I saw. My arms were tanned and toned, my legs were leaner and darker than they had ever been in my adult life and my tummy had shrunk noticeably since I began my gruelling sessions with my trainer.

I remember the fleeting thought that this look was being wasted just hanging out at home; I looked good and I should be on a date or just out there, maybe walking the aisles of the big box hardware stores looking for handsome and handy types. I could make the 'damsel out of her element' work for me.

Then I noticed it, a vehicle pulling up out front that looked vaguely familiar. The door opened and then I remembered. I recalled the first time I saw that tall frame unfold itself from the driver's seat. But this time he appeared quite different, quite different indeed.

Dylan was doing his usual "there's someone at the door, there's someone at the door" dance, clicking on the marble tiles and sending puffs of hair into the air. The doorbell rang and sent my hairy housemate into an excited frenzy.

Would any man EVER be that happy to see me?

I gave my breasts a perfunctory lift, checked in the mirrored closet doors for nipple alignment, glanced up my nostrils, pulled my t-shirt down around my waist so it sat just right, then pushed back my shoulders, sucked in my belly, formed a huge "what a pleasant surprise" grin and answered the door.

"Well hello. If it isn't 'Tommy-I'm-full-of-surprises-Kessler.' C'mon in, and don't mind the crazy canine. This is Dylan."

He reached down to give him a hello pat and Dylan ran off to grab his prized possession – his black rubber Kong to then drop this at the feet as a welcoming gesture to his new friend.

"What a nice surprise. What brings you up this way?"

"I just finished a Daddy weekend and dropped off the kids and thought I'd take a chance and pop in and check you, I mean your place out. He was smiling a wicked grin. "Very nice. Warm, cosy, not too girlie but inviting. Nice. I give it an A minus."

"And you're just in the front hall. Listen, I was just about to get myself a beer and go out the back and enjoy this great day. Can I interest you in one?"

"Please say it's Mexican and comes with a lime!"

"It definitely is. Is there any other kind?" I was giving him my best mischievous grin and questioning glance.

He followed me into the kitchen. When I was in bare feet, I think he could probably stand behind me and look straight down my top, given he was 6'2". Oh well, 'the girls' looked great today. I was wearing the right bra, had a nice rosy glow on my otherwise tanned chest and the ice blue tight wrap tank top showcased everything quite nicely.

I detected a mixture of cologne and perspiration evaporating from him encouraged by the day's humidity. When he brushed by me in the kitchen, I also faintly detected a wave of body heat emanating from his tanned arm, the one that had probably been out the window soaking in the sun as he drove.

I opened our beer, inserted the lime and handed Tommy his. As we made our way to the backyard, I insisted he go first so I could check him out from behind. While he had a bit of a butt, it wasn't his strongest feature. I did notice a sizeable difference in his back though, it seemed broader, more muscular and his shoulders and biceps had grown as well. He was very tanned and he looked good in the bronze coloured shades he wore. I guess I never really appreciated what nice lips Mr. Kessler had. They were full and wide and thick, but not too thick. I was thinking about how they might feel kissing mine, kissing my neck, moving further down and kissing my collarbone – when I noticed him watching me, perhaps having similar lustful thoughts. I could see his eyes looking out over the top of his lenses. He was watching with great interest as I placed my mouth around the beer bottle preparing to take a sip.

Bottle unmoved, I shot him a quizzical glance.

His response was simply a barely audible, "lucky beer bottle!"

I purposely took a longer drink than normal all the while never breaking his gaze.

Tommy Kessler was flirting with me – this time in person and not just online. Who would have thought?

"I have to tell you Kayte, this not working stuff certainly agrees with you. You look fabulous!"

"Takes one to know one," I said. You've changed a little yourself Mr. Did you lose your job and not tell me?"

"I'm trying. I guess the weight I lost through the whole marriage breakup thing is coming back on and I've been going to the gym every day, doing a mix of cardio toning and weights, some serious weights. So I guess it's going on in all the right places."

"Well you look good. You'll be snatched up in no time."

"Snatched? Only if I want to be. And I'm not sure I'm ready for another relationship yet. I think I just want to date for a while. Be single, be a cool, freewheeling, bad-ass biker, bachelor dude."

I crossed my legs and watched him watch my leg as I did it.

"Nice toe polish. I like it when a woman looks feminine. Yes nothing quite as nice as pedicured feet, manicured hands, just the right amount of makeup and pretty lingerie. Do you like lingerie?"

"Like? I've considered joining a 12-step program for my addiction to it. So yes, it's one of my indulgences. I have lots of it. The bra and panties must match and the lacier and prettier the better."

"I noticed a little blue strap there under your t-shirt. You must be wearing some pretty stuff today. Wanna show me?" He laughed and I knew he was only half kidding.

"Maybe a little later." I looked out over my sunglasses and winked. If Tommy was going to dish it out, I'd dish it back to him.

He had finished his beer. I offered him another and his response was a mature one; "I'm driving, so I better not." It was the line that came next that almost had me spit the remaining bit of mine in his lap. "But you don't have any popsicles, do you?"

I laughed and shook my head. I thought that if I did, I'd be the one enjoying it. He would just have to suffer through watching me enjoy every drop of it. I made a mental note to self… buy more popsicles.

"Chloe, you wouldn't believe it. He looked like a completely different guy."

"What's that about the sky?"

"I said," raising my voice to compete with the vacuum cleaner in the background at Chloe's place, "he looked like a completely different guy."

"Who?"

"Tommy."

"Which one is he? I can't keep them all straight."

"He's the guy I had no physical attraction to when we first met."

"And now?"

"Not so sure, but I think I do. He stopped by today unexpectedly and he looks so much different. He's like 'ultra- Thomas', the new and improved version. He looks happier, more confident and sexier. He's probably put on about 10 kilos and all in the right places. His arms are noticeably more muscular. His chest is fuller and firmer. He has a great tan, and although he didn't take off the baseball cap, I'm thinking the hairline issue wouldn't even be a problem."

"So is there a date coming out of this?"

I could hear the sloshing of water in the background that I could only assume was coming from a bucket and that my dear domestic diva had moved on from vacuuming to cleaning the floors while we chatted.

"Well I don't know, but I'm certainly tempted. We seem to get on so well in our online chats. He gets me and my sense of

216

humour. He is amusing and intelligent and seems down-to-earth, like someone we'd hang out with. And now that he's looking on the hot side, why wouldn't I want to try dating him?"

"Then make it happen, honey."

"And I think he may feel the same. There was a time when we were sitting outside and he brushed his arm slowly against mine and the heat exchanged between us was scorching."

"So what are you waiting for? Don't sit back and wait for it to be served up to you. Do what you've always done, honey, and go grab what you want out of life."

I thought about the easy banter that Tommy and I shared, the flirtation, the new and improved physique, the fullness of his lips and how I had been thinking about how they would feel exploring my body.

"You're right. I will do something. I'm not going to just sit and wait."

"That's my girl!" And with that I also heard the toilet flush. I can only assume that bathrooms had been next on the list after cleaning the floors.

CHAPTER 29

Fingers hovering over the keyboard, I contemplated the right words to tap out in the email to Tommy. I wanted the right mix of communicating how happy I was to see him, that he was looking good and that I wanted the door open for further in-person interactions. But I didn't want to appear too forward. I was pretty sure he was the traditional type that needed to take the dating lead.

My interest in dating him grew as I pondered our recent communications. I knew that the online chats were fun and entertaining but I saw them as only a contemporary means to a desired end. I wasn't prepared to live online. I wanted more. I didn't want to find my cyber mate, but my soul mate instead.

And as Roman so wisely stated that Roman's Rule #10 for online dating states, that once you've met in person you must be wary of the return to the cyber relationship. While online interactions are great, you need to move into and remain in real life, (IRL) as he puts it, for you can divulge way too much through email and online chats and rush the process of getting to know one another rather than letting it unfold in person in a far more natural and lasting way.

I sat at my desk, Dylan lying beside me, and I considered just how much time I had been spending in this online space lately. I feared that I had become a little too connected to my computer and the life that lived at the ends of my fingertips. I wanted to expand my horizons and I hoped that Tommy might want to accompany me.

I tapped out a cheery email and hit send before I could second-guess myself.

To: tomtom@socialarity.com
From: k8@socialarity.com
Subject: What a nice surprise!

Aren't you just full of surprises! Thanks for popping by – I love surprise visits and it was great actually SEEING you in person. On that - WOWSA you look fantastic. The single life is agreeing with you Mister!

Just moments before you rang the bell, I was roaming around noticing just how quiet the house was and thinking how I liked it so much better when there was company... and then... tada... there was... you... right there on my doorstep. I hope you know you are welcome anytime!

I busied myself scanning other new profiles, responding to email and keeping up my other cyber acquaintances and then came the following:

To: k8@socialarity.com
From: tomtom@socialarity.com
Subject: Re: What a nice surprise!

Hey Kayte,

Ya well... I couldn't pass by again and not say hi. Actually I was kinda curious... wanted to see your habitat and how you make your way in the world. You have a very nice home you should be proud of. I'm envious. Cool stuff... nice taste. Speaking of tasty, thanks for the beer... now if only I had been lucky enough to have had a popsicle or at least watched you have one!

To: tomtom@socialarity.com
From: k8@socialarity.com
Subject: Re:Re:What a nice surprise!

Thanks for the compliments – but the real cool stuff (like the trapeze!) is upstairs!

As for having good taste, it extends to my choice in people too! And Tommy, as for the popsicles, perhaps they'll be the special of the day the next time you pop by Kayte's Bar & Grill & Pleasure Emporium …

Hope you had a good first day back at work!

To: k8@socialarity.com
From: tomtom@socialarity.com
Subject: Re:Re:Re:What a nice surprise!

You kinky little thing!!! Now you tell me. Way to go!

Well thanks for the compliment tucked in there… far too kind.

But, I'm a cold hard biker bastard and don't you forget it!

And the first day back was slow and easy baby... just the way I like it ;-)

I couldn't let it just end there.

To: tomtom@socialarity.com
From: k8@socialarity.com
Subject: Re:Re:Re:Re:What a nice surprise!

Man, how I miss slow and easy Come to think of it I miss first days back too. Me kinda jealous that you're at the office, interacting with people, feeling like you have a place to be, that you're needed, that you have a purpose. Sometimes I honestly miss working. It was such a big part of who I was and now it just feels strange to not have that. I devoted so much time, so much attention, so much of my soul to working, not sure how to fill that void now.

To: k8@socialarity.com
From: tomtom@socialarity.com
Subject: Re:Re:Re:Re:Re:What a nice surprise!

I think you should fill the void with fun, food, fitness and lots and lots of fooling around.

And, yes, my purpose now is to attend a two-hour meeting that starts in five minutes. Today's attendees include a bunch arrogant ego-driven engineers, each with an axe to grind over the changes to this project. Let's see, there's one who's allergic to... everything and can't stop sneezing, one with tear-inducing BO, one borderline narcoleptic, one who is compelled to write everything on the white board, one nervous throat clearer, one always bored finger strummer and one nose/eye/ear/zit picker (who I just plain refuse to shake hands with)... so you're jealous, are you?

I'd trade places with you in heartbeat honey.

I repeat lots and lots and lots of fooling around!

"Dylan, he called me honey!"

I had at least two hours before Tommy was potentially back online. It was just enough time for a good long run with my loyal training partner and some new podcasts and a few tunes.

I had discovered podcasts and they had become my new addiction. Okay podcasts and my computer both helped to fill the void caused by not working. On the computer I was either IM-ing, emailing, or trolling the dating site. I was on my computer more at home than I ever had been at the office. What struck me most was how technology, once something I relied upon only in the corporate world as a tool to get my work done, had now permeated every facet of my life.

Looking back over the past few months, I don't think I had been disconnected from my computer or mobile phone for more than an hour or two at a time. Okay, while I was showering or sleeping, but even then, I'd find myself rising for my 2am trot to the potty, then popping into the office and checking for new messages. I'd even pop in for a quick email check after a 10-minute shower thinking that I might have missed something.

I wondered if this was normal, desperate or just bordering on obsessive.

Winded, wet and wobbly, I trounced upstairs after a 7K run and headed straight for the computer. Tommy was showing as online.

K8says:
Hey there Tomtom

Tomtom says:
Hey there KayteyKat! How's tricks sista?

K8 says:
Silly wabbit, twicks are for kids!

Tomtom says:
So what have you been up to while I've been meeting with sneezy, stinky, picky, sleepy, strummy and writey? (okay, that last one was lame)

K8 says:
Oh lots, I've just been out with a blonde and I'm out of breath, glistening with sweat and my legs are all wobbly

Tomtom says:
Oh a new man huh?

K8 says:
No, not quite… Dylan and I just came in from a run.

Tomtom says:
Good.

K8 says:
So Romeo have you met any new ladies online that have any promise?

Tomtom says:
no new cyber-chicklets - last one sucked huge (and not in a good way)!!!

K8 says:
Don't hold back now. Tell me how you really feel. So how come? Tell me all the dirt!

Tomtom says:
Full of herself and she was soooo not good looking

too skinny and brutal hair

K8 says:
Sounds horrid - probably had some stripper name like Tawney Scrawny

Tomtom says:
Na, normal name, normal type, divorced, mother of two but no chemistry

K8 says:
Me thinks you might be pretty hard to please?

Tomtom says:
Shuddap you!

K8 says:
You wouldn't like that now would you? You've missed talkin to me - admit it!

Tomtom says:
Ya - you make me laugh... and I'm not just saying that. I appreciate you even more with every new woman I meet

K8 says:
You make me laugh too

Tomtom says:
And you're good counsel... smart lady

Hey I drove by your place last night...

K8 says:

And why didn't you come say hi?

Tomtom says:
Would you have liked that?

K8 says:
Of course

Tomtom says:
I was on the bike and it was getting dark.

long day already

K8 says:
Gotcha - but you should come by for dinner some night after work your work's not too far from my place

Tomtom says:
True but it's not on the way home

K8 says:
WHATEVER!!! It's 20 mins D2D but hey no worries - you don't have to come sample my fine cuisine - your loss

Tomtom says:
WTF - whoa now Nelly... back your big truck up!

D2D?

I would like to really

I'll even bring wine

K8 says:
D2D - door-to-door silly.

Great - a nice fruity chardonnay or a full-bodied cab sav

Tomtom says:
I'll try to remember, which do you prefer?

K8 says:
I can go either way with my wine but do prefer the red as it makes me relax and the white just makes me horny

Tomtom says:
Two bottles of white it is then!

K8 says:
Darn. There I go giving too much info again - I really need to learn to edit

Tomtom says:
Don't you dare. How else will I learn the intimate details about you?

K8 says:
Two bottles of white will give you a good start - LMAO

So, what do you like to eat?

Tomtom says:
Me man, me like meat! Steaks, burgers (LOVE burgers) chicken, not so much on the fish, but love Thai, love Italian, pretty easy

K8 says:
Good to know

Tomtom says:
Which - the food preferences or the easy part?

K8 says:
Both! Listen I should go, but we'll do this soon okay?

Tomtom says:
I'm outta town for the next week or so, but how 'bout when I get back? Give me something to look forward to - when I'm not travelling this bachelor dining - eating out of the pot is getting a little tiresome.

K8 says:
We'll just have to remedy that then. Dinner at my place when you get back... we'll BBQ... hmmm... something... I'll think on it... for now, it's K8 out!

Tomtom says:
Later gater - or should that be later K8er?

I signed off not responding to the last comment; just a little online tease. "Always be the first to exit the conversation and leave the guy wanting just a little bit more." That was Roman's Rule # 11 of online dating. Oh yes, Roman. I wasn't going to think about him now. I had something far more important to concentrate on.

Tommy was coming for dinner. Tommy was coming for dinner! I started to plan it right there on the spot. I pondered what I'd serve him. I would need to do something tasty, but nothing too fancy... I didn't want to make it look like I was trying too hard. I thought about fixing homemade burgers on the BBQ with traditional toppings and some fancier ones like fresh grated mix of cheeses, yellow tomatoes, pesto mayonnaise, grilled red onions, grilled sweet red peppers – you could tell a lot about a man by how he dressed his burger. I wondered what Tommy's burger would say about him. Was he traditional or more adventurous? If he had two, would he fix them both the same? Was his palate tame? Or was he a fan of the spicy? I thought that I could make a big colourful salad with home-made dressing. I decided upon something cool for dessert – no, not popsicles! Maybe I'd serve a chocolate gelato, with an orange sauce or maybe a hot peanut butter sauce. Yes, chocolate and peanut butter... the thought of a dinner with Tommy had appeal on a number of levels.

What kind of music would I play that night? I'd need something sexy but not seductive, something casual and unpretentious. I thought a mix of a little latin, some reggae and some traditional rock – no, better yet, some sultry blues, heavy on the guitar.

I really needed to start thinking about going back to work. I was getting far too excited and detailed in planning a simple casual dinner. But who knew where it might lead?

CHAPTER 30

With Tommy out of town for a week, I succumbed to the nagging urge to do a little looking for any new and interesting men on the dating site, expecting full well not to find any.

It was then I stumbled on Joey.

He was just plain sexy. I remembered wondering if his sexy profile would translate to a sexy person. That was the thing about online dating and meeting someone for the first time, there were always expectations. Sometimes you were disappointed, sometimes you weren't. The night I met Joey Cuirissma, I was pleasantly surprised.

Our online meeting went well. I had been flipping through the new profiles, following Roman's Rule #12 to save yourself time in the searching for love process and claim 'first dibs' on the 'newbies'. He suggested that you make it a daily habit to go through only the 'new' profiles. Most sites gave you the opportunity to sort based on this criteria, so why not use it to your advantage? Why waste time going through the masses, most of whom you had already seen and knew you weren't interested in, when you could go straight to those who were new in the zoo? Roman made sense, at least when it came to providing advice on how to best use the online dating sites and make this process as efficient and productive as possible.

Oh yes, Roman. I had managed to squeeze even the teeniest thoughts of him out of my mind. After the 'incident' with Roman, I ran directly back to the site, after only a short respite. It was like I needed to meet new men, chat with new guys and date other men just so that I could, quite literally, get the taste of Roman out of my mouth.

I also had the Tommy diversion and that growing flirtation so I hadn't thought much about Roman, which was probably best.

Why did the evening with Roman bother me so much? Why wasn't I getting past this? Why was I still so uncomfortable even thinking about it? I still didn't have these answers.

I sought my online refuge with the other singles-looking-for-love. I saw Joey's profile online on the first day he had posted it. "GuitarGeek" was the profile name he used. Apparently, while he earned a living in technology by day, it was music that fed his soul. You could see the creativity sparkle from his eyes. Even in his photo, it was evident that he oozed passion and enthusiasm. The photo that most caught my attention showed him crouched beside a lake, one knee higher than the other, his right hand over his left wrist and his whole body leaning a little to the right. He wore snug faded blue jeans and a plain long sleeved aqua coloured jersey that emphasised his broad shoulders. His expression was a closed mouth smile, almost a smirk and his eyes twinkled. His face, especially around the eyes, resembled a certain well known, sleepy eyed, action adventure actor, producer, director who changed his name to avoid nepotism.

His profile was pretty average but he had a testimonial from a friend, a guy even, claiming he was a really good guy, the type who people were drawn to, the type who brightened up a room.

I made first contact sending him a note through the dating site mail system.

GuitarGeek,

So you light up a room huh? Apparently your friend thinks you're a pretty decent guy - I saw something in your look that I find warm and appealing and your profile seems pretty down-to-earth and honest. All wonderful qualities. Have a peek at mine and get back if you're interested - if you're not, what the heck is wrong with you?

LOL - Just kidding, hey, if I'm not your type, then thanks for reading and good luck out there!

An hour later I received his response:

Well you definitely have something to say don't you. I like that. I would imagine there's never a boring moment with you, however flattery will get you nowhere LOL. I don't know what my type is but you cracked me up with the "what the heck is wrong with you?" comment. As far as lighting up a room I guess he never mentioned that it was a careless accident with a flaming torch? OK, OK, I've never burned anything except some dinner and that only happens once a month or so.

There was a hint of flirtation in our exchange. He challenged me from the beginning. We agreed to talk immediately. He said he hated typing and had to do far too much of it at work.

Our first telephone call lasted two hours and his questions had a real depth and thoughtfulness to them.

After the initial pleasantries and the required acknowledge-ment of the sound of each other's voices and that of being a user of online dating sites and some basic experiences we had both had with it so far, we got into the to good stuff.

"So ever been married?" I asked.

"No, but was close once. Realised that I wasn't mature enough for that big a step. How about you?"

"To my job? Yes. To anyone else, no."

"It's not as uncommon as it once was. I've seen a growing trend with women who are or were in the same situation. Think that's kinda scary."

"Agreed. So happy that I've seen the light."

"Good for you. So what is the most important thing to you in a relationship?"

"Hmm... I guess it would be honesty."

"Even if the truth hurts?"

"Yep, even if the truth hurts. I'd far rather know exactly where I stand and hate it, than to be oblivious to it in the first place."

"I guess at least that way you can do something about it."

"Exactly."

"You sound like you have a strong sense of self."

"I try. Maybe it comes from spending so much time on my own."

"Are you your own best friend?"

"I would have said Chloe was my best friend, or my dog, Dylan, but ya, maybe I am."

"I want to meet you Kayte."

"Where did that come from?"

"I just have a feeling. I don't want to wait. I think there's something here, something I want to explore."

I was beaming, I agreed.

"I think I'd like that."

The discussion then jumped from musical tastes, the families and influential events and people in our lives, to questions like, "If you could name a single thing that could destroy a soul, what would it be?" and "If you were to pick one characteristic of your Zodiac sign that best fits your personality, which one would it be?"

I wondered what Tommy's answers to these questions would

have been.

Joey and I talked about past relationships, sexual appetites, preferences and expectations. We compared old family recipes, shared vacation experiences and confessed to our respective nicknames and how we had earned them. He even played me a little acoustic Clapton to tease me just a little, insisting that more would only follow as a live performance.

Did Tommy play any instruments? I wasn't sure. I'd have to ask.

Joey's voice was smooth. It had a deep, sensual lulling quality to it. It was captivating. He had a genuine laugh that was both mischievous and childlike. I was attracted to his words and his voice. I was sure that I wanted to meet him. And he wanted to meet me.

So we did, just two days later.

Tommy wasn't due back for a few days so it was good timing.

I felt a little guilty, but then I reasoned with myself. I was single. I wasn't dating Tommy. We hadn't even kissed. I liked him, yes. But from what I knew so far, I liked Joey too. So it was just fine to meet him. There was no reason I shouldn't, was there? There was nothing in Roman's Rules. There was that name again and that memory. I shook my head, like a dice, hoping it would come up with a different thought. And it did.

What would I wear to meet Joey?

CHAPTER 31

It was a Friday evening and we had chosen a spot about halfway between where we both lived. I arrived on time, parked and purposely made a call to Chloe. I gave her the details as to where I was and with whom I was having a date. In my mind this was a date, not a meeting. Roman might disagree, but that's how this felt. I shared with Chloe that I was a little nervous but that I had high expectations. She said she could hear the anticipation in my voice. This was a feat in itself because all I could hear was the duet featuring the combination of the dishwasher and the television in the background from her place.

I arrived first. I always did. Even though it provided time for my 'first date nervousness' to heighten, it also gave me the opportunity to watch him arrive.

From where I was parked I saw him approach the door. His gait was something between a swagger and a strut. Mmm… he even walked sexy.

I checked myself in the rear view mirror as I said a quick goodbye to Chloe. She wished me luck and then added, "Be good.

And if you can't be good, be good at it!"

I laughed. The smile came with me as I walked through the restaurant doors where I was greeted by Joey wearing an equally telling grin.

He was wearing a snuggly fitting pair of slightly faded blue jeans that hugged his firm butt. His shirt was mostly black, accented by bright teal and purple vertical stripes and worn casually over his jeans. The sleeves were rolled to mid forearm and the shirt moved loosely around his waist yet got considerably tighter as it reached his chest and shoulders. Black leather loafers were the finishing touch.

As I reviewed this man from the feet on up, my assessment was that he was damned handsome. He was fit and slightly taller than me. He had large well-developed thighs and a trim waist. His pecs filled his shirt and actually made the vertical stripes lean outwards from the strain. He had a hairy chest that popped out of the few top buttons undone from his shirt. He wore no jewellery but when I went in for a hello hug there was the presence of a seductive scent that hung round his neck inviting a nuzzle. I resisted.

His hair was darker than his pictures had suggested, perhaps because of the obvious hair-sculpting product that had been added. His temples were dotted with accent grey sweeps of hair that acted as pointers directing my gaze to his eyes. They were the size and shape of large olives and they glistened with the enticing colour of a sparkling fresh brewed cup of Columbian coffee. When he added a full, white-toothed smile, the total effect was that of a warm and sexy boyish demigod. He was definitely handsome... very, very handsome. Very, very, very... 'Can I touch you now?' handsome.

We had chosen a nice restaurant that had a small wine bar area as you first entered. It was casual and comfortable. There were two fireplaces warming the room and as we passed a speaker a deep female jazz voice greeted us from above. Everything about the evening was sexy. We were off to a good start.

We sat in a comfy corner booth that had caramel leather seats and a walnut table. There was a large vanilla scented candle encased in a basketball sized transparent bowl that cast a soft glow upon our faces. The ambience of this intimate little wine bar seemed to wrap itself around us.

While our bodies weren't touching, they were connecting. I felt a heat exchange between us. The conversation was flirtatious and flowed easily.

"Do you meet a lot of women when you're 'gigging'? That is what you called it, right?"

Joey grinned a wry smile. He was amused at my discomfort with the use of the musician-speak. "Yes that's what I call it. And I don't meet a lot of women gigging."

"Really? So the women in the audience aren't coming up to you and tossing their panties at you?"

"Nope, as much as I'd love that. I can honestly say that even in the bars where I'm sure there were a few ladies not wearing panties, I've never had any find their way to me. The occasional drink, yes... some phone numbers, business cards, some food... at times. But never ever any panties."

"Oh, poor you. Maybe we'll just have to change that!" I was biting my lower lip and giving him my best pout.

He laughed. "Speaking of food, you hungry?"

"Sure, I could nibble on a little something."

"Then we'll have to order a little something because all I brought with me was a big something!" He smirked.

Joey ordered us a plate of calamari rings with two sauces, a basil infused pomodoro sauce and a fresh tzatziki sauce. Our little feast also included a filo-wrapped baked Brie slice with cranberries, rum, raisins, cinnamon and rosemary served with toasted pita wedges.

"Do you like to cook?" Joey asked.

"Love it! It's one of my passions! I love getting right into it, just immersing myself in it, allowing me the freedom to be creative and try new things."

"You sound like you cook with wild abandon. Do you do anything else with the same verve?"

"Well yes, yes I do." I pursed my lips and rolled my eyes playfully. "And sometimes it also includes food."

He grinned, took a sip of his drink and just stared, saying nothing, but the twinkle in his eyes told of the many thoughts dancing through his head.

He fed me my first taste of the second dish, keeping his finger near my lips a little longer than was necessary, but exactly long enough for me to brush it with my tongue as my open mouth accepted his offering.

It was after the first large glass of wine, post appetisers and about mid way through our second drink that Joey insisted he join me on my side of the booth. "Can I come over there?" he asked. I put up no fight. It saved us both from reaching across the table to close the physical distance between us.

He slid in beside me and now I could feel the strength of his obvious well-toned muscles as his biceps brushed my arm and his rock hard thighs grazed mine.

Our gazes taunted each other. All the while I was screaming in my head "kiss me… kiss me NOW!" I was *so* attracted to this man. I wanted to taste his lips. I wanted to sample his tongue. I wanted to explore his mouth urgently with mine. I wanted him to press that rigid body against me.

I thought he was going in for the kiss. I hadn't realised that I sat there beside him in the booth and had crossed my arms over my chest defensively. Maybe this had been an unconscious defensive gesture on my part because I sensed the physical power that this man had over me. Joey reached over and opened me up. With his two hot strong hands, one on each of mine, he physically took control and uncrossed my arms, placing each one to the side. He then looked at me with raised eyebrows, and gave an approving nod. He was proud of himself. He was definitely a take-charge man.

I felt my breathing quicken.

He stared deep into my eyes, suggesting hints of an erotic journey to come while he continued to tease me by softly caressing the palm of the hand closest to him, then up inside the arm, then back down again. His continuous gaze was broken only by his taunting words, "How does that feel?"

I couldn't answer so I just bit my lip.

It felt a-m-a-z-i-n-g, but why wasn't he kissing me?

Motivated by my inability to speak, my rapid breathing and a growing dampness, I was about to end this torture, take the lead and initiate the first kiss when I felt his glance move from my face downward. He surveyed my breasts, formed the faintest of smiles and raised his eyebrows approvingly and suggested that it might be time to leave.

I was confused. I thought things were just getting interesting.

We paid the bill. He helped me on with my coat with a slow deliberate shoulder caress, then placed his hand in the small of my back, leading me to the exit where he held the door for me to step out of the restaurant first.

"Where are you parked?"

I pointed to my car.

He reached for my hand and entwined his hot, long fingers with mine as he walked me to it.

Rather than unlock the door, I turned my back to it, looking at him straight on. I was getting a kiss from this man. My lips wanted him, my tongue wanted him, my breasts, my entire body was aching for his touch.

He stared for a moment, then raised both arms up, one either side of me, and placed his hands flat atop the roof of the car. He then pushed his whole body, crotch first, I might add, into me. I felt the obvious hardness of his manhood and the tautness of his body. His cologne filled my nostrils and then his lips reached mine - caressing, exploring, opening and allowing his tongue to take the lead. Our arms and hands did not touch but our mouths and bodies were connected and combining into one. Every part of me craved this man. The heat between us was searing, even though it was unseasonably chilly and a light rain had started to fall.

Between kisses he suggested we sit in the car while it warmed up.

I had a feeling it would warm quickly. He kept kissing me as he guided me into my seat.

He came around to the passenger's side, got in, looked at me, took my face in his cold hands and kissed me with a passion and intensity that caused my foot to press down hard on the gas pedal and rev the engine.

He broke away, still holding my face, still staring into my eyes and he said, "I've wanted to do that for the last two hours. How about we spend the next two actually doing it?"

Our hands moved up and down each other's bodies. I could feel my heart beating faster, my breath quickening, my nipples hardening and the wetness seeping out of me as we did.

I wanted to feel this man's skin on mine. I wanted to hold him tightly to me. I wanted to inhale his scent. I wanted to kiss and lick and suck and explore his body with an intensity I was not used to feeling. His body concurred. He wanted the same. His member was rock hard against me and it was huge. I wanted to see it, to stroke it, to lie there breathless, anticipating it making that first thrust into me, penetrating my wetness and filling me with its presence.

We agreed. We both wanted this to go further... and soon. He got out of my car, found his own and followed me home. While the drive gave me time to regain my composure somewhat, the heat of our shared desire was soon rekindled once we were both inside my foyer.

Our lips met, our tongues battled for the lead. Our teeth bit playfully. Our hands alternated between unbuttoning clothing and exploring each other's freshly exposed steaming flesh. Clothing pieces were dropped in the hall, over Dylan, on the stairs, on the upstairs landing, on the bedroom floor, with the very last pieces taking their rightful places at the foot of the bed.

The pace changed. We stood there, naked; drinking in each other's vulnerability, slowly caressing each other's hot wanting bodies. Our kisses lengthened and slowed in their intensity. Still upright, our unclothed bodies found a hypnotic rhythm and swayed in tune with each other's touch. Back and forth, rocking and swaying, kissing, and caressing, exploring and licking, rubbing and brushing against each other. I felt his thick chest hair sweep across my breasts, tickling my nipples as he moved from side to side. The sensation was breathtaking, sending a quiver that created a wave of goose bumps rippling outward covering my entire body.

Then, without warning, the song changed. It was like the bass guitar had just charged in for its solo riff. He grabbed me around the butt, lifted me up above him. I wrapped my legs around his waist. When I looked down I could see every muscle in his chest and arms bursting to the surface of his skin. He kissed my breasts, first one, then the other, before tossing me down on the bed. He centred himself, kneeling between my now spread legs. His eyes were seducing me and his body was lit only by the faint light wafting in from the hall. Through the dark shadows of my bedroom, I could still see that the man before me had the body of a chiselled Greek god. He was masculine and sculpted and hard and perfect. Broad shoulders, full rounded muscles, a small waist, visible abs and defined hips complete with an alluring Apollo's Belt.

In surveying this masterpiece of a man, I had my first real look at this musician's perfect organ. It was truly the most spectacular penis I had ever seen. Erect it was at least 10 inches long. Its circumcised head was perfectly formed with a noticeable slit that divided a circumference more sizeable than anything I had ever witnessed. His large well-formed balls were the size of kiwifruit but they needed to be that large to balance his imposing shaft. This man's penile girth rivalled that of a fresh baked baguette. I'm sure it would not have fit in my mouth.

My passion and hunger for him was tempered by the tiniest bit of fear.

Would I be able to accommodate something this large? I had never had sex with any man that had been so big. In moments of ecstasy, would it take me places I had never been? Or would it hurt? Worse yet, would it tear me or cause some other type of damage?

As he deftly placed a condom over his penis, I stared in awe. It was beautiful. And it was huge. Everything about this man was visually stunning. He was chiselled to perfection. There in my bed was a male masterpiece. I remember thinking that his parents must have been very attractive to have created such a perfect specimen.

He was so hard and so hot. I could feel the warmth from his thighs seep into mine as they pressed against me. Our bodies were calling out for each other, wanting to connect, needing to be entwined in every way possible. Thankfully, mine was moist in preparation for his generous gift.

He licked and kissed and playfully nibbled my neck before delivering a breathy "I want you" into my right ear that resonated through to my lusting loins. His mouth was firmly in place and his strong tongue enthusiastically explored and his lips sucked mine with an unbridled vigour. He splayed himself on top of me. The full length of my body felt his intense presence. His firm chest found its place on my heaving breasts and my soft belly welcomed his taut stomach. His pubic hair was entwining in mine. The head of his stiffness met my wetness and at that exact moment, he stopped kissing me, pulled his face back and stared into my eyes as if searching for my reaction.

Holding himself up by his muscular arms, I peered deeply into his eyes. I could not ignore my desire for him, my patience was at its end, I wanted to reach down and stroke his member with both my hands, but with his arms spread wide, he held them tightly under his. He scanned my face for a reaction as he began teasing and taunting my hollowness, inserting the large head of his penis ever so slightly, then retreating, then again, just a little deeper each time.

After a few rounds of this, I was writhing in wanting and my need to have him inside, filling me with his strength and presence was erupting. My hips shifted around and ground deeper into the bed in an effort to encourage him. My vagina was circling the probing head and covering it with my dampness. All the while my clitoris was swelling with excitement as it was being kneaded by the combination of a full and soft mound of pubic hair covering a strong and assertive pelvis.

He moved to his elbows, still staring and not kissing me. My hands were free. They searched up and down his back, feeling the definition in his back, the bone, the muscle and the full strength of his torso as it imprinted itself upon me. I remained silent, as did he. But I continued to gyrate to communicate my yearning for him. It was a depth of hunger that I had rarely experienced, a wanton desire to connect with him on every level.

His gaze intensified. His hip movements stopped, mine followed suit. My hands ceased their exploration. Then, in one pointed thrust, he plunged himself inside of me. I expected heights of pleasure. I expected to welcome him and yearn for thrust after thrust. I expected to climax to heights I had never experienced.

But in that instant I was shocked. I was fuller than I had ever been. I had been pierced. The pain was searing. He did not evoke moans of pleasure but those of pain. This man was huge and it hurt. Oh, how it hurt!

There was more than ample wetness to glide him in, but he was just too big for me. I had heard of this but never had experienced it – quite often my experiences had been at the opposite end of the scale. But this was unbearable. I could not enjoy this. He was thrusting inside me and I had to stop him. I pushed him away. With my eyes wide in shock, a pained cry escaped my lips both before and after I cried, "Joey! Stop, please stop!"

His face belied a knowing yet thwarted look.

Joey pulled out of me, pulled back and in his confusion asked, "Kayte, what's wrong? Am I hurting you?" His voice suggested that he knew the answer.

"I can't believe I'm actually saying this, but, um, ah, I think you're too big for me. I've never seen, let alone accommodated anyone so… I'll say it… gargantuan."

His look was a combination of sheer pride and familiar disappointment. "I don't know whether to apologise or thank you for the compliment. I am sorry if I hurt you though." He turned onto one hip facing me and his massive member now rested in its waning firmness alongside my thigh. I remember thinking that it was almost the size of my forearm. I was fascinated by it. I had never ever in person seen anything so imposing. Never. I also remember thinking that I'd love to get a camera or a measuring tape, but knew that was way too tacky. But man… it was huge… I couldn't wait to share this one with Chloe… not literally, though there certainly would have been enough to go around!

After an awkward silence I kissed him.

We began a tactile exploration of each other with the light caress of fingertips. We sought out other ways besides intercourse to please each other and we found a way to revel in our unmistakable chemistry. It was like Joey was my chem lab partner, my bed our laboratory, and we curiously conducted experiment after experiment, testing our various hypotheses knowing that our chemistry had few limits.

We spent hours touching, teasing, tickling, massaging, tasting and treating each other to a sensual feast. We rubbed oil and then lotion; we melted ice cubes, tickled lightly across hot skin and plunged deeply inside various crevices. We dipped various body parts into hot wax then drizzled it across each other. We rubbed coarse salt flakes, tequila and lime and licked it all off. We playfully slapped and tapped each other with rubber spatulas, hairbrushes and even found new uses for a vibrating toothbrush.

We sustained ourselves by first playing with then consuming yogurt, berries, bananas, dark chocolate and champagne. We found a use for stockings and elastic bands and blindfolds, feathers and beads. We licked and sucked each other to orgasm before we collapsed together in sweet sensual exhaustion. We showered together and lathered each other - inserting soapy fingers in new hiding places. We both obviously enjoyed the experiments and there was something incredibly liberating about knowing that actual penile penetration was not on the menu. We experienced the joy of numerous orgasms. I learned that he truly was a creative spirit. I also learned a great deal about my own wants, desires and reactions. And duly noted some of the most enjoyable bits for future reference.

It was very early the next morning when Joey embarked upon his own treasure hunt. He retraced the steps of the night before to find his various articles of clothing. He dressed his Grecian Godlike body to leave. I remained naked and vulnerable as I walked him to the door.

Our kiss goodbye was long and sweet and calming, but final. Our mouths were certainly right for each other. We had chatted lots that evening, but I knew that this would be the last time that I saw Joey Cuirissma. Beyond the intercourse incompatibility I knew he was not my dream guy. During our conversations at the bar, I learned that he was probably too bohemian, ungrounded and free-spirited a soul for me and I was too corporate, settled and traditional a chick for him. While the sexual chemistry was undeniable and it was a wonderful evening, this was not a lasting love match. But there were no apologies. We were both very happy with who we were and we enjoyed our time together but both were looking for a more suitable match. So we said our farewell with a smile and sincere positive wishes for each other in finding what we truly wanted and deserved.

We both had a clearer idea of what that was and wasn't as a result of meeting each other. I felt a liberation I had never known and for that I was grateful to have met Joey.

When the door closed behind him, I wondered if Tommy was home yet.

CHAPTER 32

With the door closed on another hopeful, I was transported to a familiar place, that doubtful place where I wondered if it were really possible for me to find love. And was online dating helping or hindering the process? I questioned why love remained so elusive and examined my own worthiness.

Why did I find it so difficult when others found it without effort? How many men would I have to meet, date, sleep with until I found him? When would I be able to turn around and wave a heartfelt goodbye to my single life? Where was he? Why wasn't I meeting him? Was I doing the wrong things? Was I asking for too much? Should I lower my expectations? Should I change myself? Did I need to be more feminine? Less independent? More demure? Less confident? Had I missed my chance? Had I met Mr. Right and not known it? Was he in my circle of friends and acquaintances? Who was he with right now? Was he finding it this hard to find love? Or had it come easily for him? Was this love stuff all a trumped up romantic notion that had no basis in reality?

It wasn't that I really thought Joey was "the one". But I sure wanted to find "the one" and soon. I was tired of dating, exhausted by the roller coaster. It had lost its thrill. I wanted something more stable.

I wanted to meet my man and start our lives together. I yearned to be someone's girlfriend, someone's fiancée, someone's wife, to learn about myself through the eyes of another to have that deep emotional intimacy that can only come from that special connection, to be the smile on my man's face, to feel so connected to another that being apart felt incomplete. I longed to know that I had truly found my soul mate, to feel special and spoiled, appreciated, respected and cherished for exactly who I was, to be loved warts and all. I dreamed of being the best cheerleader, supporter, coach, caregiver, confidante, friend, lover and emotional connection that my lover had ever experienced. My aim was to be strong and tender and sensitive and wise and open and firm in my values all at the same time. I wanted to be with someone who needed all the best parts of me and from whom I needed all his strengths. I wanted to grow together and learn from and with my partner. I wanted to see the world through his eyes, but keep my vision and adjust it where the new perspective made sense, become better people together, to evolve in our own identities as we continued to develop our combined oneness. Yes, I wanted it all.

I opened my ideal mate list again and read it over and over. It contained over fifty things I was looking for in my perfect man.

Was this way too long a list? Could he really exist? If he did, what did he look like? Where did he live? What did he do for a living? What had his life been like, who were his friends, how would we meet, how would we know that it was it, true love? Should I just throw away the list and trust myself to fate?

The more I thought about it, the more I kept coming back to that notion that I simply could not settle for just anyone. I needed the man from this list. I deserved the man on this list.

But then there were those times when the loneliness was just unbearable. I spent too many days rattling around an empty home. Yes it was furnished, yes it was comfortable, but it wasn't filled with the laughter, tears and lives of a family, or even a partner – it was just me.

Then there were the times when I was faced with life's unavoidable challenges. Like those occasions when money was tight. I didn't have another pair of shoulders to bear the load. I didn't have someone to be strong for me when I felt vulnerable. No, I didn't have a partner to share the responsibility for getting through the obstacles. No one to throw their arms around me and assure me that everything would be okay. I didn't have someone who could fill my tanks back up after I had poured every drop of them out to encourage or support a friend, family member or in just meeting the demands of my day to day job.

Those were the moments I dreaded. Not only were they horrendously painful, dark and soul testing, they were also the times when I seriously considered pairing up with someone, anyone, the next man who came along. I certainly wasn't considering an axe murderer, but I considered the possibility of any number of regular Joes. These were the times when I wanted to abandon my list, just to experience being part of a couple. It was then that I felt that this loneliness might have the power to force me to surrender my dreams, give up my wish list, forget about passion and lower my expectations about the man I wanted to connect with and the life I envisioned for us.

Yes, this loneliness led me to craving someone to do one chore around the house, pay a bill, answer one phone call, take one bag to the trash, put on one load of laundry, clean a toilet, paint a single wall, make one dinner, give me one hug, surprise me with one breakfast in bed.

I would be so grateful for some help rather than always having to bear the responsibility alone. I needed someone to drive away these feelings of despair. I needed someone to hug me, hold me and love me.

I felt more isolated and unloved with every year and every time I started, then ended, another relationship. It was getting harder and harder to keep putting myself out there.

Where was Mr. Right? Would I ever find the love I desired? These were the questions that haunted my otherwise strong and happy life, mind and soul.

I made a coffee then made my way to the computer. I hadn't been near it for almost 48 hours. I found the usual spam, a joke from Chloe, a note from Alex from Ardent saying he'd quit and was starting with a new firm next week. And a note from Roman sent the previous day.

From: Bigbadwolf@socialarity.com
To: K8@socialarity.com
Subject: Just Checking In...

...'cause I've already checked you out - LOL! So where you been, sexy? I called you a couple of times today and no answer. Wondered if you wanted to do dinner and then maybe... ME!

LMAO.

PS Been on a hot date or something?

I had no idea where to even begin to answer that one. *Was he trying to ask me out on a date?* I couldn't do that. I was still regretting 'the incident'. Since then, I had promised myself that I wouldn't have any more than three drinks in an evening.

What if he really liked me? Wanted to date me? How would I be able to tell him that I had no interest in him that way? How would I be able to keep our friendship? Did I still even want to? I didn't know, so I did what anyone would have done. I put it off. I didn't answer the email. That was the beauty of it. You could reply in isolation, when, and only when, you were ready. You could say everything you wanted to say, edit it until you got it exactly right. You'd hit send and then it was gone. You weren't interrupted. You could put everything out there all at once. And then let the recipient deal with your words. You didn't have to edit if you saw a hurt look. You didn't have to explain further if they didn't seem to get it. You had done your part, the rest was up to them.

I'd think of the right response. But it would take some pondering.

I had left my chat status as away. I referred to this as 'trolling'. People can send you messages while you're away, but they can't if you're offline. This way it feeds the curiosity, that burning need to know if anyone was trying to make contact. I had one trolled message from Roman saying much the same as his email.

I would have to connect with him at some point, but it would have to wait.

CHAPTER 33

There were no messages from Tommy as I made my daily email check, but I was sure it was only a matter of time.

He had come home last night. He'd be back online today.

In the meantime, Dylan and I had a date. We were visiting a new leash-free park. I'd heard it was huge and well appointed with the latest dog playground equipment. It was nothing but the best for my Dylan.

"C'mon boy. You ready to go to the park?" He was at my side in seconds. His mouth hung open, his eyes were glistening. He was a big golden ball of exuberance and energy.

We leapt into the car and drove off in anticipation. He knew he'd be free to run with a pack of canines and I'd be touched by his sincere boundless joy.

As we got close, Dylan could smell all the other dogs in the air. He stood up in the back seat and started pacing back and forth across the bench. Even over the radio I could hear his excited cry. It resonated in the base of his throat. He ran from window to window. He stuck his nose out the crack in the window with quick shorts sniffs against the glass, covering the top two inches of the window with his damp nose prints.

We arrived at The Ruff and Tumble Dog Park and I could not have opened the door fast enough. Dylan bounded out and didn't even look back. True to form he went right for two other Goldens who were battling for the power position in order to claim the bright purple rubber disc soaring through the air.

I scanned the park, heard barks and whistles and laughter and the faint jingle of dog tags as the dogs ran and jumped beside, beneath and atop each other. This was a place of fun, of freedom and love. These canines came here and their spirits soared. They were free to be themselves, to find friends and explore. Dogs have a way of reminding us of what's really important, of being present only in the moment and squeezing as much enjoyment out of it as possible.

I spotted Dylan with a mouth full of rainbow-coloured rag bone, heading my way. I was calling him now. "C'mon boy, bring that to Mommy". He stopped, looked at me, and ran off to his left.

Dylan slowed his pace until he stopped and dropped the rag bone at the feet of a panting one-eyed Bernese Mountain Dog and his very handsome owner. The man crouched down low and gave Dylan a thank you pat with both hands – one behind each big droopy ear. Dylan was smiling and soaking in every bit of attention. Then Dylan did something I had never seen him do before. He sat back on his hind feet, placed his front paws around his new friend's neck and gave him what looked like a great big hug.

Sure, Dylan got a hug from Bryan. What did I get? Stood up.

I guess Bryan wasn't all bad. It still didn't mean I was going to talk to him, especially the way I was dressed.

Maybe, just maybe, it was time for me to go back online and send him an email or dig out his phone number and make contact again. Or maybe not. After all, he did stand me up. No call, no explanation, no email afterwards. Nothing.

I looked at him again, standing there with Wink and tossing toys for the other puppies to retrieve. Maybe. I'd consider it. Or at least wear makeup and a better outfit next time I took Dylan to the dog park.

CHAPTER 34

Showered, changed, makeup applied, I checked a couple of emails, deleted a few rogue spam messages, learned that the word of the day was 'disinclination' and without any further keyboard foreplay, found myself back on wheresinglesfindlove.com.

Now where was Dylan's new boyfriend's profile? I had favourited him at one point, but after the no-show, I thought I might have deleted it.

What was his profile name? It was powerful - it had something to do with passion. I typed in 'Passionate'. No such name. 'Pashinate'. Nope. Then 'Pashinate1'. Still no. What if he no longer had a profile up? What if I couldn't reach out from the safe distance of my keyboard? What if I had to get dressed up and visit the dog park every day for weeks in the hopes that I'd run into him? Not that I would, even though Dylan would love it.

I think we ended up chatting off the site so I'd have his email. Do I even remember the date? Sorting through my conversation history was very telling indicating how many hours I'd been spending online. I thought of it as time well invested. If this was what it took to find my dream guy, if it worked, every word, every false start, every non-connection would be worth it.

Tommy showed up in my online chat window

Tomtom says:
Murrr… rowwww… KaytieKat… murrr…rowww"

K8 says:
Hehehe - well hello there - I have to admit, you never cease to bring a smile to my face

Tomtom says:
would that be a Cheshire grin?

K8 says:
It would indeed

Tomtom says:
good - 'cause that look is right up my …alley

K8 says:
Oh really?

Tomtom says:
Yep and I've been known to enjoy a little _____

K8 says:
DON'T you DARE say it… or TYPE it!

Tomtom says:
Ah, Kayte, that's the great thing about us, I don't have to - you and I both know what I'm thinking

K8 says:
Yes, already I can read your mind

Tomtom says:
That's not hard. I'm an open book. I'll never be able to keep anything from you

K8says:
And I wouldn't want you to

Tomtom says:
that's so true - in a relationship, it's so much better when
you feel comfortable sharing everything - okay maybe not
EVERYTHING, I don't care how close we get, I don't think I could
get used to you sharing my underwear, and come to think of it, I
call dibs on the red lifesavers too

K8 says:
You're safe - the underwear? Not a good look on me - but you
may just have to share a red one once in a while

Tomtom says:
oh baby, I'll share a red one...

K8 says:
Ohhhh geesh... we're not back there again are we?

Tomtom says:
yes Kayte, we are, now move over, this is MY gutter!

K8 says:
Then stop draggin' me in there... hehehehe

Tomtom says:
So missy, what are you up to? sorting through your online
suitors and lining up a few dates?

K8 says:
Ya caught me. So many men, so little time!

Tomtom says:
If you can fit it in, did you still want that tap fixed? I'm around
this week and would be happy to strap on my tool belt and have
a look at it for you.

K8 says:
That's so sweet. Yes, it's even worse now than before, constantly
leaking.

Tomtom says:
Then we better see to it. How about Tuesday? I could come by
after work.

K8 says:

That'd be wonderful. How 'bout if you fix my tap, I'll fix us
something for dinner for your trouble?

Tomtom says:
Not necessary.

K8 says:
Not necessary, but might be nice.

Tomtom says:
Nah, I'd rather have you all beholden to me. Kidding! Seriously,
sounds good. Just don't go to too much trouble.

K8 says:
Okay - something basic. Maybe barbequed burgers.

Tomtom says:
I like basic, but I LOVE burgers. Burgers and beer... mmm. Better
yet, burgers, beer and boobies...

K8 says:
OK, I'm not going there. I'll see you Tuesday.

Tomtom says:
Yep about 6-ish. I'll be the guy wearing the tool belt... wink wink

K8 says:
I'll be the gal wearing the boobies! Kayte - out!

And with that I signed off before he could type another word.
My heart leapt a little. I was flush with anticipation. I so enjoyed
our online exchanges. I felt challenged and flirtatious and
energised all at once. He hadn't even been here for a meal yet, but
I was already making a mental list of other home improvements
and repair projects that would serve as fabulous excuses to get
him back again and again.

Now what would I wear?

"Okay so I need something sexy but casual, something flirty but not trying too hard… something that showcases 'the girls', but doesn't look too slutty."

"First date?" The sales woman was giggling as she sifted through the racks helping me to find the perfect piece. I was obviously entertaining her with my list of requirements.

"How'd you guess?"

"I've been doing this a long time." She was nodding knowingly. "How about this?" She pulled a royal blue, flowing, rather sheer blouse from the rack directly in front of us.

"Hmmm… I like it, but I think it might be a bit froufrou for what I'm looking for. I want to look feminine, but feminine and strong, not feminine and delicate, not that I could really pull off delicate."

"Okay, cleaner lines, still somewhat sheer but less fluid, more cling?"

She was holding up a black three-quarter sleeved sweater that had a subtle sheen to it. While I hadn't gone with the intention of buying yet another black top, I was captivated by the obvious quality of the piece, demonstrated by its unique texture. The material had the finest ribbing I had ever seen and the fabric was almost shiny. The combination just begged you to reach out and touch it. When you did, instead of ridges it delivered a soft, smooth yet dense and cool experience, not unlike the feel of satin.

The cut was a simple tunic style with a deeply formed v-neckline that exposed most of the chest, but not too plunging. The sleeves hung loosely, but the bodice was intended to be rather tight fitting. I was intrigued by its simplicity and immediately made off to the fitting room to try it on.

I slipped it over my head and felt its coolness tickle my shoulders, then my back, my arms, then my stomach. It was tight but not binding. It was chic and sexy, but not overly enticing. Most of the flat part of my chest was exposed and the cut displayed just the right amount of recently tanned cleavage.

It fit perfectly. This was the one. My skin came alive under its touch. I wanted to wear it out of the store and never take it off. I settled for a few more minutes standing there in its reassuring embrace. I enjoyed a rare moment of admiration in the fitting room mirror. I was proudly staring at a happier, more relaxed, fitter version of myself. I was pleased with where I was. I had the time and focus to appreciate it. And I was excited about where I might be going.

"So?" There was a tentative tap at the door… "How'd we do? Are you in love?"

"Yes, yes, yes… this is definitely coming home with me"

"Let me have a look before you take it off."

I stepped through the door. Sarah, the sales clerk, just stood there with a pursed lip smile, nodding her head up and down. "I think we found a perfect match. You were meant for that and it for you."

"Yes, and I have the perfect skirt at home to match it. This was definitely easier than I thought. I might just go looking for a new bra and panties to match or is that being too optimistic?"

CHAPTER 35

"Okay boy, let's get you some water." Dylan was panting hard, his tongue almost dragging on the ground, yet he still maintained that silly grin on his little doggy face.

My muscles were humming, my t-shirt was drenched, my face crimson and I, too, was panting. If I could've hung my tongue out of my mouth to cool down like Dylan did I would have. Instead, I'd have to settle for a cold shower.

According to my running app we had run a new personal best distance today... 12K.

"We did 12K today boy. That's a record!" And one I was quite proud of because I had never been a runner, but I was almost enjoying it now. Dylan had dribbled a trail of water droplets from his dish to where he now lay splayed out on the cool tile floor, his whole body heaving with each pant. He was tired. Thankfully this would last the rest of the day and he'd be calm that night when Tommy was there.

I felt good. My body was abuzz from the hour-plus run. I had purposely had very little to eat. When you combined both of those with a long steamy shower, a stunning new outfit, date underwear and lots of time to get prepared, I was ready for Tommy that night. Very ready.

He'd be there in less than two hours so I had better get started. I didn't want to rush a thing.

Dylan let out a short announcement bark. I glanced at my watch; it was Tommy time. I gave one last glance in the bedroom mirror. I was very pleased with the final result. My hair was full and curly. I had applied makeup with the detail and intricacy of a painter. The vision staring back from the mirror had dark, captivating and sultry eyes, cherry sun-kissed cheeks with a glow that extended across the top of my nose. It was punctuated by the shiniest and most luscious lips you could ever want to kiss. And the skin on my neck and chest – everywhere, for that matter – was so soft that it screamed to be caressed. I had massaged a half bottle of moisturiser into my entire body following my shower. For the final touch, I had just applied another dab to my hands.

The new top was paired with a clean straight-cut black and white print skirt that fell mid-shin and had a long slit reaching up to mid thigh exposing just enough well tanned leg. The skirt was one I had not been able to fit into for months so it added an extra air of confidence to the ensemble.

I drew in a long breath, threw back my shoulders, did the bat check then the tooth inspection (visions of Roger and his tooth refuse still haunted me), scanned the bedroom and bathroom to ensure I hadn't left anything telling lying around.

The doorbell rang again as I reached the top of the stairs. I could feel my heart beating hard in my chest, harder than during my run earlier that day. I didn't think I'd be this nervous. All that was left between Tommy and me was for me to descend the stairway that led directly to the foyer. From the front door he could see halfway up the staircase so I had an opportunity to make a grand entrance. Hopefully, as I descended each step he'd be getting more and more excited, just as I was.

My heart had almost reached my mouth. I hesitated. Then, quelling my inner date critic I gathered my composure, set one foot in front of the other and began down the stairs. I took the next step, took a breath, the next step, another breath. My chest was heaving. I could feel my cheeks high on my face from my animated grin and I knew my eyes had to be sparkling with excitement. I could see Tommy's frame filling the doorway from my perch. I was noticing his broad shoulders and full chest, giving him a good look over as I took the next step. The adrenalin was pumping. I was just about to welcome him into my home. Hopefully he'd greet me with a strong lingering hug.

I took another step closer to this sexy man who had captivated me for weeks now. My right foot hit hard rubber where carpet should have been, twisting to the right and throwing me off balance. The object rolled from beneath my foot and Dylan's favourite chew toy, his black Kong bounced randomly down the remaining five stairs. I grabbed for the handrail to steady myself and my newly moisturised hand found it then slid right off. In that instant I knew I was going down. My butt hit the stairs. Then it was my back's turn, then my left shoulder blade. I slid down the remaining steps, twisting and pulling my skirt up around my waist, exposing both of my freshly shaven and well tanned legs. I landed in a thud onto Dylan's bed that sat at the foot of the stairs. Given it was nothing more than a big material cushion that sat atop ceramic tile floor, both it and I then slid into my final resting place, knees pressed against the glass front screen door where Tommy stood watching every moment and taking in every excruciating detail.

I was mortified, but happy I had purchased new underwear.

I looked out the door and was staring directly at Tommy's crotch. After a cursory inspection, I timidly raised my humiliated gaze up his chest to his face.

Tommy's expression was a mix of shock, concern, helplessness and I think I detected a wee bit of laughter.

I was speechless. Thankfully he broke the ice. "Well I've had women fall for me before but none quite so enthusiastically. I'll tell you what, I'll definitely give you an 8.5 for artistic impression."

I wanted to cry but I couldn't quell the laughter that was erupting inside me. I knew one thing. This was not the impression I had planned on making, but I could sulk and make it worse or laugh and get on with the evening.

Dylan licked my face as Tommy opened the door and helped me to my feet, almost losing a grip on my still slippery hands.

"So do we need to call an ambulance?"

"No. It's too late to save my ego and the body is a little stiff, but I should be fine." I was rearranging my skirt, and adjusting my top as I sheepishly stood facing Tommy in the doorway.

"Nothing wrong with a little stiff," I heard him claim softly over my right shoulder. He had turned me around and was guiding me into the living room. "Well Missy, I'd suggest we get you to a soft seat, apply some ice to reduce the possibility of swelling, and get you a big glass of wine to dull the pain - sound alright to you?"

"Sounds perfect." I glanced over my shoulder with a grateful smile.

"Okay, sit," Tommy commanded. I turned to see Dylan had immediately complied with the order that was meant for me. I laughed as I took a spot on the sofa leaving plenty of room beside me.

"Ow... laughing hurts!"

"Uh oh, this may require more wine than I thought. Now, where are your glasses? And will we be having red or white? Oh yes, I remember. I suppose the white is chilling here in the fridge." Tommy winked and smiled.

I felt tingly. However, not in any area I had bumped down the stairs, but in a hidden, less obvious spot. It felt so good to be fussed over. I had planned on doing the fussing but this felt so much better. It made me sad to think how rarely I experienced this feeling.

"Here we go." Tommy handed me a chilled New Zealand Chardonnay I had chosen especially for this evening. His hands were large and vascular. Strong man hands. I noticed that the glass was filled to its widest part – I wondered if this was accidental or whether he actually knew the proper way to pour. I wish I had watched to see if the bottle had touched the glass and whether or not he twisted the bottle to prevent stray droplets as he removed the bottle from the glass. I'd take more notice on the next pour.

"Thanks. I should have done that but given that my back, butt and legs were beginning to throb, I was happy to let you. Will you be cooking dinner too?" I giggled and winced all at the same time.

He sat down beside me, close enough that I could feel heat emanating from his long muscular arm. "Geesh woman, do I have to do everything? Find my tools, drive to your house, pick the lady up off the floor, serve the wine, make the dinner and fix the tap? Some hostess. The next thing you'll be asking is for me to walk the dog."

"Nah, he doesn't need one. He's still exhausted from our run today."

"How far did you go?"

"12K."

"Wow, that's incredible. So let me get this straight, the lady can run 12K but she can't walk down a single flight of stairs?"

"It's a gift!" With that we raised our glasses, clinked, laughed, took a sip of the woody chardonnay and then laughed some more.

"Owww… this really hurts." I had to dull this pain or stop

laughing. "I think I can feel the bruises forming. I hope I didn't break anything." I took another mouthful of wine.

"Do you want me to take a look?"

"No thanks, Tommy, I'm sure I'll be fine."

"Cause you know I don't mind." It was his eager seductive grin that was hitting me harder than either the stairs or the wine. I thought, I'd better be careful with this one.

"Perhaps a little later." I wanted to present myself to him as perfectly as possible. My back, butt and legs covered in a mosaic of greens, blues and yellows, was not exactly the colourful Kayte I had in mind.

"How about after I fix that tap then?"

"Perfect."

He got up and went to the kitchen to assess the situation. "Easy. I'll just go grab my tools and have this done in a jiff. I'd better be fast, because I've got lots to do – making dinner, filling wine glasses and all."

I felt bad. This was not how the evening was supposed to transpire. When he was out at his car, I pulled the homemade burgers from the fridge (simple, he said he wanted simple) and when I bent down to reach for the huge salad, I couldn't believe the pain. I actually shrieked. It was at that moment that Tommy returned, toolbox in hand and tool belt hanging on his hips. It's a cliché, but it was quite a look.

He rushed to the kitchen, placed the toolbox on the floor, grabbed the salad bowl from my hand, put it on the counter and asked if there was anything else we needed for dinner. I directed him to the buns and the foil packet containing sliced potatoes, onions, garlic, parsley and grated old cheddar.

"Okay Missy, I will get to barbequing this fine feast in just a minute. But first little lady, I want you to sit and do nothing while I fix this." Tommy took charge and I obediently moved to the sofa, sitting purposely in a spot where I had a clear view.

When he opened his toolbox, I saw that it was incredibly well organised, neat and clean, especially for a toolbox – check! He whistled while he worked. I don't know if this was for my benefit or a habit, but he genuinely seemed to be enjoying the task. A naturally happy guy – check!

He seemed to know what he was doing; very methodical, and I didn't hear any swearing or frustration along the way. Check!

I watched as his muscular arms tightened the tap back into place. He was bent over slightly so I had the added benefit of a good clear view of his butt. Well rounded, firm, very nice. Double check.

"Are you staring at my bum?" He was laughing as he looked over his left shoulder. I didn't think I had been perving on his backside that long. Had I been that obvious? Could he have felt my eyes on him?

"Me? Would I do that?"

"You're a woman aren't you? I do have a rather nice one, or so I've been told. So I understand it may be hard to resist." I could see his shoulders moving up and down and, while I couldn't hear it, I knew he was laughing his handsome hiney off. He had a good sense of humour and it seemed he could easily amuse himself. Check!

"Not that I'm an expert but, yes, I'd have to agree."

"There. All finished!" And with that declaration, he put on a little show for me. He picked up each tool individually then, in exaggerated motions, bent over, holding the pose for far too long, giving me a full view of his dashing derrière. And then he picked up the next and the next until they were all packed neatly away again. Snapping closed his toolbox, he turned around and stood there. He was quite a sight, his six-foot-two broad-shouldered frame with his tool belt hugging his hips. With a big smile, he said, "Now that the tap is fixed, how 'bout I fix us some dinner?"

I felt so looked after, so content to just let go the reins and let someone else take over for a while. He was easy to surrender to. And he took up the challenge willingly and with great delight.

"Thanks. That would be perfect." I uncrossed my legs and motioned to get up.

"You just sit back down. Let me wash my hands, get you some more wine and then I'll put dinner on. You stay put." Wash his hands? Get me more wine? Cook dinner? Check, check, check! Tommy was thoughtful and attentive. I was so glad he was there. It was so comfortable, almost familiar.

"And that's an order" I heard echo from the bathroom down the hall.

The burgers were delicious and juicy and the potatoes so tasty and filling, but the most enjoyable part of the dinner had been the conversation. It flowed easily, no uncomfortable pauses, just a pleasant tour from topic to topic. Tommy and I had similar upbringings. We shared many of the same references, seemed to have similar values about money, family, morals, religion, sex. Where we differed was that he had married relatively young, had a family, two kids, and I had been married to my career with Dylan being my only dependent. We pondered what it might have felt like for each of us had it been the reverse. It helped us both to see the benefits of our respective realities.

He had an engaging way about him, a hearty laugh and a sparkle in his eyes as he spoke and a calm intent in them as he listened. I noticed this shy boyish quirk when he was revealing something about himself where he would suck in the left corner of his lower lip while he changed his glance slightly downward and to the left with a half closed left eye. It was almost as if he wasn't sure he should be sharing that information, but it appeared that he was comfortable enough with me to do so. I took that as a great compliment. In turn, I shared more with him about my past and my hopes for the future than I had even with Mike.

We had sat over empty plates for over an hour when I made the suggestion to move to the sofa. Instead of going directly there, he headed to the kitchen counter with plate and a serving bowl in hand. I followed. We stood together in the small kitchen, no words, just a shared sense of connectedness and contentment from the enjoyment of each other's presence.

He reached around and took the plate from my hands. I noticed his large, strong hands, watching as his long fingers wrapped themselves around the plate and placed it down ever so gently. I wondered how these hands would feel enveloping mine, how they might excite my skin as they made their way up my arms. I wondered how it would feel to be held in his muscular embrace. I couldn't tell whether it was the wine or the presence of this intriguing man that made me feel so giddy and aroused, but I was and I wanted to stay there, in this tiny kitchen, sharing this small space with this large man.

He must have felt it too. He turned to me, said nothing and looked shyly, yet curiously into my eyes. His left hand reached down to my right wrist turning my hand so that it rested open yet protected inside his large outstretched palm. At the same time, his right hand with the index finger outstretched had reached up and was lifting my chin and my gaze. Our eyes were locked on each other. I could feel my lips parting slightly in anticipation. There was a soft tingle making its way down my body. I felt my heartbeat quicken, and my nipples tighten. My stomach was whirring and there was a growing sensation between my legs. I could feel my heels lift lightly off the floor as his finger raised my chin more firmly, drawing my mouth up closer to meet his. I stared into his eyes. I could feel my heart beating at the back of my throat. My breasts and hips were screaming to press themselves against him. I could feel the heat from his fingers on my chin and neck, then from his breath, then from the softness of his lips as they slowly reached down to meet mine. I wasn't breathing. I could feel myself begin to kiss back, tentatively at first. Then my body moved closer to his. His left hand had moved to the small of my back and I could feel him guiding me to him. My mouth opened wider, I could feel the heat and moisture from his tongue as he began exploring my willing mouth. Our tongues found a rhythm and hungrily explored each other. He tasted familiar. Our lips had moved from soft gentle encounters to more eager and firm connections. He wrapped both arms around me now and my hands moved up to explore his face and neck. I felt my body surrender and meld into his, my nipples thrust against him just below his own and his growing hardness pressed firmly against my belly creating a growing heat, hunger and moistness below.

I could feel his rock hard erection fighting with his pants as they grew tighter and tighter around it. I wanted to liberate it, but knew that would be premature. I didn't want things to go any further on this date. Okay, I did want them to go further but I knew that looking longer term it would be better if we waited. Especially given that almost half my body was likely black and blue by now.

Tommy pulled me even tighter and while I wanted to get as close to him as possible, I winced in pain as his hand found one of the more sensitive spots from the fall, at the top of my buttocks, just below my waist.

He felt me cringe and then pulled away.

"Oh did I hurt you? Kayte, I'm so sorry. I guess I was getting a little carried away, caught up in the moment."

"It's okay. You were carrying me away right along with you."

"Is your back really that sore?"

"I think it's my butt that's that sore."

"You poor thing, your back is probably all bruised and here I am grabbing at you and poking you in the belly with a…"

We both erupted in laughter.

"I'm not complaining."

"Me neither, that was nice. Not where I had thought things would go, but nice."

What did he mean, "Not where he thought things would go?" Where did he think things would go? He was obviously interested. Wasn't he? Of course he was. I had a glock poking me in the gut as a firm indication of his interest. He enjoyed it. I enjoyed it. And it was where I was hoping things would go, even if he hadn't thought they would. Even if he didn't plan on going there, I'm sure he's glad they did.

"Kayte, Kayte… oh Kayte… "

"Yep, ya, I'm here."

"Do you want me to have a look, see if anything's really swollen? You could need to ice it if it is."

"No, I'm alright, really."

"Are you sure?"

"Hmmm… okay… I guess." I didn't want him to think I was jumping at the chance to show him my bare skin, but truthfully I was aching for his touch and couldn't wait to feel his hands directly on me.

He gently raised my top halfway up my back.

"Oh girl, you are going to be sore tomorrow. There's a big bruise that goes up your right side, not sure how far." He was lifting my top even more, exposing my back and my bra. At least he was getting a glimpse at the pretty lingerie.

"Very impressive."

"The bruise?"

"No, the lacy bra – very sexy. And I just happen to know that there are matching panties."

Maybe I should check your boo-tay to see if it's bruised too."

"No, that's quite alright." He gently pulled my top back down covering my exposes skin.

I turned to face Tommy. There we were standing just inches apart. I could feel the flush rise from my chest, up my neck and on through my cheeks.

I looked up and was met with the most gentle and sympathetic gaze looking down at me. I just stood there looking into his huge blue eyes trying to understand what he was thinking and feeling. I wanted to know him. Know how he thought, what he was thinking about me, how he was feeling about our evening, whether he wanted more or less. I wanted to know what frightened him, what he was unsure of. I wanted to know what excited him, what drove him, what he needed, what he needed in a mate, in a friend, in a woman, in a lover. I wanted to know how he wanted to be touched, where his weaknesses were, how he felt, whether he talked or moaned or was quiet as he made love, I wanted to know how he looked in that moment of ecstasy.

"Whatchya thinking there pretty lady?" His deep voice cut the silence. His eyes were sparkling with a warm and curious smile.

"Just thinking that I'd like to get to know you better."

"Really? Well know this, as much as I've enjoyed this evening, I do have to get going, it's a fair drive home. The street lights have been on for hours and it's far too late for me to be out on a school night. If I stay out too late, I certainly don't play well with others!"

I enjoyed his childhood references. It showed that he was in touch with that part of himself and I found that appealing as I had when I read his profile.

We made our way to the door and Dylan rose from his sprawled state and fell in behind. Standing in the front hall I sadly started the goodbye dialogue. I didn't want this night to end. Bruises and all, it had been a fabulous night with a wonderful guy. A guy who I knew I liked and found attractive. I wanted more, much more.

"Thanks for everything. I do appreciate the help. I can do a lot of things but I've never mastered plumbing." He was nodding. "Apparently, I have a tough time with stairs too!" I reached around and placed my hand where my now throbbing bruise was forming and shook my head.

He laughed. "That was all the butt plug's fault. That Kong thing really does look like one you know."

"Yes, I've heard that before. But here's a question for you. Just how come so many people know what butt plugs look like, yet so few ever admit to using them?"

"You make me laugh Kayte. And that's a good thing."

He bent down and gave Dylan a pat goodbye, ruffling his ears. "See ya little buddy. Look after your Mother and don't be expecting any walks tomorrow."

And on the way up, he placed both hands on my hips then ever so gently up my sides, then into the small of my back. I could feel myself tingle under his touch. He drew me closer to him. His face moved tentatively at first, then purposely, right to mine. My smiling lips partly slowly and his full, hot soft mouth met mine.

He stopped, slowly placed his large hands around my shoulders, looked deep into my eyes and between light soft kisses said simply and slowly, "You... sure... know... how... to... kiss!"

He opened the door, picked up his tool belt and left.

I steadied myself against the door and watched him drive off. Neither of us saying a word.

I closed the door and stood there reliving the night's events – the arousal, the playfulness, the hunger, the raw yet gentle exchange. I don't know how long we explored each other with our tongues and hands but the irony was it felt like it went on forever, yet when it was over, it felt like it was much too short. I guess that's what keeps us coming back. That's what leads to next time.

"Dylan, I think I could see myself spending a whole lot more time with that man. A lot more time."

CHAPTER 36

I woke with a smile added to my usual routine. I raised myself slowly out of bed and instantly the pain brought me right back to the mattress and back to the embarrassment from the previous evening's fall from grace. The routine was the same but today everything was in slow motion. I let Dylan out to relieve himself, put on the coffee, relieved myself, let Dylan in, gave him a few pats and then grabbed a big cup of coffee, hobbled up the stairs to the office where I settled myself as comfortably as possible into the office chair. I knew it wouldn't be a long sit so I got right to opening a number of new emails and began typing one to Tommy:

Hey Handsome, How are you doing today?

Thanks again for all your help last night. And for the wine, making dinner (sorry to be such a poor hostess), the witty repartee, the laughs, the great conversation and just for being you! You're an intriguing man and I really do enjoy your company. In fact, I was a little surprised by just how much! No complaints though - sometimes surprises are REALLY good - this was one of those times!

K8

Five minutes later,

Hi Kayte.

Happy to have helped. No worries about doing the cooking. Just sorry you had to fall for me in the process. How's the back today btw?

I was a little surprised by where things went too. Not where I intended them to go. Did you?

I needed clarification.

Tommy,

Not where you intended to go, huh? Did I? I had no preconceived intentions or expectations. I was just looking forward to seeing you. But I'm not sorry it went that way. I was a little surprised, but pleasantly so. It felt right, not awkward, not planned, not expected - just spontaneous and sincere and I really enjoyed it. How about you? What are you thinking/feeling about how things went?

Come on. Reply would you. Don't keep me in suspense. Tell me that you love me, that you can't live without me, that I rock your world and that you think we have a long, bright, sexy future together. Tell me you'll cook for me, fix whatever's wrong with our house, tend to me and make love to me like no man has before. Tell me that that those big hands of yours will hold mine and I'll never feel lonely again. Tell me that your big shoulders will help me carry the burdens I've been managing on my own up until now. Tell me I'm the one. Tell me that you've fallen hopelessly in love.

I looked down at the golden glob of fur that lay a few feet from mine. "And, dear Dylan, what do you think he'll have to say?" He just looked at me reassuringly with those warm understanding brown eyes of his as if to say, "Exactly what you want to hear."

His response took eleven minutes and thirty two seconds to arrive.

Kayte,

How am I feeling? I'm not sorry it went the way it went at all, it felt nice and you are a very sexy woman... obviously, judging by what you made me leave with ;-)

Although I don't think we should pursue that avenue any further... I think it would get a bit awkward as I think we're at different places in what we want. Don›t want to hurt you, you know? I consider you a good friend, a smart woman, a funny lady, attractive and built for sex... but I'm not looking for a relationship right now of any kind and I think you are... perhaps I›m assuming too much. Does that make sense?

Anyway, I'd like to think we can continue as friends and support for each other... and the flirting is damn fun.

I think you know this already... and understand.

"NO!" I screamed at my computer screen shocking Dylan to all fours. "No, you can't be serious." Dylan was staring at me. "No, I don't know this already." Dylan was now at my side, providing some well needed calming. What about last night? I was now using my 'indoor voice' and Dylan now had his head in my lap and I automatically stroked behind his ears.

I thought he was letting me in. I thought we had an unbelievable chemistry. I thought we felt the same way about each other. I thought we had a chance. "Continue as friends?" *What the hell!* "Friends?" *I have enough "friends" thank you. I don't want more "friends". You don't kiss "friends" like that. You don't boner up like that with "friends". You don't flirt like that with "friends". You don't share deep feelings, sexual attraction, real emotions or a lifetime with "friends".*

I don't want to be friends. I want to be lovers. Or I at least want to be friends AND lovers. "But I'm not looking for a relationship right now of any kind and I think you are." *Yes of course I was. That was why I put a profile on a dating site... duh! Or the fact that I was almost forty fucking years old and I wanted to find the love of my life before my life hurled me all alone into middle age. I wasn't afraid to commit to a relationship.*

Afraid... maybe that was it. Maybe he was just scared. He'd been recently hurt. He'd been dating only for a little while. Maybe he was afraid of getting hurt again. Doesn't he realise that's something I would never do to him. But that had to be it. He was scared.

As I replayed our past conversations, our e-exchanges, our connection, our previous evening together, the passion we had both felt when we kissed, I knew he had some feelings for me.

He might have thought that he wasn't looking for "a relationship of any kind". But, he didn't know what kind of relationship he could have with me. He didn't know how wonderful we could be together. He was afraid to trust his feelings. He was scared. He had been hurt.

So if I wanted a relationship with Tommy Kessler, I had to take away his fears. I had to make him realise that he wanted this. I needed to make it comfortable for him to come to his own understanding, his own realisation.

As much as I hated to admit it, that journey might just have to start with us being "friends". Just like my running had to start with walks with short bursts of running before I was up to running without walk breaks – it had taken lots of effort to be able to run 12K in one go.

There may need to be some training, some goal setting involved with Tommy too. You don't just decide to run a marathon and do it, there's a foundation that needs to be put in place, there's progress and time invested, there's the celebrations of milestones, but it has to start somewhere. Just like love needs to start somewhere and maybe this love needed to start at friends. Maybe that was the only place Tommy was comfortable.

Okay - first of all, Tommy Kessler, I am honoured to have you as a friend. Truly. I know some great people and "you is right up there baby". It's funny - some people you meet, you feel so comfortable with, like you've known them forever - I feel that way with you. Secondly, I know you are not looking for a relationship

right now. This is "you time" and, as your friend, I know how important this is for you and respect and support the fact that you need it. Everyone needs some time on their own to truly connect with who they are, especially after going through what you've just been through. I'd never do anything to take that from you - in fact, quite the opposite.

As for how I feel about you beyond platonic friendship, I'd be lying if I said there wasn't a part of me that would like to explore things further with you on a physical level. I find you funny, interesting, warm and welcoming, and apparently SEXY! (Who knew?) Judging by my own physical reaction last night, albeit not as apparent as yours (sometimes it's great being a girl!), I enjoyed the physical too! ;-). But do those feelings always have to be within the confines of a relationship? Maybe not.

As for me wanting a relationship - I do and I don't. I've obviously not been in too much of a rush so far!!! I do want a relationship - eventually, when all the right things are in place - the right person, the right time, the right kind of relationship. But I'm VERY selective about that. I do eventually want to settle down with someone, but I'll never settle. You never know when or even if, you'll find that. My occasional bouts of loneliness will never outweigh my need for the right kind of relationship.

I have a lot going on that is taking my attention right now - getting back into shape, re-establishing my career, finding the right work/life balance. Those things are my priority right now, but I've also learned to keep myself open to relationship possibilities, because you never know when that person may appear in your life.

So, I guess what I'm saying is, yes I want to be your friend, and I do understand exactly where you're at, I think I needed to clarify a little more as to where I'm at - I think it's a different place than you may have thought.

I have a tough time with laying down rules and to how we will and will not interact though. Too much of a free spirit for that, I'm afraid - I've never been good at following the rules.

I do understand and appreciate you being respectful of my feelings and trying to avoid hurting my feelings though. Thanks for that.

Can I suggest we don't put any limitations and expectations on our friendship - we'll see what happens and continue to be open and honestly communicate how we feel and think and just enjoy each other's company. Whaddya think about them apples?

Tommy, now that I've found your friendship, I'd hate to lose it!

And, as for flirting thing, I'm with you man - any day, any time - 'cause it IS fun!!

With that email sent, it was a great time to take Dylan for a walk and think about my strategy in approaching things with Tommy.

I knew the walk would be painful, but I also knew that it was required to keep me from stiffening up completely. We walked four kilometres but it was hot so both Dylan and I were in serious need of water when we returned home. I filled his bowl, put his leash in the closet, grabbed a glass of water and headed straight for the computer to see if I'd heard back from Tommy.

I had. His email was encouraging:

Ok... so let's see... HOLY FREAKING CRAP LADY WHAT A NOVEL!!!! But phew... you is cool baby... cool. I am surprised by how you are seeing things and it's a good surprise. I was afraid that you may have thought that I led you down the wrong path and then left you there. But you do understand and I underestimated you and where you are at and what you are looking for.

I appreciate too how you understand and appreciate where I'm at, and you put it well... connecting with who I am. I'm not looking for a relationship but if one slaps me in the face (or on the bum ;-o) then that's cool too. As far as the sex thing... I did wrestle with that last night... I mean, you were such a tease! Looking so hot, being so warm, funny and vulnerable all at the same time. Those full soft lips and that mouth that knows how to kiss, those boobs pressing against my chest, and let's not forget the legs up around your ears as you came barrelling down the stairs... all not fair! And that bra was the kicker... argh!

But when you said "But does that always have to be within the confines of a relationship? Maybe not"? What exactly do you mean by that?

So I'll be briefer than you and agree with the bulk of what you said... I too would hate to lose your friendship, it deserves no limitations or expectations and we'll roll with it. I like them apples... or perhaps grapefruit is more accurate? I came home, went straight to the shower last night tho... all that work making the meal, serving it, fetching drinks, fixing the plumbing and, playing doctor made me work up a bit of a sweat... and that kiss at the door just got me worked up - let's just say that well I didn't use a whole lot of shampoo, I went through a fair bit of uh... CONDITIONER! :o)

Later Kayter... glad weez cool.

I wanted to keep the response cool, playful and much shorter than my previous message.

Yes I is cool and don't ever forget it!! And WE is cool too.

And for the record, I'm not a tease - and even if I was, "takes one to know one!!!!" (said in my best nanananana voice!)

In answer to your question, let's just say relationship or no relationship, sex is never COMPLETELY out of the question! Thanks for the visual of you in the shower. Nice. Speaking of showers, I should head there. I am still so sore so a long hot one would probably do me good.

His reply came back within minutes.

I'm sure a long hot one would do you good, but I digress!

But let me put something to you straight Miss Smarty Pants... I didn't do nuttin to tease... untucked shirt for comfort, wore the tool belt for effect, bent over a few times showing you my best ass-et, but nothing more...so there!

Thanks for clarifying my question... I see what you mean now... (Actually, I saw it all along. I just wanted to make you say it)

I couldn't resist responding once more before showering:

That's 'Miss Very Pretty Lacy, Matching Bra and Smarty Pants' to you!

Now off to the shower for my long hot one. You know that steamy place where droplets of water and rich soapy lather will cascade down upon my naked flesh and bathe my skin in a layer of glistening moisture that sneaks its way from my face, down the length of my neck, trickling further down my chest, across my heaving bosom, dripping from my hardened nipples and...

When I returned from the shower I found only this in my inbox:

Ah, thanks for the ah... visual! Apparently you've just put something straight too. Now I need to find a file folder before I can leave my desk or perhaps I'll just sit here for the next hour until things... hmmm... die down!

I'll get you for this...

CHAPTER 37

It was an early rise the next day. I just couldn't sleep. Dylan had received pats, been out, given a treat and some fresh water. The happy boy followed me upstairs to the office as I took my seat at the computer.

Coffee in hand, checking email both in my inbox and on my dating profile had become part of my morning ritual. It felt strangely comforting to know that even when I was home alone, it didn't have to feel like it. At any time I could tap a few keys and feel as surrounded as I wanted. Knowing that there were so many others in the same situation was reassuring.

I logged into wheresinglesfindlove.com and found that I had three new messages. One was from a man, or boy, rather, half my age and proclaiming his love of older women. The second was from a man who sounded like he had some potential until a quick peek into his profile details indicated that he was five inches shorter than me.

The third email appeared to have some merit. It said simply,

You sound like a woman who knows what she wants. I'm a man who does too. Interested?"

The message was from 'AdventureGuy' who, according to his profile, was a 42-year-old consulting professional who played racquet sports, ran marathons and did fencing of all things. He had grown tired of games and wanted to experience a relationship that was deeply intimate, compelling and undeniably passionate. I could relate.

There was no photo, but he went on to say that he enjoyed wine and travel and proclaimed that life could never serve him up enough of either. He wanted an intelligent woman, who knew herself intimately and wasn't afraid to commit to adventure in life and in love.

I deleted the first and second message immediately and then saved message number three just in case I was ever in need of some future adventures.

There would be no running or gym today. I was still quite sore from my fall and the bruises were painful and ugly. So, I settled in at the computer where the seat was comfy, I didn't have to move to go places and I could connect with people without having to see them. Or, more importantly have them see me.

I perused the dating site to see who was new and met my basic criteria. Not that I was looking. My sights were set on one Tommy Kessler, but I did have a natural curiosity about others like me who were single and seeking. My latest search results uncovered some interesting profile names: 'loneturtle', 'youthfulindiscretion', 'Johnnyfunkypants', 'in8lycurious', 'NRGinspades', 'hoping2findU'.

'Loneturtle' was a self-described introvert who enjoyed spending time alone (so why on earth was he on a dating site?). He read a great deal and was proud to have reached the top level for a number of online games I had never even heard of. He sought social refuge in his shell, a.k.a. his home, and spent most of his time in his brand new multimedia room. Not sure why I even looked but, of course, there was no picture.

However there was certainly one created in my imagination, just not one I could ever see myself dating, let alone responding to.

Next!

'Youthfulindiscretion' was half my age, even though he put himself in a category 10 years his senior (the bottom of my acceptable dating range) because he wants to date older women exclusively. Very handsome and fit, he was undeniably also just too young.

Next!

Now 'Johnnyfunkypants' was tall, dark haired with a mischievous grin and decidedly offbeat.

His profile got my attention:

Ladies, I wear mismatched socks, have long hair that has a mind of its own. I sing in the checkout lines at the grocery store. I make a decent living, but don't own anything of value. In fact, I don't think anything of real value can be owned. I don't drink coffee, tea or anything with caffeine. I'll eat dinner for breakfast and vice versa. I'll see far more late nights than early mornings. I read poetry, paint when the mood or insomnia strikes (usually once or twice a week). I play sax well (and often) and the bagpipes badly (thankfully for my neighbours not nearly as often) and still have my first recorder. I'll kiss you for no reason and invent back-stories and role-play when we're out in public. I'll say things to shock people just 'cause I enjoy seeing their reactions. I take baths. I'll lose track of time trouncing around town exploring and watching. I'll not join, watch or cheer on a sports team, but you'd have a good chance of spotting me at the opera, a jazz bistro or a street festival. I'll open my heart once I feel I can trust you, but be forewarned that might take a while. I live in disorder but find comfort in it. I don't have a television or a full fridge and prefer to feed my mind with the literary classics. I drive but don't have a car.

If you're looking for a man who doesn't fit neatly in most modern day conformist boxes (and that's not just 'cause I'm 6'4), I might just be your guy.

If you want someone to love you forever and the above sounds like a forever that might make you happy, say hello.

Sincerely,

Sir Johnny Funkypants

I thought back to a time where Mr. Funkypants and I might have had a chance. I used to be far more hedonistic, unpredictable, reactive and far freer wheeling than I was now. But I have grown to find a certain comfort in order and see how predictability isn't always a bad thing.

I think it was the combination of being almost 40, living alone for so long, managing a demanding career and having to be so damned independent and self-reliant that had caused me to lose some of that youthful freedom and become so responsible. Not boring, but responsible.

While I think Sir Johnny would have been a fun date, I don't think we would have been a long term fit. Maybe if we had met 10 or 15 years ago, but not today. I needed more stability and maturity - fun, passion and a sense of humour too, but someone I could trust with my heart and my life. Someone I could rely on.

'In8lycurious' was a redheaded Scot whose profile asked simply, **Who are you? Why are you here? How do you know you're in love?** His brevity was intriguing mostly because he got right to the point, cut right to the chase, distilled the discussion down to 14 words.

While I didn't respond, I did spend some time considering the questions posed by 'In8lycurious' as they and their Scottish r's rolled around my head.

I had a much clearer vision of who I was, what was important to me, what I would tolerate, what I enjoyed, what my priorities were. The last few months had taught me more about myself than I could have imagined. Between focusing on me and what I was looking for in love doing this online dating thing and losing my job and being forced to examine other priorities in my life, I had come to a place of deeper self knowledge and felt that I knew myself better than I ever had.

The answer to question two was simply, I was here to find love. It was time. I was ready. I wanted my turn. I wasn't happy being alone anymore.

That said it had been so long since I had been in love. I struggled with the last question. "How do you know when you're in love?" I wasn't sure, but hoped that I'd have my answer very soon.

I didn't read the profiles of the others that turned up in my search. I sat there staring out the window and considered that last question. Somehow the popular response, "You just do" was not enough of an answer. It had been a long time; would I even recognise it?

CHAPTER 38

Dylan and I had just returned from a 20K hike at a local conservation area. I chose the hike over a run so I could still get the exercise but with longer pants and sleeves so the bruises weren't visible. It was a truly refreshing change and it unearthed some fond memories. It was the same park Mike and I had visited a few months before. I didn't usually go on such long treks alone but I had my phone and I had my Dylan and I felt like I just needed to get back to nature and spend a few hours thinking and drinking in the fresh air.

I arrived home later than I thought. I had only 30 minutes to shower, grab the goodies and go if I were to arrive on time to Aaron and Andrew's. Thankfully it was only a two-minute walk.

It wasn't like I'd be fussing over what to wear or ensuring that my makeup was just so. That was just another great thing about going to dinner with incredible friends. No airs needed. They love you just the way you are. I stopped by the bakery where Mike and I enjoyed a lunch what seemed like so long ago. I picked up two freshly baked wood oven breads. One was a kalamata olive, rosemary and feta loaf and the other a garlic loaf, but not just any garlic loaf. It must have been stuffed full of three whole garlic bulbs. The ones that popped through the crusty layer were caramelised and I was so tempted to pick one out, convincing myself that no one would notice. Both smelled divine. I had to hide these away while I had my shower as Dylan was quite the connoisseur and might try helping himself in my absence.

I was so inspired by my communing with nature that I also picked up a couple of bottles of organic Californian Chardonnay. Aaron and I were the only Chardy drinkers but if it was a typical dinner at their place, we'd have no trouble getting through the both of them.

We settled in the living room and while Aaron was filling everyone's glasses and the focus moved to me.

"Okay spill it. Not the wine. What's new on the dating scene? And we want ALL the details!"

Aaron just enjoyed this a little too much. But when he gave an order (and he was in control of the wine bottle) you didn't deny it so I started talking. I knew that they wouldn't let me go until I shared every detail, so share I did.

"He emails me every day. Some days it's 10 times in one day. He tells me about what he's been up to, asks tons of questions about what's going on with me, suggests we do this or that the next time we see each other. He's flirtatious too - he makes comments about my breasts and my legs and my lips. Not rude ones, but playful ones. He's very playful. He wants to know what I think about things. He shares his thoughts. He's even comfortable sharing his fears, things he feels uncomfortable with, the hurt he's still dealing with the breakdown of his marriage."

"First off, who's got that kind of time?" Wanda asked.

"Well I do, 'cause I'm still not working, and getting paid

handsomely for it I might add! And I guess when you're tapping away at a keyboard at work, who is the wiser? But most of our conversations, if you can call them conversations, are outside of work hours."

"So he obviously likes you," offered Andrew.

"Yes, I'm pretty sure of that. What's not to like?"

"But does he waaaaaannnnnt you?" Aaron added.

"It sounds that way often. It certainly felt that way the night he was at my place, but then why hasn't he asked me out again?"

"Simple solution. Ask him." Melissa popped an olive into her mouth. "Take charge, don't wait for him. You could be waiting forever."

"It's weird. We've only seen each other four times. Back when we first met and there were no sparks, that time he just popped by my place, and the night he came to fix my tap."

"Don't you mean your plumbing? And isn't that only three times?" Aaron piped in.

"Well then a couple of days ago, we were emailing and it was nearly lunch time and I teased saying I'd be in the parking lot in 15 minutes so he could take me for lunch. And… he took me up on it."

"So he is interested, maybe he's just shy." Andrew was getting up to check on dinner in the kitchen.

"He seemed a little uncomfortable when we went for pizza. Don't really know why. It was weird because he didn't seem nearly as easy-going as the interactions we have online."

"Did he buy lunch?" Wanda asked. "Cause if he didn't buy, I'd be wary. When guys like you they put skin in the game. They pay."

"No, we paid for our own. It was just weird. It seemed a bit awkward. Maybe because there were lots of people from his work around there, but who knows?

"That's the trouble with meeting online and having so many

conversations online. It's Rule #10 - Beware of the return to the cyber relationship.

"We chat about everything online. I like him. He's gentle and funny and bright and normal. He's got a big heart and he's man enough to admit his fears. He knows a little about a lot. He had a similar upbringing to me. He's a great big tease and he brings that out in me. And funny? He cracks me up. We get along so well. It's like we've been dating for a while. Honestly, I probably know more about him than I do about some of you right here in this room.

"And I think I have feelings for him. I trust him. I open up to him. I look forward to our conversations. I like who I am when I'm with him. He brings out the best in me. Good heavens, I could really be falling for him. But we've only physically been in each other's company four times. How weird is that?"

"I say play hard to get. Disappear for a while. If he is interested, it'll drive him crazy and he'll be very attentive. And if not, at least you'll know for sure," Aaron offered. "One thing I know for sure – this wine is fabulous!"

Andrew, the ever-objective balanced one, countered with, "Just be patient with him. The poor guy is new to dating after being married for so many years. It's completely understandable to be giving off mixed signals. He probably doesn't even know what he wants. Let alone how to go about getting it. But I think you make a good point about too much of your interactions being online. Shouldn't you being trying to focus on in-person exchanges?"

"If it were me, I'd keep talking to him. Talk to other guys too, go on dates with a number of them and when and if this Tommy guy is ready, you can decide on exclusivity. In the meantime, think of the fun you could have," Wanda offered.

Melissa said simply, "Men! They are just way more trouble than they're worth." She hadn't dated in years so I guess she believed what she said.

"I really like him so I guess I can be somewhat patient – I've waited this long!"

"You may just need to dance the dance a little," Aaron
continued. "You probably have to find the right balance between
showing interest and being available and keeping him guessing,
making sure he doesn't see you as a sure thing. He needs to know
that you're going on some other dates, that other men are interested in you and that he's got some competition. Guys like a little
competition. That's how I got this one!" He winked at Andrew,
who rolled his eyes.

"He probably needs to feel really comfortable with you Kayte.
Sounds like he may be in need of a friend, but a very playful
one who can add a certain passion to the friendship. I think that
might just describe you. Just be patient with him. Good things
come to those who wait." Andrew nodded and shot me one of his
insightful glances. He was a wise man.

"But I'm sick of waiting."

"More wine?" offered Aaron.

"Yes, at least I don't have to wait for that!"

Everyone laughed.

The dinner conversation moved to everyone comparing their
latest home improvement projects, movies they had seen and
dreams of travel and adventures in far away places.

Once the dating inquisition was over, it was nice to slip into
a night away from dating, away from the computer, away from
thinking about being single, away from wondering if I'd ever have
the kind of relationship that I had always dreamed of.

I looked forward to the day when I could share this supportive
group of friends with my partner and introduce him to them. I'm
sure that they would embrace him as they had me.

In the meantime, I may not have physically introduced Tommy
to them, but they had all introduced me to some ideas that I'd
work into a plan to give it the best shot of making that happen.

CHAPTER 39

I hadn't even showered, dressed or had anything to eat and there I was at the computer looking, hoping, needing some validation, some evidence that I was desired, missed or thought about - I was hoping that Tommy had been thinking about me as I had about him.

I recalled Rule #13: be wary of how much time you give this and don't let it become a substitute for real life experiences. So many people get a payoff from their online interactions and fail to make meaningful connections in person. Roman summed it up this way; "it should be a means to an end, not an ongoing practice and part of your daily life. That's how addictions are formed."

No new men had stumbled across my profile and fallen immediately in love. No Romeos had found their Juliet. No public declarations of undying love arrived through the night. No invitations. No messages on the dating site from Tommy.

Nothing.

Maybe my profile had become tired. I thought I might need

to tweak it and then republish it. It would then show up in the search results as a new listing. Fresh and new got noticed. There was a certain competitiveness in wanting to be the first to connect with the new guy or girl. Once your profile got old and tired, it wore a certain stigma. If you were on there for too long, it was assumed that there must be something wrong with you. And if there really was something wrong with you, why would anyone want to connect with you? Old got old, fast!

Roman summed it up in his Rule #7. He said, "Kayte, you gotta keep it fresh girl. Don't let your profile get stale. You have to change a heading, change your message, your photo, your age group, your preferences, your dating category… something. You have to do this every couple of weeks or so, or you will get passed over. New meat gets devoured here. Old meat just gets left to rot."

After a few weeks on the site looking through the profiles myself, I saw that Roman made a good point. Not an eloquent one, but a good one!

Part of me thought I should update my profile, part of me just wanted to take it down. I was developing feelings for Tommy and I didn't want him to think I was still looking.

Or did I?

I kept playing over the conflicting advice from my friends. I then found myself looking for a new photo to update my profile and pondered a new headline. I came up with, "I'm on here to get off here", realised the double entendre and wasn't prepared for the sexually graphic responses that it might create so I settled on, "I came here on my own, perhaps we can leave together." I thought twice about that too. I decided to change the word "came" to "arrived" for much the same reason and hit the update button. Was it too lame? Did I sound too hopelessly romantic?

Okay, Roman said it had to be new. He didn't say it had to be good.

I knew that I had to spend more time away from the computer so I opened a new window and began searching for running events in my area. Being relatively new to the sport I didn't know much about them, where they were held, or how often. I was astounded by how many there were close by. There were marathons, half marathons, fun runs and walks, 5Ks, 10Ks, fundraisers, qualifiers, family events, pet friendly events and even fancy dress runs.

I had clicked through to a 10K that was on the following weekend when I saw the highlighted message window indicating that I had an unread chat – the time stamp indicated that it must have come through the night before while I was over at Aaron and Andrew's.

Tomtom says:
K8 u there?

Woo hoo… O Kayte…

Calling Kayte…

Come in Kayte…

Come in Tokyo, maybe I should have done that to your boobies the other night

Which are really nice by the way

Very firm

Very large

Great fit for my as you called them "perfect C cup hands"

Nice boobies

Me likey boobies

I could go on and on and on about boobies

Or about just about anything

Can you tell I'm bored?

I'm not much of a TV watcher

I've already done a two-hour blade down by the lake

I cleaned my wittle apartment and she's spic and span

Now I gots nuthin' to do

So I figured I'd chat with you

But,

YOU'RE NOT THERE!

The nerve of you

I don't know where you are

Maybe out with Dylan or Chloe

Maybe out socialising with your neighbour friends

Oh, maybe you're out on a hot date with some other online man who has seduced you with his sense of humour, good looks and fetching photos

But that couldn't be, I'm right here

Or MAYBE, you're just pretending to be away like it says

And, MAYBE you're sitting back with a glass of chardonnay in hand and reading this, laughing at me blathering on like an idiot

If that's the case, (and I suspect it just might be) I wouldn't want to disappoint you, so I shall continue.

I wonder just how much you can type without a response before your chat gets cut off?

Sounds painful!

Hmmm

Apparently at least 4 minutes worth, which is where I am already

Okay okay, I KNOW, I'm a slow typer, or is that typist?

Hang on

Have to take a sip

Mmm… rum and coke, yum

Almost as yummy as those burgers you made

You sure can cook sista!

Mmm. I'm surprised that with those boobies and your cooking expertise that you don't have the menfolk bashing down yer door.

HMMM, wonder what would make the womenfolk bash down my door?

Sometimes I just feel like a great big fish outta water in this dating world

I was married soooo long, it just all feels so very strange

Even though it's been almost a year since me and the ex split, when I kiss another woman, like, say, um, YOU for instance, it still feels a little like I'm cheating

I know that sounds weird, but it's true

And not only is getting back into the dating world a whole new ballgame for me, this online dating stuff is so different than the dating I remember

There are some crazy ass chicks out there – I'm almost a little afraid of it to be honest

But it's also interesting and certainly not dull,

And we both know I'm in NOOOOO hurry to hook up again

Plus who would have me?

C'mon ladies, step right up... get your broke, balding, beer drinking, burger eating, boobie loving bachelor who's not looking for marriage and already has two kids and the child support payments to go with them. And did I mention he's got no savings and no investments to speak of?

Well at least he isn't living with his parents

OMG – I sound pathetic, I'm really not, damn, wish you could go back and erase things you type in here – oh well

This is kinda therapeutic though, almost like seeing a shrink but at no cost, which is just the right price for this fella!

Speaking of shrink, I just want you to know that anything you may or may not have felt through the pants the other night, was not shall we say, umm, fully inflated!!!

LOL

I kill me

OOPS ... need more Rum & Coke... BRB

K... me back

So I was saying, I was a little embarrassed when I got to thinking that you might have been thinking that what you felt while we were kissing in your kitchen, that you might not have been feeling much

Well I was aroused, and wanted to kiss you and see those fine booberellas of yours, I wasn't fully, ok, I'll say it, ERECT!!!

I don't know why... sex and stuff has been a little weird, but I guess it's just going to take some getting used to - I was a long time married

I know the one-eyed trouser snake isn't going to stay hidden for good, he's just been transplanted into unknown territory so it's gonna take him a while to get his bearings

Man, what am I saying... you must think I'm nuts

I wonder if I could go over there, break into your place, bribe Dylan with some raw meat, jump on your computer and erase this whole blab-fest before you get a chance to read it.

Unless of course you're already reading it as I type - are you?

Ah what the heck, I trust you... sort of... just please don't share this with your girlfriends or worse, your boyfriends... I beg of you...

Hmm begging of you... I could beg of you one other thing... Man those lips of yours and the way you kiss... Do you know where my thoughts were going?

I so wanted to feel those large, soft wet lips somewhere else

Oh man, I miss BJ's

Did you know that March 14th is officially Steak and BJ day? It's a man holiday. Made up by men, enjoyed by men, kinda like the testosterone-induced response to Valentine's Day.

don't believe me?

I kid you not, my lady... c 4 yourself... go ahead and search for it - it'll come up - first hit

I really, really miss BJ's

Oh there's another B to add to my b-urgeoning list

Do you do that?

I bet you do.

I know that's a personal question, but humour me... I've spilled my soul here (thanks to a few of rums)

I can't believe how long I've been typing. But I'm not stopping now

So do you...?

Ah, do you give good BJ's?

With those lips, I hope so. I would suspect so.

So assuming you do pleasure your man, do you like it?

I always wondered if women really enjoyed doing it or just did because their guy likes it or because they think it might get them jewellery credits!

How many of you actually give them?

Do your girlfriends?

Are there some guys who don't like them?

I have so many questions about sex and dating these days and I just have so few people to talk to about it... obviously if I had lots of people to talk to I wouldn't be at home drinking R&Cs by myself, typing away to a person who isn't there...

Man, this single life is da bomb!!

N-O-T!!!!

So back to BJs and boobies... me so horny tonight

Face it, me so horny every night!!

Do women get this horny?

Do they fantasise like we do about sex? Or do they fantasise more about romance, about falling in love?

I've been married so long I have no idea what the modern day single woman thinks, what she thinks is normal

At least when I was married I never had to go without sex this long.

Not that it was always good, but it was there if I really pushed for it.

So now that I'm bachelor stud, what should I expect?

How many dates will it take to have sex?

So how often do you have sex? I know it's personal, but hell you're not even there so I can ask.

Or change the question, how often, in a perfect world, would you like to have sex?

I know we're not in our 20s anymore, but I'm curious as to what a low/high sex drive is these days

And is it different for single women versus married ones?

I have so many questions...

so few answers...

so little Rum left...

Sigh.

Double sigh

Well thanks for listening... I should head to bed

Alone,

Well at least there I can have a hand in creating my own happiness...

If you get this message soon, come by...

Wow!

Even though it had been only a one-sided conversation, I felt like I had learned so much about Tommy. His words in all their honesty and vulnerability made me laugh, made my heart go out to him, made me fall for him even more. I had no idea that his mixed signals were driven by so much angst and uncertainty. Being single and dating must be such a strange and disconcerting concept for him at this stage of his life. I just wanted to reach out, put my arms around him and reassure and remind him what a wonderful person he was, how hard it was for decent women like me to find someone with such a good heart, who was also hard working, so open, so funny, strong, sexy and sincere. I wanted to dispel his fears and show him that dating and finding love didn't have to be so scary. Especially if he were to find that love with me. I had real feelings for him and I didn't want to see him ruined by the darker side of dating in this age. My wish for him was that he was able to remain the great person he was and that whatever amount of time he spent being single served him well and helped him to become an even better person rather than chip away at the fine man that he was.

Then there he was.

Tomtom says:
Hey there, Kayte

K8 says:
Hey yourself!

Tomtom says:
What are you up to? No good?

K8 says:
Oh contraire monsieur - it's ALL good!

I've just read a rather lengthy rum-influenced yet curious, entertaining and enlightening soliloquy from a very intriguing and sexy man.

Tomtom says:
Oh gawd. You did get it.

All of it?

K8 says:
If it ended with an invitation to come by, then yes, I got all of it.

Tomtom says:
I'm sorry if I offended you. I had a few of rums and was looking for some companionship, feeling a little sorry for myself and guess I got a little carried away.

K8 says:
Tommy seriously, nothing to apologise for - I enjoyed reading it - it made me laugh (with, not at, you) and gave me some insight

into how all this must feel for you.

Tomtom:
Damn strange to be quite frank.

K8 says:
I understand that now.

Tomtom says:
So you'll still be my friend?

K8 says:
Of course Tommy, you're a pretty special guy and yes, you can count on that!

And PS - I give good friendship!

Tomtom says:
Wowsa - do you give good anything else?

K8 says:
You'll just have to wait and see, now won't you...

Tomtom says:
Ah shucks... K8 you're makin' me blush and other things! I really don't know how blood can go in two directions at once.

K8 says:
hehehe

Tomtom says:
I digress

This is serious Thomas now - so, what were you up to before I interrupted?

K8 says:
Firstly Tommy, hearing from you is never an interruption.

I was just about to sign up for a 10K run? Care to join me?

Tomtom says:
Not if I want to live to tell about it.

K8 says:
You're in pretty good shape. You could do it. Have you taken part in any runs before?

Tomtom says:
Kayte, you've seen me. I'm not the least bit aerodynamic. I'm 6'2" with broad shoulders, big clunky legs and the only fast thing about me is my ability to concoct a witty retort at lightning speed.

K8 says:
I hear you. I certainly don't have the typical runner body either. My ample bosom has a tendency to slow me down!

Tomtom says:
Oh Kayte the vision I'm creating in my head... You and your ample bosom are running toward me bounding up and down, up and down, up and... ahhhhhhhh... Ample bosom! I love ample bosom. How are 'the girls'? I miss them. Please give them a hug and a kiss for me! And if you can seriously do the latter, please take a photo and send it!

K8 says:
There's a 5K run. You could do that. C'mon Tommy, it'll be fun. I'll race ya! I'll even make it interesting. Winner gets to choose their reward.

Tomtom says:
Oh that does sound enticing. I know what I'd pick. Are there any limitations to said reward?

K8:
I would think that as long as it doesn't hurt anyone, damage anything and is legal, it's pretty much open.

Tomtom:

Oh Kayte, the places my mind is going right now. The rewards I'm imagining are inspiring, or should I say, ahhh... stimulating me to want to take part. I might well, ahem, rise to the occasion. In fact, I might just be doing that now!

K8 says:
Then, you're in?

Tomtom says:
Ohhhhh yessss... I definitely want to be in.

K8 says:
For the run, I mean!

Tomtom says:
Oh ya, the run. When is it?

K8 says:
Next Sunday morning

Tomtom says:
Darn. Sorry Kayte I can't

K8 says:
Sure you can. It'll be fun.

Tomtom:
I'm actually away for the weekend.

K8 says:
A kid weekend is it?

Tomtom:
Ah... no.

K8 says:
Boys' weekend?

Tomtom says:
Nuh-uh.

K8 says:
Okay, spill it

Tomtom says:
Uhhh, I'm going on a, I have, uhhh, a... date.

A date? I must be cool. Stay cool Kayte.

K8 says:
Oooh... Tommmmmmy has a daaaate...

Tomtom says:
We leave on Saturday morning and don't come back until Sunday night.

Oh, even better. It's a sleepover date, is it?

I was experiencing a flood of different emotions. I was hurt, I was angry, I was jealous. I was screaming in my head.

If you're going on an overnight date, why the hell isn't it with me? But I had to play it cool. Just friends remember. I couldn't let on. Must stay in control. Humour. Use humour. It always helps!

K8 says:
Ya, so I guess you have your own version of breathless, hot and sweaty planned then. No worries.

Tomtom says:
Here's hoping. Sorry, but these plans were already made.

Anger, hurt and jealousy just connected with disbelief, depression, disillusion and frustration. I couldn't believe it. Tommy should've been be overnighting with me – not someone else. Who was this?

K8 says:
Listen there's someone at the door, I gotta run.

Tomtom says:
It'll be good practice for the race!

I logged off without responding.

"Well Dylan, what do you think of that?"

The golden boy had been lying in the hall looking in on me. My voice made him lift his head from the floor. His ears perked up and he look directly at me.

"Can you believe it? He goes and opens all up to me and I'm feeling so close to him, feeling like we're making progress and now he's going on a weekend date. An overnighter - with a woman. There will be more than 24 hours spent together in person, face to face, and who knows what else to what else! There will be bonding. There will be laughter and there will be flirting. There will be kissing and touching. There will be sex. And there will probably be even more sex! But do you know what there won't be? Me. That's what!"

I needed a run. A long one!

CHAPTER 40

I had spent the remainder of that week focused on preparing for the run. I purposely found all kinds of things to keep me busy and off the computer.

I set two goals that week. The first was that I was limiting myself to 30 minutes computer time per day until the run. The second was that I would run my very first 10K. I would run it for me. I would be able to say, "I did it!" I would be able to say I set a goal, prepared for it and accomplished it. I would then provide myself with an appropriate reward.

It was challenging. There were a number of times around the seven to eight-kilometre mark where I wanted to stop or start walking but I kept pushing on, one foot then the other. This was something I had to do for myself. I pushed through those defeatist thoughts and made my way to the nine-kilometre mark where something changed. I looked around and saw the determination on other runners' faces. I saw people cheering from the sidelines, urging us all on; I saw my goal so close to being accomplished. I knew I could do it. I poured whatever I had into that last kilometre and then there it was, the finish line in full sight. I was steps away from crossing it and I soaked in every detail. My foot hit the finish line pad. A glance at the race clock, a quick calculation and I knew that my time was under my goal of one hour. My first 10K at almost 40 years old was completed in 58:45. While I wasn't heading for the Olympics, I was going home with a finishing medal around my neck, and a full (and healthier) heart knowing I had just completed an important milestone.

I was exuberant, but I was alone. I had not invited anyone to come today other than Tommy. When he said he couldn't attend, I decided this was something I wanted to do on my own. But there at the finish line watching others being hugged, congratulated and applauded by their loved ones, I felt not only alone but very, very lonely.

There was nothing like a long hot soak in the bath after a long run. Not immediately after the race, but a few hours later. You had to time it just right. I had developed my own post long-run routine. After the run I'd towel off, drink plenty of liquids, change into warmer clothes, have something healthy to eat and more liquids, then gradually wind down through the day.

At the right moment I'd treat myself to the steamiest bath I could stand. I'd trade the harsh bathroom lights for soft candles, turn on some soothing music, pour myself a wine, nibble on some chocolate and then slide into a steamy bubble bath just as my muscles were beginning to constrict and tighten. The heat would seep in to warm them while I did stretches in the tub to get them back into a more pliable state.

Lying in the tub, naked, happy, here on my date with myself I was at peace. I found a state of total relaxation. I was proud of achieving this goal. It was in moments like this that I felt so connected to myself, so connected to my body. I felt the throb of my muscles from my toes up through my shoulders lessen as the heat from the water seeped through my pores. When I opened my eyes I observed the soft flickering glow of candlelight as it danced around the room. I was lulled by the rhythmic tones of jazz playing softly in the background. I inhaled the sweet smell of the coconut bubbles. I savoured first the creamy morsels of milk chocolate then the smooth buttery texture and fruity notes of the wine as it slid slowly down my throat.

I had created a decadent sensory buffet for myself – for me, alone, to enjoy. I had earned it.

One thing was certain; dating or not, in love or not, married or not, I had learned to enjoy my own company and I could be alone. I just didn't want to be.

It was almost midnight and I felt warm and relaxed. I had topped up the hot water in the tub twice, soaked for what felt like hours, then wrapped my hot skin in the cuddliest pyjamas and a terry robe complete with the fluffiest socks to keep the heat trapped for as long as possible.

I was relaxed but not tired. My daily limit of 30 minutes on the computer had not been used up.

My choice was either TV or computer. The choice was easy.

I logged in to email and found just one new message.

I was surprised when I received this telling note from Tommy:

Hi Kayte.

I looked for you 'you know where' tonight and didn't see you pop in. You didn't appear in the chat so I thought I'd contact you old school and send you an email as my inkwell and quill were nowhere to be found.

How was your run today? I thought about you and really hoped that you enjoyed yourself and did well. I should have been there with you. I could have used the exercise and the company.

You know, you are one impressive lady. I am really inspired by you. You don't rest on your laurels (or your hardys either... hehehe). You seem to always be trying to better yourself, taking on something new, being open to new experiences, meeting new people, learning new things. So many people around our age just get so stuck. I admire that you don't. I wanted you to know that.

Look at me waxing on (wax on, wax off, grasshopper!)

I had hoped we could talk tonight. I'm here alone, having a couple of rums, thinking about life and wishing I hadn't had such a shithouse weekend.

I almost joined you at the run today, but I didn't have any of the details. Maybe the next one.

Kayte, I just wanted you to know that I was thinking about you. In fact, I've been thinking about you a lot today. Hopefully we can see each other soon.

Okay, my glass is empty, the weekend's almost over and I guess I should go do some manly stuff and then take myself off to bed. Had hoped we could chat before I did :-(

Good night KaytieKat. I hope you did well in your run today. I'm sure you did. Seems you do well in everything.

Sweet dreams dear Kayte

xxx

Thomas

That was an interesting twist. I had so many questions. I wondered what had happened to ruin his sexy weekend. I reread the email and then reread it again (okay and again!) and got all warm and fuzzy on the inside too. With that reassuring feeling I, too, went off to bed.

CHAPTER 41

There are some mornings when coffee just tastes better than others. I made my daily brew, poured a cup and made my way to the computer, sat down half hoping the soothing heat from this blessed liquid that warmed my stomach could find its way to soothe the muscles in my aching lower back, buttocks, legs and feet.

I was sore. But it was a great run yesterday and I achieved a long standing goal and a new personal best, so the pain was well earned and worth it. But I'd have still killed for a massage.

I signed on to find a few spam emails, a possible job lead passed on from one of my old team and an email from Tommy with no body copy, only a subject line that read:

Want to accompany me to a wedding?

As long as it's ours!

Between sips, I replied to his email.

Perhaps. Where? When? And should I wear white?

Seconds later the chat window opened up.

Tomtom says:
Got your reply. Where? A resort up north.

When? Six weeks from now.

And with that tan, white would be stunning on you, especially with a plunging neckline. So is that a yes?

K8 says:
That depends…

Tomtom says:
On what?

K8 says:
Are you down on one knee?

Tomtom says:
LOL – kinda hard to type that way and I might get some strange looks here in the office, but you can imagine that I am…

K8 says:
Oh, I'm imagining it, baby!

Tomtom says:
And?

K8 says:
Yes, I'd love to accompany you to a wedding.

Tomtom says:
Great – the resort's about 4 hours away, so we'll have to stay overnight, if that's okay.

No. That's not okay. It's friggin' fabulous! I can't wait.

K8 says:
I guess that would be all right.

Tomtom says:
So how are you doing after the run?

K8 says:

Good, very pleased with myself – one less goal on my list and a new personal best, but I'm sore... so very, very sore.

Tomtom says:
If you ask nicely I could pop by after work and give you a foot massage.

K8:
Oh would you please, pretty, pretty please?

Tomtom says:
OK. I'll be there around 7. Have to head to a meeting now.

K8:
See you then.

Now wasn't that a pleasant surprise? I liked the way this day had started out. I'd better get booked in for a pedicure so that Tommy's not massaging rough runner's, chipped-toenail feet.

The doorbell rang at 6:57. I loved it when a man was on time. Secretly, I liked it even more when they were early and eager!

Tommy arrived with two packages in hand. One was obviously a bottle of wine and the other was more intriguing. It was a small green gift bag that was only slightly smaller than his large capable hand.

"A man bearing gifts! Well you can certainly come in!"

"Why thank ya l'il lady," Tommy offered with a cowboy twang all while Dylan sniffed at his crotch. "Dylan, while I like you and you're cute and all, I just don't roll that way. Okay?"

I chuckled.

Tommy placed the smaller gift in the same hand as the wine. The now unencumbered arm found its way around me, drawing me close. He bent down and gave me a very hot, very wet, very intense hello kiss. I must have counted to 25 steamboats before his lips slowed, the time between kisses lengthened, the pressure lessened, all signalling the imminent end of what was an incredible kiss. He stood back and just smiled.

I caught my breath and when I gained composure in my wobbling knees, I whispered, "Well, hello to you too!"

"I've been wanting to do that all day."

Secretly so had I - that and so much more.

"These are for you." He offered the wine first. I opened the bag. It contained an already chilled lovely Australian Semillon from the Barossa Valley.

"Mmm. Thank you Tommy. This looks great. Shall we open it?"

"Definitely. I've been waiting for that all day too! But open this first."

He had a silly schoolboy grin plastered across his face.

What could this be? It was way too early in our relationship (that couldn't really be referred to as a relationship at that point) for jewellery. I hadn't dropped any hints. He hadn't either so I was stumped. I untied the ribbons and removed the tissue paper to find a small bottle of massage oil and two votive candles in a matching scent. It was a fresh citrus aroma that delivered an energy and freshness upon inhaling it.

"These are wonderful. Thank you. How thoughtful of you." I reached up and gave him a kiss on the cheek.

"Well I promised you a foot massage. For a good foot massage you need both atmosphere and oil, so I brought both. But for a great one, you need atmosphere, oil and wine. But for an absolutely awesome foot massage, you need atmosphere, oil, wine and me!"

"Then we have everything we need for awesome."

"Yes we do." He smiled. "How about we start with the wine?"

We sat on the sofa and talked about my latest run, how running had become a great release and a challenge. We discussed his two boring meetings that day and the amusing things he did to entertain himself. In one of them, he confessed to imagining what I might be wearing and then after a few more sips of his wine, also admitted to imagining himself taking every article of clothing off me slowly and deliberately. After blushing, he also sheepishly admitted that he had to stop that game when certain un-office-like physical manifestations started as a result.

He was so cute, so open, so willing to share. He looked up from his sheepishness and I couldn't resist reaching out and grabbing his head and kissing him solidly on the lips. My tongue took charge. I separated his full lips while we matched lip for lip and kissed deeply pressing into each other. I pushed my breasts into his chest and moved from sitting to straddling him on the sofa. Within moments I felt his physical manifestation grow.

I kissed up his neck to his ears and whispered, "That's okay, manifest away. You're not at the office now."

His large hands started at my waist and began rubbing and massaging up my back. When they reached my shoulder blades, in unison, they both moved forward to cradle my breasts, one in each.

I wanted him so much. Right there on the sofa. I wanted to hike up my skirt, tear off my panties, unzip his fly, liberate his manifestation and have him manifest me. I wanted to ride him hard until we both reached the peaks of ecstasy. Then I wanted to collapse into each other stroking, and caressing and continuing with soft, wet, reassuring kisses and then stay right there forever. I wanted this man in my bed. I wanted this man in me. I wanted him in my life. I wanted him to be my future. I wanted him. Oh how I wanted him.

He continued to fondle my breasts. His kisses moved from my lips up to my ear, down my neck, across my collarbone and down to my breast – first one, then the other. His hands had undone my blouse and opened it. He reached around and undid my bra liberating my heaving bosom so that he could explore them with his mouth and tongue.

I was wriggling in ecstasy. My crotch was damp with anticipation for him. *Was it actually going to finally happen? Was I finally going to make love with Thomas Kessler? Could it finally be the night?* I couldn't ever remember truly liking someone so much and desiring someone so much all at the same time and in the same person. He was the one. I knew it. I knew it in my head. I knew it in my heart. I knew it even lower.

I felt his heat and hardness beneath me. I knew he wanted me too. *Should I play hard to get? Well as hard to get as I could now that I straddled him, my blouse open, my nipple in his mouth? Or should I just keep going?*

Should I stop?

Or go?

Stop?

Go?

My desire for him was peaking.

Should I pull away and make him want me more? Or should I continue on?

I pulled back even though I wants so much more of this. "Maybe… we… should… slow… … things… down…"

He lifted his head quizzically and looked gently into my eyes. "Maybe you're right. But, maybe not. How about another glass of wine and we'll think about it? I'm so glad I brought the white."

My chest was heaving and heaving, my breaths were so shallow. "Yes… please."

I stood up and let Tommy do the same. I pulled my bra and blouse together and said, "I'll be right back," and headed to the bathroom.

My breathing still hadn't returned to normal. I stared in the mirror, dishevelled and glistening and I noticed the biggest, happiest smile. I knew good things would happen with this man. I didn't have to rush it.

I had put bra and blouse back in place and when I returned from the bathroom Tommy surprised me. Most guys would have tried to pick up right where things left off. Most guys would not have stopped in the first place. Most guys would have just sat there doing nothing just waiting for me to return and then there were some guys I would have returned to find laying naked on my couch. But Tommy was not most guys.

Soothing new age music was playing, the votives from the gift bag were lit and on the coffee table, the lights dimmed and a towel from the upstairs bathroom laid out on Tommy's lap. He had removed his tie, untucked his shirt and was obviously making himself comfortable, but he was making me comfortable too.

"Here's your wine, Kayte. Now sit here with your back against the arm of the sofa, I'll do the same at the other end. You extend your legs and then all you have to do is sit back, sip your wine, close your eyes, listen to the music and enjoy the most awesome foot massage of your life."

I said nothing. I just complied with his instructions and put myself in his hands. Good things would happen with this man. I didn't have to rush it.

CHAPTER 42

"Chloe, I had the best foot massage EVER! On both of them! They feel like they could run a half-marathon."

"He must be good. Send him to my place, would ya?"

"No way, I'll never send him away. He's mine, mine, all mine!"

I went on to tell Chloe all about my date with Tommy the night before, how he initiated it, how focused he was on pleasing me, how he had brought wine and presents, how his foot massage was the perfect indulgence and how the night moved from us fooling around to talking to laughing to fooling around to falling asleep in each other's arms on my sofa.

"Chloe, we didn't have sex but it sure felt like we made love. I just feel so connected to him, so comfortable, so aroused, so safe, so challenged and so understood."

"So things are looking up with Tommy then?" Chloe sounded so very happy asking this question to which she already knew the answer.

"Yes, they are. In fact they were up about three different times last night!"

We both erupted in laughter.

"And we're seeing each other again tomorrow night."

"Awesome! Where are you going? What are you doing?"

"He knows a new Thai restaurant he's been keen to try so we're going there. He brought it up, he asked. All I had to do was say yes."

"Mmm… I love Thai."

"Me too. Can't wait."

"And I love you. Have fun Kayte. It's so great to hear you so happy."

"Thanks Chloe, you're the best."

"No, you are!"

"No you are!"

We were both laughing as we hung up the phone.

It was about 10pm and I hadn't heard from Tommy all day, but hadn't expected to as he had travelled a few hours out of town for a meeting. I found myself missing our daily contact. Even if only a brief message or chat, these interactions added another dimension to my day, a highlight I was coming to rely upon. They helped me feel connected and it was reassuring to know that I was being thought about, especially by someone I contemplated often. Plus, Tommy made me laugh. There was something in the way he expressed himself, the way he saw the world through a childlike innocence that always seemed to arouse a giggle and make me feel a little more like all was right with the world.

I spent the day in preparation for the following day. I lathered my body in moisturiser, drank extra water, made sure I ate lightly and didn't eat any strongly flavoured foods. I ran 8K and did 100 crunches. I organised my date outfit, gave Dylan a bath and a brush, vacuumed and dusted the house, cleaned the bedroom and bathroom, washed the sheets (just in case), replaced old candles with new ones, picked out some of my favourite tunes and made sure everything was organised, clean and perfectly welcoming, all on the off chance that we ended up back at my place, or better yet, in my bed.

Could the next night be the one when Kathleen and Thomas finally consummated their growing desire? It had to be. This would be a very telling date. I knew it would. It was time. It had to be time. I so wanted it to be time.

I couldn't wait to talk to him though. I needed to connect with Tommy before then. Even if only briefly, just to confirm that things were set and dispel the nagging fears that started mounting. I had met a few really good men in my search for Mr. Right but I was afraid. I was afraid that the potential would once again turn to disappointment. I just needed some reassurance from him that he was as excited as I was about tomorrow, that he was looking forward to connecting in person. We needed more in-person time and less online chats, because as great as all these online connections were, there needed to be the in real life interactions, side by side, face to face, body to body. Oh how I wanted there to be body to body.

K8 says:
Hey Tommy U there?

Helllllloooooooooooo

Red rover, red rover, I call Thomas over…

Anybody home?

Yoooo hooo…

Oh, I get it, now that you've finally got cable, you're probably watching the game

Thought I'd see if you were around, but it appears not.

See – you're not the only one turning to your computer for friendship

Not much on so I'm not watching TV, don't feel like doing any more housework, my neighbour friends are out.

I'm home alone (ok with Dylan). I was hoping I might have a cyber-visit with one very funny guy but seems you're not there.

Or maybe you are, and you're just sitting back watching, reading, wondering how long I could go on.

Well settle in baby, I can go on for quite a while I assure you.

On and on and on and on…

I can't believe we've actually come to this.

Not we as in you and me specifically but society, people in general.

When did technology come in and take such a huge role in our communication and, as a result, in our relationships?

I'm not that old, but man, I NEVER EVER would have thought, back when I was a teenager and fantasising about love and the man I would eventually marry, that I'd be searching the net, scanning through hundreds of profiles of men, looking at photos, reading profiles, having online chats, wondering if he was the one? Could he be the man I might fall in love with?

I never thought that I'd be maintaining friendships through chats and messages and emails all around the world rather than face-to-face, over coffee at the kitchen table.

I never thought that I'd be almost 40, not married, home alone and turning to my keyboard and computer screen to reach out for companionship, comfort and to keep the growing feelings of loneliness at bay.

I guess it doesn't hurt as much if you can take comfort in the fact that there are so many others just like you in the same boat.

But whatever happened to friends setting up friends? To meeting the love of your life serendipitously?

Are we just too busy now?

Or are we afraid because so many marriages fail? We just can't be bothered setting people up because we don't want a 50/50 chance of being blamed for the inevitable demise? Or we don't want to lose half our friends as a result?

What happened to seeing someone in a bar, supermarket, gym? Sharing a look, mustering the courage to have a chat, asking for a phone number then agonising over when was the right time to call?

Now when we feel lonely, it's just so easy to jump online in the hopes of finding someone similar to us or at least another lonely person.

We spend hours chatting with people we connect with this way without ever physically meeting them at all or in place of being together with them in person.

We use emoticons and acronyms in place of real emotions and words.

While I am as guilty as the next gal, I still wonder what this is doing to our ability to communicate, to relate, to actually fall in love?

I sometimes feel that through all the choices, efficiency and entertainment that technology has availed us, it has also driven us further and further apart.

Even if you've seen photos and connected really well through your cyber chats, there is such an emphasis on the first few meetings that it almost overwhelms.

Maybe it's putting too much pressure on the first date, maybe rather than being the great solution to singledom, it's reducing the quality of our relationships.

Sometimes I truly doubt its viability in the quest for love.

But online dating is a tool. It's another option. So I guess I had to try it, if for no other reason to say that yes, there is not a thing that I hadn't tried to find true love.

And, hey, I have met a wonderful man, who I doubt I would have met any other way, so hey, if all this means I got to get to know you, it was all worth it!

Wow... that was quite a rant, now wasn't it... whew, glad that's over. I feel purged

I feel better.

Well, kinda.

Who am I kidding?

No I don't.

I guess I'm still yearning for simpler times,

I think I'll go hug the dog.

Thanks for reading Tommy... I guess it was my turn to share... now we're even.

I missed you today.

Can't wait to see you tomorrow.

Just one more sleep!

I think I might get started on that now.

K8 out

CHAPTER 43

Tommy was five minutes early – good thing I was too.

There was the usual mayhem at the door as I invited Tommy in while Dylan danced around looking for his own greeting. Luckily I got the kiss and he got the pat.

"Don't you look lovely tonight."

"Thanks for noticing."

"How could I not? You look hot… and spicy. In fact, I think you'll go perfectly with our dinner plans. Hope you're hungry."

I was starved. I had hardly eaten anything over the past 24 hours.

"Oh I could eat!"

"Good. Well then, let's get going. I can't wait to try this place. It's been getting rave reviews."

As we drove, I listened attentively as Tommy took great joy in sharing the details of his client meeting the day before. He went on to tell me a bit about the small town where he grew up as he had passed through it en route.

"Kayte, I was just flooded with memories, coming at me every which way. At one point I just pulled over by my old school and just stood there in silence listening to all the voices and watching all the images of my past play through my mind. It was a surreal experience."

He relived some childhood adventures and pranks; the perpetual kidnapping of his neighbour's garden gnomes and leaving ransom notes demanding a piece of pie, a penny, a ride in the volunteer fire truck. He spoke fondly of family time spent with his now deceased grandparents. He reminisced about school and favourite classes, least favourite teachers and friends (sadly a number of whom he lost in the divorce). I was pleased that he trusted me with these intimate details of his life. It gave me a greater insight into how he had come to be the man he was today. And it made me like him all the more.

Before I knew it, we had arrived at the restaurant. On the outside it resembled the traditional houses of central Thailand with a series of peaked roofs and the entire structure was built on stilts above ground level and surrounded by a massive water feature dotted with lily pads.

He opened the car door, took my hand, helped me out of the car and guided me into the bustling restaurant. The smells were incredibly seductive – I inhaled the deep spicy curries, the fresh-ness of lime, the salty scent of seafood and the heavy sweetness of coconut cut by a slight zing of vinegar wafting by. Even though the restaurant was large, the seating appeared intimate with each table having its own dark wood booth for six or eight, each with padded bench seating, an array of multicoloured throw cushions and a candlelit lantern adorning the table tops. The walls were bright and colourful. The whole restaurant was a feast for the senses. I could hardly wait to try the food.

"Wait here. I'll be right back." Tommy made his way through the foyer to the hostess desk. I watched, but couldn't hear, as he conversed with the petite Asian woman. He frowned, said something else, then it was her turn, then a huge smile replaced the frown. He nodded, turned and met me back exactly where he had left me.

"Want the good news or the bad news?"

"Good."

"They have a table for us that's right in the back." Tommy pointed to a very cosy table in the back right-hand corner where the only lights were those from the candles. There was no one on either side and it was surrounded by greenery.

"I'm almost afraid to ask for the bad."

"We can't be seated for another hour. And the tiny bar waiting area is already overflowing."

"Hmmm… so what do we do?"

"Let's go outside and see what's around. Maybe we can go have a drink somewhere and come back."

"Sure."

We walked outside.

We both spied it at the same time.

"Do we dare?" Tommy asked.

"Hells ya, I'm sure we can kill an hour in there."

"And heck, I'm going to get a bonus from re-signing that client from yesterday, so shopping it is!"

He grabbed my hand and walked me toward one very large adult toy store.

To be truthful, as open as I was to exploring this place with Tommy, it was slightly uncomfortable. It's not like we were deep into a relationship and we were going through the rite of passage that every pairing seems to. Either out of sheer curiosity or to combat growing boredom, they ended up in a similar place at some point in their relationship.

But, sharing in this would be a good test to see if he had any hidden fetishes or strange sexual practices I should be aware of.

I was struck by just how colourful the place was. And by the almost overwhelming smell of plastic and rubber. There were walls and shelves and racks donning a prism of colour – purple, pink, white and blue vibrators, racks of red, black and white lace panties, bustiers and full body suits, black leather straps and harnesses complete with silver spikes, dainty little pink furry handcuffs, all sizes of flesh coloured dildos, blow-up dolls and various masturbation aids, yellow, orange, green and red thin, flavoured and textured condoms. There was a rainbow of tubes and bottles containing lubes, gels, oils, edible body paints and colours. There were dress-up outfits that included naughty nurses, policemen and women, pirates, Santa's little helper, and even Little Bo Peep. There were staphs, feathers, wigs, body jewellery and 5" heeled boots and leather sandals to complete the look.

I was mesmerised.

Tommy appeared awestruck and a little nervous but was the first to speak. "Here's a bit of adult store trivia for you. Did you know that adult stores in Sydney, Australia cannot have their doors at ground level?"

"No. I did not."

"They have a city ordinance or something that states that they have either 12 steps up or 12 steps down from street level. Something I learned when I was there on a trip for work. Or the guy I was with was just pulling my leg, but the three I went into you couldn't access from street level."

"Three? So shopping in adult stores around the globe is a hobby of yours?" I teased.

"No, actually, the marital bed needed a little spicing up around that time. The shopping fell to me because my ex would never set foot in a store like this. In fact, Kayte, I think you are the very first woman I've ever gone adult shopping with."

"Well, let's make our first of many enjoyable then shall we?" I winked and picked up a huge black dildo that seriously could have doubled as a baseball bat.

Tommy's eyes widened. I grabbed it with both hands, crouched into the hitter stance and made the batting motion with it. He laughed and I placed it down.

Tommy picked up a box containing a "mega masturbator" which could only be described as a large set of breasts on a lifelike torso complete with the required openings.

Tommy was reading more about its features. "Maybe I could ask my friends for this as a housewarming gift. This living on my own can get pretty lonely and she wouldn't take up much room under the bed."

"It's almost $400!" I was aghast.

I whispered, "Oh, and Tommy, I predict you won't be alone for long."

Tommy ignored the comment and went on, "But look Kayte, it comes with its own lube, and DVD to set the mood." He was chuckling as he put on his best infomercial announcer voice. "And wait there's more! It also comes with its own bottle of toy cleaner. C'mon, it's a steal for $400!"

We erupted in laughter.

Tommy tried on a long blonde wig and tossed his locks around from side to side as he blew me kisses from pouted lips.

I shook my head.

"Not doing it for ya?"

"Nope. Sorry."

"Should we get one of these for Dylan?" He was cradling a selection of butt plugs.

I was really enjoying Tommy's shopping enthusiasm. "Nice thought, but he has enough toys thanks."

"How bout this?"

He was holding up a couple's shock therapy sex kit in one hand, demonstrating it like a game show model with the other.

My eyes widened.

"Thought this might shock ya!"

"Ouch!"

"No. You're right, Kayte. I'm not into pain either. In my mind, sex and making love is all about feeling good. Don't quite understand all that S&M stuff. Apparently there's a market for it though and there are lots of people who are right into it."

He put on a bewildered face as he looked at the entire display devoted to pain inducing gadgetry.

I was so relieved to hear his admission because I felt very much the same way. Making love could be curious and fun and experimental but my preference was to avoid pain and pursue pleasure and pleasure only.

With a very purposeful expression, Tommy came over and gently patted me on the butt. "Okay, Missy, let's get down to some serious shopping."

I didn't know if he was kidding or not but I was curious about a few of the items I had been scanning.

I stood staring up at the wall of vibrators. There were so many choices, so many offering variable speeds, so many features, and so many colours. There were straight ones, twisted ones, curved ones and bendable ones. I had secretly hoped that having sex with something that didn't run on batteries was in my immediate future. But it also might be fun to have a little something for us both to play with or that I could have to enjoy on my own as I recalled this milestone with Tommy.

I had narrowed my choices down to four options. I had taken two of them off the shelf to examine them further. Tommy was gone again, disappearing down another aisle.

My decision was between a purple silicone stimulator with dual vibrating motors and a pink three-motor pleasure stick that came with it's own carrying box.

"I'm buying us these for tonight," Tommy exclaimed as he popped out from behind me, causing me to jump and drop my two contenders. The purple one started vibrating away. He quickly flashed his new toys in front of my face then hid them behind his back. His cheeky mischievous grin told of just how much he was enjoying this.

"Buying US these?" I repeated. "For us? I really like the sound of that. Us."

"Yep. If you're okay with my choices of course."

"Well that might just depend on what you have behind your back."

"Left or right?" he teased.

"Left."

"I thought this might make a nice dessert for later."

"For us?" I added.

He presented a package containing honey dust. As it sounded, it was an edible flavoured dust made from honey. Using the delicate feather provided you could take all the time you wanted dusting and tickling each other with the sweet powder until its irresistible light fragrance and taste begged you to start licking and sucking it off.

My mind raced to a naked Tommy and I splayed across my freshly washed sheets, dusting, licking, sucking, and dusting and licking and sucking. It would be ecstasy. I knew it. My growing moistness had me wondering if we could just skip dinner and go right for dessert.

He was staring, waiting for my reaction.

"What flavour?" was all I could manage. I was imagining his hot tongue licking my inner right thigh.

"I thought honeysuckle was the best option. Or maybe I just chose it 'cause I like the word suckle."

Oh how I wanted to be suckled by him.

"Good choice, Thomas." I looked at him with my best naughty smile. "Now what's in the other hand?"

"Before I show you this, I just need to say that if in any way you're not comfortable with this, we don't have to get it. But I thought it would be a lot of fun and would be a way for us to really connect. One last disclaimer, Kayte, you know that you can trust me right?"

Oh gawd. This wasn't another "join me at my swingers club" thing was it? I couldn't bear it if Tommy turned out to be like Mike in asking me to do something I just wasn't comfortable with. Please don't be like Mike.

"Yes, Tommy I do trust you. But I'm now very curious to see it. Out with it. Ah... I mean... what's behind your back?"

It was in a small package, relative to many of the products I'd been examining. It consisted of two purple pieces. After closer examination I learned that this big kid in a candy store had found something that we could both enjoy. It was a small waterproof egg-shaped vibrator with various speeds and pulsations and the kicker was that it even had a climax mode. The real fun came from the second piece – it was a wireless remote control! Apparently good for a range of up to 10 metres.

"Hmmm... this certainly has some possibilities."

"Is it okay? Do you like it? Am I being too presumptuous?"

"A little. But that's okay. This could be fun! And oh so portable."

"So I'll get them both?"

I nodded and with that Tommy proudly trotted off to the cash register.

I made a mental note to come back and buy the vibrator I had decided on at a later date.

After Tommy paid for our purchases, which included complimentary batteries, he asked if I'd carry them. I placed them carefully in my bag.

We were both smiling in anticipation as we left the store. Once outside, he stopped and stared with an intensity I hadn't seen from him. He ushered me slowly backward until my back was against a wall. He whispered, "Kayte, you get me so excited. I can't wait to try our purchases." With that he kissed me hard, then gentler, then hard again, then softer until we found a passionate rhythm that told of what was to come.

"I want so much to try this restaurant, but I could seriously just take you home right now and forget about eating. I just want my fill of you."

"I feel the same." I was soaked with anticipation and I could feel his stiffness prodding me.

"But I am really hungry and something tells me we both might need some strength for later."

"Agreed." I needed to catch my breath and I was famished.

Once we were seated in our secluded little booth, had ordered our food and been served our wine, we fell into a very giddy and animated exchange.

Somehow we combined our shopping experience with our dining one and came up with the idea that they should combine the adult store with the Thai restaurant to provide some better marketing slogans for their products. The marketer in me was having fun with this one. Tommy was keeping an impressive pace as well.

"Okay, what's your slogan for that black lacy bustier?" I asked him.

"Looking for an en-Thai-sing outfit? Look no further."

"Okay, for that masturbator thing you were looking at?" I took a sip of my wine.

"That's easy. Just Thai and resist me?" We both laughed.

Our coconut shrimp appetisers arrived.

"Okay, Miss Marketer, what's yours for a pair of handcuffs?"

"Don't even Thai and get away! Or I don't mind being Thai'd down."

"Not bad and neither are these sweet bundles of coconutty goodness - great choice! Okay, next, how about one for the whips?"

"Hit me baby, one more Thai." I groaned.

"Not sure that deserves one, but I'll give it to you anyway." Tommy lifted a shrimp from the plate and held it to my mouth, stroking my upper lip with his forefinger every so slightly as he did.

"Mmm... these are good." Just then the waitress arrived with chicken satay in hand.

"Okay, I've got one for that dildo, strap-on thing. 'Want to spice things up? Thai one on!' Or 'Thai it, you just might like it!' Or simply, 'Thai something different.'"

Partially because I was famished and partially because I had a need to continue building this sexual chemistry, I reached for a satay skewer, dipped it in peanut sauce and slowly brought it to my open waiting mouth. I inserted it, encircling it with my lips, tightening them until Tommy could see from the tautness of my cheeks that I had a good grip around it. I held it there for just long enough to get his full attention. He just stared silently as I gently sucked a moist morsel of peanut and coconut flavoured meat from the skewer, deliberately removing it from my mouth and then seductively licking my lips before inserting it again.

"Oh Kayte, you don't play fair. Lucky skewer!"

I repeated the display until I had consumed the contents of my two skewers. Tommy watched every second of my performance.

"Kayte, you've just made me so hard."

I was proud of the reaction that I could induce. "Then you'd better stay seated huh?"

The Massaman Beef Curry with potatoes and peanuts and the Green Curry Chicken with vegetables and basil arrived with rice for two. The aromas from both dishes and their creamy curry and coconut sauces created a hot and sweet and enticing cloud around us.

Being the gentleman, Tommy offered me the rice, then the chicken, then the beef. His serving size was about twice mine, but we both enjoyed the depth of flavours.

I was almost finished when I broke what had been the longest silence of the evening. "I think I might invite Chloe to go shopping with me there again. Who knows, I might just pick up another toy or two."

"Oh really. Well I'm glad we stumbled upon it. Whaddya gonna get?"

"Maybe one of those vibrators I was looking at, maybe some fancy dress-up clothes. Not sure."

"I really liked the sexy nurse's outfit, just in case you were wondering."

"Duly noted."

"Kayte, did you know that doctors used to prescribe a form of vibrator for women to treat hysteria?"

"Really?"

"Yes, back in the day, female hysteria was thought to cover a myriad of conditions including sexual desire and the tendency to cause trouble."

He placed air quotes around the "tendency" bit. "Women diagnosed with it were prescribed a pelvic massage for treatment. Apparently it didn't take long for this medical treatment to gain attention and make it into the pleasure-seeking mainstream. Its inventor was horrified by it being used on women as his life's work had been devoted to treating mental disorders and improving memory. His invention, the vibrator was intended to stimulate male nerve centres in the spine."

"Well who knew?"

"I did."

"Just where do you pick up all these things?"

"I'm a sponge, what can I say?"

With that I excused myself to find the restroom. All that talk about vibrators had given me an idea.

I returned a few minutes later. I sat back down at the table, placed my right hand in the centre of the table, picked up my half full wine glass with my left, downed what was left, stared Tommy directly in the eye, removed my hand to reveal a small purple remote control and said, "Doctor, doctor, I think I'm becoming hysterical. I'm feeling the need to cause trouble. Is there anything you can prescribe to help me?"

The light went on in Tommy's eyes. He immediately got the waitress's attention and motioned for the cheque.

He picked up the remote, smiled widely, and with a flick of a deft left thumb, my loins began to quiver.

Once in the car Tommy explained that he wouldn't be playing with the remote as he drove. Okay, maybe a little at the red lights but the real fun would start once we arrived at my place.

"I feel like champagne," he announced, as we were part way home.

"It's a good thing I just happen to have some for us in the fridge."

"Kayte, you think of everything."

"I try." I really hoped I had because I wanted this night to be so special.

We pulled into my driveway and Tommy flicked the remote to what I only could guess was medium speed. It provided a constant hum that was obvious as I walked to the door. Just as I tried to insert the key, Tommy obviously cranked it up a little, jolting me and making it difficult to unlock the door.

As the door closed, Tommy pressed me against it. His mouth was on mine, his curry-tasting tongue was exploring and his growing hardness was pressing into me.

Dylan tried to wedge himself between us, first from one side then the other.

Tommy began cupping my breasts in his hands and playfully flicking my nipples with his thumbs. I was squirming beneath his touch.

Dylan began to whine.

I ignored him and my hands began exploring Tommy's back and then down to his firm buttocks.

Dylan whined some more. Having received no attention, he started barking.

Tommy broke our embrace, stepped back and asked, "Poor thing has been stuck inside for a few hours. Shall I take him outside for a minute, or do you want to and I can pour us some bubbly?"

Dylan had placed his paw on Tommy's foot.

"There's your answer. Just a quick run to the corner and back would be fine. Then get back here as fast as you can!"

I attached Dylan's leash.

"C'mon boy, let's hurry up and get this done and over with. Your Mummy and I have some new toys to play with."

The door closed behind them. Tommy delivered a slight parting buzz to me, serving to spring me into action.

I ran up to put the music on in the bedroom and light the coconut scented candles in the bedroom and bathroom.

I ran back downstairs and got the glasses, the champagne bottle and ice bucket and ran them up to the bedroom. I placed the newly purchased honey dusting powder on the dresser. I quickly brushed my teeth, adjusted my cleavage and finished freshening my makeup just as I heard the door open and felt the vibrations growing inside me.

"We're back!"

"Up here."

Tommy bounded up the stairs, turned the egg to high and said, "Now for my favourite part of the meal – dessert!"

I stood in the centre of the bedroom, mildly vibrating from the waist down and nipples erect with anticipation. My breathing had quickened at the sight of him standing there. He placed an arm on each of my shoulders.

"Kayte, let me just stand here and drink you in. The way the candlelight is bouncing off your cheeks in this light, the gentleness of your curves in the shadows, the seductive look in your eyes, it's all so incredibly entrancing."

I stood there taking the opportunity to appreciate the man that stood before me. His body was imposing, his height made me feel feminine. I felt so connected to him even though we just stood there staring, saying nothing.

I moved closer to him placing my arm around his waist. He mirrored my movements. With his other hand, he lifted my chin and then approached ever so slowly placing his full searing lips on mine. Our mouths opened and our tongues began twirling and twisting and joining us together. He drew me closer. His muscular chest pressed into me and his growing member was not shy in making its presence known.

His hands stroked my back, my shoulders and down the length of my arms. I reached up and my hands explored his broad shoulders and up his neck to his face and behind his head.

With a slight clumsiness he freed me from my blouse by pulling it over my head rather than undoing the buttons.

He kissed down my neck and across my breasts and then up my neck again.

He was placing light kisses in my ear when he spied it. He whispered, "Ooh, champagne. Can we open it? Can I pour you a glass? Can I pour me a glass?"

I nodded biting my lip.

Pop went the cork. I heard it fizz into the glasses.

"To a wonderful evening." He handed me a glass and clinked it.

"And to many, many more." I offered as a follow-up.

I noticed a momentary pensive look on his face, but a split second later it was replaced by a gentle smile.

"Mmm. This is good. Kayte, do you mind if I take a few minutes and have a quick shower?"

"Not at all. Go ahead. I want you to feel at home here. I'll bring you in a towel."

"Mind if I take this?" He held up his almost full flute.

"Tommy, mi casa es su casa."

He left the bathroom door slightly ajar and chose to shower by candlelight. Through the dimness I could see his pants hit the floor, then his top, then his briefs. I wanted to see his naked body and had for a while now. I sat on the bed for a spell, anticipating what was to come.

Champagne still in hand, I found a clean fluffy towel and tapped on the door. "I've got your towel. Can I come in?"

"Of course."

"I'll leave it here on the counter."

The sweet scents of the coconut candles and the coconut scented soap filled the steamy room.

"Thanks, but aren't you going to join me?"

"Uh… ok!" I took a sip of my drink and placed it on the counter next to the shower - right beside Tommy's.

I stepped out of my skirt and let it fall atop his jeans. Standing there in just my bra and matching red lace panties I was greeted by a wet, glistening and very naked Thomas Kessler.

His chest was wide and hard and sculpted as were his ample arms and shoulders. His waist was slim and there was just a hint of an Apollo's belt. His legs and pubic area were covered with more dark hair than I'd imagined and his penis, which had somewhat softened at this point, had a reasonable length and girth. It had been snipped at the tip and had a slight curvature. He was a lefty. All in all, a masculine vision that I'm sure I'd never tire of admiring.

"Kayte, you're staring… but that's okay. It gave me a chance to have a good look at you as well. You're so beautiful. I thought the blue one was nice, but that red lacy outfit is S-M-O-K-I-N'! It's almost a shame that I'm going to remove them."

He reached out and pulled me into the shower toward him with one hand, the other undid my bra and it fell to the floor beside my skirt. The panties were not as easy to remove. They clung to my skin as we stood together and the hot droplets moistened our bodies, allowing them to glide against each other. Tommy placed a single kiss on my mouth then one on my neck, then one on my chest right over my rapidly pounding heart. He paused, lowered himself to a kneeling position and kissed me so very softly once on each erect nipple, then down the centre of my belly while his hands lowered my panties to the shower floor.

He kissed my belly button then the top of each hip bone. He exhaled a lengthy spray of hot breath and kissed my mound before returning to his feet and grabbing the bar of soap. He turned my back to him and with arms around me began lathering me, covering my neck, arms, breasts and belly in a foam of coconut-scented bubbles. I could feel his hardness prodding the small of my back. He kissed the side of my neck, across my collarbone and shoulders. I was experiencing a plethora of invigorating sensations. The image of naked Tommy was burned into my brain. The sweetness of coconut permeated my nostrils. The hot water pellets pricked and tickled my skin as they fell. Tommy's hands delivered a strong and hungry sensation as they slid up and down my torso, claiming it and me. The jazz saxophone hummed in my ears. I was wet with anticipation and longed to feel him inside me. Seemingly sensing that taste was the only sense not totally aroused at this point, Tommy reached out for his champagne glass and emptied it in one huge gulp. He placed the glass down and pulled my head back by tugging playfully on my hair until my mouth was directly beneath his. He kissed me first, then with slow and deliberate pursed lips he surprised me by streaming the cold bubbly liquid into me, filling my mouth. I let it trickle slowly down my throat enjoying the contrast of its coolness compared to the growing heat of our exchange.

I turned to him and kissed him hard. My tongue was now in control. He returned the vigour as he grabbed my buttocks, squeezing them firmly but gently.

"Do you know how much I want you?" He mouthed between kisses.

I took his hand and placed two fingers deep between my legs. "Oh, I think I have an idea."

He smiled while his fingers explored, tickling me just a little.

"Should I remove your new friend?" He asked referring to the still present egg.

"That might be wise for now but let's put him on the night stand for later."

Tommy smiled a wry wicked smile as he pulled it out.

It was time. I couldn't wait any longer. I turned off the shower, took Tommy's hand, grabbed the white fluffy bath sheet and wrapped it around us both and we shuffled to the bed, kissing all the while.

I let the towel fall. Tommy took a long look and then gently pushed me back until I lay across the bed. He took another approving glance before he blanketed me in his heavy, hot, still wet and wanting body. He kissed me passionately. The fingers of one hand were lightly tickling my side as they travelled from my underarm to my waist. The other had started at the opposite ankle and was making its way up the inside of my leg.

My ecstasy was raised to new heights, half fuelled by the emotional connection I had with Tommy and half by my sheer lust for him. I was completely aroused, alive and in love, lying there with him. He had teased me by pouring cold champagne first over my breasts and lapping up every drop with his wide soft tongue. He trickled it onto my mound, giving it a moment before licking it as it dripped down into my clean-shaven crevice. He then turned his attention to giving me searing kisses that told me of his passion.

My body was tingling with wanting. His was hard with desire. He quickly found his way between my legs. I had to spread them wide to accommodate him but I was ready to receive him. His penis knocked at my vaginal door tentatively at first. With some eager moans of encouragement, he found the audacity to fill the doorway and then forge his way inside. He explored his new surroundings moving left then right then back again. He retraced his steps, backing in and out until he found a comfortable rhythm. He circled round and played with the tempo, first slow and deliberate then faster and more forceful.

I felt full and complete. The frenzy of his forceful pace was causing me to writhe and moan and beg him to go faster. He did. My pending orgasm was verging on eruption. I heard him groan each time he thrust inside me. His pace got harder and faster. In then out. In then out. The friction on my clitoris was explosive, the hair on his heavy chest teased my nipples as it brushed against them with each consecutive thrust. I wanted to burn that moment into my memory – my first orgasm of a lifetime of orgasms with Thomas Kessler.

"I'm… so… close… Kayte."

"Me too." And then it hit. "Oh gawd… oooooh… oooh… gawd, yes, yes, yessss!" My screams were loud and guttural. The searing friction ignited a forceful and explosive orgasm. I was thrashing and wriggling and twisting. He was groaning and coming in long explosions inside me. I was drenched in my own response. I lay breathless. He was surrendered and spent. With our passionate cries and movements abated, he collapsed on me then angled himself beside me, lying on his side. I looked up. We stared at each other, each fighting to catch our breath.

"WOW!" was the first word we both uttered, at the exactly the same time.

We laughed.

"Sorry that was so fast."

"No apologies. We both got there. And we'll have lots and lots of opportunities to slow it down next time and the time after that and the time after that."

"Uh. Ya. I guess so."

"Tommy, we go well together. I could get very used to this." I backed into him and he encased me in his arms.

He said nothing.

With a huge smile and an incredibly connected and accomplished feeling I just lay there soaking in the moment.

I must have drifted off because I awoke to a light tickling sensation across my chest. It was followed by another that started with a caress of my left breast and ended with a swipe across my belly. I squirmed into consciousness. I could feel the goosebumps form across my skin.

My awareness grew. I was in bed with Tommy. I was in bed with Tommy Kessler. He was tickling me. He was tickling my naked body. Holding the feather that came with the honey dust that he bought for us! His naked hand was attached to his naked body that was sitting up in my bed next to my naked body. We had finally made love. Hot, sweet, passionate, burning love. Finally. After all this time, we were together. It wasn't email flirting, it wasn't IM chats. It was a real life skin-to-skin, heart to heart, connection. And here he was, teasing me. He was initiating another round. He hadn't woken up, made some excuse and put on his pants to leave. He stayed. He wanted more. He wanted more with me. I wanted more with him too.

This had been a fabulous start but it was just the beginning. There would be so much more, so many nights together in the same bed, so many shopping trips, so many dinners out, so many laughs, so many moments of connection.

Being with Tommy made me so happy, so complete. I had been concerned that our playfulness and great cerebral connection wouldn't translate to the bedroom but it did. We had obvious physical chemistry. And for our first time together we demonstrated some pretty incredible timing too.

The tickling had moved to high on my left thigh where I could now feel the presence of the light powdery coating he had applied.

I smiled. He smiled back.

"Hey sexy, you don't mind if I start on dessert do you?" He slid down and began licking the honey dust from my belly and with wide tongue stroke after tongue stroke was making his way up to my breast. He stopped, glanced up, licked his lips and said, "This stuff is really tasty and I'm starving. I hope you don't mind me taking my time and lingering over dessert, Kayte. I want to savour every lick."

"So do I, Tommy. So. Do. I."

The fire between my legs was beginning to reignite.

"Oh, and Kayte, after dessert… we're going to try a little eggs-periment!"

All were fine by me. This was my time to lie back and enjoy.

I had been waiting a long long time to share my bed with this man so I was happy to surrender to Tommy's plan.

I trusted that he knew what he was doing and that he'd let me know what he needed.

With a feathery dust of the fine powder across my nipples, followed by a hot probing tongue and powerful lips, he was certainly well aware of what I did.

CHAPTER 44

After a quick cuddle and kiss session, Tommy stopped things before they took us down the path we had travelled three times during the past evening. He had to get to work so he showered, had a quick coffee and left with promises to call me later.

"I'll be looking forward to that." My response gushed out far too dreamily but I just couldn't help myself.

I closed the door behind him. Looking down at Dylan, his huge brown eyes set amidst his furry blond face looked at me with a certain knowing glance, almost as if to say, "you look really happy."

"Come here Dylan." He obliged. "Paws up." Dylan stood on his hind legs and I grabbed his paws and began dancing around the foyer. "You're right boy. I am happy. Happier than I've been in a long, long time." I couldn't believe the rush of feelings that were welling inside me.

"Tommy makes me happy. He makes me laugh. He turns me on. He teaches me things. He asks me good questions. He appreciates me. He's easy to talk to. He's smart. He's tall. He's sexy. He's a good man. He's everything on my list. My dream guy personified. He's... perfect for me!" Poor Dylan didn't know what to make of my silly behaviour but he was patient with me.

I let his paws go, ran up the stairs and jumped into bed. I closed my eyes and lay there reliving all the wonderful moments of the previous evening. I had definitely fallen for Thomas Kessler. Attaboy77 had captured my heart, my head and my desire. There was something different about him, something that I felt from when I very first read his profile. There was a connection to his words that made me notice him, that made his persona resonate, that made me think that he very well could be "the one".

Online dating had presented me with all sorts of men to choose from. The ones I met all had so much to offer, but with each of them, there had been something that didn't quite gel. I had learned there were things I was and things I wasn't prepared to do in the name of love. I learned that I didn't have to sacrifice my dreams. They've been tested and I've found a man that lives up to them. I was grateful for 'wheresinglesfindlove' and Chloe's introduction to it. I was proud that I took the chance to explore online dating and I was especially thankful for having met the man behind the Attaboy77 profile.

I wanted to read those words again. To glance back from where we now were. I wanted to see if the man whom I had given all of myself to last night appeared to be the same man presented in the profile I had read those months before. While I now knew him on a deeper level, I thought it would be interesting to look back and see what showed through then. To look back in hindsight can be very educational.

I leapt out of bed and ran to the computer. I thought about all the fun and flirty conversations Tommy and I had exchanged and how I was so happy that it had led us here, to a place where we could know and appreciate each other on all levels. I also thought that it was now time for me to remove my profile. I thought Tommy and I were at that stage. I wanted him to know just how much I felt for him. I didn't need to keep dating other men. I didn't want him to think he was competing for me. I was happy to invest my time and my emotions in him and him alone. He was the man I wanted. I didn't need to keep comparing and contrasting. I felt it. I knew it. I was committed to it.

I searched for his profile in my favourites and it wasn't there. There was, however, a new message from 'AdventureGuy', the marathon runner and consultant who enjoyed fencing and the finer things in life.

Dearest Katontheprowl,

I've just re-read your profile and looked again at your photos and must tell you how much you've captivated me.

You are a divine creature, so very beautiful, so searingly erotic.

We need to meet.

I'd be honoured to observe your obvious confidence and passion in person.

Your evident intelligence, wit and sensuality form a triumvirate that I find both refreshing and reassuring.

Your energy? Irresistible.

Your desire to find a deep connection with a sensual polymath is alluring.

I'm your man.

I'm the one who can deliver your deepest desires and encourage you as you develop fresh ones.

Know this – a passionate relationship entices rather than frightens me.

I run toward, not away from, commitment – so unlike most other men.

Let's meet so we can ignite what I'm sure will be an explosive connection.

Together we can form a pairing that will challenge, reward, amaze and astonish us both on every conceivable level.

Our time is now.

Let's begin.

There's no reason for us not to meet.

Is there?

In anticipation,

Everett

Wow. I was agog by this latest correspondence. 'AdventureGuy' was obviously intelligent. His confidence was powerful. His praise was generous, inviting and somewhat embarrassing. However, I couldn't resist my own narcissistic tendency to read it again. Okay, and again.

His words made me feel desired and appreciated. He could see just from my profile that I was worthy of the type of relationship I sought. He was clear about his own intentions, needs and desires. He was a man that knew what he wanted.

I was flattered by his attention. He was certainly intense and direct. I read his final question for the third time, this time answering it. I was reminded of why I was at the computer in the first place. My answer brought me back. Is there a reason for us not to meet? Yes. Yes, there was. There finally was. His name was Tommy Kessler. And I felt a tingle you know where just at the thought of him.

But where was his profile?

I typed in Tommy's full profile name and the message **Profile removed** came back with the date and time of removal being just hours before.

My initial reaction was somewhat unsettled. I wondered what that meant. Then it hit me.

"Woo bloody hoo!" Tommy's taken down his dating profile. He beat me to it. After last night, he must feel the same way I do. We had found love. Why would we need to continue looking, why would we need a dating profile?

I got up and started dancing around the office, grinning and singing, "I'm in love with Tommy and he's in love with meeeeeee". This time Dylan made a beeline for the stairs. I guess he'd had enough of seeing a gleefully happy, somewhat delirious me dancing around earlier today.

Composure regained, grin still beaming from ear to ear, tingly-in-the-pants feeling still present as I still felt where he'd been inside me, I sat back down to the computer.

I needed to do as he did.

Just as I was about to remove mine, the phone rang. "Hello stranger." It was the unmistakable deep and gravelly voice of one Roman Wolfsky.

"Hello yourself" was my rather unimaginative, somewhat disappointed 'you're not Tommy' reply. His timing was incredible. He must have sensed how happy I was and thought it was time for a buzz kill. I was still uncomfortable with Roman, but I guess given how well things were going with Tommy, I was in a better place to deal with Roman now.

The truth was that we had not spoken much at all over the past couple of months; the odd email here and there, a voicemail message left at a time when we knew the other would not be home, a text message sent every once in a while just to ensure the other was still out there and distantly connected through this technological web. It had been enough to suggest that we had wanted to connect, but not enough to actually make it happen. It was safe and at arms length. It's like we had moved to the safe haven of e-friendship.

I was not proud of myself for being what I deemed rude to Roman, but I was not sure how to deal with his advances either. In our brief exchanges after "the incident" he had proclaimed that he had apparently had some "feelings" for me. My fears had been realised. Coming from Roman, I didn't know what "feelings" really meant. He had never been the commitment type and his actions with women were downright offensive to me so I really couldn't see us ever finding a common ground upon which to build a relationship. With him, feelings could be, and probably were, all sexual, nothing more.

We had sex – that was it. I made sure that things didn't go any further. For as much as I craved a relationship, one with Roman was nowhere near what I had in mind. While I was frustrated by dating and way overdue, I still was not ready to settle. I did miss his friendship though. I missed the uncomplicated relationship we used to share.

While a bit cowardly, I guess I wanted time to step in and smooth things over. I didn't want to look Roman in the eye and say that I didn't have romantic feelings for him – sexual or otherwise – that went beyond what had now become a tenuous friendship. I didn't want to defend my stance with the rationale that I thought the way he treated women stunk – that I had regretted ever even kissing him, let alone sleeping with him. I didn't want to explain that I didn't think he was capable of forming a lasting relationship or finding true love because he didn't even like, let alone, love himself. I could not have imagined taking responsibility for that discussion or for being the one who shook him into an alternate reality, one where he might finally have seen the error of his ways.

Even though I hadn't been capable of having that conversation with him, he needed to hear it. He needed to learn that he was better than his actions made him out to be. He needed to know that people, mainly women, couldn't see what goodness lay within him because his badness turned them away before they could see deep enough.

He needed something to shock him into a realisation that the 'player' in him needed to be benched… permanently.

Little did I know that this phone call was the confirmation that the universe had set that transformation in motion and it was already happening. Something had been occurring with him, something big that had forced him down that illuminated path.

"I've been better, Kayte."

"Oh? What's up?"

"Do you want the good news or bad news?"

"Both – feel free to pick which order."

"The good news is that it's curable and the bad news is, it's still seen as an STD."

"An STD? As in a sexually transmitted disease, STD?"

"Yep, one and the same I'm afraid. It's a skin condition."

"And you have this? This STD?"

"Yes and that's why I'm calling. I've been agonising over this but I had to do the right thing and tell all my sexual partners."

Oh great, this just keeps getting better and better! Why did I have to sleep with him? Why? Why? And why did I have to get this call today? Why couldn't it have been yesterday? Why?

"And I guess I now fall into that rather large category." *Oooh. That was a catty retort. Try and have some understanding Kayte.*

"Yes, I had to make a few calls."

"I'll bet." *Stop it Kayte. Now, you're just being a bitch. But this could have a very unwelcome effect on Tommy's and my relationship. Tommy knew about Roman, but he didn't know I had slept with him.*

"Hey, Kayte, I feel bad enough about this as it is."

"Yes, I guess. Sorry Roman. That was uncalled for and uncharitable. I'm sorry. So what do you have? How bad is it? What do I need to look for?" *The reality of it was hitting me.*

"Well it's called 'molluscum contagiosum'. It's a contagious skin condition – the eruptions caused by it look like the combination of a wart and a pimple. They're curable but contagious. So make sure you take a good look."

"Where should I be looking? Uh… where do you have them?"

"The doctor said that these are viral and often sexually transmitted and usually affect the genitals, lower abdomen, buttocks, and inner thighs. In rare cases, molluscum infections are also found on the lips and mouth. So check all of the above."

Oh great, Tommy was all those places!

"What do they look like?"

"Best to go to the web and have a look yourself – it's spelled m-o-l-l-u-s-c-u-m c-o-n-t-a-g-i-o-s-u-m."

"Got it… the spelling that is, hopefully not the condition! Haven't noticed anything weird in my nether regions recently, but I'll make sure to take a good long look."

I had sex with Tommy. What if I gave him this? No. This can't be happening. No. Not now. This was not the next step I'd envisioned in our relationship.

"Good. Sorry to call you with this. But I just found out a few days ago and I'm getting treated. I wanted to make sure that everyone I've been with over the past few months knew about it and could get themselves checked out. Everyone I know how to contact anyway."

"Well thanks for letting me know. I'll have a look but I don't think I've been affected, or should I say infected?"

"Thought it wouldn't have, given our timing and that we used a condom. And I'm pretty sure now that I know where I got it and she was after you."

"I still don't know how you keep them all straight."

"I won't have to any more."

"And why is that?"

"Kayte, can I be perfectly blunt?"

"Aren't you always? C'mon, Roman, that's one of your best attributes!" It felt like an old-style Kayte and Roman conversation for the first time in ages.

"This really got me thinking. Thinking about this lifestyle, about how I am with women, what it is I'm really looking for."

"And… "

"And between that and knowing that you, or women like you, would never be interested in a guy like me, especially with these unsightly contagious bumps all over my man parts, I just think that it's time I gave my head a shake. The other one for a change!"

"Roman, you might just have something there, besides the bumpy nether regions. You've got a lot going for you, but to be equally as blunt, so many people never get the chance to see it because it's buried under so much machismo crap."

"Well, thanks, I guess. Also, I met a woman a couple of weeks ago and we've actually been out a few times. It feels a little different. We haven't had sex yet, due to this whole STD thing. It's forcing me to take things slow and get to know her before we hop in the sack. The ironic thing is I knew her back in high school and had a crush on her then. We bumped into each other when I was coming back from the doctor's. Of course I haven't told her why I was there. We're really getting along well, seem to have tons in common and she's very understanding, patient, gentle, kind and non-judgmental. We're making all kinds of plans over the next few weeks. So we're both looking into the future. You never know, maybe I'll do something different and try monogamy for a while."

"You can always try. "

"Yeah, and I may even be successful at it."

"One thing's for sure Roman; you won't know until you try. Anyways, I should get going and find myself a mirror, but thanks for making this call. It must have been tough to do it. Doing the right thing isn't always the easiest thing is it? But thanks for respecting me and my health enough to let me know. I really do appreciate it."

"Yeah, thanks Kayte. Sorry to have to make the call, but it is nice to actually talk to you. And I do respect you – our relationship is different than the ones I have with most women. I like it. I miss it."

"I do too, Roman. I do too. It's nice talking to you. And as for us, we'll find a way to regain our friendship. It's just going to take a little time. Good luck with your new woman, I really hope it works out for you."

"I think I do too. Thanks babe… later!"

Great. I was being punished for indiscriminate sex. I hadn't noticed anything that even resembled what I saw on my computer screen. Geesh the web really did have everything didn't it? Nope, nothing like that. Eeeeeeeewwwwwww and thankfully nothing like that either. Although I hadn't noticed anything, it hadn't stopped me from dropping my pants right there standing in front of the computer in my office as I bent over and took a good hard look. I had just grabbed a hand mirror from the bathroom and was contorted into a position that could best be described as a human pull knot, bent over, head between my legs looking up, arms on either side of each leg, holding the mirror in one hand and moving myself around to find the best lighting angle.

And then the phone rang.

Great.

I could tell before the caller even said hello that it was Chloe. Her 'tell' was the swoosh of water in the background. I heard it before her. She was most likely washing fruits and vegetables that would later form some gastronomic masterpiece.

"Whatchya doin'?"

"You wouldn't believe me if I told you," I replied.

"Try me."

I explained the call that came before hers and she listened supportively, with no judgement, like the friend she was.

"So what do they look like?"

"Tough to describe, but from what I'm seeing on the website they look like little skin balloons, or bubbles, like the ones you see forming in hot tar on a sunny summer afternoon, but they're made of reddish skin."

"Ick!"

"Yes, ick! Thankfully it looks like I'm clear."

"Is it treatable?"

"Yep, apparently they can burn them off like warts, cut them off, laser them off or various other topical type treatments. But hopefully I won't have to investigate any treatment options."

"Poor you."

"Yeah. I just so want all this to end. I am just so bloody sick of dating and all the crap that goes along with it. I just want to be in love, be with one man, say goodbye to this dating drama for ever."

"I wish I could wave a magic wand and find you your Prince Charming. But he's out there KitKat, just have faith. I think Tommy just might be a keeper. Sounds like things are going really well."

"Things with Tommy are going exceptionally well. Especially after last night. And given our activities last night, I better NOT have this condition because there's a chance then that Tommy would too."

"Are you saying what I think you're saying? Oh, do tell."

"Yes, yes, I am, but details are reserved for an in-person conversation."

"So this could be it then!"

"Yes Chloe, I think it is. We connected so well in so many ways. But then I start thinking and wondering, really, could it be? Is there something missing? Am I seeing all the signs, is he holding back? Am I seeing only what I want to see? Or am I just so used to things not working out that I can't just accept this as being different?"

"I wish I could answer those questions for you darling."

"I know. I'm trying not to over-think it. I just want to enjoy this warm fuzzy feeling. I think I just have too much time on my hands. Too much time to just think, analyse, ponder, question, go back and forth, replay every conversation, re-read every email. I've been thinking about starting a business. Maybe an event management business. What do you think?"

"I think you need to do something. And that's a great idea. With one caveat – as long as you can maintain the balance you've got going in your life. You don't want to finally realise that you've met the perfect guy and have no time for him. It's all about balance."

"True. I've really enjoyed having time for me and things outside of work that make me happy."

"As for the business, we can work together – you plan the events, I cater them! I need some help promoting my catering business. Maybe we could create a big fundraiser for a charity, maybe for animals and that would give us both great exposure. I've got my eye on a Vespa and I want to buy it with my own money. Boomer says if he's forking out for a motorcycle, it's going to be a Harley or nuthin.'"

"Oh honey, I can't quite see you on a Harley."

"Exactly my point. Me neither, so with my own cashola I can buy whatever I want and that happens to be a powder blue Vespa."

"Okay, so we'll be talking date details, event planning company, fundraiser and scooters. I'll see you at your place in just three sleeps"

"Can't wait."

"Love you."

"Love ya back and hope you don't find a bump on ya!"

"Oh, darling, me too!"

How was I going to tell Tommy? Was I going to tell Tommy? If there were no signs on me, would I even need to tell him?

CHAPTER 45

There had been no phone call from Tommy all day.

I didn't know if he had tried to reach me online as I had taken Dylan for an 8K walk. We walked instead of running today because I was physically tired from not having much sleep the night before. Something I'd willingly repeat night after night into perpetuity.

With each step, I felt where Tommy had been inside of me and I smiled at the thought of it. I strolled most of our walk on autopilot as I replayed the silliness of Tommy's and my shopping expedition, our laughs and intimate moments at dinner, our sexual tension building in the shower and the repeated times we released it by making love. Each time was different but each brought us to heights of pleasure. It was no wonder I was tired. I'd bet Tommy was too. Thankfully I didn't have to work today and I felt a little sorry for him that he did.

What I did do after my walk was get in to see a doctor, given the news from Roman. I thought it best to have a professional opinion. The doctor said that I appeared fine and had I been exposed I most likely would have seen evidence of it by now.

That was a relief on so many levels.

It was past 7pm and I realised that I hadn't yet had a shower or eaten. I was tired and if I was to keep my eyes open and stay awake to speak with Tommy or find the energy to make myself a meal, I certainly needed a second wind.

I stepped into the hot stream, the water drizzling down me, grabbed the soap and began lathering when the scent of coconut brought the entire evening flooding into my consciousness yet again. I felt Tommy's large hands exploring my slippery skin. I recalled his hot warm tongue spread wide and licking up my spine from the small of my back. I relived the smile of contentment on his face as he lay back after his initial orgasm. I was tickled by the honey dust being feathered across my nipples. The hum of the egg delivered sensations vibrating inside of me. The warmth and wanting from his eyes pierced mine again. The warmth from his chest and arms burned into my skin as he held me to him. I felt the happiness bubble up inside of me, the contentment soar, the connection solidify while all the waiting and wanting for that one true connection wafted away, freeing me to enjoy the wondrous gifts from this incredible man. I desperately wanted to speak with him, hold him, connect with him again. I wanted more Tommy and Kayte.

I towelled off, checked the phone – still no messages. I went directly to the computer. Nope, he wasn't showing as online in the IM window either.

There it was. A new message had just arrived in my inbox. The subject read, **I've been thinking...**

My mind raced through the possibilities.

I've been thinking about just how much I adore you. I've been thinking, I've waited all my life to find someone like you. I so enjoyed our night together last night, I'm having a shower, stopping to pick up some wine and I'll be right over. I've been thinking that I'd like to come by and do a little role playing and strut around bare-chested in my tightest jeans and tool belt and fix everything that needs fixing, including your plumbing. I've been thinking about whisking you away to a sunny destination where we can swim, drink and eat all day and make love all night. I want to introduce you to my family and friends so that they can start loving you as much as I do. I've been thinking that it's time I gave you a full body massage and that we should go back to that store and see what other things we can buy to play with. I've been thinking I want to dress up, go to the theatre and tease you all night by remote control. I've been thinking that I just can't stop smiling today. I've been thinking that you make me so happy that I want to spend the rest of my life with you. I've been thinking that we will grow old together.

And then I read his email.

Kayte,

I don't know where or how to start.

I've been thinking a lot today. In fact, I left work early because I just couldn't concentrate.

I went for a long drive. It always helps me to get clarity of thought. After my marriage broke up, I clocked some serious mileage.

Ok, focus Tommy, focus.

I guess I should start with a huge THANK YOU for last night.

I'll probably come off sounding more like a gushing girl than the bad-ass biker dude I am, but you deserve my full disclosure.

I'll be able to say far more in writing than I'd ever be able to get out in conversation

I had an incredible time. You are so easy to get along with, so open, so smart, so funny and so… okay, I'll say it… SEXY. What man could resist? I enjoyed every second of it. It was HOT. I felt comfortable enough with you to explore and to experiment. It's been tough, having been married for so long, to even think about being with someone in that way, let alone take it to the level that we did last night. I am so very grateful for that. I feel it's helped

me to turn a corner. Maybe soon I'll be able to move past my past and take real steps toward my future.

You are a supportive and strong woman who has helped me in more ways than I can ever express and I hope you know just how much this means to me. And how deeply grateful I am. I know that doesn't sound too manly, but it's the truth.

And it's because of this that what I have to say next is so difficult. I've looked at it up and down, across and sideways, inside and out, but keep coming to the same conclusion.

Kayte, I don't think we should see each other anymore.

I'm sure you're going to be shocked by this, but that will just further prove my rationale as to why I think this.

Please try and hear me out (or read me out as the case may be).

I went back and re-read your profile today and in it the same phrase kept playing over and over in my head:

"But know this, I'm looking for a relationship. I may be ready to settle down, but I'll never settle. If this scares you then I'm probably not the woman for you. However, if you too are seeking an amazing and passionate relationship, then introduce yourself."

Kayte, you deserve to find love so much more than anyone I know. You deserve someone who is ready to give you all the love and support that you are so worthy of. You need someone who is not only a great fit personality-wise and sexually, but in readiness. Someone who is prepared to give you 100%.

I think we connect on so many levels, but last night it was clear that you want so much more than I can give you. When we clinked glasses and I was very much in the moment holding no future expectations, you immediately referenced the future, our future. You kept referring to what we'd do next. You've done this on a couple of occasions prior to last night too. First I just tried to look past them, but then it really hit me, that you are looking for 'happily ever after' but, to be truthful, I'm still stuck on "once upon a time."

This is all so new to me. I've been so lucky to meet someone like you so early in my new single state, but it's early days. You've probably gone and ruined me for other women though – you've set the bar so high.

I'm just not ready for a relationship, Kayte. I am still hurting from the breakup of my marriage. I'm still redefining who I am. And I need time on my own to do that. I need time to get to know who I am now, before I can commit wholly to someone else. I hope you can understand that. I took my profile down today. I know that now, so I'm going to just give myself some time. Forget about dating for a while.

And you are looking for and are so incredibly deserving of a great relationship. I want that for you.

I wish you all the luck in the world in finding it. It's out there for you. I know it is. There is such a big part of me that wishes I was ready for what you were prepared to give me. I'm honoured and somewhat overwhelmed that someone as wonderful as you even gave me a second glance.

Kayte, I'm sorry. I'm sorry if I've led you on, sorry if I've hurt you, which I suspect I have. I'm sorry I'm not where you need me to be yet. I'm sorry that I can't look forward to a future with you in it. I'll miss you so very much.

I wish there was a way that together you could have what you need and that I could have what I need and together neither of us would be hurt in the process.

But, I just can't see a way to make that happen.

I think it's best that we don't have any contact for a while. It would only confuse things if we did.

Just know that this decision was not arrived at lightly and I hope that you know how difficult it was for me to make. But I tried to consider both our needs. I don't want to be careless with your heart. It's huge and loyal and loving and someone else deserves it. As long as they are good enough for you because you deserve the very best.

Kayte, I want to thank you from the bottom of my still broken heart for everything you've taught me, for the good times and

the laughs, for the attention, for the friendship, for the intimate moments.

They and you will stay in my memory forever.

Goodbye Kayte, and good luck in finding a lover worthy of you.

Please give butt plug boy a pat goodbye for me, will ya? I'll miss him too. I'm going to go now and have a big rum and a little cry.

Thomas

"N-o-o-o-o-o-o-o-o-o-o-o-o-o-o-o!"

My scream was long and primal.

Dylan came running to my side.

The tears were streaming from my eyes. I just sat there, unmoving, numb, stung and broken by his words, yet reading them over and over and over again.

My gut wrenched, my smile disappeared. My shoulders slumped. My images of our happy future together shattered into a million sharp teeny chards. The happily-ever-after page had been ripped from what I thought was shaping up to be my ultimate love story.

How could I have been so wrong?

I was shocked.

I was perplexed.

I couldn't move.

I just stared blankly at the screen.

I couldn't understand how we could have been where we were last night only to end up here today, how 24 hours ago his mouth explored mine and today his words cut right through my heart.

I was confused by the discrepancy between his words of today and his actions of last night.

I wanted to turn back time. I wanted to stay in the moments where I was cocooned in the reassurance of his arms.

I wanted to hear his laugh and see his smile and believe in all the joy we could bring to each other.

I wanted to lay together in a future where we drifted off to sleep and woke each day in each other's arms.

My dream was over.

The belief that I had found love, that I had met Mr. Right in Mr. Thomas Kessler had vanished.

Could I do something, anything, to save this?

What if I spoke with him?

Could I tell him it was okay, I understood what he was feeling and I'd wait until he was ready?

Should I tell him that we could have any kind of relationship that he was comfortable with?

What would happen if I told him that we could just be friends?

Maybe I should say that I'd help him put his broken heart back together until it was whole enough to love me.

Could I tell him that I'd help him to find himself?

I could.

But I wouldn't.

That wouldn't benefit either of us.

The truth was that I was ready for him. I was ready for love.

But he was right.

He wasn't. And on some level I knew that.

I saw signs, subtle ones. There was a glance here, an uncomfortable reaction to my words there. There had been confusion and mixed messages during our online chats.

I guess I just chose to ignore them because I wanted him so much. I wanted love so much.

I thought together we could get past them. I thought that there would be enough of a connection to overcome his lack of readiness. My optimism was fuelled by the dramatic changes I had already seen from the Tommy I first met. He was a good man – moral and smart and funny and affectionate and he was coming into his own.

But no, he wasn't there yet.

Maybe I had just been a fool.

Maybe I just wanted it too much.

Maybe the two of us just couldn't distinguish between the flirtation, sex, friendship and love.

Maybe I just couldn't understand, why I wasn't finding true love?

I knew that I deserved someone who was ready. Someone who wanted love, someone who was whole and complete enough in themselves to give it freely. Someone who knew who they were, what they wanted and were sure of their feelings for me.

Tommy was right. That was what I wanted and what I deserved.

And he deserved his own brand of happiness. He needed to take his own journey.

I knew he was right, but why did something so right have to feel so wrong and hurt so damn much?

I sat there bawling. I plummeted from the high I had been on all day to the very deepest darkest cavern of despair.

I was alone again.

I had experienced yet another false start.

Why was love so elusive for me?

When would I find my soul mate?

Where was the man that was destined for me?

Did he even exist?

Beaten, deflated, broken and sad, I dragged myself off to my lonely bed.

Hours of sobbing wore me into a welcome sleep. It provided freedom from the pain.

CHAPTER 46

Looking through blurry swollen eyes, the clock read 11:42am. I had been in bed for almost 15 hours. If I hadn't have needed to get up to let the furry one out and feed him, I probably would have stayed in bed for another 15.

I swung my feet around and out of bed. They landed in a mountain of tissues. There beneath my feet lay dozens of little white wads, each little ball holding bits of disappointment, pain and broken hopes and dreams. The crying had stopped but my eyes were puffy and stinging and told of my anguish from the night before.

I went downstairs to open the door for Dylan and I put fresh food and water in his bowls. I opened the fridge, looked around and closed it again. I had no appetite. Glancing at the coffee maker, I refrained from making coffee. It was too much work. I poured myself a glass of water and dragged myself back up the stairs into bed.

As I passed the mirror, I observed the dramatic change in myself from just 24 hours before. Yesterday my eyes were shining brightly, there was a huge goofy grin plastered across my glowing face, my shoulders were back, I walked tall, I looked and felt as if I could take on the world. Today I was a lifeless bundle. My face was grey and there wasn't the hint of a grin anywhere to be found. I walked slowly, dragging my feet with shoulders drooped. My eyes told all. They were empty and swollen, half closed and pink and puffy.

At least I looked like I felt.

I didn't care how I looked. Why should I? There was no one to look nice for. There was no one to impress.

I looked around my lonely bedroom. I remembered the passion that had filled it when Tommy was here with me. I remembered how comfortable it felt having him here, how it felt like he belonged, how wonderful it felt to be one part of a couple.

Then I spied them, the little lilac gadgets taunting me from across the room. They and the open package of honey dust sat on the nightstand on what I had already been thinking of as his side of the bed. I picked them up and threw them down the hall. What was left of the dust erupted in a billowy cloud. Yup, there go my dreams, up in smoke.

The tears came in wrenching waves. I let them flow. I didn't dare try to stop them.

I knew from experience that the only way past it was through it.

Box of tissues in hand, I sat all alone in what was supposed to become our bed and built another tissue mountain.

The next 48 hours were a blur of sleep, tears, Dylan cuddles, water, sleep, tears and more Dylan cuddles.

I hadn't gone near the computer since receiving Tommy's email. Dylan hadn't been on a single walk because I hadn't left the house, hadn't got dressed, showered, spoken to anyone, eaten or done anything that used to fill my routine.

Everything had lost its appeal.

I had let myself fall into a hole. I knew it. I gave myself permission to go there, but I also knew enough not to stay there.

Chloe would come by tomorrow and I would climb my way out of this hollow darkness by then.

If I hadn't, she would offer a hand.

The sound of the doorbell rang into my dream. On the second ring it succeeded in rousing me from my slumbered escape. I was groggy. I heard Dylan dancing around at the front door.

Chloe!

Damn, I must have slept in again!

I jumped out of bed, grabbed my robe and peeked out of the upstairs window to see Chloe standing on the stoop digging through her purse while she waited for me to answer the door.

"Kayte, you look like shit!"

"And I love you too."

"Seriously, what the hell?"

"Believe me, I feel much worse than I look."

"What's going on? The last time we spoke you were on cloud nine!" Chloe was giving me her mother face; authoritative yet concerned and she was sincere in wanting an answer.

I burst into tears again.

"Oh KitKat, what's wrong?" She was giving me the tightest hug. All I could do was sob, shoulders bouncing up and down, nose running, lips quivering and no words could find their way out.

She held me until I got my sobbing under control. Then she walked me over to the sofa, covered me in a blanket, put on the coffee and went about cooking me an avocado, salsa and green onion omelette - my favourite. She filled Dylan's bowl, found his treats and sent him, his treat and his bowls outside.

"What's happened?"

"T-T-T-Tommy doesn't, sniff, want, sniff, to see me, sniff, again…" Through the tears I managed, "Chloe, it hurts so much."

"Kayte, I know. I can see that. But you know what? You're going to be okay. You'll see."

"I wish I believed that. It's just…"

"I'm going to stop you right there. First we eat then you shower, then we talk. In that order. Now here's your coffee. Sit up and drink it. It's made with Chloe love. It'll help, trust me."

I was grateful for her tending so I dutifully drank it. The hot liquid warmed my insides and I could feel hints of energy begin to form. I finished the first cup and then asked for more.

Chloe had been expecting to be greeted by exuberant over-the-moon, walking-on-air Kayte and instead was met by dishevelled, disillusioned, heartbroken, dragging-her-sorry-ass-around Kayte. I filled in the gap for her sharing the exhilarating highs of that one wonderful night with Tommy and the gut-wrenching lows of the past few days as I came to terms with his words and his wishes and tried to pick up what was left of my scattered romantic notions.

"Chloe, it's not that he's wrong. I know that it's the right decision for him and I know how brave and principled he must have been to make it. But it sucks. It really sucks. And it hurts. I thought we were forming a great bond, I thought he was finally the one."

I sat there dumbfounded.

I devoured my omelette and mustered a "thanks."

"My pleasure. Now off to the shower with you."

We trotted upstairs.

Chloe noticed the dust and little purple pieces scattered through the hall. Bless her, for all she said was, "Where's the vacuum?"

I stepped into the shower, turned on the water and heard Chloe yell, "Do you mind if I read the email?"

"Sure. As long as you promise me that you won't send a response."

"Oh Kayte, I would never do anything like that!"

"Yes you would and we both know it."

"Seriously Kayte, you have my word."

My depression was falling away as the droplets carried it down the drain. I was feeling stronger. The combination of friendly support, coffee, food, time and distance was helping.

My body was warmed through. Soap in hand I lathered myself. The smell of coconut permeated my nostrils. The sweet seductive smell instantly transported me and my thoughts back to that night with Tommy. Every touch, every moment, every taste, every notion, every emotion was running like a film on fast-forward through my brain. But this time I did not cry. I wanted to but I stopped myself. I gave myself a mental 'attagirl' and made a note to toss the coconut soap and candles into the trash.

Standing in a towel, drying my hair with another, I joined Chloe in the office.

"Feel better?"

"Ya. A little. Thanks. Did you read it?"

"Yes. He sounds so very sincere."

"He is, uh, was."

"It must be really hard for him. I just couldn't imagine having to return to the dating scene after being with Boomer for so long.

It would probably just go into the too-hard basket."

"It's a challenge for me so I could only imagine how it must feel for Tommy. I just don't know how I could have been so wrong."

"Kayte, sometimes we just want things so much that we can't see the full picture. Maybe that was the case. But it sounds like he really likes you, respects you and really enjoyed everything you shared."

"I think you're right and that's what makes it so hard. He is the type of man I can see myself with. He has so many incredible qualities and I don't think he even knows it. We were so good together." I could feel a lump growing in my throat.

"Honey, this much I know for sure. When it is the right one, it happens to you, you don't have to force it. It's easy. Nothing can stop it. But you both have to be ready for it. Sometimes love can take your world and turn it upside down, like in those snow globes. The clarity you had before gets clouded by the deluge of snowflakes, but it's so beautiful you don't mind being shaken up and turned on your head.

'I know you want to find love and it really sounded like Tommy was a fabulous man and you and he had a great time together, so it was natural for you to have such strong feelings for him. It sounds like you helped him to grow and to learn more about himself, his circumstances and what he needs and wants from his future. I'm sure he's thankful for that. But it goes both ways. I think he may have even taught you a little something too."

"Like what smarty pants?"

"Think about it, Kayte."

"You're right. I guess Tommy showed me the clearest vision I've had yet of the kind of man I need and want to find as my life partner. He personified the mate I had described on my list. He brought that wish list to life."

"See. I knew he had. We learn something from everyone, Kayte. Anything else?"

"That timing is key? I guess he taught me that if you're not ready for love, you can't do anything to force it. That just doesn't work. For when it's time and when it's real, like you say, it happens naturally. It's easy. Things just fall into place. Maybe I just need to trust in that, huh?"

"Attagirl!"

" I guess I also learned that even though when I started this online dating thing, I thought that I was ready, I really wasn't. I learned so much more about what love means, what it includes, what I will and won't do and with who, than I ever knew before. I guess that can happen when you have 337 to choose from!"

"I think you may be right."

"Tell me something Chloe. How'd you get so smart?"

"Baby, I was born smart!"

I giggled for the first time in days.

"Chloe, I don't want you to think that I didn't appreciate you getting me on to this online dating site. Because I did and I probably never would have done it without your coaxing. I met some wonderful guys, found great comfort in the fact that there were so many people out there, just like me, looking for love and looking for a way to connect with new and different people. It's been a really interesting experience. It's come complete with its shocks and awes and even provided some valuable ahas. I've learned more about myself and I think more about love and what I'm ultimately looking for. But that said, I think it's time for this single gal to take down her profile. Maybe I'll just let fate chart my course for a while."

"Think that's a splendid idea."

I logged in to wheresinglesfindlove.com for the last time. It indicated I had one message. Was it from Tommy?

No. Of course it wasn't.

Katontheprowl

Let's get started on our tomorrows today.

Everett

"What's that you're reading?" Chloe probed.

"Just a note from this consultant who has been messaging me. He wants to meet. He's a little intense but seems to really understand what I'm looking for."

"Are you going to meet him?"

"I don't know. Don't know if I'm up to it."

"Might do you good to get out of the house."

"True. But I'm just not sure about him. Or about men or about dating."

"Go for a drink, you never know."

"I guess. Ah, what the hell. What have I got to lose?"

"But, like always, let me know the details as to who, where and when!" She had donned her motherly face again.

"Absolutely. Always adhere to Roman's Rule #4."

I sent him a note with my email address, explaining that I was taking my profile down so he wouldn't be able to reach me on the site.

Then, with Chloe at my side, just as she was when I posted it, we removed my profile from wheresinglesfindlove.com.

CHAPTER 47

I found my way to the hotel that Everett suggested.

I was a tad wary of the suggestion to meet at a restaurant in a hotel, rather than just a restaurant, but I figured what the heck, it was still a public place. And why not meet him? He seemed educated, driven and had a professional job. He was polished and handsome. Not tall dark and handsome, but shorter and reddish hair and handsome. From what I could tell from his one photo, he was quite muscular too. He wouldn't have been my first pick, but then again, look what had happened with my first pick. What did I have to lose? It was better than sitting at home alone (sorry Dylan, you can be great company but never much of a conversationalist). What was the worst that could happen? I'd meet someone new that didn't fit in the "love-you-long-time" category. Maybe I'd learn something from him, maybe I'd have a laugh, maybe I'd have a nice meal, maybe I'd make a business contact or maybe he had a friend who was a better fit. Maybe I'd walk out of there feeling a bit better about myself and dating. Or maybe I just wouldn't spend another night alone. While I wasn't really "Jonesing" to meet him, I did feel good that during our brief conversation he appeared to have really understood my needs, what I wanted from a relationship, what I truly longed for. He could articulate it all so well.

I has disclosed this rationale with Chloe on our daily call earlier when I also followed Rule #4 and shared all the details of the date – who, where and when. I also told her of my reluctance but she then convinced me to finally commit to going. So I figured I might as well go ahead and actually meet him.

I mused at how the feeling I had in preparation for meeting Everett was nothing like what I had felt for Tommy. The day I was going to meet Tommy for the first time (and the second and the third) I was excited, nervous, energised, hopeful and as far away from rational as you could imagine. I chose every piece of my outfit, my makeup palette and the jewellery I donned for meeting Tommy with painstaking detail. I started getting ready two hours before I was to leave. I styled and primped and touched up and primped, then preened and primped some more. This time I had opened the closet, chose something comfortable and put it on. There was no trying various outfits and creating a growing mound of choices that weren't just right. I wore my standard everyday makeup and put my hair up rather than spend anytime styling it. That was it.

I arrived right on time. The parking lot was very full but I found what must have been the last spot way in the back. I checked myself one last time in the mirror; makeup… check. Nothing in the teeth… check. Nothing elsewhere that shouldn't be showing… check.

I closed the car door and began walking toward the hotel. Part of me wanted to just turn around and drive right back home, crack a bottle of Chardy, make a big bowl of popcorn topped with truffle oil and sea salt, find a chick flick and escape, with my trusted furry partner at my side.

Then there was the other part, the part that made a commitment to trying to find Mr. Right, that knew it was necessary to be open to the possibilities, that truly wanted to find love and knew the only way to it was through it and that dating was the path to get me there.

The front doors of the hotel opened as I approached. I was not consciously aware of walking from the car, but when I had parked, I remembered noticing the orange glow low on the horizon as the sun was just setting and when I reached the lobby it appeared decidedly dark.

I could see the restaurant in the far right corner so I straightened myself, planted a smile on my face and strode purposely in that direction. The restaurant wasn't even half full. Empty tables dotted the centre and it seemed that patrons had chosen the perimeter to occupy. I did a quick scan of the room and in the far right corner I saw a 40ish gentleman, with well coiffed strawberry blond hair sitting alone strumming his fingers on the table with a partially drank beer and mobile phone as his only companions. He took up a good deal of space in the corner bench seat as his shoulders were broader than I had expected. His tie had been removed but the remainder of his outfit told of his professional occupation and discerning taste. The fabric was expensive, the suit jacket a cocoa brown with a faint cream fleck, the tieless shirt a light pumpkin (Egyptian cotton was my guess). I could only assume the pants matched the jacket but I couldn't see below the table as the dim lights of the restaurant illuminated the table tops and punctuated the walls, but beneath the mahogany tables it was dark and shadowy.

He saw me approach, gave a warm smile, stated my name rather than asking for confirmation that it was me, got up, pocketed his mobile, placed a hand on the small of my back and ushered me into the corner bench seat following very closely behind.

He smelled familiar. He radiated a hint of citrus, what might have been sandalwood or patchouli with just a strange but slight hint of Christmas tree pine.

"Hi, have you been here long?" I asked.

"You are even more beautiful in person." He was turned facing me, staring directly into my eyes, his large muscular arm now resting below behind my shoulder and he was angled sideways, almost touching me.

I could feel the warmth emanating through the expensive wool suit (I guessed was designer Italian).

Rather than face him directly, I sat beside him facing out from the table, so I had to glance his way occasionally.

"Why thank you." I fluttered my eyelashes playfully.

"And the poise and assuredness of your stride as you walked to the table, very sexy, very confident, very refreshing, very..." He pursed his lips and shook his head where a word should have been.

"Thank you again."

I had picked up the goldenrod cloth napkin from the table and began twisting it.

The waiter appeared, "What can I get you?"

"I'll..."

I was quickly interrupted, "She'll have a New Zealand Marlborough Chardonnay, only slightly chilled, not too cold. She knows that when a fine vintage heats up, the true depth of its offering becomes apparent. It's that intensity that beckons you back for more."

He was looking at me now and not the waiter. *Was he suggesting what I thought he was suggesting?*

Strangest order I'd ever heard.

The waiter was confused but remained attentive, scribbled a note on his order pad and set out to find my wine. He probably wrote down only what I would have said if I had I been doing the ordering; "New Zealand Chardonnay."

He slid in closer and I recognised his scent – it was the one Simon had started wearing just before we broke up. Everett was staring into my eyes, glancing down at my chest, up at my lips, back to my eyes, then down at my hands and all very appreciatively. I moved back angling myself toward him. He liberated the napkin from my hands, placed in on the table and covered my right with his left and began stroking it. I had been in the restaurant five minutes by this point.

He just grabbed my hand. We just met. But it's better than spending the night alone in front of the TV. Isn't it?

This immediate physical attention felt a little creepy, but, by the same token, it was also a little flattering. It was refreshing to be so adored, especially after so recently being so rejected. He could just be an intense type. I told myself to give him a little time, enjoy a nice glass of wine, relax, get to know him a little more, see where it goes. I had found the strength to show up even though Tommy had just ripped my heart out. I deserved so much better. It was a success even just being out on another date. And a little attention would be good for me.

"What really inspires you Kayte? What is it that stirs your soul? What drives you?"

"I might need my wine before I answer!" I giggled out.

"Seriously, Kayte, I want to know you on that level. There's no sense in wasting time. It's real intimacy that I'm after and I sense you are too. I don't want to play games and I know that you don't."

"True. One thing that inspires me is creativity. I am moved by the creation of something new, by seeing things differently, by finding new meaning in the existing."

"What else motivates, arouses you, Kayte?"

I bit my lip. "Passion."

"Why?" I felt his firm leg slide right up against mine. My immediate reaction was to pull back, but I also found the immediacy and intensity of this direct man somewhat intriguing.

"Because of its energy, its commitment, its intensity. Greatness cannot be achieved without passion. Passion makes the difference."

He was staring at my mouth when I spoke as if watching each word escape. He whispered, "You are an incredibly passionate woman, aren't you Kayte? I sensed that from your profile. I suspected it when we spoke online. I am sure of it now as I watch you express yourself. You need to find the heights of that passion, don't you Kayte?"

"Your wine, ma'am."

I caught my breath and then used the interruption to create a little space between us. With my free hand I raised the glass to my lips and took a large sip and swallowed fast. *Are there red flags here? Is this all moving just a little too fast? Or am I just in the presence of an articulate powerful and passionate man who knows exactly what he wants and seems to know what I do too?*

"Yes, I try to be."

"I'll bet you have incredibly high standards. And I'd bet you've been disappointed. Kayte, have you been disappointed by love?"

"Yes, I have." *Oh yes, so very disappointed by love, far too often, far too recently and it hurt. It really hurt to want something so much and have it not only elude you but wound you in the process.*

"I won't disappoint you, Kayte. Especially if you, first, do not disappoint me."

His phone rang, or vibrated rather, in his chest pocket. He apologised for the interruption, pulled it out, looked at who was calling and said, "I need to get this. It'll only take a moment."

His expression changed from somewhat serious to intensely so.

"Yes?"

The caller stated their case. He nodded and remained expressionless. He listened some more.

His voice was low, imposing and unwavering.

"I don't care if it takes you all night, the entire team on it all night or the whole division on it all night. It needs to be ready for first thing tomorrow. The meeting starts at 8:00am. The presentation will be ready. It will be polished. It will be perfect. It will win us this business. I want this business. We will get this business. Do what has to be done. Understood?"

He waited a few seconds, clicked off the blackberry, placed it back in his pocket, grabbed both of my hands and slid in closer to me.

"Now Kayte, let's talk about what we both want."

"Actually, I could use some more wine."

"Yes, your wine is almost empty and I could use another beer. Waiter..." He motioned the waiter to bring two more of the same.

"So, what do you do for fun? What are your hobbies, your interests?" He was taking the last sip of his beer so I took advantage of the opportunity to pose a few questions and change the direction of the conversation.

He dismissed my question without taking even a moment to consider it. "I'd much rather talk about us, our connection, how we can arouse the depths of desire between us."

His hand was now stroking my thigh.

I wiggled back in the seat and clutched what was left of my first wine.

"Well, I'd like to know more about you. I know you're passionate, but what do you enjoy doing?"

"Truthfully Kayte, now that I've met you, I think I might relish taking you with me on an adventure into ecstasy."

"That's all good but c'mon Everett, be reasonable. You need to give me some indication as to who Everett is beyond the passionate man whose hand is making its way up my thigh." On the surface I donned a scolding smile but a very real and wary frustration was growing beneath.

"Kayte, I work hard. I have a very demanding job. I need to play as hard as I work. So I play competitive squash and run marathons for fun."

The waiter delivered the drinks.

"I'm doing Boston for the fifth time next year. I enjoy the succulent delights of gourmet food and fine wines from around the globe. But my driving passion is the exploration of the elements that propel passion, determining what it is that ignites intense attraction, what creates that ultimate combination of emotional, intellectual and physical connectivity – the connectivity that erupts in the most incredibly intimate sexual experiences possible."

I took a big sip of wine, fanned my face and added, "Well I asked!" Jokingly I tried to break the extremity of the exchange.

"I think I've become aroused just thinking about it. See what you do to me, Kayte."

He looked down at his crotch where an obvious erection had reared its head. "Would you like to touch it?"

He was sliding my left hand to the edge of the table.

"No!" I snapped. I didn't want to appear too rude, so I added, "Not right now, thanks." *What was this guy's problem? Did I really just get asked to touch his penis after 15 minutes together in this very open, very public place?*

"I think you'd like it. I can feel it grow harder and bigger just thinking about exploring you and your moistness, about being touched by you, about..."

"Enough, Everett. I'm not comfortable with the direction this conversation is taking."

The waiter noticed my agitation. He shot me a questioning glance as if to ask, "Do you need my help?" I shook my head gently to indicate no, but hoped that my face also displayed my appreciation for the gesture.

"But Kayte, I find you so incredibly attractive. You ooze passion and I just wanted to share with you the effect you're having on me."

"I'm flattered." *Actually, I was a little... no... a lot, weirded-out by it.* "But I'd really like to change the topic to something a little less intimate and a little more appropriate for a first meeting in a public venue."

"Okay, so other than give me a raging hard-on, what do you excel at?"

One more crack like that and I'm out of here.

"I guess that's a start. I think I'm good at a lot of things."

"What are you great at?"

"I'm a great friend."

"What else?"

"I'm creative."

"I'd agree. I saw that in your profile. It also had a sense of purpose to it, yet it also suggested a sense of humour. Oh, and a healthy balance and passion. And speaking of passion, are you sure you wouldn't like to get a room, go upstairs and push the boundaries of we've defined as passion up until now?"

"Thank you for the compliments, but no thank you on the suggestion to go upstairs." *This guy was certainly not letting up.*

I'm finishing my drink then I'm leaving.

"Kayte, how do you like to be touched? Do you enjoy soft, long sensitive caresses and slow wet exploratory kisses? Or do you prefer a quicker, harder, more direct approach? Do you want to it to build with anticipation or would you prefer to be surprised by my touch?"

I had been scanning the restaurant rather than looking directly at him and when my gaze returned to the table to take another sip of my wine, I noticed that only one of his hands was on the table.

Thankfully the other wasn't stroking my leg anymore.

However, to my utmost shock, it was stroking something else.

I was aghast.

"I've had enough. Goodbye Everett!"

I grabbed my bag and sprinted out of the restaurant.

I couldn't believe what I had just witnessed. This was not what I wanted, not like this, not on a first meeting, not in a restaurant and not without some sort of lead up. How disgusting!

It was dark as I marched back to my car in disappointment and disgust. I fumbled through my purse for my phone. Chloe was not going to believe this one. My left thumb had just dialled her number and my right hand was about to insert the key into the door when I felt a presence, smelled the familiar mix of citrus and pine and knew who was behind me.

His large hand covered mine and he took control of the keys.

"Leave me alone," I shouted. "I'm not interested!" I tried to sound as in control as possible given I was terrified.

I heard Chloe's voice faintly in the background. "Kayte, is that you, are you okay?"

"Leave me alone Everett," I screamed again.

He was holding my hand so tight that it was starting to cut off the circulation to my fingers.

"Kayte, you know you want me as much as I want you."

"No, no I don't." My voice was cracking but I thought if only I could reason with him maybe I could get out of here.

"Kayte, are you in trouble?" I could hear the urgency in Chloe's voice.

"Please take your hands off me, you're hurting me," I said loud and firmly. I scanned the parking lot for help. My heart was beating out of my chest. The adrenaline was flowing freely.

I thought I heard, "Boomer, Kayte's in trouble, we have to help her." Or maybe I imagined it or just hoped I'd heard it.

I was only hoping that Everett didn't hear Chloe, I could barely make out her voice escaping from my mobile.

I was in trouble. I needed help. Another look and there was no one in the parking lot, no one to jump to my aid. I was on my own.

"But Kayte, you're missing the point. I want to put my hands on you, all over you, I want my fingers to explore every inch of your body, I want you to explore mine, I want us to find the passion and the desire for each other that I know is there. I think, no, I know, you want that too."

"Even if I did, which I don't, especially now, it certainly wouldn't be like this, not this fast, not this forced. No, not like this at all."

I was pushing him away and saying anything that I thought could buy me time to figure out what to do, time for a passerby to appear that could help, time to hopefully talk some sense into this man. I hoped that I wasn't making matters worse.

Did I have anything in my purse I could use as a weapon? My mental inventory came up empty.

He was so strong. While not overly tall, he was exceptionally muscular and he was being physically forceful.

I was petrified.

I was strong too but there was no way that I could defend myself against him.

He pinned me against the car. I could feel his entire muscular frame pressing against me.

I was panicking. I was in pain, the moulding of the roof of the car was pressing into my back.

I thought that maybe if we at least stayed outside the car, I'd be fine.

Don't let him push you into the car. Don't let him push you into the car.

I just wanted to burst into tears but I had to stay focused on thinking as clearly as I could. If I kept him talking I might get out of this and avoid being raped – avoid what I saw as the worst-case scenario. Then came the sting of the realisation that rape wasn't the worst case here. He could actually kill me. I had no idea what to expect from this man. He was intent and forceful and he had a vision of how he wanted this evening to go.

No, I'm not ready to die. I'm not. I'm not going to and I'm not going to be raped either.

I tried wriggling from his grip. I couldn't free myself.

I have so much to live for, so many things to still accomplish, so much of life to live, so many other goals to tick off my list. I like my life. No, actually, I love my life. And, yes, I haven't found Mr. Right, but I have an incredible life without him. I would have a perfectly rewarding life on my own. I couldn't see myself with someone like this just to be with someone, to be part of a couple. If I'm going to be with someone it's going to be a man who is good enough for me. And I am going to meet him. I'm going to have that chance. This freak is not going to take that from me.

Still terrified, I made a promise to myself right there. I was going to walk away from this. I was going to walk away unharmed – shaken, terrified, changed no doubt, but unharmed. I had to think of something. Still no one in the parking lot to come to my aid.

Where was help? Why was I so alone?

"You asked me what I was looking for. Can I tell you that?"

"Why don't you show me instead?" His hips were pressing me into the car door; my tailbone was being jabbed by the door handle. His face moved closer. He was trying to kiss me now. My stomach churned. I was repulsed by the thought.

I tried to wriggle away but he held me there with the force of his burly body. His lips were still cold from the beer. The smell of hops and cologne made the nausea inside me rise.

I didn't kiss back. Trying to get a reaction, he moved his lips from kissing my lips to my cheek, to my ear, then back to my lips again, then down to the left of my neck, then the right, and then back again.

When his lips made their way back to mine, he found them pursed shut. His firm and prodding tongue was intent on prying them open so that he could enter and explore. I was revolted by him and his persistence. There was still not a passerby to be seen. I began making deals with our creator. *I had to get out of this. I just had to.*

"So you want to play hard to get do you? I can play that game to. It just builds the excitement and the anticipation of having you, Kayte. And I will have you."

He pressed his fully erect penis hard into my pelvic bone as he said this. I wanted to run but couldn't. With flight not an option, the only remaining one was fight.

"No you won't. Never. Not with this approach. You're far too presumptuous and far too pushy. You've decided what you want and not even given a thought to how I'd like things to proceed. You've leapt way ahead of where things should be at this point and in doing so you've proceeded on your own as far as I'm concerned."

"C'mon Kayte, I know you want me. I can tell by how you look at me. I'm just moving things along to the good part. Why waste time?"

"No, Everett, you're just pushing yourself on me. Trying to take things to a place I haven't the slightest desire for them to go."

I was beginning to feel some suggestion of just a hint of control of the situation. I scanned the parking lot again. No one!

Where was everyone? Where were the people staying in the hotel, eating in the restaurant, working there? Where?

He took a step back but still stared intently at me. "So you don't want things to go any further? You don't want for our bodies to connect, meld and explode into each other with the passion and hunger I know is there from both of us?"

"No." I felt even stronger.

"Well I do. And, Kayte, I make it a habit of getting what I want."

He grabbed me around the waist and pushed me into the car. I was sprawled across both seats. My head hit the passenger's door handle. The gearshift was digging into the small of my back and my side at the same time, my butt was in the driver's seat and my feet were still hanging out the door.

"NO!" I screamed as loud as I could.

He was holding me down with one hand and undoing his belt with the other.

"GET OFF ME. HELP." I was screaming so loud it hurt my own ears.

In one well-practised motion he opened his zipper and liberated his appendage.

"PLEASE SOMEONE HELP ME!"

I was trying to fight him off me, wriggling, trying to punch him, honking the horn, trying to open the passenger door but gravity, his obvious strength and determination were all working against me.

I will walk away unharmed. I will walk away unharmed. Somehow I will get out of this. Some way... somehow... I will...

He was kneeling into me now, smiling and rubbing his exposed member on my stomach and my leg and then my crotch.

"I'll help you, help you get to heights of ecstasy you've never experienced Kayte. Heights you can reach only with me. Then, I promise you, you're screams will be for more."

"CAN ANYONE HEAR ME - SOMEBODY PLEASE HELP ME?"

Where was everyone? Why was there no one around?

Then I remembered... Chloe. My phone dropped to the floor when he pushed me into the car. I fumbled one hand around trying to locate it.

He was kneeling on the driver's seat. He pulled my head forward by grabbing at my ponytail and thrust his swollen weapon into my face.

I screamed, "NOOOOO!" I then quickly switched my efforts to clenching my jaw and pursing my lips so that nothing was going past them!

"Kayte, you know you want to take me in your mouth and suck me with those large luscious lips. I want to feel your Chardonnay-soaked tongue wrap itself around me. I want to feel you hunger for me, drink me in, plead for me. I want to thrust my dick deep into your throat and choke you with it. I want you to swallow me and... "

Then I heard it. "Whooooop, whooooop, reeer."

I had never been happier to hear a sound in my life. The first car thundered in and came quickly to a halt directly in front of my vehicle. I heard doors open and a number of purposeful steps approaching. Then another car screeched to a stop. I heard more doors, more footsteps.

I felt Everett immediately lift himself off me and I watched as he tried to fold his hardness back into his imported wool pants.

Then the beams shining their glorious rescue light danced in from a number of directions. I let out a huge sigh and could feel the tears welling up inside me.

"Sir, move out of the car please. Slowly." An emotionless male voice barked directions at Everett.

"Of course, Officer. Is there a problem?" Everett replied.

The same officer's voice asked, "How about you tell me what's going on here." I could hear a few pairs of footsteps move away from my vehicle.

I assumed that one cop escorted Everett and guided him to the other side of the second police car where he and his partner began questioning him. I could hear murmurs but couldn't make out the words.

A light shone directly at my grateful face. A deep yet gentle voice asked, "Ma'am, are you okay?"

"Ah, yeah. I guess I am. Now. Thanks."

Then a woman's voice, "Are you hurt? Were you assaulted?"

"No, not really hurt. Terrified, but not really hurt." The magnitude of what I had just been through and what could have happened was starting to hit. I was trying to raise myself to a sitting position but I felt like jelly. I was becoming increasingly overwhelmed.

She continued her questions as she reached into the car to help me out. "Do you want to be here? I mean, is what was going on here consensual?"

"No. It definitely was not. Not in the least."

I was struggling to get up.

"Do you need some help?" The man's voice asked. "Let me give you a hand." His voice was smooth yet commanding.

"Ya." I nodded and then felt a strong hand reach ever so gently under my right arm and the other behind my back to help pull me out of the car.

The woman reached in as well so there were two officers gently pulling me from the vehicle.

"Thanks."

I stood outside the car now, leaning on it for support. The two officers stood one on either side, blocking my view of what was happening with Everett.

The female officer grabbed her notepad from his belt and was looking down at it. "So what was happening here?"

"That jerk was trying to rape me – forcing himself on me even though I had made it very clear that I was not interested. He just wouldn't take "no" for an answer."

My eyes adjusted from the flashlight. The lights from the police cars cast a glow and I could now clearly see the officers that stood before me in their matching uniforms.

I recognised the male. *I knew that I knew the face, but from where? How did I know him?*

"Do you know him?" the woman asked.

"Uh… the guy attacking me? Yes. Well sort of."

And I know you too. I surveyed the handsome yet gentle face of the man standing to my right. *Where do I know this man in uniform from? Where?*

"And how do you know him?" She looked up from her notepad, directly at me.

"We were meeting for a drink." I answered her while continuing to look at the very familiar officer.

"Did you know him prior to this. Have you met him before or is the first time?"

The male officer was silent. When I glanced at him, I detected a reassuring look in his eyes as if to say, "It's okay. You're going to be fine."

"I had spoken to him online from an online dating site but this was the first time we had met in person."

That was it! That's where I knew him from! The officer standing in front of me was Bryan; the first guy I chatted with on that very same dating site. Bryan who stood me up, Bryan who I had seen many times at the dog park but was always too shy to talk to, Bryan the handsome dog lover who was Wink's dad.

I thought I detected a hint of recognition in his eyes too.

"Ma'am, I'm going to need to get a few details. May I get your name, address and telephone number please?"

"Yes, it's Kathleen, Kayte, Wexford, I live at… "

"Kayte? It is you. I thought I recognised you," Bryan broke in.

"Hi. It's Bryan, right?"

"Constable Bryan Dailey actually. So we finally meet."

"Yes. Finally. I must admit, your timing is incredible."

"Sorry it wasn't under better circumstances."

"You two know each other?" The female officer asked as she pointed at each of us with her pencil.

"Yes." We both nodded in agreement.

I detected a hint of a smile from Bryan. But I think I also detected a hint of guilt so we moved back to procedure.

"Can we get your complete name and address details please?" the lady officer asked.

I provided them.

She looked at Bryan, he gave a single head nod and then asked ever so gently, "So, Kayte, please tell us what went on here."

After providing all the details I could remember from Everett's profile, I recounted the evening's events to them – I bounced between embarrassed, disgusted and comfortable in revealing these details. Both Bryan and the lady officer were very professional, thorough, understanding, delicate yet direct and detailed in their questions. He seemed very easy to talk to, more so than her, even about an evening like the one I had just been through.

I remembered that from our online exchange. I recall that he responded at the right time, he asked questions, he was genuinely interested, he shared details of himself easily, he had a great sense of humour and appeared to be really grounded and didn't take himself too seriously. That's why I was so surprised when he stood me up.

When they were done asking their questions, both officers excused themselves and went over to check with the other officers.

I had almost forgotten that Everett was still there.

I stood alone leaning on my vehicle replaying the evening's events. I bounced from emotional wave to emotional wave. I got pulled under by disgust and horror. I got tossed around by my ignorance to the signs and my inability to have seen this coming and by the apparent disappearance of my usual intuition. Then I found myself drowning in a pool of pity, feeling like I deserved so much more but that I was just treading water, trying just to stay afloat until I could find the right shore to swim into when there was no land anywhere in sight. First the news from Roman, then Tommy so abruptly ending things, now this. It had not been a good week.

Bryan returned on his own. He said that he thought that they had all the information that they would need for now.

He explained my options and the next steps in the process.

"Kayte, I think that's about it for now."

"Good." I could feel the tears welling up inside. "Because I just want this horrible night to be over."

"I'll bet you do. Is there anything else that you think might be relevant? Any other detail that you think might be important? Or any other questions on your mind?"

"How did you guys know that I needed help?"

"We were dispatched after an emergency call was received from…" He flipped back through his notes, "a Chloe Collins who said she could hear what was going on and she was fearing for your safety."

"Oh that Chloe. Always looking out for me." I owed her big time!

"Anything else?"

This was my chance. I had the opportunity so many never do. If I didn't ask now, I'd lose the chance. If I didn't ask, I'd always wonder. It certainly was not the best timing, and it was so irrelevant, but it was probably now or never and I felt I deserved to know. Not that it would change anything. Not that it would make a difference one way or another but I just couldn't keep the question in.

"Bryan, I know this is going to sound bizarre given what has transpired tonight, but why did you stand me up? Why didn't you show up for our date?"

"Kayte, I'm sorry about that. That night work got in the way as it seems to do at the most inappropriate times. I was working on a case that actually included a few persons of interest from the site we were on, so it all got very complicated. That's why I took down my profile. Not only was it a conflict of interest but I just couldn't take the ribbing I would have got from the guys and the girls at the station about being on a dating site.

I'm so sorry. It was rude and you deserved better. I know that. It was just too complicated to explain so I just let things go.

I've thought about you a couple of times, even went on the site and was going to send you a message one day after I came home from the dog park. I had seen a woman there who reminded me of you and thought it would have been nice to connect but I would have had to start with a huge apology and then I figured it would just be easier if I left it alone. Figured you probably would have been snatched up by then."

"It doesn't sound that complicated. But thanks Bryan. I appreciate your honesty."

The other officer came over and said, "I think I have all the information I need. You?"

Bryan nodded.

I could only imagine what Everett had said to them about his account of the evening.

She looked directly at me. "Are you okay? Do you need us to call someone, give you a ride home?"

"Thanks. I should be fine… I think." I'm sure I didn't sound convincing.

Bryan broke in with, "Why don't I drive her and her car home?"

"Sure. I'm fine with that." She responded. "I'll follow you."

My grateful face made another appearance. "Thanks, I'd appreciate that."

"The other officers will take this guy in until we decide what we're going do with him."

Out of nowhere I started to shiver uncontrollably. And then came the tears.

The officers exchanged glances, she returned to the vehicle and opened the trunk, pulled something out, walked back and handed it to Bryan.

He gave the blanket a shake, placed it ever so gently around my shoulders and said, "Into the passenger's seat with you."

He pulled the keys from the driver's door, unlocked the passenger's door, made sure I was in securely buckled in, picked up my phone from the floor, tossed it in my lap, closed my door, then went around and took his place in the driver's seat.

I could see that the other officer had taken Everett and placed him in the back seat and closed the door. Their car was the first to leave.

Bryan's partner was in position behind the wheel ready to follow our lead.

On the way home Bryan explained that they had enough information to charge him with assault, especially given that Chloe thought to keep the phone line open so that the emergency operator could record the whole ordeal.

They would need me to charge him with sexual assault. I wasn't compelled to. That was up to me. I could take a little time to think about it, but only a little.

As we drove, the conversation took an interesting turn.

"Kayte, I wasn't completely honest before."

"Oh?"

"There was another reason, actually, the real reason I didn't show up for our date."

"Go on." This night couldn't get any worse so I encouraged the unprompted disclosure.

"The truth is, I thought I was ready to date but I just wasn't."

"Ready?"

"You know I was married before, right?"

"Yes, now I do remember. So the split was just too recent? I can't remember, how long ago? Are you divorced or just separated?"

"Widowed."

My heart sank.

"No. Oh, I am so sorry Bryan."

Silence.

Awkward silence.

The awkward silence had to end. It was too painful for him. I had to ask the question. I had to ask the obvious one. I couldn't just ignore that bombshell.

"Can I ask what happened?"

"Of course. To make a long story short, Kayte, I was married to my high school sweetheart and she was snatched away from me by a drunk driver."

"Oh, Bryan, that's so sad."

"Yes. It's so ironic because she was always so worried about me because of my job. Every day before I left for work she would give me a hug and a kiss and then smile and wink at me and say, 'Stay safe, honey'. Every day."

I could see the pain of that memory as it invaded his face.

"It must have been just horrible for you to deal with. I could not even begin to imagine."

"Kayte, it was devastating. Toughest thing I've ever had to deal with and believe me in this line of work, that's saying something. It got to the point where I just dreaded coming home to an empty house. Then a friend suggested I might get a dog. So I went to the pound, initially just to entertain the idea. I peeked in cage after cage, so many dogs just begging for a new home. There were so many cute lovable faces, so many barks, yips, yelps and excited dances vying for my attention, so many options. I almost wanted to take them all."

"Breaks your heart, doesn't it?"

"I must have seen 20, maybe 30 dogs before I found my girl. When I first approached the cage she was just a big blob of fur pushing into and poking through the wires that made up the cage's front door. She was obviously biting at some itch in her hinds. Just as I was almost past her cage she turned completely around and looked out at me, her mouth half open in a big toothy grinned, panting smile. Then I noticed that she only had one eye. At first glance, it looked just like she was winking at me. I knew in that instant she was the dog for me."

"Oh that is so sweet!" I had tears in my eyes. "I'll bet she's the best dog. Rescue dogs and their owners seem to have such an incredible bond, a connection on a deeper level."

"Let's just say she has been very good for me."

"I know that feeling."

"I think she rescued me rather than the other way round."

With that he pulled into my driveway.

"So, Kayte, that's the real reason I didn't show up for our date. I just wasn't ready. And you seemed like, in fact, now that I've met you I can tell you are, a great lady who deserved better than a guy who knew he wasn't ready for any sort of relationship."

On that we agreed.

Bryan opened my car door, helped me out, locked the car, walked me to the door and handed me the keys.

"Kayte, keep the blanket for now. If you come into the station tomorrow, perhaps you could bring it. If not, we could have a patrol pick it up."

"Thanks Bryan, oh, Officer Dailey, for all your help."

"You're welcome. It's been a big night for you. I'm sorry Kayte, sorry about everything. You deserve so much better than what you experienced tonight."

"True, but the last hour has certainly been a marked improvement." I let loose a flirtatious smile. But given Bryan's recent disclosure, I held back my signature smile and wink combo.

On a more serious note, I said, "Thanks for sharing that with me Bryan. I appreciate your honesty and respect how difficult it must have been to admit that, let alone get through it in the first place."

"Kayte, thanks, but the good thing is I do think I am through it."

I opened the door to the house and a panting Dylan bounded out. I was so happy to see him. He looked at me then at Bryan. Both of Bryan's substantial hands immediately reached in for a great big scratch behind both ears. Dylan soaked in every bit of attention. Then he did something very uncharacteristic; he leaned back on his hind legs, jumped up and took his front paws and placed them on Bryan's shoulders. Just like he had done at the park that day.

"I forgot you had a dog – he's gorgeous and apparently very affectionate."

"Thanks. This is Dylan. Actually I think you two may have met at the park a few weeks ago."

"I seem to have a vague recollections of a very friendly retriever retrieving Wink's toy and looking for some pats from me."

"He's not shy but he's also kinda cute, don't you think?"

"Just like his owner."

Did he just flirt with me?

"Goodnight Kayte."

He was making his way back to the waiting patrol car when he stopped and said, "And, Kayte… lock the door."

"Goodnight Bryan. Thanks."

I closed the door, slid down in into a crumpled ball on the floor and freed the tide of welled up tears. Interspersed between the sobs, I had a conversation with myself.

That's it. I'm done. I'm done with dating. Done looking for Mr. Right. Done searching for my soul mate. Finished. Finished with looking for love. I will never go on another date. Never. Ever.

My phone rang and I looked at the number. It was Chloe.

"…lo," was all I could get out through my sobs.

"Are you okay?"

"Yes, (sniff), thanks to you (sniff). Chloe, how can I ever thank you?"

"You can start by opening the door. I'm right outside."

I looked out the window to see she was standing there, fidgeting, still with her phone in her hand.

I opened the door and then fell into her warm reassuring arms.

And the sobs erupted again and again.

She let me cry. Not asking or saying anything. She guided me up the stairs, into my bedroom, put me into bed, added an extra blanket, got me tissues, the cordless phone and a big glass of water and then just lay there until I fell off to sleep.

CHAPTER 48

I didn't know how long I had been asleep but I awoke to Dylan standing beside me licking my face.

It felt like I had been asleep for just minutes, but it was 8:15am.

The phone broke the silence.

I picked it up. In the background I could hear the radio, the sound of running water and someone yelling."

My voice cracked out, "Hi Chloe."

"How did you know it was me, I haven't said anything yet?"

"I just do."

"Just wanted to check to make sure you were okay."

"I'm fine, Chloe."

"Are you sure?"

"Yes. And Chloe, thanks again, you're the best. Have I told you that lately?"

"No, and that's quite remiss of you. You call yourself a good friend… hmm… Seriously, honey, I'm just glad that you're okay."

"Hey, weren't you here when I went to sleep?"

"Yes, but once you drifted off, I had to leave to see to the kids this morning. I hope that's okay."

I sat up in bed and all the details from the previous night began whirring around in my head.

"Thank you – I don't know what I would have done if you hadn't heard what was going on."

"Let's just both be glad I did. I still can't believe it."

"Me neither Chloe, me neither. And just for the record, I'm done with this online dating thing, done with dating in general, done looking for Mr. Right. I came to an epiphany last night. You can't find love on a schedule. You can't force it. If I can't find it, then on some level I'm just not ready for it. If after all this, I haven't found it then it's not the right time. I'm not giving up, just think I'll stop looking for a while and maybe it'll find me."

"Wow. You have been thinking. There may well be some truth to that hon, but we can talk about things this afternoon. I'll be there by three. Can I bring you anything?"

"Just a great big Chloe hug."

"Okay, but be forewarned I may be packing a few extras!"

"You don't mind coming to the station with me, do you? I've decided that I am most definitely going to press charges. That asshole is going to get what's coming to him."

"I don't mind at all, my friend. I'll be right beside you. Maybe we can get them to show us a holding cell or a gun, or go behind a one way mirror, or let us question a 'perp.'"

"Don't get your hopes up Chloe."

"And Kayte, we're going to make sure that jerk rues the day he messed with the likes of Kayte "Kicks King-sized Ass" Wexford and her trusty sidekick Chloe "Caught Ya In The Act" Collins!"

"Thanks sweetie, I can always count on you."

I hung up the phone and looked at Dylan.

"Like I told you last night boy, it looks like it's going to be just me for a while longer pal. How about I get myself a coffee, then we'll go for a good long walk and then I'll go get Chloe the biggest bunch of stunningly beautiful flowers she's ever seen?"

I took it from the swoosh of his tail and the perk in his ears that Dylan was in agreement.

CHAPTER 49

We parked among the police cars at the station as there didn't appear to be any defined visitor parking. Bryan had given me his card last night and this was the address. I had never been there. In fact, I had never been in any police station and had no references other than those I saw on TV.

Chloe and I walked through the sliding glass doors under the navy-blue and white POLICE sign. We stepped in unison into the sterile and functional building. There was a long stainless steel counter to our left that joined a locked gate that went on to meet the long cream-coloured brick wall that appeared to our right.

A young officer on the other side of the counter looked up at me and asked, "Can I help you?"

I nervously croaked out, "I'm here to see Constable… ". Honestly, I could not remember Bryan's last name. "Uh, Constable… " I had to look down at his card in my hand, "Ahem, Constable Da… Dailey," I said with a little more authority.

"Oh, do you mean me?" Bryan popped out from behind the

young officer's right shoulder. He was wearing a big grin, dressed in a loose brown t-shirt that hung from his well-developed chest and exposed his tanned and strapping arms. His jeans were dark with fade marks in all the right places and they were just tight enough to accentuate the physique that lay beneath. He wore well-loved tan canvas sneakers to top off the casual attire. Quite a difference from the uniform he donned last night.

"Hello Bryan." Then thinking that might be too familiar, "I - I mean Officer… " Oh shit, I did it again. I snuck another look at the card. "Constable Dailey." All the while Chloe was looking at the floor, playing with her purse on her shoulder, tapping her foot, biting her lip and doing her best to stifle a growing giggle. She knew I was nervous.

"How are you today, Kayte?"

"Much better. Thanks."

"I assume you're not here just to drop off the blanket?" He motioned to the grey blanket that I was clenching under my arm.

"No, I think I want to press charges. In fact, I know I do. Yes, I'm here to press charges."

"Good decision, Kayte." He gave me a supportive and reassuring smile.

Chloe was staring at me with a very determined look on her face.

"Oh, how rude of me. Bryan, this is my dearest friend in the world, Chloe Collins."

He smiled. He transferred the big stack of papers he had been carrying to his left hand and reached out with his right to shake hers. It looked so petite compared to his large mitt. "Chloe Collins? Chloe… oh yes, you were the friend who called in 'the assault-in-progress.'"

"Yes, that was me." Chloe was beaming and still had not let go of Bryan's hand.

"Kayte's lucky to have a smart friend like you."

"Yes, she is, and I remind her of it daily. Well, I didn't mean you, 'Dailey', but "often" as in, like every day." Chloe was crimson with embarrassment but still holding onto his hand.

I nudged her and she immediately let go. Bryan was chuckling. I was enjoying the entertaining exchange. They would get on so well I thought.

"Well, ladies, c'mon back. Coffee? Water?"

"No thanks, we're fine." I spoke before Chloe had the chance to embarrass herself further.

"Over here." Bryan motioned for us to enter a small glassed in room with one table and about five chairs around it. Chloe and I sat down. Bryan laid the stack of paper he had been holding down in a thud.

The stack immediately got my attention as it featured a big bright-eyed, golden retriever. It also included an officer, a schnoodle and a few joggers, all under the heading "Laws & Paws for a Cause! Furry 5K Fundraiser & Fun Run".

"Be right back ladies, I'll just go get the paperwork."

He wasn't even out of the door and Chloe had turned to check him out.

"He is HOT Kayte. Very handsome indeed. And definitely your type – tall, handsome, broad shoulders, strong arms, nice butt… "

"He is good looking isn't he?"

"Yes, but don't tell Boomer I noticed!"

Chloe picked up the top flyer from the stack and handed me one. She read for a moment and then burst out with, "You have to go to this."

"Sounds sort of interesting and it is to raise money for local animal shelters."

"No, I mean you have to go to this with HIM!"

"Chloe, stop it. I told you I'm done with dating, at least for now."

"No, it would be perfect, or should I say, furrfect. It's not like a date, but you guys could get to know each other. Maybe he really IS ready now. And if he is, honey, he's not going to stay ready and single for long. Not looking like he does in those jeans!"

"Chloe!"

Bryan came back in the room. We went through all the paperwork. I filled in forms, answered questions. Chloe filled in witness forms and answered questions. And when we were done Bryan explained a little about the process and about the fun run because Chloe just couldn't help herself from asking about it.

"After I saw so many dogs needing to be rescued, I thought that I should do something about it. A few of us from here came up with this to raise some funds. Thought it would be a good community event and help the force to get a greater visibility. Both people and pets can get some exercise and the animals at the shelter get some well needed funds."

"I only wish I ran!" offered Chloe. "But Kayte's the runner!"

I knew exactly what she was doing. And I knew she was lying. She did run, just not nearly as much as me.

"Is there anything else you need from me today?" I asked Bryan.

He smiled a slow broad smile and his eyes twinkled as he answered, "Nope. I think we have everything."

"Okay Chloe, we should go and let Constable Dailey get back to work."

"Part of that is distributing all these." He tapped the stack.

"We could post some around our places," the always-helpful Chloe offered.

"Thanks, that'd be great. Here." Bryan handed a bunch to Chloe.

"Kayte, could you hold these for me please? Bryan, is there a ladies room I could use?"

I stood there reading the flyers while he directed Chloe to the toilet.

I didn't hear him return.

I felt a warmth envelop me and looked up to see Bryan with his arm raised above my head, leaning on the doorway encircling me. He looked at me, then at the flyers then back at me. In a very quiet tone, almost a whisper, he said, "Kayte, it should be a great event. You and Dylan should think about coming."

His bright blue eyes were sparkling with promise as they stared deeply into mine, not with lust, but with sincere interest, with hopefulness, with understanding, with a quiet confidence that I found unnervingly sexy.

I looked straight back at him and nodded, "I'd have to check Dylan's calendar, but I'm pretty sure that both he and I would really enjoy this." I wasn't sure if he was just suggesting we go, or suggesting something more.

"You both will. Especially if you join me and Wink!"

That made things clearer.

Chloe came back to find us both standing intimately close and just smiling at each other.

I nervously dumped the flyers back into her arms. "Ahem, well, shall we?"

Bryan placed his hand as near as he could to the small of my back without touching it as he walked us to the door. Thankfully he didn't make any further reference to the run because I had no idea what Chloe might come up with if given the chance. And I wanted her out of there before she had the chance. I let her leave first.

As I stepped after her, Bryan whispered in a hot breath that sent shivers from my ear through to my toes, "Kayte, absolutely no pressure. Please just think about it. It's the first time for this event and I'd be honoured to share it with you and Dylan. Who knows, it may become an annual event and we can run it year after year."

"Just like an anniversary."

"Yes. And I don't know about you but I think anniversaries are worth celebrating." He smiled and winked.

Chloe dodged a patrol car as it entered the lot, "Did you see the way he looked at you?"

Yes, yes I did and it made my knees wobble and my heart race and my…

"What way? What are you talking about, Chloe?" I didn't let on how much I had noticed.

"The way he watched you as you filled in those forms? The way he held out the chair for you and brushed your back as he pushed it in closer to the table? The way he just lightly touched your hand as you handed back the pen? The way he kept looking over to see if you had completed the forms? The way he stared so intently at your lips as you spoke? Did you actually even see ANY of it? And what was that big grin all about when I came back from the toilet?"

The big grin was the result of some incredible sparks, some sensual connection, some feeling that needed to be explored.

"You have quite the imagination Chloe."

"Kayte, I've seen that look before. I know what it means."

It means that I must see him again.

"What, Chloe? If there was a look, and I'm not saying that there was, but IF there was, what does it mean my delusional yet well meaning friend?"

"What it means is that this online dating thing just may have worked for you after all. You can thank me at the wedding! Dum

dum de dum, dum dum de dum, dum dum de dum dum, de dum dum de dum."

Chloe had rolled one of the flyers into a funnel and was holding it in both hands like a bridal bouquet while she hummed and marched all the way to the car.

"I better be the maid of honour."

"If I ever get married, Chloe, you know you would be the only person I'd have as my maid."

"Of honour!" she reiterated.

"Actually I think it's actually Matron, given you're all happily married and matronly."

"Happily married yes, matronly, no way – I'm far too young for matronly!"

We giggled.

I drove home considering the experience I'd had over the past few months with online dating, the array of unique men I had met, those I chose not to meet, the great experiences, the exhilaration and the excitement, the challenges, the disappointments, the heartbreak, the things I learned about myself and about those I had met. It had helped me to create a far clearer vision of what I ultimately wanted and needed from love and the type of man who could provide it.

These experiences also taught me a greater appreciation for the incredible importance of timing in finding love. It cannot be forced or rushed. If you're not ready, you're not ready. Tommy was the kind of man who I knew I could love, but he just wasn't ready for it or me.

While I had thought I was ready when I embarked on this journey, in hindsight, I realised now that I needed to learn more about myself, more about love, more about what I was and wasn't prepared to do to achieve it. I was happy to say that I was ready now. As worthwhile as online dating can be, I was done with it for now. It was time I trusted in my readiness and let fate play her hand.

I looked down at the flyers for the Furry 5K Fundraiser and Fun Run, cracked a smile and let my thoughts take their own run as they began pondering the question, "Just how would one go about incorporating a couple of big hairy dogs into a wedding party?"

L. A. Johannesson

eloves me, eloves me not

Visit us on the web at **elovesmeelovesmenot.com**

Here you can connect with other readers, join the
eloves me, eloves me not community, share your thoughts
on the book and connect with the author.

If you know someone who'd enjoy this book, then please
spread the word! We're on most of the social media
channels to make it as easy for you as possible.

Happy reading!
L. A. Johannesson

eloves me, eloves me not